THE MUSIC WAS NOT HIS ...

No, no, no, he told himself. *This cannot be! A dead man cannot be in his body. Rabinowitz cannot be playing. I am Rolf Geiger and I am alive and Isador Rabinowitz is dead!*

But he heard the unmistakable touch of his master upon the keys. In every note, in every bar and syllable. It was the interpretation of the dead man.

Rolf tried to compensate with his fingering, but he was helpless. His own brillant touch at the keyboard—the one that has made him the most popular pianist in the world—had deserted him.

The old man's vicious spirit was moving in his hands now ...

<u>BOOK YOUR PLACE ON OUR WEBSITE</u>
<u>AND MAKE THE</u>
<u>READING CONNECTION!</u>

We've created a customized website just for our very special readers, where you can get the inside scoop on everything that's going on with Zebra, Pinnacle and Kensington books.

When you come online, you'll have the exciting opportunity to:

- View covers of upcoming books
- Read sample chapters
- Learn about our future publishing schedule (listed by publication month *and author*)
- Find out when your favorite authors will be visiting a city near you
- Search for and order backlist books from our online catalog
- Check out author bios and background information
- Send e-mail to your favorite authors
- Meet the Kensington staff online
- Join us in weekly chats with authors, readers and other guests
- Get writing guidelines
- AND MUCH MORE!

Visit our website at
http://www.pinnaclebooks.com

THE PRODIGY

Noel Hynd

Pinnacle Books
Kensington Publishing Corp.

http://www.pinnaclebooks.com

Readers may contact Noel Hynd at NHy1212@aol.com

The author is indebted to the late Irwin Shaw for the use of one ball of lightning in the skies above France.
The author wishes also to thank Mr. Michael Joy, distinguished teacher of music at St. Peter's School, Philadelphia, for his invaluable assistance and knowledge which helped shape this manuscript.

PINNACLE BOOKS are published by

Kensington Publishing Corp.
850 Third Avenue
New York, NY 10022

First Kensington Hardcover Printing: January, 1998
First Pinnacle Printing: January, 1999
10 9 8 7 6 5 4 3 2 1

Printed in the United States of America

for my good friend
Irv Schwartz

"When you
perform
Beethoven, you have to transform
yourself and commit yourself. You
have to
believe
that God
exists,
that
there is
a soul,
and that
you can
change
the world."

Yo-Yo Ma

one

―――――――――――

―――――――――――

The Air France 777 shuddered as it climbed through the dark gray ocean of clouds above Normandy, ninety miles northwest of Paris. All around the sky there were the streaks of lightning and severe wind currents that sometimes defied even the best in-flight computers. Mid-March rain streaked the outer windows of the aircraft like supernatural tears shed for a distant unseen sorrow.

The thrust of the plane's engines changed abruptly.

The young blond man with shaggy hair, huddled into Seat 2-A by a window in the *Première Classe* cabin, looked to the flight crew for reassurance. He found none.

The nearest stewardess—a dark French girl with a lovely face and slender body—was gripping one hand with the other, nervously twisting a paper tissue. She was frightened.

The young man looked away before she caught him watching her. He stared out the window again. The palms of his hands were sweating. No one anywhere nearby spoke. The aircraft was acting as if it was in trouble.

Suddenly the plane lurched severely downward. There were loud gasps from several travelers behind him.

No! he thought to himself. *No! Not today! I do not wish to die today!* He drew a breath. "I want more time," he whispered aloud, half in prayer. "There's so much I want to accomplish."

The airplane gained altitude, or seemed to, as it wrestled its way upward. The seat-belt signs in French and English remained lit.

He sighed. He wished he still had religion, but hadn't since he was a boy. His stomach clenched. His insides didn't believe in God, either.

Then—amidst more gasps, then screams—there was a loud bang, followed closely with a ripping, bursting noise. It sounded like an explosion. Transfixed, the passengers watched in horror as a ball of lightning emerged from the cabin to sizzle down the center aisle before exiting through the wings. It left 152 passengers on the brink of terror.

"So that's the way it's going to be," the sandy blond man said to himself. "This will be Isador Rabinowitz's final revenge. I'm going home to attend his funeral, but I will never reach it. I will die a fiery death en route."

He searched for something to be content about and found only one thing. At least Diana was not on board. The woman he loved was back in New York. Waiting for him.

She was safe. Presumably.

The airplane fought for its position in the sky. Then it gradually steadied. The blackness within the clouds disintegrated and the gray became lighter. A few minutes later, to the relief of everyone on board, the jet broke from darkness into a clear blue sky. The aircraft tipped its starboard wing toward the morning sun and continued to climb gently. From the flight deck, in French and English, came an announcement that there was no reason for alarm.

The woman in 2-B sighed. She was in her fifties, with dark hair pulled back. She wore a smart navy blue Donna Karan suit.

"We were hit by lightning," she said, still shaken. Her slight New York accent told him she was American, and, from her reading matter, he could guess that she was in the fashion industry. "Can you believe it? *Hit.*"

"Yes. I know," the blond man answered. His nerves remained scrambled. His heart beat like a kettledrum.

The woman shook her head. "This is the second time that's happened to me," she explained. "I fly New York to Paris and back once a month. I suppose I shouldn't be scared. But I am. Every time."

"Understandably," he answered. His accent was American, also. Flat. From almost anywhere.

He looked out the window. The view was reassuring. The clouds were far below and so was the electrical storm. He turned quickly and looked back. She was studying him intently. She smiled with slight embarrassment at having been caught.

"You're the concert pianist, aren't you?" she asked.

"Yes, I am," he answered softly.

"I'm completely enamored of your approach to music," she said. "The way you have such *fun* with it. I've been to several of your recitals. Two in New York, one in Chicago, and the one in London at the Royal Albert Hall in 1993."

It was his turn to smile with mild embarrassment. "Thank you," he said. She looked at him without speaking for several seconds. He knew what was coming.

"I wonder . . ." she said. "No one will believe I flew back to the United States with a celebrity, unless . . ." She fumbled with her purse. "Do you mind if I ask you to—?"

"I don't mind at all," he said politely. "I'm always flattered."

"You're very kind."

She produced a Mont Blanc pen and a fine blank note card.

He signed the card, asking her name and autographing it personally to her. His penmanship was big and assertive, handsome in the deep blue ink. Ten big, bold sweeping script letters.

Rolf Geiger

On the bottom of the card, for fun, he drew a quick little sketch of a man playing a grand piano.

She looked on with pleasure and smiled widely when he handed the card back to her. At the same moment, the seatbelt signs went off. The once-frightened stewardess was preparing the drink cart.

Absurdly, the service of beverages after bouncing perilously around the skies made him think back to the old joke:

In the unlikely event that we land on water, your seat cushion doubles as a flotation device—and the drink cart can be used as a shark cage.

Yeah, sure, he told himself. Thoughts of the absurd frequently followed him. Sometimes he thought that his whole life was a journey through absurdities.

"I'm thrilled," the woman beside Geiger said, looking over the autograph and the sketch. "I'll treasure this."

"It's my pleasure," he said.

"I wonder if you could tell me something," she asked.

"I'll try."

"I love your recitals, but I haven't seen *any* advertised recently. Have you been abroad for a long time?"

"I've kept an extremely limited schedule of late," he said. "Maybe a date every few months at a small venue. I just played a tiny hall in San Remo, Italy, for example. Fewer than two hundred in the audience."

"Such a shame," she said, shaking her head. "Your talent—and I know I'm flattering you here, Mr. Geiger, so beware—is so enormous. So *unique.* I know you know what's best for you, but we as an audience *love* to enjoy you in person."

"You're very kind."

"I loved when you used to do those huge extravaganzas," she said. "Like you did a few years ago. Oh, they were simply *wonderful!*"

"Thank you. The press and the critics used to kill me for them."

"Does it matter to you?" she asked. "Do you take what they say as important?"

He shrugged. "I shouldn't."

"No, no," the woman agreed after a moment. "You shouldn't. *Audiences* love you. People who are enthusiastic about music love you. But the classical establishment?" She opened her hands as if to dismiss the entire universe of serious criticism. "I know they have problems with you."

"They do," he agreed. "Major problems."

Major, indeed.

Following his tour in 1995, the critics all over the world had turned on him with such ferocity that he had stopped playing, other than small quick hit-and-run *cache-cache* recitals. The reviews about him had turned so vicious and even so personal that he could barely endure reading them.

He just didn't take his gifts seriously enough, they all wrote. He just kept fooling around.

Smiling, she leaned to him and spoke beneath the sound of the airplane's engines.

"My feeling is that the music establishment is full of *shit!*" she said cheerfully and conspiratorially. "So *screw 'em all!*" she said loudly enough to be heard throughout the first-class section. "Come back to your audiences. We love you."

"You're very generous," he answered. "I'm taking some time to think things over. There may be some changes soon."

"I hope so," she said. "I hope so."

Rolf Geiger politely looked away from his new best friend. He picked up his seat's headphones and donned them before she could continue.

He closed his eyes and pumped up the volume. He was tired and distressed and needed no more conversation.

Actually, he felt relieved. He had been hit by lightning and would live to tell about it. Outside, the brilliant yellow sun seemed to be perched harmlessly on the tip of the 777's wing. All in all, he told himself again, he was once again a very lucky man.

The thought helped him relax. And with relaxation came a calming, satisfying sleep.

Rolf Geiger came out of his sleep to the steady droning rhythm of the airplane's engines, the headphones having slipped away from his ears somewhere over the North Atlantic. Tired beyond reason, Geiger had been in Europe for only five days this March, just long enough to play as a last-minute surprise guest at the annual music festival in San Remo.

This had been such a quick trip that Diana had chosen not to accompany him. Not like the previous summer, when she had come with him and they had joyously explored Europe on those days when he was not required to play. There had even been four days when they had slipped away from everyone and bicycled through Provence. Best of all, no one had recognized him.

Rolf had missed Diana on this junket to San Remo. But he knew she was waiting for him in New York. That thought, too, reassured him. In his hand luggage, he had an exquisite pair of gold-and-ruby earrings that he had purchased for her, plus several French perfumes unavailable in the United States, and—almost as a joke because it was so inexpensive—a thin silver neck chain with a piano pendant. It had cost him a crisp American five-dollar bill from a street vendor on the Via Contessa Ferrara.

Much as he had missed Diana, however, he might have preferred to have missed her phone call that morning, the call that had compelled him to return home to New York forty-eight hours earlier than planned. The call that had put him on this aircraft.

Isador Rabinowitz, the great concert pianist, was dead at eighty-two. The funeral was to be held at once. And there was no way, considering the manner in which the lives of the old Rabinowitz and the young Geiger had already intertwined, that Geiger could not be present at the funeral. He prayed that the normal hassle at U.S. Customs at Kennedy International would be minimal. Thinking further ahead, he hoped that his car and driver would be waiting at the airport.

The descent into New York was as bumpy as the ride over Normandy. But at least there was no lightning, and after a six-hour flight he was safely on the ground again. He passed through customs easily, paying duty on what he had bought.

His car and driver were waiting. So was Diana, who had come to the airport to meet him. The sight of her—a tall, slim, beautiful woman with shoulder-length dark hair—sent his spirits soaring. The couple broke into wide smiles upon spotting each other and fell into a long embrace.

"Missed you," she said.

"Missed you horribly," he said to her in return.

The chauffeur stood by awkwardly.

Geiger finally relaxed in the car as it drove into Manhattan to his current home. The touch of melancholia upon him he assumed stemmed from the death of Rabinowitz. Diana, sensing his mood, sat very close to him, her hand on his, comforting him.

At one point in the ride, he turned and found her looking right at him. So she leaned to his ear, and whispered. "I know you're upset," she said, gently teasing. "But I'm incredibly horny today."

He smiled. "I'm glad," he whispered back. "Me, too."

He kissed her. When his eyes found the driver's rearview mirror, he saw the driver's gaze quickly shift back to the Long Island Expressway.

And when their limousine hit heavy inbound traffic on the Triborough Bridge, Geiger had some extra time to examine his feelings toward Rabinowitz.

Time that he did not want. Or need.

The housekeeper had prepared dinner for them and then gone home. Rolf and Diana enjoyed the light supper. She helped him unpack. They had from time to time discussed marriage, but were both content with the present setup. There was no pressure to it, only affection. Both had been in brief unsuccessful marriages when younger. Now, if the time ever came that one of them wanted to leave, departure would be as easy as packing a few bags.

But tonight, there was only love.

They showered together and tumbled into bed, attacking each other as if they had been apart for months, not days. The sex, as always, was deeply physical and deeply passionate. She fell asleep beside him, wearing only the gifts that he had bought her. The earrings. The neck chain with the piano pendant. And a dab of one of the perfumes.

He lay awake for several minutes, feeling how lucky he was to love such a woman and have such a woman in love with him.

But equally he was troubled. Anxious. Tomorrow would bring an occasion when he could finally escape from the stark, ominous shadow of the old man.

Instead, what would come with the next dawn was the beginning of an unspeakable terror. Perhaps this notion was at the edge of Rolf Geiger's consciousness. Perhaps, because something deep within his soul already dreaded the next day.

Somehow, deep down, he knew . . .

two

On the cold morning that followed his return from Europe, Rolf Geiger stood by the grave of Isador Rabinowitz with the other pallbearers. He was by twenty-four years the youngest member of the funeral party. And inside him were aches, anxieties, and fears that would not go away.

The world was burying the "old man" today.

Rabinowitz.

Suddenly dead.

In his youth, at a Catholic school in West Virginia, Geiger had had a fine teacher and counselor. Brother Matthew had always said that a man's life can only be understood at the moment of his death. Geiger was certain that was true today, here in this burial ground. But Rolf had no idea what he understood.

The world would lay Isador Rabinowitz to rest that day in an aging Jewish cemetery in upper Manhattan among people whom he had never known and where the burial sites were so crowded together that they screamed out for relief. But that was the physical part. Rabinowitz would go into the earth amidst the accolades that he had earned over a lifetime. Geiger, as a pallbearer, was one of six who would actually help lower the coffin into the ground. Already Geiger knew the downside: Burying a great man was not something that came easily. Burying a legend was not something that ever came completely. And burying a soul was impossible.

Isador Rabinowitz. The so-called Dark Angel of the modern piano. Lucifer of the black and white keys. No one who knew music had a neutral position on the man.

Until the coming of Rolf Geiger, Rabinowitz had been the most renowned classical musician in the world. Probably the greatest pianist of the twentieth century. The question could start vehement arguments. There had been Arthur Rubinstein before Rabinowitz, and Vladimir Horowitz. Rudolf Serkin, too, if one wished to start another argument. For technique, earlier in the century, there had also been Rachmaninoff, as well as Prokofiev, nineteenth-century men who played their own compositions and who had wandered into the twentieth century almost by accident.

Rabinowitz, the young Geiger's onetime mentor and teacher. Rabinowitz, who had sacrificed his humanity for his art. As Geiger stood in the Beth Zion Reform Cemetery in upper Manhattan on this cold day in March, a sharp breeze off the Hudson River slashed through his overcoat. Rolf Geiger was not a happy young man.

Geiger's blue eyes were wells of sorrow, mixed a little with fear, an unusual emotion for him. When he raised his eyes again and the rabbi was still talking at the graveside, Geiger's gaze settled upon the pine coffin. Then his eyes lowered again.

It was better that way. Lowered eyes. Sometimes in life it was better not to look. Not at what one feared the most.

For Geiger, time spiraled. The old man had been eighty-two when he had died. For Geiger there were many emotions, but one prevailed. One that he dared not speak of to anyone except his closest intimates.

As the service continued, Geiger held in his mind an old vision of Rabinowitz. It was sepia-toned and came from an old family snapshot that Hilda Rabinowitz—the old man's third and final wife, who had died two years earlier—had once displayed. In the photograph, one saw a handsome tender young man, a citizen of Vienna in the late 1940s, having returned to central Europe after spending the war years in London. This was before Rabinowitz's emigration to Montreal in 1950 and then to the United States in 1956, where he had found both celebrity and wealth.

In the old photo, Rabinowitz's head is thrown backward in laughter, his hair is thick and dark, and his eyes are merry. His strong right arm is wrapped tightly around a pretty young Viennese woman who eventually became his first wife.

A nice memory. A nice slice of the past. But the reality had not been like that for the last three decades. Two marriages had failed and five children—two outside the two early marriages— grew up learning to hate him, as did both women whom he had divorced.

These and the other women in Rabinowitz's life—and there were many—had called him cruel, cunning, manipulative, tyrannical, and abusive. No one had any doubt that these assessments were correct. Of the five Rabinowitz offspring, none possessed any of their father's recordings. All, for that matter, disliked him so intensely that they made a point of *not* owning any of his recordings. They were unable to separate the man from his music, the despot from their father.

The mature Rabinowitz—acknowledged by many to be the greatest pianist of the century by the time he was thirty in 1946—had been tortured by a thousand demons, each of them given existence by his greatness. Over the years, something glacial had replaced the merry face. He wore a mask in his later years, an aloof icy public expression frozen from lack of warmth and the absence of humanity. One of his characteristics, and one of the few benign quirks that Rabinowitz had allowed himself, was a massive six-carat emerald ring worn on his left hand. He had worn it when he played, signature jewelry on signature hands.

Some of his fans tried to explain away the surliness of his behavior. Rabinowitz, some said, had never fully shaken the sadness, horror, and paranoia of a European Jew who had survived World War II. Nor did any of these fans expect him to. The man's passion *was* his music and was *in* his music. So what if he was also known as the Dark Angel of modern classical music?

"Greatness exacts an incalculable price," Rabinowitz had said to Geiger when Geiger was seventeen. This was a much-referred-to statement that had been reported when *The New Yorker* had profiled the man. "I paid it, Rolf. And so will you."

"No, sir. I won't," Geiger had responded.

"You must. For your art."

"I won't."

Rabinowitz had snorted. "Don't be a damned idiot. Eventually, we all do. One way or another. Genius is a blessing *and* a curse." The split between the two men was often attributed in public to that particular exchange.

Moreover, Rabinowitz was impossible both personally and professionally. He frequently broke concert dates and recording contracts and then everything would be set right again because of who he was. He was habitually churlish and belligerent. He was once arrested for trying to throttle a man who had beaten him to a parking place in New Canaan, Connecticut. Charges were dropped because this was, after all, the great Rabinowitz, and the "assault" was settled out of court. In the latter years of his life, he insulated himself from the public with "assistants" and secretaries, all of whom were dedicated to him and most of whom, in appreciation of their loyalty, he would eventually dismiss. He lived on a remote converted farm in northwestern Connecticut—a farm with no animals, for the great man hated animals. The property was surrounded by an electrified fence. In his enclave, he practiced in a soundproof studio away from all human ears. He had been dead for a week when his body was found by his maid.

In the last twenty years of his life, Rabinowitz had only one student. One protégé. One young man to whom he wished to pass the torch of genius.

Geiger.

"He will be greater than I but only if I counsel to teach him how," Rabinowitz once said in his never-quite-perfect English. Like most of his pronouncements, this one was a ukase. It came from the summit of a musical Olympus. "And then only Rolf Geiger will be great if he wants to be."

Rabinowitz had taken on Geiger as a student when the younger man was thirteen and had won a full scholarship to

Julliard. Even at that point, when Rabinowitz was sixty-five years old, he allowed himself to be grudgingly impressed with the younger pianist. Geiger played with an evident romanticism and a haunting crystal clearness which never failed him, even in the most complicated passages. It was not something that anyone could ever learn. It was intuitive.

"This boy is very good," Rabinowitz remarked at the time. "It is as if he can photograph extraordinarily complex pieces and exactly imprint them upon the ear of the listener."

The maestro thought further. Then he pronounced further.

"It is apparent that he will soon master his piano. We will eventually learn if he can also know to make music." This was said *after* Geiger had won the Tchaikovsky competition in Moscow. And these were the first words of praise that Rabinowitz had been known to utter for *anyone* other than himself for several decades.

Rabinowitz would then spend weekly two-hour "apprenticeship sessions" with Geiger at Rabinowitz's place in Connecticut. He would stand behind the young man, his powerful hands on Rolf's shoulders, for the entire time. If Geiger made a critical mistake, the hands would move roughly toward Geiger's neck in a gesture of potential strangulation—Rabinowitz's way of saying that Geiger had profaned something holy. This technique persisted for a year until Geiger threatened to stop coming unless the hands-on-neck technique ceased. Nonetheless, Rabinowitz was part of the younger man's life for seven years as an instructor, professor, and on-the-spot tormentor.

Seven years. There even seemed to be something Biblical about that number. Like a plague. Or an increment in time in which a god's wrath could be measured.

Eventually, the relationship between Rabinowitz and Geiger became more than mentor—protégé. It was also love-hate. Over the last years, the men had parted company. Rabinowitz criticized Geiger relentlessly in the press. He said he was turning into a latter-day Liberace, not serious about his work. His art. His craft. His music. His life. His gift. Not taking what talent he had—and Rabinowitz began to question whether Geiger had any—seriously.

The old man and the young man had encountered each other at the Kennedy Center in October 1995.

Unsolicited, Rabinowitz had approached Geiger.

"It's all right, these things you're saying, these ideas you have," Rabinowitz had said to Geiger before a dozen witnesses. "I wouldn't *want* you to be as great as I. Not that you ever *would* be. Not that you could be, the way you remorselessly *fuck* great music. On the best day in the life of yours you will never approach the artistry I could command on the worst day in mine."

The old man had snorted and walked off. Geiger had held his tongue. The younger man had performed live before close to three million people on his latest tour. He had made two television specials (loved by audiences and reviled by critics) and commanded more than a million dollars to make a single recording. There were those who suggested that the aging Rabinowitz was jealous.

Thus had concluded their last in-person meeting. Since then, Rabinowitz had been Geiger's harshest and most savage critic. Geiger had never understood if these were the master's true final sentiments. Or were these his methods, his way of goading him onward to more celestial things?

Geiger would never know. But he—and the rest of the classical music world—would endlessly hypothesize.

"If being like Rabinowitz—old, angry, and alone—afraid to play in public, is what it takes for greatness, then maybe some people are correct. Maybe I question whether I *do* want it," an unusually irritated Geiger told *Gramophone* magazine in a celebrated interview before Christmas 1995.

The statement was not meant as a personal counterattack. But it was received as one. Rabinowitz read the article and filed a ten-million-dollar lawsuit for defamation of character, a suit that he had no chance of winning, and which still remained unsettled at the time of his death.

The men never spoke again. When Rabinowitz died suddenly and the instructions for his funeral were read, there were gasps. The old man had never changed his instructions from five years earlier, before the rift, even though Rabinowitz had updated his will monthly. He had many ways of always having the last word.

So the burden—one of many—then fell to Rolf Geiger. What to do? Avoid the funeral? Or participate?

Geiger felt he should honor Rabinowitz's written request. Perhaps the young virtuoso could use this final association with Rabinowitz to make peace. Anything else could have been construed as a snub. And even if Rabinowitz didn't have any friends, there remained legions of starchy older musicians who were his admirers and apologists.

So Rolf Geiger stood on the hard earth of upper Manhattan on a raw March day, freezing as the wind tore into him, clutching his long navy wool topcoat to himself as tightly as possible.

Geiger was dazzlingly handsome. Tall, lean, athletic with dark blond, shaggy hair and gorgeous blue eyes. His all-American looks made him stand out like a mannequin among the rumpled, middle-aged and old European men who were the other five pallbearers. Geiger wondered if Rabinowitz had orchestrated that, too, and decided that he had.

Geiger's gaze involuntarily drifted back to the pine casket time and time again. A rabbi whom Geiger had never met spoke briefly about the artistry of Rabinowitz, the brilliance of Rabinowitz, the "hidden humanity" of Rabinowitz. The wind off the Hudson increased, and the one thing Geiger could be glad about was that he could barely hear. But the ferocity of the wind made the occasion even colder.

Darker.

More unpleasant. There were even a few brief snow flurries.

It was a heavily ominous day in ways that no one could precisely place. It was an occasion of silences and foreboding. Even the sun had gone behind the clouds at the precise moment that the mourners had assembled at the cemetery. It was as if, from somewhere, Rabinowitz was suggesting that the world would be a diminished place without his music.

Geiger sighed.

He scanned the other mourners and found the face in which he could always find solace: Diana's. On this cold, uncomfortable day, Geiger found comfort in her eyes for several seconds.

His thoughts drifted. Suddenly the wind subsided and Geiger realized that the rabbi was finished.

Mercifully.

Geiger shifted his feet and moved slightly to get warm. He was increasingly uncomfortable. He felt too many eyes were on him. A few moments later, the pine coffin was on its final journey, and so was Rabinowitz. The great one's remains were lowered into a small dirt chamber. Four walls without windows, down, down down, contained by a simple wooden box until it rested.

Geiger heard the sobbing of Rabinowitz's sister, the last human who could muster a tear for him. At the appropriate moment, Geiger moved forward to throw a flower into the open grave. In keeping with custom, other members of the party stepped to the graveside to throw a shovelful of dirt upon the deceased. With reservations, and understanding the heavy irony of his act, Geiger also took a shovel and gently threw dirt to his onetime mentor's grave.

Moments later, everyone stepped in different directions. There were condolences exchanged and handshakes. Solemn looks and words of support. There were dozens of renowned orchestra members present. Some of them were of Rabinowitz's generation and had come to the United States at about the same time. Geiger sensed hostility from this quarter, but ignored it. He was used to it from them.

Phrases floated everywhere.

One stayed with Geiger.

"The torch is passed, Rolf," said William Baumann, the arts editor from New York's newspaper of record. "Now you're the greatest alive." The critic spoke softly, but his words were tinged with a whiff of breakfast gin.

"You're very kind," Geiger answered.

"Rabinowitz would have said so himself," Baumann continued.

"He also would have said that I 'need to be more serious.' 'Not prostitute my talent for popularity.' Not only would he have said that, but he *did* say that on several occasions."

Baumann shrugged. "He wasn't alone in that notion."

"I know. I'm quoting your reviews in the *Times,* Bill."

"He would also say that you should start playing again. Real concerts without all the show business claptrap. In big halls. Before demanding audiences. Instead of sneaking off to Europe to play a date or two in some remote music hall."

"San Remo is hardly remote."

"You know what I mean," Baumann said.

"Yes. I suppose I do."

"Are you looking for a quote?" Geiger finally asked.

"Have one?"

"Rabinowitz hated me," Geiger said.

Baumann snorted. "I can't believe that he really *hated* you. Resented, maybe. I know what's been said and written. But I still can't fully believe it."

"I know you can't. He wanted me to fail."

"If he hated you and wanted you to fail," Baumann proposed, "why would Rabinowitz have had you here today as a pall—?"

"I'm not at ease with this conversation," Geiger said softly. "Not here. Not now." He walked away.

Baumann was taken aback and followed, apologizing profusely, but bird-dogging Geiger at the same time.

"It's all right," Geiger finally assured him. "I'd just rather discuss something else."

"Then may I quote you, Rolf?"

"If it 'fits in print,' quote me, Bill," Geiger said.

The young pianist excused himself from the critic a final time. He moved through the crowd. Unlike the deceased, and notwithstanding the coterie of Rabinowitz's remaining peers, Geiger was personally well liked, even if he drove the music establishment batty. He felt many hands of comfort upon his shoulders as he moved among scores of people he knew from concerts all over the world.

He nodded to several. He heard many kind words. None negative. The eyes and faces of strangers followed him as he walked. But that was nothing new.

More words floating on the wind.

Thoughts.

Snippets of overheard conversations. There was a discussion of the massive emerald that the old man used to wear and some of the mourners wondered if Rabinowitz had been buried with it. There was a rumor that a pair of biographies of Rabinowitz had been commissioned this year by competing London publishers; it was only a matter of time for an American house to grab the U.S. rights for one of the works-in-progress.

Again, Geiger kept his eyes low, the better not to catch anyone's eye. Then another phrase came to him.

A thought. Or a particularly intrusive overheard line. Amidst all the voices, he really didn't know which it had been—a thought or something someone had said—though it was male in origin and tinged with a *mitteleuropa* accent strangely suggestive of Rabinowitz's.

"... *the greatest pianist in the world. And now it's Rolf Geiger. If he wants to be.*"

The same old mantra. The same old suggestions, over and over. The legend to live up to. The talent never to live down. The apparent obligation to be "serious" about great music rather than to have fun with it. Unhappily, the old man had been correct about a lot of things. Among them, genius was a blessing *and* a curse.

"... *if only he would start doing serious recitals again* ..."
"... *if only he would concentrate* ..."

He knew he couldn't resist the notion much longer.

Geiger spotted his agent in the crowd: Brian Greenstone, an affable Englishman in his fifties. Greenstone had represented Rabinowitz, also. Geiger's eyes kept traveling. He found Diana next. He went to her and took her hand. He paused to say the right things to Lena Rabinowitz, the one attending daughter. Lena embraced him. Rabinowitz's son Jonathan, who lived with a clothing designer and scored art films in San Francisco, had not seen fit to attend. Nor had the others.

Geiger felt a gentle hand take his elbow. He turned.

"Hello, Rolf." It was Brian Greenstone.

"Hello, Brian."

"I know you're uncomfortable here, but you were wise to come," Greenstone said.

"I'm here because I thought I should be," Rolf answered.

"You thought correctly. Hello, Diana."

Greenstone gave Diana an embrace and a kiss on the cheek.

Rolf's agent was a big, good-looking, heavyset man with dark hair, graying only at the temples. He was gracefully navigating his mid-fifties with slightly rounded shoulders and some extra pounds as the only toll of the years. A good hairstylist and an excellent tailor managed to hide much of the bad news.

"I'm glad you're back in America," Greenstone said. "We need to talk very soon." He spoke in the faded cadences and tones of south London.

"I know."

"How was San Remo?"

"It went well."

"As planned?"

"Yes," Geiger said.

"I read a press clipping from *Corrierra della Sera*. Or at least I read the translation that my London office sent me. You behaved yourself and played Mozart. Only Mozart."

Rolf nodded.

"You felt good with it?"

"Yes, I did."

"Have dinner with Sarah and me sometime soon," Greenstone suggested. "It's very important."

Geiger nodded again. "When is good?"

"Tomorrow?"

"Perfect."

"Take care of him, Diana," Greenstone said, turning to her. "God knows he won't take care of himself."

"I'll look after him," she answered softly.

"I know. You're looking beautiful."

"Thank you, Brian."

Then Rolf Geiger found his car and driver. Across the street, a group of fans spotted Geiger and screamed. They yelled to him, seeking autographs. Geiger normally would have obliged. This time he shook his head.

"No. Sorry," he called back. "Any day except today."

His fans, moments ago so expectant, looked at him with disappointment. Geiger felt bad. There were only a few dozen of them, and they had waited for him specifically in this dismal cold weather. So he darted across the street and walked to them.

Diana stood outside the car and waited.

The legion of Geiger fans were mostly young, white, and well educated. A heavy concentration of college students. They handed Rolf programs and pictures and magazine covers. He patiently signed all of them. The crowd slowly thinned as the satisfied autograph seekers—almost reverently—stepped back, each after having been satisfied.

Then an uneasy feeling overtook him. He felt a presence. Something strange. Something not quite right.

"Rolf Geiger?" a male voice asked. The voice rasped slightly.

His eyes rose and he was startled. Amidst all the teenagers, amidst the crush of fans in their twenties and thirties, was an older man. At first he looked as if he were aging and homeless. Geiger was taken aback. He felt as if he were about to be accosted for a few dollars. Mentally, he prepared quickly to fish into his pocket for a five-dollar bill to buy his escape.

Then he realized that he wasn't confronting a homeless individual at all. Rather, just a strange man, in his sixties or even older.

"You're the best now, aren't you?" the man asked.

"I . . . I really wouldn't know."

Geiger found the exchange awkward. The younger fans gathered to hear.

"Yes, you would."

"That's not for me to determine."

"Oh, yes it is," the old man affirmed. "I've spent my life in concerts and music halls. Seen all the great ones. You're the best alive today."

"You're very generous," Geiger said, signing the last item pushed toward him.

"No, I'm not."

Geiger turned fully toward him. The man gave him the creeps. He smelled bad. An offensive mixture of tobacco, alcohol, and poor hygiene. He wore a rumpled brown coat and looked like he lived in it. Very slightly, Geiger recoiled.

"Did you want me to sign something?" Geiger asked.

"No," the man said. Then, as if thinking it over, "No. What would be the point? Signing is foolish. What would I have you sign? What would I do with an autograph?"

Some of the kids smirked. "Sell it," someone mumbled in jest. There were a few titters of laughter.

"Have a nice day," Geiger said.

The man didn't answer for several seconds. Then, "I'm going to follow your career," he said. "Carefully."

His old eyes were upon Geiger like those of a terrier. Geiger had difficulty pulling his own eyes away and breaking contact. But he managed.

"Thank you," he said. "That's very nice of you."

The man grunted and said something unintelligible. Geiger thought he caught part of it:

". . . not nice. It's an obligation . . ."

It sounded half-crazy and Rolf didn't ask for a repeat. Geiger left his admirers with a short wave and crossed the street again. He could feel the strange man's gaze upon him as he walked. Then Geiger heard footsteps. A handful of late arrivals, spotting Geiger, had fallen into stride with him and pursued him for signatures.

Geiger hastily accepted programs and pictures as he walked. He never bothered to count how many there were, but he figured there were four or five. He arrived at his limousine and the driver held the rear door open.

"It's all right," Geiger said to the driver. "I'll sign, then we go." He nodded to the chauffeur to go back to the driver's seat. The driver did, leaving the rear door open for him.

Geiger signed twice, then a third time for his fans. He was now trying to leave. He had been in situations like this so many times before and knew how they could get out of control. Even those for whom he had signed now stayed close. Sometimes he could feel a hand brush against him. A caress. A touch. A little shove. Fans liked live contact.

The crowd pushed in on him. He steadied himself with his free hand by resting it in the doorframe.

Nothing more was pushed toward him to sign.

"Thank you all," he said, establishing eye contact with none of those who surrounded him. He moved his body toward the limousine and made the first motion of getting into the vehicle.

Then, he felt a surge in the crowd. A disruption of some

sort. He felt himself jostled, as if someone within the crowd had pushed hard.

He steadied himself against the limousine. Then, seeing something moving, he recoiled quickly and moved his outstretched arms back close to him.

Two of his female fans screamed. The limo door slammed so violently that the entire vehicle shuddered. Incredibly, it just missed Geiger's right hand, which had been in the doorframe.

He was so stunned and startled that he said nothing. But when he searched the faces of those near him, all expressed shock and terror. No one had seen who had pushed the door. But the bizarre gnarled man in the brown coat had a piercing look in his eyes as he stared at Geiger.

Their eyes locked upon one another. And there was something there that bothered Geiger anew. Something familiar? Hatred? Or just intensity?

Had the man pushed it? Or had he not even understood what had happened? Geiger didn't wish to stay long enough to find out.

"Rolf! Rolf!"

Diana's voice beckoned him from within the car. She reached across the backseat, unlatched the door, and pushed it open. The chauffeur attempted to come to his aid, but he signaled the man back to the steering wheel once again. Geiger just wanted to be out of there.

This time those around him gave way, and Geiger slid to safety into the backseat.

"Jesus!" he gasped. "Did you see what nearly happened? Did you see how close that came to my hand!"

Some of those in the crowd realized that something serious had happened. They could see how alarmed Geiger was. But when Rolf looked back to them and searched suspiciously for the old man, he had disappeared into the crowd. Or he had gone somewhere, because Rolf couldn't find him. Nor did he know from where he had materialized in the first place. It was scary—in these days of dangerous obsessed fans—how close the old man had come without Geiger seeing him.

"I saw," she said. "Did someone do that intentionally?"

"I don't know!" he answered, calming slightly. "I thought someone slammed the door at me. But I don't know."

He nodded to his driver. His fans continued to wave from across the street. Even the police who were maintaining the traffic line glanced for a final look at him. Then his vehicle moved onto the street and was safely away from the crowd within seconds. He gave his more peaceable admirers a final wave.

"Jesus," Geiger said a second time. He flexed his hands and fingers before him and shook his head. "What a world when your own fans just about maim you."

He leaned back into the leather seat and slowly gathered himself, his breathing evening off.

"Thanks for coming with me," he said.

"Who *was* that?" she asked.

"Who? Which?"

"The man who looked like an aging degenerate," she said. "God! Rumpled old coat like that. I thought he was going to flash us."

Rolf allowed himself the thinnest of smiles.

"I have no idea," Geiger said. "A fan of some sort, I guess. They come in all sizes and shapes and varying states of mental lucidity."

"Was he a nut?"

"Only creepy," said Geiger. "In fact, he probably wasn't even strong enough to push the car door that hard. So forget about him."

"Are you sure?"

"I'm sure."

"Creepy fans scare me," she said. "Ever since John Lennon. And that soap-opera star who got killed by a fan."

He sighed. "They scare me, too," he admitted after a moment. "These days, who knows what they're carrying, what they're going to do."

The driver had left the motor running on the vehicle and the interior was already comfortable. Diana leaned against him in the back of the limousine. Her once-frigid hand, now warming, came to rest on his knee.

God, he thought, how he hated that cold, and how funerals

depressed him! And God, he thought, how he loved the warmth of Diana next to him.

"Let's not dwell on this, Tiger," she said to him.

He smiled.

"Wish granted," he said. The vehicle moved from a side street in Morningside Heights to upper Broadway and turned downtown.

Tiger.

The nickname that Diana had accidentally invented for him and which she alone called him. The first night they'd gone to bed together, she had said afterward that he had made love to her "like a tiger."

"You mean I smell like a big cat?" he had asked, teasing her.

"I mean you drove this girl wild," she had said. "Tiger."

The nickname had stuck.

He had no nickname for her. Not that he needed one. Diana, the name her parents had given her, fit as if it had been tailored.

His mind was a compendium of all sorts of music. So it was not surprising that he often thought of her in terms of the old Paul Anka song by that name. "Diana."

. . . Goddess of love that you are

Even the refrain was with him this day of the funeral, this date when he felt he needed her so much.

Oh, please, stay by me, Diana . . .

Fortunately, she was right there.

He put his hand on hers and wrapped an arm around her. She snuggled closer to him and the thought arose that human love and kindness might be more important to his life than any score or any performance. He smiled ruefully. The old man would have skewered him alive for such a thought.

Love—the word, the thought, the very *notion*—had never been in the crabby old man's lexicon. Many times Geiger had heard Rabinowitz speak of his passion for music, his enthrallment with his instrument, his dedication to the art of the piano.

But Rabinowitz had never spoken of love. Not in front of Geiger. Never in his life had Geiger ever heard Isador Rabinowitz use that word or discuss the concept.

Not even once.

three

From the cemetery in upper Manhattan, the drive back to East Seventy-third Street began in a weary silence. But for Rolf, who was always mentally turning over some intricate piece of the past or the future, silences always gave way to introspection. And introspection precipitated brooding. Today was no different from any other.

Geiger watched the city go past him. The limousine cut through deteriorated sections of Morningside Heights, old neighborhoods that once were famous for kosher pickles, pastrami, and egg creams, but which now were marked by dilapidated storefronts. Signs in Spanish, Hindi, and Vietnamese announced the newest wave of merchants.

The driver came to a stoplight. Geiger studied a trio of men sitting on the steps of a crumbling tenement, drinking beer from quart bottles covered with paper bags.

Geiger's eyes left the men and he stared off into the middle distance. In his mind, a montage of bitter unhappy memories was before him, one of growing up, one long, lingering, aching recollection of an unhappy childhood in West Virginia.

Coal country. About fifteen miles west of the Pennsylvania

border. Intellectually, the middle of nowhere. An American Siberia.

He shuddered, and, for the time, he buried the long series of thoughts and associations. He turned to Diana and began to tell her about the beauty of the Italian coastline around San Remo and how much he hoped she'd accompany him on his next trip.

Before he knew it, they were back on the east side of Manhattan, traveling down Fifth Avenue in the Eighties. She nodded to the Metropolitan Museum of Art, indicating a huge sweeping blue-and-yellow banner above its front steps. The museum was one of her favorite places. The banner had just been raised that morning. It proclaimed the opening of a Renoir exhibit, several weeks hence, which she wished to attend.

"Will you go with me?" she asked.

"Maybe," he said.

"If you're not interested, my art teacher will go with me."

He looked at her. "Whatever you want," he answered. "I'm happy to go with you."

She squeezed his hand again. A squeeze was always her way of telling him he had done or said the right thing.

Fifty minutes later, the limousine came to a stop in front of Geiger's town house. He stepped out. Diana followed.

There were two photographers waiting, plus a woman with a television camera who worked for local news.

Geiger acquiesced to giving a brief on-camera statement. His words were kind, fitting for the day, recalling an earlier time when Rabinowitz was still Geiger's teacher.

"In the past few years you'd been apart," the reporter stated. Geiger cringed slightly. "Some unkind things were said by Isador Rabinowitz about you. Do you have any thoughts on that today?"

"I've already forgotten the unpleasant things," Geiger said. "Isador Rabinowitz was one of the giants of modern music. I prefer to remember him that way, just like everyone else."

"You were his only student for the last fifty years. Was he a great teacher?"

"I learned more from him than anyone, so, yes. I'd have to say so."

"And he was the greatest pianist of his time?" she pressed.

"Indisputably," he answered. He could feel the next part coming. Always the same next part.

"And now you're the greatest," she said.

"That's not for me to decide or even discuss."

Geiger tried to move away.

"One final question?" she pressed.

"Just one."

"With all that he said about you, why do you suppose he selected you as a pallbearer?"

"I would interpret it as a final gesture of kindness and friendship from a great man," Geiger said diplomatically.

"But he selected you in the place of his own son, who's your age," she said. "Was he suggesting something by that?"

"I couldn't speculate," Geiger said, "and you shouldn't either. Thank you."

He finally won his freedom.

Geiger had long ago decided he would always handle himself in public with grace, and he found himself reminding himself of that decision here. Yet in the back of his mind, even as he was fishing his house keys from his pocket, feeling the hit of a television camera upon his back, a little voice was warning him.

Rabinowitz, too, had been kind and charitable as a young man, the interior voice told him. Then something in the maestro had changed as the years had gone by. There had been excesses in his pursuit of excellence and greatness and the public had demanded too much of him personally. Rabinowitz had probably not set out to transform himself into the monstrous bitter man he had eventually become. But he had become it, anyway.

I will not turn out the way he did, Geiger found himself thinking. Thinking, but not saying. *I will not sacrifice life for art.* It was his mini-mantra and had been for years.

He and Diana entered the town house. They both drew long breaths and felt relieved as the door closed behind them. And at least *this* door missed his fingers by several feet.

"I don't know why you even speak to people like that," Diana said, irritated. "God. You should have earned membership in the Vatican diplomatic corps from the way you handled that bitch.''

He kissed her on the cheek. ''I'll settle for sainthood,'' he answered. ''Hello, Edythe.''

Mrs. Edythe Jamison, his housekeeper, appeared and collected their coats. She was a nicely mannered woman in her late fifties who came in for six hours five days a week. Today, she had a light lunch waiting.

The house felt warm and splendid. It had a large foyer on the first floor, flanked by a living room and dining room on one side and a large room behind two oak doors which Geiger had had converted into a library.

The room was a den and his studio, too. His personal Steinway sat in it, jet-black, dominating the room. The walls were lined with bookcases overflowing with biographies, works on music, books about the great composers, scores, and essays on theater, art, and cinema. There was even a sprinkling of books on sports—tennis and baseball in particular. Geiger had been fascinated by the New York Yankees since he was a kid growing up in West Virginia. He loved to read about their wonderful history as it transported him into another world and another time. There was also a collection of books on world politics. Geiger sometimes liked to buy books by the armful, and this room reflected that penchant. Unseen, behind all the books, Geiger had had special soundproofing installed. If he wished to, he could completely contain the sound of his music. Or he could leave open the doors and windows and fill the air with his playing.

A stairway in the front hall led to the second floor, where there were three bedrooms. One had been converted to his home office. The master bedroom was at the front of the house, overlooking the tree-lined Seventy-third Street. The guest bedroom was rarely used. The third floor was almost empty—two large rooms whose fate had been left undecided. One room, however, had recently taken purpose with paints and an easel: Diana had begun art lessons. She studied twice a week in SoHo with a handsome Lebanese expatriate named Maurice Sahadi. Rolf liked her work and encouraged her.

Diana had appointments in the afternoon. Geiger stayed

within his home, reading scores, occasionally listening to music on compact discs. A few business calls came. He took them in the second-floor office. He didn't touch his piano all day.

In the evening, toward eight, he met Diana at Audrey's, a small pub on Madison at Seventy-fifth Street. He sat in the back with her. The only people to recognize him were regulars, who didn't approach him. There was a jukebox in the pub and someone kept playing Sinatra. Sad Sinatra. Point-of-No-Return Sinatra. Geiger liked Sinatra and the music fit his mood perfectly.

Almost too perfectly. Rolf fell silent. Sometimes when Geiger brooded too much, he felt that Diana was his lifeline to reality.

"A penny for your thoughts," she said, trying to draw him out. She placed a hand on his, her usual gesture when she saw that he needed support.

He shrugged.

"Rabinowitz?" she asked.

He sighed. "Of course," he said.

"What about him? Everything?"

"When Isador Rabinowitz gets into your head, you're finished," he said to her. "You never get him out. Imagine how deeply he's already in mine."

"He's gone now. Maybe it's time to work on getting him out," Diana suggested.

"Not easy," Rolf said.

"But worth the effort," she said. "Don't you think?"

He smiled. She reciprocated. She leaned to him and kissed him on the cheek. He placed an arm around her and held her tightly, then released.

"Definitely," he said.

They left Audrey's between nine and ten and walked home. The night was raw and a drizzle had begun. They shared an umbrella. Geiger had three locks on the front door of his home, but once past them the building felt warm and secure. This was his redoubt, one of Geiger's two secure sanctuaries in the world. There was his small pink house in Malibu, and if it hadn't slid into the ocean in his absence, that was the other.

Diana went upstairs and retired toward eleven. Sometime

after that, as was his daily habit when he was in New York and not performing, Geiger wandered into his library.

He closed the windows and closed the doors. Tonight he would make music away from all human ears, other than his own.

He sat down at his Steinway and thought for a moment. Then he began to play. He liked to play at night, when no one would disturb him. To get into the proper mood, he played melodies from Paul Simon and Billy Joel. Then he played some Scott Joplin and, to screw around, some Kander and Ebb. Then, to mess around a little more before getting serious, he played Chopin interlaced with themes from Springsteen and he played Beethoven with motifs from Jerry Garcia.

He smiled. He felt better. Acid-natured old Rabinowitz would probably have already been kicking at the lid of his coffin if he could have heard this.

"You have mongrelized some masters!" the old man would have said. "You are a slut, young man! You have the morality of a musical whore!"

"How is that?" Geiger answered aloud.

"You fuck with many and love none!" Rabinowitz raged in his imagination.

Geiger thought about it. "Maybe," he answered. "But musical promiscuity is its own reward."

He had an image of the departed maestro slamming down the lid above the keyboard. Slamming it down and locking it, lest further sacrilege occur. A similar incident had occurred at a lesson that Geiger had taken at age nineteen when he had sprinkled themes from Def Leppard into some Schubert, which Geiger had announced impetuously, "needs some livening up."

The old man had stormed from the practice chamber. As Geiger thought back, he broke into a full smile for the first time that day—even though he could almost feel the old man's hand on his neck.

Several minutes passed.

After a few measures of introduction, Geiger took one of the dramatic themes from Wagner's *Tannhäuser* and by degrees worked himself up into a cyclone of rainlike runs, hail-like trills, lightning arpeggios, and thunder chords. But these were mere exercises, physical and technical.

Only when he was satisfied his hands were limber enough did he settle down to serious business, alternately attacking and caressing some Chopin.

The music soared in the enclosed room. He was pleased, though aware that he had no audience for this performance. He knew that he had picked up that one small trait from Rabinowitz—playing where no one could hear, lest there be a witness to a mistake or a badly turned phrase. It bothered him when he found himself doing things that the old maestro had done. He wasn't completely sure why. But it bothered him.

Now, sufficiently warmed up, he sank deeply into a major work by Chopin, the Fantasie in F Minor. He spent an hour on it, occasionally toying with or improvising on certain themes. Before he grew too tired, he switched to the Beethoven. The Piano Concerto No. 1 in C Major. One of his favorite works, as well as one of the composer's favorites.

Fatigue wrapped itself around him like a heavy blanket. He thought of Diana sleeping one floor above him. He was anxious to shower and slide into bed with her. If he felt like making love, he would wake her. She never turned him down, and he loved her all the more for it.

His gaze drifted around the room. There were awards and photographs, and plaques and souvenirs. Booty from his many artistic triumphs on five different continents. Unending testimonials to his brilliance. A thousand memories and not a bad one among them.

He took stock.

He was young and—despite the funeral today which brought back a flood of mixed emotions—he felt increasingly good about life. The anxieties and fears that he had entertained earlier in the day didn't seem so monumental now that he was back in his own place, comforted by his own things, secure in his Manhattan fortress.

Life was fine, he decided. Just fine.

Aside from the challenges of his few small upcoming appearances, which were significant, he had nothing in the world to worry about. To fear. To feel bad about.

Or at least, that's what he kept telling himself. But deep down, he knew something was troubling him. He glanced at his watch. It was 1:30 A.M. He finally admitted to himself what it was.

Against all reason, against all logic, against all knowledge, he didn't believe the old man was dead. *That's* what was bothering him. There were so many things left unfinished, and not all of them were symphonies.

He rose from the piano and walked quietly across his library, pursued by this notion and trying to dismiss it.

His hand found the light switch.

He turned it off.

Simultaneously, one of the strings within the piano—he recognized it as the A above middle C—snapped of its own accord.

Geiger flicked the light back on and turned toward the Steinway. He stared for a moment.

Strings snapped all the time, he told himself. But he continued to stare. He would repair the instrument tomorrow, he told himself. There was no rational reason to be alarmed.

Uneasily, Geiger clicked off the light again. He left his library and walked up the steps to his bedroom. Diana, beautiful Diana, was sleeping soundly, breathing evenly.

He sat down on the edge of the bed for a moment and gazed at her. She was the woman of any man's lifetime. The type of woman who would make any man feel lucky to be alive. She wore a blue silk nightgown. It was bunched up high on her thighs as she slept. The neckline had fallen away and one of her breasts was visible.

He smiled the smile of a man deeply in love.

Sometimes, when sleeping next to her, he would awaken slightly and look at her. He sometimes thought his emotions were the purest at these moments, before the other complexities and complications of his present life could crowd in upon him. At these moments, all he could feel was his love for her. He leaned forward and gently kissed her on the lips.

Her eyes flickered for a second, then opened. She saw Rolf and smiled in the mistiness of her half sleep.

"Come to bed," she whispered invitingly. He said he would.

"I want to feel you on top of me. And inside me," she said.

"Just a second," he whispered in return.

He undressed.

Rabinowitz is dead, he reminded himself. *That chapter in my life is over. It's finished. A new reality begins tomorrow.*

True enough.

He settled into bed next to Diana. He put his arm around her and she responded warmly to him, moving her body as close to him as possible.

She smelled wonderful. She always showered before bed and he had no idea what she used on her skin, but it aroused him to no end.

She came fully awake. Her lips met his and her arms wrapped themselves around him.

Half an hour later, everyone in the house was asleep.

There were no disturbances overnight. No intrusions from outside the house.

At one point, however, Rolf Geiger had in his mind the very realistic image of himself on his feet and moving through the house. He was walking as if in a trance, taking himself back downstairs to where he stood in front of his Steinway for several seconds.

Thinking. Ruminating. His head filled with music, his soul filled with challenge.

He was gently rubbing his fingers across the keyboard, so lightly that not a single note was struck. He felt that the eyes of his master were upon him, which was silly, because Rabinowitz was neither any longer his master nor alive. But in a chilling moment, Geiger struck a chord with his right hand. No music emanated from his piano.

He stared at the instrument and didn't understand. When he raised his eyes, Rabinowitz was smiling. Gloating. Then, like the grin of the Cheshire cat, Rabinowitz receded into nothing.

I'm dreaming, Geiger was conscious of thinking. *This is okay, but only because I'm dreaming.*

Then he had gone back upstairs and settled into bed.

When he opened his eyes in the morning and thought back, he realized all the more that the dream had been just that.

A dream.

He was certain that he had never left his bedroom. He also

knew that he had made a decision. The time had come to go before the public again—which, inevitably, he knew, was exactly what Brian Greenstone wanted to discuss.

Outside on East Seventy-third Street, on the opposite side of the block from Geiger's town house, late on the cold evening that followed the funeral, a new presence—a watcher—had taken up position.

The figure that had Number 112 under surveillance was small and sinewy, a ragged little whippet of a man. His eyes were intense and dark, the same color as his spirit, the same color as the night.

He sat in the shadow of a big old tree several houses away from Geiger's. He was one of the feral figures of a New York nighttime, the type of human form that lurks in shadows and doorways and startles passersby with sudden movements. The type of figure that New Yorkers steel themselves against, the sort of presence that one keeps one's eye upon, but never allows to catch one's eyes—though his own eyes had widened significantly when he had spotted Rolf Geiger standing in the frame of his second-story window, if only for a minute.

The figure down on the street was heavily into tobacco. Puff, puff, smoke, smoke, hack, hack, cough, cough.

The watcher sat on the steps of a house with three brick front steps, working a pack of unfiltered Lucky Strikes—the perfect nicotine delivery system—through the night. A little orange glow pinpointed him in the shadows, a glow on the end of his cancer stick.

He kept his eyes on the second floor of 112 East Seventy-third. He had already noted the times that the downstairs lights went off and the times the upstairs lights went on.

There was an old woman who worked in the house, the watcher had noted, and a twentysomething woman who lived there with the famous concert pianist. These people were young and beautiful, both the man and the woman, the figure in the shadows had decided, and were undoubtedly undeserving of their wealth. Well, they had ways of paying.

Already, the watcher knew much of their schedule. The old

lady arrived in the late morning and often stayed until seven-thirty or even later. Then she left and didn't come back until the next day.

What made the house unusual was the unpredictable figures of the pianist and his girlfriend. They would come and go at their apparent whim during the day. The only thing that was predictable was that when they went out during the day, they usually would be met by taxis or private cars. They would leave the neighborhood and they tended to stay out for several hours.

Knowledge of that helped.

The watcher noted that this morning the lights had gone out at one-fifteen. A nighttime pattern would eventually emerge, too.

The watcher stayed till 3:00 A.M. Then, with the streets very quiet, he was certain that no further activity would occur in the pianist's home that night.

The watcher looked down at the small pile of cigarette butts that he had created. He brushed them out onto the sidewalk and rose.

He walked westward toward Madison Avenue, thinking of how if he had nudged the limousine door just a little harder, a little faster, he could have crushed that too-talented right hand and ended Rolf Geiger's career the afternoon of the funeral.

Tsk, tsk, he mused. What a shame he had missed.

Oh, well, what the hell, he told himself. *There's always a next time.*

The watcher had nothing else good on his mind either, and so disappeared into the night.

four

Up until two years earlier and the time when he decided to withdraw from most public performances, Rolf Geiger had been the splashiest, most dynamic, most famous musician in the world.

When the twenty-seven-year-old American virtuoso played the piano, women often hurled bouquets, candy, and even lingerie onto the stage. They shrieked and sometimes fainted. When he played New York, London, Rio de Janeiro, Tokyo, Berlin, Rome, or any of the innumerable other points of the world which he mesmerized, many in the audiences surged toward the stage following his recitals. His fans wanted to gaze closely upon the most handsome, talented, and engaging musician of his generation.

In Rome three summers previously, during his world tour of 1995, the stage was overrun with fans following a rocked-up performance of Prokofiev's Piano Concerto No. 3 in C Major. Geiger's fans pulled apart a Steinway and fought for broken strings and keys. Someone made away with the white tie that he had worn during his performance. The woman who had first seized the tie fainted when she realized that she had it.

Geiger well knew the impact he was making and the hold he had over his fans. He was a rock star in a field of classicists. And he was not averse to adding his own touches, his own drama, his own sense of impact to a concert.

In Stockholm on the same tour, he played for five days at the majestic new state theater. During his booking, the stage was lit entirely by candles—a special dispensation from the fire marshal. The candles were powder blue, matching his formal suit. Then he continued on to Paris where, on Bastille Day, 1995, accompanied by l'Orchestre Nationale de Paris, he played a superb jazzed-up Debussy on a tricolor Steinway *supergrande*. The instrument had been specially constructed for the occasion, the only one of its kind in the world—right down to the alternating red, white, and blue keys.

But that was only the beginning.

His stage in Paris had been built at the northern base of the Eiffel Tower. The tower itself was backlit as he performed, and his roof was a canopy of radiant stars. Before one million French men and women and assorted others who had traveled from all points of the world, giant-projection television screens were set in every direction across the Champ-de-Mars all the way to the Seine. As an encore, he played an impromptu "La Marseillaise," seamlessly weaving in and out of it alternating strains of Tchaikovsky's *1812* Overture and Gershwin's *An American in Paris*.

Fireworks followed, igniting the sky a second time. It was the most dramatic appearance of a Yank in the French capital since Lindbergh in 1927 and Kennedy in 1962.

Even if critics and purists hated what he was doing, Geiger had a way of taking the music of a nation and bringing it to its citizens in ways that made it pulse with new life. In staid, cautious Warsaw, he was followed by a mob of one hundred Polish women on the street after he played his own variations on Chopin. In Prague, he was hailed as the philosophical descendant of Dvořák as he, visitor from the new world, played his own piano transcription of the *New World Symphony*, interpreting Dvořák in ways that had never before been heard.

In Vienna his arrival was akin to the second coming of Mozart. There were also serious whispers in the Austrian capital that Geiger was the reincarnation of Franz Liszt and that he possessed the resurrected genius of Beethoven. Around the world, he was more popular than Presley, Sinatra, or the Beatles had ever been. Grenada, where Rolf Geiger had played for free at a charity event against world hunger in 1990 when he was twenty-three, put him on a series of stamps.

All this for a young classical pianist, though Geiger was far from a classicist. He was unafraid to experiment, contemporize, or popularize venerated works. His arrival on the music scene had begun to reverse the trend of popular music for the last half century. By the time he was twenty-one, he had been on the covers of two hundred publications around the world.

From Rolf Geiger's fingers, musicologists heard sounds that they now said had been dead for two centuries. His performances of Beethoven—when he played Beethoven without monkeying around with him—caused hardened critics across the world, seated in dark music halls, to look up from their notebooks and feel the hair raise on the back of their necks. That was standard, and that was why the critics hated it so much when he extemporized. Also standard was the eye contact he would often establish with his audiences. He would sometimes play an entire concerto or sonata without ever glancing at the keyboard. Once, as a stunt at one of the big gambling palaces in Atlantic City one balmy June evening, he played his own transcription of Brahms' *Academic Festival* Overture while blindfolded. He didn't miss a note.

Rolf Geiger was that good. And Geiger, who had grown up poor in a failing, rusting, industrial town in West Virginia for the first thirteen years of his life, had a problem with none of this.

Sometimes he would perform with three pianos onstage, using them as his whims dictated during a performance. He played every important city in the world. Concert halls were not large enough to hold his audiences. Sometimes stadia weren't, either. His performances, like the one in Paris, were *events* that transcended music.

He played Beethoven and Rachmaninoff in full formal attire. But every bit as often he played in white tie, tails, and blue jeans, depending on the venue. He played in green velvet in

Dublin. He wore a tricornered Minuteman hat and a Red Sox jersey when he played Sousa on the Fourth of July 1992, on the Esplanade in Boston. And once—to shock—when he played the Chandler Pavilion in Los Angeles, he performed in tight black patent leather jacket and jeans, no shirt, and sequined boots. He liked to perform on blue Steinways and red Yamahas. It barely mattered.

Equally, he was given to the odd acerbic one-liner, occasionally even off-the-cuff comments to his audiences during concerts. At the Chandler concert he noted that the great Beethoven physically stood only five feet four inches in his lifetime.

"In the film business," Geiger told the Hollywood audience, "that would have made him an Outstanding Short Subject."

It didn't hurt that Geiger was young, blond, and dazzlingly handsome, with a face ruled by his eyes—blue, darting, and intense. Yet his eyes were also romantic and mysterious, at once drawing you in but not letting you past. His cheekbones were high—Tartar cheekbones, Rabinowitz once called them—and his dark blond hair was shaggy as it fell just past the top of his ears.

His hands were powerful. Large and strong, yet sensitive. Veined and fleshed versions of something sculpted by Michelangelo. He could reach a twelfth on a standard keyboard. His legs were long. His body was lean but athletic. As a youth, once he took up the piano seriously, he had won every important piano competition he had ever entered.

The musicality of his life was nonstop.

He could do everything with a piano except make it fly; but he didn't need to. His music, his musicianship, his showmanship, the persona of Rolf Geiger soared by itself. At the end of his 1995 European tour, as a conceit for European television, he presented himself at a television studio in Monaco and played Chopin's "Etude for Black Keys" with a lit votive candle balanced on the back of each hand.

Sometimes, his talent could scare the daylights out of everyone, including himself. The problem was, eventually such events caused the fiery backlash among the self-anointed "serious music critics" of the world. They had turned on him with a pyrotechnic vengeance, almost to the point where some would no longer even consider him an artist.

"One doesn't *hear* the onetime prodigy Rolf Geiger play, so much as one *sees* him play," wrote the arts editor of the *San Francisco Chronicle,* putting in words what many musicologists privately felt. "This whole 'cult of performance' thing has gotten completely out of control. Geiger has become the sociopath of the symphony."

"Rolf Geiger," wrote another scribbler in *Time,* "is ruining classical music when he could be saving it. Because of his enormous popularity, much of the concertgoing public knows the great music only by the corrupt variations Geiger plays. They know it not by the way it was written. He uses great music the way Evander Holyfield and Mike Tyson use a sparring partner."

"A fraud," wrote the *Toronto Globe & Mail.*

"An out and out sym-*phony,"* maintained the *Dallas Morning News.*

"If all these people knew so much about music," Geiger was once quoted in response, "they'd be *creating* music instead of writing about it."

But, over the last two dozen months, and as he viewed the distant approach of his thirtieth birthday, Geiger had become elusive, then reclusive. Militantly so, playing only at small dates in remote concert halls while he sorted out his life, his talent, and his art.

"Time to think," he called it. "Time to consider the direction of my life."

Time to decide what he wanted to be. At least now, he had finally made that decision. And the passing of Rabinowitz had only underscored what he felt to be the correctness of his choice.

At 10 A.M. on Friday, in his home, the day after the Rabinowitz funeral, Rolf Geiger telephoned his agent, Brian Greenstone.

Greenstone maintained a huge office on Seventh Avenue at Fifty-seventh Street and represented most of the top classical artists in New York. Geiger had always been represented by the fifty-five-year-old London-born Greenstone. As in all endeavors, Geiger was infinitely loyal to the people who had always been loyal to him.

Habitually, Greenstone lunched and frequently dined at the Trattoria Dell'arte on Seventh Avenue, and often used that venue for meetings with clients. Yet, when something truly monumental was afoot, such as it was now, Greenstone liked to avoid meals in restaurants. One never knew when they were going to be interrupted by fans or, worse, talkative friends.

So at the funeral Greenstone had invited Rolf and Diana to dine with him and his wife, Sarah, the next evening at Greenstone's home. Geiger had accepted. But on further thought, Geiger realized that he owed his agent several invitations. So he reversed this invitation and asked the Greenstones to come dine at East Seventy-third. Greenstone courteously protested, then accepted.

Later that morning, Geiger turned his attention to his Steinway and its ruptured string. He had become quite adept at applying emergency first aid to his own equipment. He replaced the string, fiddled with the tuning, and was pleased after about forty minutes of effort.

He selected several of the various editions of Beethoven's sonatas from his library and refamiliarized himself with several movements for the rest of the morning.

Shortly after noon, he went to a health club in the East Fifties where he worked out three times a week when not on tour. Playing concerts was as physically demanding as it was mentally exhausting. It was imperative to stay in top physical shape, though, as a matter of personal pride, he would never have allowed his flesh to deteriorate without a fight.

He returned home for lunch, and a short nap. The jet lag and the end of the trip to San Remo were still having their effects. He dealt with some business matters over the phone while Diana was at appointments during the afternoon. She had agreed to write a long article for each of two of the better New York magazines and was out doing interviews and research.

Toward five, he went out into his neighborhood for a brief walk, mentally running through his feelings toward the possible proposals that his agent was likely to make that evening. Obviously, Greenstone wanted to nudge him back toward the major recital halls. *A lot* of time had passed since Geiger had performed on a major tour.

Walking on Madison Avenue, he smiled to himself.

Would Brian *nudge* him back? Or would it be closer to a firm shove? Or a hard push?

Rolf needed to make an important decision. Was it time to play again? Was it time to embrace audiences and let them embrace him? Moreover, was it time to drop the jazz, pizzazz, and rock and try to take his place among the finest pianists of the century?

He had never *really* become what he had shown promise of becoming. Something about the whole situation scared the living hell out of him.

But then again, there had been the most recent trip to Europe . . . the lightning in the airplane . . . the death of Rabinowitz. . . . all this coupled with his long absence from the world's most demanding recital halls. These things—each one complex within itself—were factors in a new equation for Rolf Geiger, leitmotifs in the composition of the present.

There was a light rain falling as he strolled alone on Madison Avenue.

Just as one note leads to another in a composition, one memory primed another until he was sorting through a whole array of them. The past always caused a pain that was never far from him.

He had endured a childhood of abuse and poverty. A home with plastic sheeting across the broken glass of his bedroom window, sheeting that failed miserably against the brutal winters of West Virgina. He could remember lying in bed at night and feeling the wind seeping through the walls. The winters had been like an enemy that always had one surrounded.

Rickety furniture. Sears, previously owned. Naked lightbulbs. Heat from a failing coal stove. Threadbare carpets from Goodwill. Chipped paint throughout the house. Not enough food many nights. He was the only child, and for the first years of his life he thought everyone in the world lived like this.

Frank Geiger, his father. A drunken, violence-prone man.

Geiger Senior worked in an anthracite coal mine when he worked at all. Half the time he drank his weekly paycheck. He had so opposed Rolf's musical affinities that he had once taken a miner's hammer and smashed his own grandmother's piano, the only object of worth the family owned.

"Pianos are for fairies. Music's for fairies. No son of mine is going to grow up to be a fairy."

Frank Geiger figured his son should work in the mines. If cracking coal was good enough for him, it was good enough for his damned kid. The boy had been an accident, anyway.

So Rolf had played at Catholic school, the one his mother insisted he go to and for which his mother's parents paid. Dorothy, Rolf's mother, was the Catholic in the family. Frank wasn't anything. He worshiped only beer.

The nuns thought Rolf had good musical instincts. Sister Mary William had arranged some time each week with the school piano. When his father found out about it, he'd smashed his son. But Rolf continued to play. There was no teacher, so Rolf figured it out by himself, with help from books in the town library. The nuns also familiarized him with some of the great composers. Music appreciation was handled well at St. Agnes'.

Dorothy Geiger was a plain, uneducated woman who walked with a limp and always carried a green plastic rosary in her apron pocket. She might have been able to keep a job if her husband hadn't continually smashed her, too. He beat her more times than anyone suspected, enough times to have caused the limp. She grew old with sinus damage—the result of one of those blows straight to the face—which contributed to a breathing problem which brought on respiratory problems which—along with too many packs of Marlboros and lousy health care—brought on sinusitis which would bring on a blood infection. Her death came at age forty-four. At least Rolf was grown by that time. Her son was the one thing that legitimized her life. Rolf sent her money, but by that time a mild form of derangement had set in, and she wouldn't spend any of it.

Smashing things. That was always Rolf's father's solution to everything.

Once he had even given such instruction to his son.

At age eleven, Rolf was to change schools, going from a lower-middle-class district in Shenandoah City to a tougher, grittier blue-collar junior-senior high school in Wales Valley.

St. Agnes' School. Parochial. Franciscan.

His father dropped him at the new schoolyard at six-fifty on the first morning. "Find the biggest toughest kid in the schoolyard at recess," Geiger told his son. "Then go up to him and punch him in his fat fucking face."

"What?"

"Do it and everyone will leave you alone here for six years."

"But—?"

Geiger slapped his son. "Do it, God damn it, or don't frigging come home."

Then he shoved his son out of the car.

Rolf agonized. He stood on the empty asphalt of the playground. He waited. School started. Then recess. Eventually, he saw a good-looking but rugged young man throwing a football to some of the seniors. Rolf worked up his courage. Then he walked up to the young man and smacked him. A sucker punch from the left, hard across the jaw. Just as his father had requested.

It loosened two of the recipient's teeth and drew blood from a cut lip. It was quite a shot. The young man stared at him in shock. He didn't retaliate. The recipient of the punch had been a young seminarian, Brother Matthew, just assigned to teach at St. Agnes'.

Rolf found himself sitting in the school's front hall five minutes later. He was terrified, waiting for an audience with the school's principal, Monsignor Kelly. He expected to be beaten in return, because that's how it would have gone at home.

He finally had his audience. Monsignor Kelly listened. Rolf explained what he'd done. And why.

The priest looked at him thoughtfully, then spoke. "Go into the next room for a moment, young man, and think about your actions," Kelly said. "There's a lesson to be learned today."

"Yes, sir."

Rolf went into the next room, a small study. There was a piano. Geiger looked at it and stood near it, running his hands across the keyboard but afraid to sound a note. It had been a long time since he'd had access to an instrument.

A few minutes later, Brother Matthew came into the room. Rolf looked up quickly and abruptly pulled his hands away from the piano.

Rolf was frightened. He looked at the young brother. Matthew smiled. They talked for several minutes. Then the brother picked up on the way Geiger's eyes frequently slid sideways to the piano.

"You like music?" the brother asked.

Geiger nodded.

"Can you play?"

Matthew opened the keyboard.

"A little."

"Do you have an instrument at home?"

"I used to."

"What happened to it?"

Geiger shrugged. "It got broken," was all he said.

Matthew reached to the keyboard. With one strong white hand he found the melody from a concerto by Mozart. It lasted fifteen seconds.

"Can you do that?" Matthew asked.

Geiger looked at the keyboard. He hadn't touched one in years. He set his hands haltingly to it and repeated the melody. The second time through he added chords.

"Impressive," said Brother Matthew. "And I think God would say that this a much better use of your hands—creating something beautiful instead of perpetrating violence. Okay?"

In great relief, Rolf nodded. "Okay," he said.

"We're friends?" Matthew asked.

Rolf nodded. "I'm sorry."

They shook hands.

Monsignor Kelly went to the Geiger home to discuss the incident. Frank Geiger came to the door. He didn't like the look of the cassock. Profanely and drunkenly, Frank Geiger took a swing at the priest. The school then understood what Rolf faced at home.

Sometimes in dark moments, long after becoming a star of the recital stages on five continents, Rolf Geiger thought back to the crushing poverty and oppression in which he had been raised. And when he did, he sometimes wondered whether his piano playing was some colossal act of fraud: deep down he questioned if he was really as good as he thought he was, or if he deserved the adulation that came his way.

Of course, he'd then pose himself the next question: one which defied a logical answer. He thought of Frank Geiger, who died at forty-seven with a sixteen-ounce can of Old Milwaukee in his hand, eight crumpled bucks in his pocket, and a bullet in his neck. A white-trash life and a white-trash death. So how in heaven's name had Rolf's mind and hands been touched with such genius? Where had it come from?

And where, for that matter, was it leading?

Today the future and the past seemed to be on his mind concurrently. He shuddered when he thought of his childhood. The ten-block walks to school in the winter in a coat that was threadbare and a pair of shoes with no insulation. Shirt and pants that were repaired beyond belief, that other children in the school ridiculed. The memory hung around him like a fetid rotting odor that was unbanishable.

Time spiraled. As he walked in Manhattan on the day following the Rabinowitz funeral, along the expensive shops of Madison Avenue in the East Eighties, his mind continued to drift.

Brother Matthew had been the first to show Rolf how this one black dot on the treble clef corresponded to C on the keyboard. The same dot, or note, on the bass clef corresponded to E. Within a few minutes Rolf could plunk a tune from the paper. The next time he sat down, he could pull a tune out of the air, then write it down with all the proper notation.

Eventually, Brother Matthew sent Rolf to see Stanley Kraus, who lived in the next town. Kraus was a learned man in his seventies, gentle in demeanor, with wise old-world eyes behind wire-rimmed glasses. He was stocky and walked with a cane. A kindly Yiddish version of Benjamin Franklin. He had built a career in Philadelphia, giving lessons, and for a while playing under the gifted baton of Eugene Ormandy at The Philadelphia Orchestra.

"So? You're going to play the piano for me?" Kraus inquired, settling into a chair by the side of a baby grand that consumed all of his living room. "Did you bring your sheet music?"

"No."

"Then how will you play?"

"From memory."

The old man raised another eyebrow. He smiled indulgently, expecting little. "Then *what* will you play?" Kraus asked. "Do you have a favorite piece?"

" 'Für Elise,' " Geiger answered after a moment's thought.

"Ah. Well, then. By all means, please play."

Mr. Kraus settled into his Queen Anne chair. He closed his eyes and waited. Twelve-year-old Rolf Geiger sat down at the piano bench. He smiled sweetly. His fingers found the keyboard.

Then, gently, he began.

A few measures and Kraus felt his pulse quicken. He looked at the intensity on the boy's face, the knowing run of the fingers across the keys. There was a clearness, a precision, and a facility to Geiger's playing which were beyond astonishing. It filled the room.

Goose bumps traveled up and down the teacher's arms and kept him in a mixed state of torment and awe. Stanley Kraus was swept away by the feeling, the passion, the immense talent. Kraus was almost frightened. The raw talent, the genius, was prodigious. And no one seemed to have picked up on it yet.

Geiger came to the end of the piece. He turned to the old man.

"Was that all right?" Rolf asked.

"Young man? Are you unaware of how good you are?"

Geiger shrugged.

Kraus thought for a moment, then reached to a pile of music books that lay nearby in casual disarray. "I would like you to try something else," he said. He prowled through the books. "Have you played a lot of Beethoven?"

"Which piece are you looking for?"

"*Moonlight* Sonata."

Kraus found the book.

"I'd like you to play the last movement," the teacher said. He opened the book.

"It's all right," Geiger said. "I know it."

The boy played. And again Kraus froze, barely moving until Geiger had finished. Eventually the boy looked up and saw the teacher staring at him.

"Was that good?" Geiger asked.

"I *expected* 'good.' What you demonstrated was in another realm."

"Thank you, sir."

"Has anyone heard you play other than the priests and nuns in your hometown?"

"No, sir."

Kraus waited for a moment as he formed the next question.

"I want you to tell me something," Kraus asked at length. "The piece you just played was not a child's piece. How do you grasp the poetry and passion of Beethoven? How is it possible in one so young?"

"You won't laugh if I tell you?" Geiger asked.

"I won't laugh, Rolf."

"The music speaks to me, sir. It communicates."

"What does it say?"

"I don't know how to explain it. But I feel something in it."

Kraus thought for a moment and sighed. "But how do you know so well how to interpret a certain piece?"

"It's very clear to me. It's obvious."

"But if no one has showed you? Or if you have never heard it before?"

"It's still obvious, sir."

Kraus settled back. He looked down for a moment and seemed to be thinking. Then he raised his eyes, having arrived at a decision.

"I am going to telephone a friend who is a conductor in New York City," Kraus said softly. "He will need to hear you play, also."

Geiger felt confused, almost as if he had done something wrong. Mr. Kraus seemed like a kind, intelligent man. Why couldn't he stay here? Why must he be again passed along?

"You must be taught by one of the current masters," Kraus said. "Rubinstein. Or Horowitz. Or Rabinowitz."

"Who are they?" Geiger asked.

"You've never heard of them?"

"I think I heard their names a little."

"Have you heard their recordings?"

Geiger shook his head.

"I will find you some tapes. This will be my gift to you. Rubinstein, Horowitz, and Rabinowitz are the greatest pianists alive today," Kraus explained. "One of them must instruct you. You will have to go to New York."

"Oh." Geiger thought about it. "What if none of them want me?"

The teacher laughed. "That is not the problem. They will fight for you."

Stanley Kraus was right. But it took almost eighteen months to move Geiger to the proper audience. During this time Rolf's academic studies at St. Agnes's were accelerated.

Geiger went to New York. The Julliard School prepared a special program for him. The word "prodigy" was used for the first time. A few notes appeared about him in newspapers that covered the classical music world.

Eventually, he found an audience with Isador Rabinowitz at a rehearsal chamber at Carnegie Hall on a sultry August afternoon.

Rabinowitz, like Stanley Kraus, was stunned at what he heard on his first meeting with the young man. Even more astonishing was the fact that at age thirteen, Geiger remained primarily self-taught, unspoiled by the techniques and philosophies of others. He was a brutally raw but immeasurably gifted talent.

On their first meeting, Rabinowitz sat and listened to Rolf Geiger play ten different pieces, five of them new. Toward the end of the visit, Rabinowitz stacked the deck, presenting Geiger with a pair of fantasias he had never seen before—both by the difficult Sigismond Thalberg. One featured a cantabile section with rugged right-hand arpeggios and left-hand octaves. The other was marked by Thalberg's normal lack of harmonic imagination, and was exceedingly obtuse, with a section of *leggierissimo* octaves that passed from the left hand to the right, while its theme still rang out in the tenor range.

Giving the piece to a young pianist was the musical equivalent of a bear trap. It had been written for a mature virtuoso for the sake of showing off virtuosity.

Geiger didn't miss a note.

He played flawlessly and with the virtuosity that Thalberg had demanded, filling the rehearsal space with an explosively brilliant rendition.

Rabinowitz sat silently as the echo of the final notes resounded into oblivion. The boy turned toward him and waited.

Rabinowitz said nothing.

"Any good?" the boy finally asked.

After another moment, almost grudgingly, Rabinowitz answered.

"Yes. It was considerably skilled. Thoughtful. Highly competent," Rabinowitz said calmly. The maestro pondered for a longer moment, then replied in his never-quite-perfect English. "But you have much for to be learned. For example, you hold yourself the fingers rather too high."

"I do?"

"You must hold them more closer to the keys, in especially the legato passages. You will that way make the music more completely finished, with a rounder and more ringing tone."

"Oh." The boy shrugged, deciphering the man's strange accent. "All right."

"More than all right," snapped Rabinowitz. "This you will do."

Obediently, Rolf placed both his hands above the keyboard again, measuring the new placement with his eyes. Then he dropped his fingertips an eighth of an inch. The gesture, the slight drop, would have been imperceptible to most observers.

"Yes! There! Better! No farther!" Rabinowitz snapped.

Rolf smiled and turned to the maestro, expecting at least a smile of approval. None came.

Rabinowitz's eyes were already lowered. The old man was carefully studying the unusual academic résumé that Rolf had brought with him. Two remote parochial schools. Lessons from the nuns. Acceptance to Julliard. He turned to him with cold calculating eyes.

The old man then spent twenty minutes describing the indignities and persecutions he had suffered as a Jew in Europe, frequently with a wink from the local Catholic clergy in Poland, Hungary, and Russia, he said. All this through the briar patch of Rabinowitz's English, which was always a crazy quilt of stray flaws, false stops, and strange consonants. Much to the boy's shock, the maestro's English was strewn with the word *fuck,* and its gerund.

These pieces of language, Rabinowitz pronounced as, *fock* and *focking.* Such usage sometimes gave even some of Rabinowitz's most brilliant observations a comical undertone.

Faced with Rabinowitz, Rolf knew enough to sit, listen, and absorb, but not to disagree or take issue, any more than he would have corrected grammar or punctuation. At the end, Rabinowitz made another pronouncement.

"I will take you now on as a student," he said. "Not because I so want to. Not because I so need to. But because I see no one else would be capable."

Then he left the room. He slammed the door. Geiger wondered what he had done to offend the great but formidably intimidating man.

Today, years later, as he ruminated through Manhattan in the aftermath of Rabinowitz's funeral, the image came galloping back to Rolf Geiger:

He could still see Rabinowitz charging angrily out of the rehearsal chamber following their first encounter. It was an image that recurred to him a lot over the years, like the echoes of his bitter childhood. Sometimes on very cold lonely nights he could hear all these echoes simultaneously, wheezing through the chambers of his heart like an ill-directed wind.

Spooks.

That's what they were, he mused to himself.

Little mental spooks.

They were like the unanswered questions that also resided in that quarter of his mind. Where, for example, had Rabinowitz's soul gone? Where had the talent gone that was in the dead man's head? Or his hands?

Was it out there somewhere, waiting to inhabit another human being? Or was it gone for good, disintegrating with Rabinowitz's remains?

Geiger entertained similar thoughts about himself.

From a poor working-class background, a home with no culture, and an unplanned birth had sprung Rolf Geiger, the musical prodigy of his age.

How could that have happened? How could he—of such a compromised background—have been born with the hands and the intellect to summon forth angelic music in a world that no longer believed in Heaven?

How could this have been possible?

Or was this the way it always happened?

Well, he had decided long ago, it was no less plausible than the way music had picked him up and transported him from dirtball white-trash squalor to a world of art and beauty.

Geiger's attention drifted back again to the present.

He passed a small French bistro, recalling his first trip to Europe a dozen summers earlier.

There had been an overnight flight to Paris and then a plane ride to Nice. Then a car and driver had taken him into Nice, where he would compete for the prestigious Grand Prix du Piano de Nice, the French city's most competitive musical award.

But there had been much more than the music and the competition.

There had been the sun. The excitement. The people.

The sex.

He had been seventeen years old and was seeing this part of the world for the very first time.

Nearing the end of the competition, he had sat out on the seaside veranda of the Hôtel Negresco one afternoon and gazed out at the blue Mediterranean. He watched the lithe girls walking along the beach, flirting with young men in cars, young men not too much older than he and with much less to offer. He glanced back up over his shoulder to a balconied suite he had been blessed with in the hotel and thought of the prices that these people charged.

Highway robbery. In French. A glass of fresh orange juice cost eight dollars, for Heaven's sake. He was glad that a New York foundation was paying to have him entered. He hoped that their accountants didn't look too carefully at the itemized costs of the trip.

God, he thought to himself, emphatically rather than in prayer. To live a life like this it was necessary to have money. Not just simple money, but real wealth.

He smiled slightly, because now, sitting on a terrace in the south of France, one of three finalists in the competition and the only non-Russian, he was old enough to realize that his life would, or could, be different than the lives of blue-collar drudgery that lay before his onetime tormentors.

Dead-end jobs and lousy paychecks. Nagging fat wives. Premature aging. Bowling leagues and bulging porcine waistlines. Nicotine addiction and strokes at age forty-five.

Well, screw all of that, he decided. He would have none of that for himself. He had sampled enough nice clothes, fine hotels, expensive restaurants, and air travel to know that there was another universe out there, one for which he now felt he was destined.

This gift in his hands would take him there. So would the intricate cadences within his mind. Wherever the genius came from, whoever had sent it in his direction, he would gladly accept it and nurture it.

And how about all the elegant women who were always hanging around? He could already see how habit-forming all of this could become. And he knew that for Rolf Geiger, there was just one key to the vault.

Music.

Not just music. There were armadas of musicians in the world, and legions of fine pianists. Anyone could tickle the ivories and bring forth some melodies. There was even a small coterie of the best and finest pianists in the world. Geiger had nothing against these other artists, he decided. Nothing at all. They were free to live their lives and play their music as they saw fit.

But for him, things would have to be different. Many of the others had had a head start, having been born into musical families, having taken training from the time they were two years old.

No, he would have to arrive from a different direction. He was a raw, unspoiled musical talent. He would listen to his mentor Rabinowitz. He would entertain what the old man had to say. But he would do things his way. He would account only to himself.

First, Geiger mused, he would have to be the best. Not just the best alive, but the best ever. Accomplishing that, he would have to take it to an even higher level. He would have to *entertain,* as well. He would have to be the most exciting keyboard artist ever to draw breath.

Chopin mixed with Roger Daltry.

Liszt mingled with Elton John.

Beethoven with Elvis.

That would get him where he wanted to go in life.

Well, he thought to himself at age seventeen, why the hell not? The previous night, he had knocked the European music world flat on its derrière.

Geiger had played Tchaikovsky with a bold sexiness that had pianists in the audience studying his fingering to try to decipher how he did what he did. The pyrotechnical conclusion had sparked the audience to its feet in a standing ovation.

But he wasn't finished. As an encore and as a near conceit, he administered a knockout punch to the vast hall at the Salles des Philosophes. He treated them to a rousing improvised piano transcription of Sousa's "Stars and Stripes Forever," intermingling into it the melody of "Auprès de Ma Blonde," before morphing both themes into a fiery but sweetly beautiful concluding impromptu composition based on romantic themes— eternally popular in France—of Camille Saint-Saëns.

The encore precipitated a fifteen-minute ovation to end the evening. No one present had ever seen, much less heard, anything of the sort. The next morning, that morning as Geiger sat on the terrace of the Negresco, the daily *Nice-Matin* carried Rolf Geiger's picture on its front page, breathlessly proclaiming him *le jeune chevalier américain du piano, sans peur et sans reproche.* And with one taste of world-class adulation, he never doubted the direction he wanted his life to take.

Today in New York City years later, walking a final block in the rain on East Seventy-third Street, he thought of the conversation he would have with his agent this evening. He had been detoured from his long-term ambitions over the last few years, but now his proper time had come. Even his hands seemed to be itching to play again.

To play and *really* play. No horsing around this time.

He would listen very carefully to what Brian Greenstone had to say. Then, when Brian was talked out, he would say yes or no to whatever direction for his future Brian wished to propose.

His thoughts were so intent, as he walked the final hundred feet down his own block, that he never noticed the gnarled man in a rumpled coat sitting in a doorway across the street, gazing at Geiger intensely.

The watcher's gaze was so intent that Geiger could almost feel it upon his back.

Almost, but he didn't.

five

Sarah and Brian Greenstone arrived punctually for dinner Friday evening at seven-thirty.

Sarah Greenstone was a third wife, the most recent in a succession of very pretty brides who increasingly got younger and thinner as Greenstone got older and stouter. Sarah was fifteen years younger than her husband. She was a petite contemplative woman with black hair. She was about forty years old but could pass for her early thirties with her gentle, unlined face.

Intellectually, she was as sharp as a razor. She had an MBA from the University of Chicago and a big office in the Chrysler Building. She held a challenging job in public relations for a famous Swiss pharmaceutical company that always seemed to be under indictment for one thing or another.

Geiger invited his guests into his library when they arrived. Mrs. Jamison had filled the town house with excellent cooking aromas. Dinner was served shortly before eight.

Geiger and his agent spent the meal speaking about social matters and the dire state of the classical concert business. Sarah and Diana talked quietly between themselves, tuning out the men's conversation when it suited them.

After the meal, Mrs. Jamison cleared, amidst compliments from all four diners. Over dessert and coffee, Brian Greenstone moved to the purpose of the meeting.

"Obviously, Rolf," Greenstone began, "I came here for an ulterior reason this evening. I'd like to suggest to you a very specific career move. May I tell you exactly without you falling out of your chair?"

Greenstone had moved to the States as a nineteen-year-old, entering the country on a six-month visa and staying a lifetime. His speech still bore the cadences of south London.

"Please do," Geiger said.

"I think the time is right for you to start performing again. But in a different way than ever before. I think you should perform a world tour on a *grand* scale. But you should drop the pizzazz and the pop music. Just do classical. Pure and simple."

Geiger smiled slightly. His round blue eyes glided sideways, and he looked at the two women. Then he looked back to his agent.

"Where is this coming from?" Geiger asked.

"From me as a friend and from me as your most trusted business advisor, Rolf," Greenstone said. "I'd like you to do a world tour in which you finally establish your rightful place at the pinnacle of pianists."

A moment passed. Geiger did not blink. Greenstone paused slightly, then set down his coffee.

"What are we talking about, Brian?" Geiger asked.

"I'm talking about—*strictly* classical music—a tour to end all tours. The principle is very simple. I want you to establish yourself as the greatest concert pianist who ever lived."

Geiger raised an eyebrow. "That's *all?*" he asked.

"That's all," said Greenstone. He smiled slightly. "And I know bloody full well that the same thought has gone through your head. Hasn't it? Be honest."

"Maybe," Geiger said, being half-honest.

"It's attainable, Rolf. It's attainable for you *now*. Fascinating prospect? No? And the current equation is perfect. The passing of Rabinowitz. The dreadful state of the classical music industry which *desperately* needs a new hero with some sex appeal. Your age. Your current following. Your immense talent.''

Geiger thought things through for a moment.

"You have to do it," Greenstone said.

"As you said, I've already been thinking about something like this," Geiger confessed. "But I want to hear your own words. What exactly are we talking about? What music would I play, for example?''

"All the great works for piano. Every one. The great sonatas and concertos. Beethoven. Prokofiev. Mozart. Schubert. Ravel. Liszt. Rachmaninoff," Greenstone answered. "God! Why are you asking me, my boy? You'd know better than I!''

Geiger glanced around as he spoke. Both women had their eyes set firmly upon him, like a pair of terriers.

"You would circle the world and play the greatest works by the greatest composers in the history of civilization," Greenstone said. "Perhaps three dozen dates. Or four dozen. Whichever is necessary. All the greatest piano concertos. All the finest sonatas. *Everything.* But only one performance of each work. Different dates all over the world, backed by the greatest orchestras and conductors alive. North America. South America. Europe and Asia. Maybe even a date or two in China and at least one date in Africa. Probably Egypt. Maybe that would be the final date. Still with me?''

"Yes.''

"Is this making sense?" Greenstone asked.

"For the sake of argument," Geiger mused, warming quickly to the concept, "I could play Saint-Saëns's *Egyptian* Concerto in Egypt. But I would want to close the tour with Beethoven. The *Emperor* Concerto at Luxor with the Valley of the Kings as my backdrop.''

Rolf paused for a moment and savored the thought. "I'm wondering if we could draw a *live* audience of half a million people to that one.''

Greenstone shook his head in admiration as well as astonishment. "I love this man," he said to the two women. "You don't think on a small scale, do you, Rolf?''

"No. I suppose not. And you're thinking exactly the same way.''

"You're brilliant, and we all know it," Greenstone said. His own thoughts were in overdrive. "So that makes me brilliant by association."

"Certain pieces would lend themselves to certain venues," Geiger said, thinking the idea further along. "I would play Rachmaninoff and Prokofiev in Russia. Chopin in Warsaw and Paris. I would play Mozart in Vienna. Scarlatti in Milan and Rome. Beethoven in Berlin, Munich, and Tokyo." He smiled wryly. "Maybe even some Aaron Copland in New York and some Scott Joplin in Kansas City." He paused. "Am I getting the right idea?" he asked.

"There you go," the agent said in admiration. "You have *exactly* the idea. Not even Isador Rabinowitz would have dared to do something like this."

"Exactly."

"Then you find the idea attractive?"

"Yes."

The two women exchanged a wary glance.

"Hell, Brian," Geiger continued, "you read the press I get. You know what people say in the industry: I quote bastardize unquote my quote immense unquote talents. I got ripped like hell the last time I played big venues, and it shut me down for two years."

"I dare say, Rolf," Greenstone said, "that when your encore in London mixed themes from Madonna with themes from Mozart, you may have titillated your audience but you *did indeed* bloody some snooty noses in the classical music world."

"I thought that was brilliant," Diana said. "Particularly since Madonna was in the audience and the whole repertoire was spontaneous."

"I agree," Sarah Greenstone chipped in.

Geiger shrugged in self-effacement.

"Look, I agree, also," Brian said. "I'm just stating that it's no arcane mystery why my favorite client gets the impertinent reviews he gets, even though every woman in the audience seems to want to have his children."

"Well, I'm tired of hearing about it, too, Brian," Rolf continued, remaining very serious. "Maybe it *is* time to shut people up. What you're suggesting is so damned challenging and so spectacular that it would establish my place forever in the history of the piano.''

''Sure. Your place as 'the greatest who ever lived.' That's what you mean, right?'' Greenstone asked. ''You'd be happy with something as humble as that.''

''That's correct.'' Geiger paused.

''Would this also indicate that you will agree not to—dare I say?—screw around on this tour? No mixing Presley with Paderewski?''

''No mixing,'' Geiger said.

''And no red-satin suits with string ties when you play Rome. God! I saw a picture of you when you just played San Remo. You may have played the music straight, but you looked like you were performing in a fancy cat house.''

''I'll dress appropriately on this tour,'' Geiger promised.

''I'll believe it when I see it,'' Greenstone said.

''The greatest music ever created played by the greatest musician who ever lived,'' Geiger said thoughtfully, looking at Diana. ''I *like* this. I'm aboard,'' he said. ''How would we set this up?''

Greenstone leaned back in his chair. Mrs. Jamison reentered the dining room and cleared the dessert plates.

''Every time a baton drops, you would have to be paid three times,'' Greenstone said after a moment of thought. ''Three times, at least. Live performance revenue. Recording. And television.''

''I know.'' Geiger nodded. ''But this isn't about money. This is about musical respect. 'Establishing my place,' right?''

''Of course. Absolutely!'' the agent answered. ''But money is involved. Yours, mine, and those who would promote you in dozens of cities. So we need to be spectacular, artistic, *and* careful.''

''If I'm only playing classical, I'm going to be sacrificing something, am I not?''

''Short-term, yes, Rolf. You'll lose some of your audience. And you won't make as much money. But you will come out of this very wealthy. The entire classical music industry will get a boost, and in the long run you will regain in prestige and respect what you might—*might*—lose short-term in audience and revenue.''

"I have a few current commitments. What about them?''

"In most cases, I think I can convince the committed promoters to amend their existing contracts, in terms of the music to be played,'' Greenstone said. "They would cash in on the publicity that the entire tour would generate.'' He paused again. "Rolf, you're going to sell out worldwide. We're talking about something that's even beyond a 'superstar' program: 'The greatest pianist alive plays the greatest composers who ever lived.' ''

Geiger raised a jaundiced eyebrow.

"Sorry,'' Greenstone said, correcting himself. "The greatest pianist who *ever lived* plays the greatest composers who ever lived.''

"Much better.'' Geiger grinned.

"The Italians might have problems with it,'' Greenstone concluded. "But they'll relent when they understand that you'll be playing Italian music for them. The Germans, the English, the Asians—they'll all buy it immediately. As for domestic, it's not a problem. Put Beethoven on the program with some American composers and the sheer accessibility of the music will sell out the tickets immediately.''

For a moment Geiger glanced at Diana, reading her thoughts, making sure he had her support. When he saw that he did, Geiger pondered further for a moment. Then he asked Greenstone, "What do you think old Rabinowitz would have thought of a tour like this?''

"Why do you ask me that?''

"Because you represented him. And you were his friend as much as anyone.''

"He would have hated it,'' Greenstone said without having to think much about it.

"Why?''

A slight chill held the room.

"Because Isador always hated the fact that you could eventually supplant him. He was jealous of his position. He didn't want anyone to be greater. You know that as well as I do.''

"Is that why you waited until he was dead to propose this?''

Greenstone shrugged.

"Maybe. Partially," the agent said. "Maybe the atmosphere wasn't right for this while Isador was aging ungraciously."

He paused.

"Look, Rolf. I've always been honest with you," Brian said. "I'm suggesting this first as a friend. Then as a businessman. Long-term, this is what *you* need to do even if you had had no relationship with Isador Rabinowitz. A huge tour makes creative sense, and it makes business sense. And right now is *the* time."

Diana saw a shadow come across her lover's face. The entire room was eerily silent for several long seconds. Greenstone finally broke it.

"So tell me your thoughts, Rolf," the agent asked gently. "If you're not up for this, it's not going to work."

Geiger looked away for a moment, then came back. "If I did this, I could be ready to play the first date in the fall," Geiger answered softly. "Maybe spread the performances and travel into the spring. Maybe conclude the tour with the *Emperor* next spring. If not in Egypt, then maybe in China. At the Forbidden City, for example."

"You feel that you could be ready to make the emotional, physical and intellectual commitment?"

Geiger shrugged. "What if I were?"

"Then I would get on the phone Monday," said Greenstone. "I make the right calls locally here in New York first. Then I call Paris, London, Tokyo, Vienna, and Rome and start talking to people. I'll try to keep things quiet for a while, but I'm under no illusion. We'll start seeing things in the press about this within a week."

Geiger grimaced good-naturedly. "That's all right," he said.

"So what do you think?" Greenstone asked in summation. "If we did this right and if you succeeded creatively with your playing, you would come out of this hailed as the greatest pianist who ever lived."

"What if I failed?" Geiger asked.

"You won't, Rolf."

"But if I did?"

"If a tour like this failed," Greenstone said, speaking cautiously, "if it were a catastrophe, if the critics savaged you and the audiences felt ripped-off, or if it failed to generate the excitement that we're anticipating . . . I suppose it could *destroy* your reputation. It could also wreck you musically, destroy your nerves, and demolish your creativity.''

Greenstone studied his client as he spoke.

''Thinking back upon the unfortunate fact that Mozart died at age thirty-five and was buried in a pauper's grave, and that Beethoven himself also died a sick, broken, unhappy man, I suppose it could physically kill you, too. That's what happens when immensely talented men overstep their own mortality.''

Greenstone paused.

''You would leave an enormous estate, however,'' he concluded with an irreverent twinkle in his eye. ''Many charities would erect tacky plaster statues of you in loving fiduciary memory.''

Geiger ignored Greenstone's humor. He looked coldly at his agent for a moment. Then his expression lightened. He smiled and scoffed.

''Oh, hell,'' he said. ''This is the type of tour I've always wanted to do someday.''

Greenstone smiled. '' 'Someday' is *now,* Rolf.''

''I know. So let's do it.''

''Excellent! You know what? Forget Monday. I'll start making the calls tomorrow,'' the agent said. ''Never mind that it's Saturday. If you change your mind, let me know before 10 A.M.''

For a few moments, a queasy frightened feeling was upon Rolf Geiger. He credited it to nerves. And excitement. Then, moments later, it was gone.

''I plan to be asleep tomorrow at ten, Brian,'' he said mischievously. ''Feel free to make your calls.''

Later in the evening, after his guests had gone, Geiger sat down again at the Steinway in his library. He felt refreshed. Renewed. A new and immense challenge was before him, and he loved that feeling.

He began his warm-up exercises. He had played only a

measure or two when he realized something was wrong with his instrument.

"What the—?"

Another string was badly out of tune. The coincidence, on top of fixing the first broken string that morning, was startling. He stood and looked into the interior of the piano, wondering if he had damaged the second string while repairing the first.

Diana came by on her way upstairs. She sat down next to him on the bench. Her fingers found the piano chain and pendant that hung from her neck.

"Where did you find this little guy?" she asked, indicating the pendant.

"One of the finest silversmiths in Europe," he said with a straight face. He continued to play. He loved to have her sit next to him as he played. "Okay, a street merchant," he amended.

"I love it," she said. "Not as much as I love you, but I love it."

He patted her on the knee, a touch that was enough to arouse both of them.

"You're precious," he said.

She kissed him.

"Does this tour scare you?" she asked.

"No," he said thoughtfully. Six bars of Chopin blended together nicely. The music was immense when he played. Or, if he wished, soft as a lover's promise whispered on a spring breeze. "What scares me now is *not* doing something like this. I need to show what I can really do with the great music. Then, my lady, I can do anything I wish with my life."

"And what would that be?" she asked.

His fingers shifted to a melody from Andrew Lloyd Webber. Just for fun.

"Don't know yet," he said. "But I was hoping you'd help me decide."

She smiled and leaned on him. "Deal?" he asked.

"Deal," she said.

He played the theme from *Dragnet* and made her laugh.

"Was anyone in here today?" Geiger asked next.

"I was," she said. "I put out some fan mail for you."

"At the piano, I mean," he said.

"No one that I know of. Why?"

"I have two busted wires in one day. I don't think that's ever happened before."

He tapped at the key with the out-of-tune string. The string hadn't broken like the other. It had been stretched to the point where it had lost all its tension. That was so unusual, it defied ready explanation.

"One of those things," Geiger eventually said. "Like two lightbulbs that flash and disintegrate within minutes of each other. It happens. But it's a remarkable coincidence."

Something made him think of the lightning on the Air France jet that had brought him home. The lightning and the woman next to him who had been struck by lightning twice.

A scary, uncanny coincidence, once again.

"You coming upstairs soon?" she asked.

"Not for an hour. Maybe two."

"Good night then," she said.

He held her and kissed her. Then she went upstairs.

He repaired the second string and made a mental note to call the professional tuner in the morning. The Steinway Company always sent their best man right away, even on weekends. Geiger was, obviously, an esteemed customer. He wanted the piano tuned perfectly by noon.

Later, he read for a while in the quiet sanctity of his library. But he found his mind drifting. First, it tiptoed to the late Rabinowitz and then it gave itself to his world tour. That's how he now conceived of it. His World Tour.

What *would* the old man have said, he wondered. What would the old tyrant have thought? They had never perfectly agreed on the interpretations of many composers. They had once nearly come to physical blows over Beethoven, particularly the *Hammerklavier* and the *Pathetique*.

Well, Geiger concluded, it barely mattered. Who cared about Rabinowitz's opinion any longer?

A disquieting notion followed: Why did he keep asking himself who cared?

Rolf turned the lights off in his study and sat for a moment in the darkness. He had always found the darkness consoling, not frightening as others might have. There was something about it that reflected an aspect of his personality. Darkness reminded him of a perfectly blank sheet of music, before the written notes create a new composition. He sometimes thought of a quiet keyboard as a sort of darkness, too. A black-and-white evenness out of which a new reality could be carved.

Geiger stood.

He functioned well in darkness. He liked to take the stage in darkness during a concert, seat himself at the piano, and let the lights slowly rise as he played, creating a unique world, a one-time-only experience. At no two times did he ever dress alike, feel alike, or play alike. Every appearance was unique. And every appearance was redefined out of that same darkness.

Some critics called it showbiz.

Pizzazz.

Showing off.

The critics liked to beat him up in this area. He conceded that they had a point. Yet Geiger felt a philosophical bond to it, also. Out of blankness, he created a new musical reality.

A line always came back to him. Victor Hugo. *"D'avoir été Lutece, et d'être Paris."*

To have been mud, and to have become Paris.

He turned the lights out in his library. Darkness embraced and comforted him.

He walked through the den and entered the front hall. He went to the stairs, found and climbed them. He walked to his bedroom.

Still no lights. But a window shade was slightly askew.

He went to the shade. As he began to adjust it, he looked down onto the street. Something caught his eye. A pair of lovers, it appeared, were leaning against a parked car. The young man was kissing a woman, who was accepting the kiss with equal enthusiasm.

Geiger stood at the unlit window for several seconds watching them, almost envying the newness and freshness of their passion. He wondered sometimes how people married and made a life together and somehow kept the passion going. A little dismal feeling overtook him, wondering whether over the years, his love for Diana, and hers for him, would run its course.

Or would they even have *years* together? Would it be only

months? He believed in the future but was old enough to know that there were never any assurances.

Where, he wondered, were self-destructive thoughts like that coming from? He shook his head and tuned out the young couple who were still smooching down below. He reached to the window shade to pull it down for the night.

Then something remarkable and memorable happened.

As Geiger watched from above, a clown suddenly appeared on the block. Geiger couldn't tell if he were watching a male or a female, as the figure had a graceful feline glide to its gait.

There was something else strange about this clown, too, something intensely surreal. There was something very much out of sync for this time and place.

It didn't look like an *American* clown, for example.

As Geiger studied the figure carefully, the clown increasingly reminded him of pictures of European circuses from the middle part of the century. The clown's outfit was very dark, either black or navy, patterned with large white dots—about the size of tennis balls—all over the baggy, sack-shaped outfit. The individual also had grossly oversize shoes, a floppy hat that matched the suit, and carried a violin. It was in white face, which was part of what held Geiger's attention. The individual's whole appearance had been in very stark black-and-white and almost seemed to be illuminated unnaturally, like a winter landscape of dead trees, snow, and moonlight.

The clown walked halfway down the block with obvious deliberation. The visitor appeared to know exactly where he or she was headed. Geiger was startled when the figure stopped right across the street.

The clown turned and faced Geiger's building, looking up almost directly at the second-floor window, oriented so carefully toward it that Geiger almost felt as if he were the special intended audience.

Then the clown turned into a street musician. He mounted the violin, which was as white as his face, to his shoulder and made the motions of playing.

Geiger cocked his head.

Strange!

He couldn't hear anything.

Fascinated, Rolf reasoned that the clown was going through the gestures of playing, but was not really creating any music. Who knew? The city streets saw many strange things at night. This was no weirder than a lot of others, though it did have that unnatural aura around it.

The bizarre display went on for a minute, this soundless near-hypnotic mime show with a vanilla violin. The minute seemed to Geiger like a very long stretch of time.

And who, Geiger wondered, *was the intended audience?*

Amused slightly, Geiger smiled. He lifted his gaze. He saw a three-quarter moon hanging in the sky above the buildings across the street. Then he looked back down to the sidewalk and the clown was gone.

Geiger knew he had not dreamed this. As he scanned the block, he couldn't find the clown a second time. The apparition had vanished as strangely as it had appeared, though Geiger did note some sort of vagrant sitting down the block, smoking on the doorstep of another two-million-dollar property. But the clown had left one thing behind. Or, Geiger thought he had.

It was a notion in Geiger's head.

Recalling the vision of the polka-dotted clown, Geiger felt a name form at the forefront of his mind.

Umberto. The clown was Italian and his name was Umberto. *Re Umberto.* King of Italy.

"Well, who knew?" He shrugged. The clown looked like a refugee from a production of *I Pagliacci,* Geiger mused. So why shouldn't Geiger have assigned him a nice Italian name?

Umberto. As red, white, and green as a fresh, cholesterol-laden cannoli.

Geiger tried to assimilate all that he had just seen. But his mind felt foggy. His body felt sleepy. The night felt bumpy. Sometimes there was no explanation for what one saw on the streets of New York. Searching for explanations was a waste of time.

So why bother?

Geiger shook his head. He finally pushed the shade back into place, blocking the light and the city out of his bedroom.

He climbed into bed beside Diana.

He felt the warmth of her sleeping body and pulled her to

him. He thought about how much he loved her and how precious she was to him.

She responded slightly and her body moved to his. He put an arm around her and started to enjoy a relaxing descent into sleep.

She kissed him lightly and he thought again of how much he loved her. It was a reassuring notion, though a mildly spooky one. It was the last thought in his mind as he drifted comfortably off to sleep.

six

───────────────────────
───────────────────────
───────────────────────

The Monday following his dinner with Rolf, Brian Greenstone was in his office early, busy with a calendar and a globe.

His client's tour would be anchored by mega-dates, he had decided. New York, Los Angeles, Rio de Janeiro, London, Tokyo. Paris. Munich, Rome. He tentatively prepared a twenty-four week calendar which would allow Geiger to play an average of two dates a week, using these cities as the focal points of the tour. Greenstone sent out faxes to the top classical promoters in each city, suggesting the possibility of a concert date by Rolf Geiger and inquiring as to which venues might be possible in each city.

The reaction was immediate. Within the hour, the fax machine was humming with incoming responses. The promoters in each city were adamant on wanting Geiger for the dates proposed. Concert halls or stadia could be arranged easily for such events. Several of the promoters requested information on how to contract for the dates and what type of deposit would be necessary. The World Tour now had its first semblance of shape and agenda.

Geiger stopped by Greenstone's office in the afternoon. Greenstone's inner office was paneled by dark wood and deep leather chairs with theatrical, concert, and classic-film posters, all of them flamboyantly autographed by one of Greenstone's clients. Included in prominent locations were one by Rabinowitz from when he played Covent Garden, and one by Geiger when he had played Alice Tully Hall at Lincoln Center.

"So we're off to a good start?" Geiger asked.

"Couldn't be better," Greenstone asked.

"There are a few other details," Geiger explained. "Things I didn't mention last night."

"Go ahead," Greenstone said.

"I want these dates to be accessible to everyone," Geiger said. "I want to make sure that whenever possible the cheapest tickets are maybe only two dollars. The balance can be made up by the wealthy people who'll pay more to sit up close."

Greenstone rolled his eyes in would-be annoyance. Not that this was anything he had never heard before. Such requests were rare from most clients, but they were *de rigueur* from Geiger, who liked to be "accessible" to all his fans, even if it kept his concert grosses lower than they might have been. It was Geiger's feeling that he was already making obscene amounts of money, sometimes more for one concert than his father had made in a lifetime. If he ever became *too* rich, Geiger frequently maintained, he would only have to spend undue amounts of time giving the money away. It was also not unusual at a Geiger recital for a pair of two-dollar rows to be positioned right through prime real estate at the center of the orchestra, rather than in—as he referred to it—the "nosebleed section" way up in the rafters. At other times, the cheap seats were sprinkled randomly through the house, much the way on airlines full-fare business travelers often found themselves next to cheap-fare students going home on spring break.

"The usual quixotic pseudodemocratic Rolf Geiger price scale," Greenstone chided good-naturedly. "I'd already thought of this, so you don't even have to mention it."

"You get 10 percent of the money I make as well as the money I don't make," Geiger answered. "That's fair, isn't it?"

"Bloody populist," muttered Greenstone.

"Am I beloved or not?" Geiger retorted, gently teasing, his blue eyes alive and sparkling.

"Beloved?" Greenstone shrugged. "By music students, yes. For the matrons who have to sit with unwashed young people, you are both admired in principle and rebuked in practice. Accountants and business people, on the other hand, have a steadier opinion and consider you a Bolshevik. We would have you executed if we weren't already getting fat on your concerts, recordings and deplorable T-shirts." He paused. "You're a problem. You break the rules. We don't know whether to love you or hate you."

"Try both."

"I do. Every day."

"Fine with me," said Geiger, keeping the banter going.

Claire, Greenstone's new secretary and assistant, entered the office bearing a just-received fax. Like all of the women with whom Greenstone surrounded himself, either as employees, wives, or occasional sex partners, Claire was very young and very pretty. She had shoulder-length dark hair and jewel blue eyes. She wore a simple blouse and a red skirt several inches above the knee. Like most young women who encountered Geiger, she could barely take her eyes off him.

"Have you met Rolf Geiger?" Greenstone asked her. Then quickly seeing the way she was looking at the pianist, Greenstone answered his own question. "No, apparently you haven't, but you certainly would like to."

"Hello," Rolf said to her, rising and accepting her hand in greeting.

"Hi," she answered, mildly embarrassed by Greenstone's introduction. She handed the fax to Greenstone.

"Claire just graduated from Smith this past June. She'll be working here as my assistant until she engineers a revolution, has me decapitated, and takes over the place later this month."

She laughed.

"Well, please keep me as a client," Geiger said to her, continuing the joke. "And I don't think you should shoot Brian after you seize control. Exile would be more appropriate."

"I knew I could count on you, Rolf," Greenstone said, taking the fax.

"Actually," Geiger said as his agent read the communication, "if you *do* choose to have Brian decapitated, I would think over the entry door would be an excellent place to mount the head."

"You're such a good friend, Rolf," Greenstone said, still reading.

"For starters, I'm just trying to learn the business," Claire said.

Greenstone fumbled with a pair of reading spectacles for a moment. "Yes. Right. These Smith girls are such slow learners," he said without intonation. He arched his eyebrows with the irony of the remark and pushed his eyeglasses into place.

"What did you study at Smith?" Geiger asked, turning back to Claire and making small talk as Greenstone read.

"Psychology," she said. "Primarily the psychology of early adults and disturbed adolescents."

Geiger nodded. "You're in the right place. With musicians and booking agents you'll do very well."

She smiled again. "Thank you," she said.

"Actually, I'm sure you'll do very well no matter what."

"Thanks," she said again. She reminded Geiger of a younger version of Diana.

Greenstone's eyes remained on the fax before him. He had the most remarkable faculty for speaking in complete inanities while considering something very serious. And here was another opportunity.

"Maybe there should be a Rolf Geiger action figure also. So you could sit on shelves like Daffy Duck," Greenstone teased absently. Then he folded away the message before him. He removed his glasses and his gaze, then slowly rose and met Geiger's again.

"Do a contract and I'll sign it," said Geiger, continuing the joke. "I won't even read it. I'll just sign it."

"Your usual practice, huh?"

Geiger grinned. He hadn't read a contract thoroughly in five years. Once, to prove the point that Geiger should be more careful, Greenstone had sent over a contract for Geiger to "sign," along with a covering letter strongly suggesting that Geiger read it carefully. It was actually a dummy contract, which, among other things, sold all of Geiger's future performance rights for one dollar and promised his firstborn daughter to a Saudi sheik. Geiger returned the signed contract and never knew what he had agreed to until Greenstone had phoned him.

"See? You have to be more *careful!*" Greenstone had pleaded.

"Not at all," was the lesson that Geiger had taken from the episode. "Now that you know how careless I am, I know you'll read everything for me all the more meticulously."

Somehow Geiger had come away from that exchange as the winner. And equally, somehow it had been a defining moment in their business relationship. Geiger would create music as he wished. And Brian Greenstone would handle all of the business and watch his client's back.

Returned to the present, Greenstone hefted the fax in his hand. "The drumbeats are carried very quickly across Manhattan," Greenstone said. "Look at this."

He handed the paper to Geiger. Already the news of a new concert tour had escaped the offices of the few promoters who had been informed just that morning. The cable TV industry had already caught wind of it.

Geiger read the message. It offered him a weekend of guest appearances on a music video network.

"Interesting," said Geiger.

"Yes. It could be," Greenstone said. "A touch of missionary work, bringing an awareness of Beethoven and Mozart to the proles. You and Billy Joel. I'll keep it on file."

Greenstone folded his thick arms. "We're off to a fine start and we're only four hours old. Now let's talk about playing some tennis, you and I."

The door opened again. "Mr. Greenstone?" Claire asked.

Brian looked in her direction and nodded.

"You wanted me to remind you about the writer who called."

The agent frowned for a second, not remembering.

"The one who wanted to speak to Mr. Geiger?" she continued. "You said we'd inquire and call him back."

"Oh. Yes. Right," Greenstone said. Claire stood by and waited. The agent turned back to his client.

"An English journalist called yesterday from London. Said he was going to be in New York and wanted to interview you."

"Magazine? Newspaper?" Geiger asked.

"Neither." Greenstone glanced to his assistant again to have his memory refreshed. "Claire? Help me out? What the hell was the bugger's name?"

"Phillip Langlois. He maintains that he's writing a biography of Isador Rabinowitz," she said. "He wanted to interview you for the book."

Geiger turned to Greenstone. "Ever heard of him?"

"I checked him. He's a solid biographer, actually. Not your usual British tabloid sleaze. Done respectable newspaper work in the U.K."

"How come I've never heard of him?"

"He hasn't been published in the U.S. yet," Greenstone said. "Claire made a phone call or two."

"His book has a contract in the U.K., but none here," she said.

"Not yet, anyway. I know the proposal is getting some interest at a couple of publishing houses here. But there are two other Rabinowitz biographies in the works, also. Unless you feel like being foolishly generous with your time, you shouldn't give three book interviews." Greenstone thought for half a second, then continued. "Plus you might want to hold on to anything good or dramatic or intimate that you know about Rabinowitz for when you want to write your own book."

Geiger blew out a breath. "I don't feel like talking to anyone right now. Particularly a biographer."

Greenstone turned mischievously to Claire.

"Phone Mr. Langlois collect in London and tell him that Maestro Geiger cordially asked him to blow it out his ass."

Claire flinched, then blushed slightly.

"Actually," Greenstone amended more seriously, "tell him that Mr. Geiger is regrettably unavailable for interviews right now as he is in the planning stages of a major new series of recitals. But we might be able to arrange some time if Mr. Langlois happens to be in New York. Don't phone Langlois. Send him a fax. Make it polite."

Greenstone looked to Geiger for approval.

"Who knows?" Greenstone asked. "Phillip Langlois writes for the *Telegraph* in London. It's sort of a fascist rag, as you may know. But it has an influential following. An audience who buys books, recordings, and concert tickets. So you might want to do him a favor down the road and create some friendly press in London. In case you ever need it. Okay?"

"Okay," said Geiger.

"Plus he might nail a good publishing contract here and end up as my client someday. So again, who knows?" He looked to Claire. "We've decided to stroke him. Can you follow up on that?"

Claire nodded and left the room. Greenstone intently watched her go.

"Lord above," he said after the door was closed. "If I weren't married and paying for two ex-wives already . . . and if I were only forty-five again . . ."

His voice tailed off, not that there was any need for him to finish the unspoken thought.

Geiger left Greenstone's office shortly after three. He wandered across Fifty-seventh Street and was recognized only by a fellow musician, a violinist named Martin Loew who had studied at Julliard at about the same time. Loew stopped to talk. Even the violinist had already heard of Geiger's impending tour and inquired about it.

"Nothing's set yet, but I'm sure it's going to happen," Geiger explained.

Loew mentioned a few words about the passing of Isador Rabinowitz. Loew had played at Carnegie Hall a few years earlier when Rabinowitz had done one of his all-Chopin concerts. He still remembered it in glowing terms, even though Rabinowitz had made it all the more memorable by not acknowledging the Swiss-born conductor at the end of the evening.

Geiger went on his way, taking a detour down Fifth Avenue to browse through some of the stores and buy a pair of new CDs and a recently published biography of Picasso. On impulse, he stopped in Tiffany and Company on his way home and fancied a small golden penguin on a gold chain. The penguin had a slight smile and a tiny diamond for an eye. It was just under eight hundred dollars.

The saleswoman recognized him after a few moments and addressed him as "Mr. Geiger," though she made no small talk about music or concerts. Instead, she explained that part of the proceeds from these particular items went toward a world wildlife preservation fund.

Geiger liked the pendant anyway and also liked buying presents for Diana for no particular reason. He bought it, took it home, and placed it on the pillow on her side of the bed. Fun surprises made him happy.

He spent the final part of the afternoon examining the books he had purchased and browsing through some music at his piano. There was also a fresh stack of fan mail waiting in his downstairs den and half a dozen new CDs sent over by courier from the offices of his recording label.

Diana didn't arrive home till after seven, but immediately found the small blue box with a white ribbon on her pillow. She opened her gift immediately and loved it, putting it on right away.

Mrs. Jamison stayed long enough to prepare dinner. Toward eight, Mrs. Jamison went home and Diana and Rolf spent a quiet evening undisturbed.

A few hours later, after fitfully falling to sleep, Rolf Geiger tumbled through time to one of the most unsettling points in his life.

His father, Frank Geiger had died not long after his wife Dorothy. Rolf was in New York at the time. One of Frank's brothers phoned collect. Tonight in a dream he would live through it again.

"Your pa's been shot dead, Rolf," the uncle said. "I think a colored guy done it, but nobody knows."

The venue was a bar in Wheeling. The event surprised no one.

Silence from Rolf. He had long since stopped searching for love or acceptance from a father who had none to impart.

"Ain't you got nothing to say, Rolf?" the uncle asked.

"No. I don't have anything to say."

"Your pa gets whacked in a bar by a nigger? Ain't you at least sorry?"

There was a horrible silence from Rolf. Then a much deeper sorrow followed when he realized there was such a void within him. He turned in his bed. He had no love for a man who had no love for him, and it would forever haunt him.

"There's a funeral service we got scheduled," the uncle began slowly. "This next Saturday."

"I have a performance in Boston."

"See, the thing is, Rolf. Your dad's gonna be buried in potter's field if somebody don't do something. The liberals in Washington closed down the mines and your pa died with eight dollars in his pocket."

"Uh-huh."

"Now, listen. Your pa's at a dago funeral home in Wheeling, but they won't release no corpse until—"

"Give me the phone number," Rolf said with a sinking feeling. "I'll take care of it."

He paid for the funeral, but didn't attend. He never heard from any family member again.

Except in dreams. In dreams he attended the funeral over and over. And his father would emerge from blackness to berate him.

Tonight, it was a double funeral—a deathly double feature!—because Rolf stood again at the edge of Rabinowitz's grave.

Or was it Frank Geiger's grave?

Or were they the same?

Images merged and meshed. He shook himself in his sleep, but the dream images were so very real!

He gazed down. The bitter wind off Morningside Heights tore into him again, colder and icier than ever before. Icy as his childhood bedroom with the flapping, useless, depressing plastic on the window. The cold cut through his flesh and knifed into his soul.

It wasn't day or night, but all around him was a cold gray, gray as the icy West Virginia mornings that he had hated as a boy.

West Virginia on Morningside Heights.

He could hear the music in the background. He could hear Rabinowitz playing. Grand, sweeping music. Beethoven. A melody standing out in bold relief. A wonderful unique sonority.

In the background, his father was shouting in a drunken profane rage.

As Geiger stared at the marker above Rabinowitz's tomb, the marker seemed to quiver. Then it broke away. The earth moved and Geiger thought he heard a second human voice.

The voice of Rabinowitz.

The earth swirled away from the tomb. The headstone tumbled away. The pine coffin rose to the surface of the earth, broke open with a sickening rumbling threatening creak. Frank Geiger shut up and Isador Rabinowitz stepped angrily from his tomb. Isador was running this dream now. It was his!

Rolf cried out. He trembled.

"Why are you back?" he asked.

"I'm not dead!" Rabinowitz insisted.

"You *are* dead!"

"Not for you! Not for you!"

Rolf turned away. He closed his eyes so tightly that they hurt. He could hear his own voice cry out. And he could hear the music in the background. Beautiful melodies turning hellish.

The piano. The master's hands upon the keyboard. He would recognize that legato, that cantabile, anywhere.

Geiger opened his eyes again.

Blackness. He was in the blackness of his bedroom.

He closed his eyes, trying to settle comfortably, but he returned to the same dream, unable to escape it.

Rolf was in a strange, uncharted territory. It was between 3 and 4 A.M., and he tossed incessantly midway between wakefulness and sleep. The same dream pursued him like a demon. And this was unlike any dream state that he had ever experienced.

He saw Rabinowitz standing before him.

Rabinowitz laughing.

Rabinowitz suddenly behind him with his hands on the young man's shoulders, powerful hands moving toward Rolf's neck.

The hands of an artist. The hands of a strangler.

Which was it?

Something in Geiger's head flashed. A big ominous bright whiteness. Then it dissolved and Rabinowitz appeared before him in a new vision. This time, the old master was sitting placidly in the conservatory at Julliard, sipping tea from a green-and-white porcelain cup, the emerald ring glistening.

"Which *am* I?" Rabinowitz asked rhetorically. "Artist or strangler?"

He sipped more tea. The strong Russian jasmine tea. Geiger remembered the powerful aroma from many afternoon lessons. Tea so pungent you could run a car on it.

"Why both, of course," Rabinowitz answered. "I'm a musician *and* a murderer."

"No," Geiger called out in his sleep.

"Yes," Rabinowitz answered. "And you will be, too."

Fitfully, Geiger rolled over in his bed. He tossed some more. The Manhattan night outside his home was quiet. The last thing Rolf Geiger had seen when he had looked out the window was stars, plus a yellow-white moon hanging in surrealistic splendor in the sky above New York.

A big fat wafer in the sky. Communion for eight million. This is the body, this is the blood.

This is your damned curse, Rolf.

The young Brother Matthew was standing in front of him again, blood running out of his nose, mystification and incredulity upon his face.

"Why did you do *that?*" Matthew demanded.

"Do what? Hit you?"

"No. Become a musician?"

Geiger sat up in his bed, coming awake with a tremor in the present day. His brow was wet.

God, he thought. *What's going on in my head?*

All around him, the darkness of the familiar room was a comfort. The wonderful thick blackness, the consoling nothingness of the night.

So why couldn't he sleep? He was safe in his home, wasn't he? Diana was near him. But a lover and a home were physical protections within the tangible world. It occurred to him now that what was approaching him was emanating from another plane of reality. The one inside his head. Or an unfathomable one that could travel through walls, doors, or even flesh.

It was a thought. A notion. A feeling.

A vision.

A horrible one was coming together in his subconscious mind, and he didn't like it.

Nightmare stuff. The vision of Rabinowitz as an old man, much as he'd looked in the final days of his life. But in the vision, Rabinowitz was as spry as a fifteen-year-old girl. And he was dancing on his own grave.

Dancing!

Jesus! Rolf thought to himself. He was awake but the nightmare in his head would not cut off. He couldn't evict it from his mind.

He turned again and forced the pillow against his face. He knew there was going to be a further vision that would be even more unsettling. He knew it was on its way but he knew he couldn't stop it.

He rolled again in bed.

He could almost hear himself thinking.

Oh, God . . . help me. . . . . Someone. Help me!

Geiger experienced the sensation of rapidly tumbling and he knew he was drifting off into the scarier regions of sleep. And there was a musical leitmotif to all of this. There were strains of Wagner. *Götterdämmerung.* Acid-spirited old Rabinowitz's valentine to a world that he hated.

Then Geiger's eyes flashed open.

It was unmistakable! Music. Someone was downstairs in his library, playing his piano!

Playing brilliantly.

''What the—?''

He looked around the dark room and realized that he was not dreaming. Not anymore.

He was no longer in the bizarre nightmare that had placed him at the enchanted graveside of Rabinowitz. He was in his home. And he did—or thought he did—hear music.

It was coming from downstairs, from the piano in his den. Rabinowitz, the dead Rabinowitz, was playing.

Rolf sat upright in bed. He placed a hand on Diana next to

him. She was an anchor of love in a harsh reality. She was there, breathing evenly. But the tinkling of the piano was still emanating from his den. He held his eyes shut, trying to escape.

It was Chopin. Other than Rubinstein, no one ever played Chopin like Rabinowitz. The touch on the keys was as distinctive as a fingerprint.

"What am I hearing?" Geiger whispered to himself. "It can't be? *No, it can't be?*"

"**Yes, it is ... !**"

His eyes popped fully open again, a jarring full reentry into the real world. The dream's message still in his mind, that insane graveside image dancing through his head.

"Isador Rabinowitz," Rolf said aloud.

The words formed on Geiger's lips and escaped in a soft whisper, a password at the hour of the wolf.

"**Yes, it is ... !**"

In the darkness, someone had twice whispered to him. *He had even recognized the voice.* And yet, as his eyes became accustomed to the darkness, he knew no one was there. . . . Or, no one he could *see*.

Yet that voice had come to him so clearly. Those words had summoned him so boldly from the realm of bad dreams, that he could have sworn that the voice had been real. In all its insanity, he was certain that *someone* had spoken *something*.

"Diana?" he whispered.

She didn't answer.

"Anyone?" he asked, almost involuntarily, coming up on his elbows in bed. "Who's here?"

Abruptly, the music downstairs ceased in mid-phrase. Like hands frozen at a keyboard. Or lifted suddenly in distraction.

Or dropped lifelessly to the player's side.

Distantly, very distantly, almost subliminally, Geiger thought he heard laughter.

But Diana was silent, other than an even heavy breathing. She was soundly asleep.

"Anyone?" he asked a second time.

"**I'm here, Rolf! I'm back!**"

"No. No, you can't be," Geiger answered.

He broke into a violent sweat. But he was too frightened

even to reach for the bedside lamp. For several seconds he waited, scanning the darkness of his own bedroom.

Waiting. Waiting.

For what?

A possible explanation occurred to him, and it comforted and soothed him. In the course of most nights, even in Manhattan, there was small window of time that was a respite from all disturbance. There were usually twenty minutes, half an hour, or some small expanse of time when not a taxi screeches its tires, not a pair of angry lovers scream at each other on a public sidewalk, and not a single car alarm wails into the night.

No sirens. No fistfights. No screams.

Geiger glanced again at his clock radio. It was 3:36 A.M. This morning, the window of tranquillity had come early. The city was very still. And through this quirk in a quiet night, oozing through some window left a quarter inch ajar, the distant unseen melodies of a lonely insomniac musician were seeping into his home.

That, and some attendant conversation, perhaps from people on the street, perhaps just passing by, and most likely unrelated to the solitary distant music.

Rolf Geiger's fear dissolved.

Then, just as abruptly, it surged back, for the music downstairs started again. And this time, it was clearer than ever that the piano music emanated from his own home, his own den.

What *was* it? A radio that he had left on? A tape? A CD?

There had to be an explanation.

As he picked up the unmistakable cadences of the music, thoughts flew at him in milliseconds.

Oh, no! Impossible! he said to himself.

He recognized the finger work.

"What *is* this?" he demanded.

Again Chopin. Played by Rabinowitz.

"No!"

"*Jawohl!*"

Damn! He heard it very clearly. Same as he thought he heard a voice, like a faint whisper of male lips not far from his ear. It was so disconcerting this time that Geiger swiped at the air.

His arm caught a big cushion of nothing.

"Missed!"

Jesus Christ!

Geiger cursed to himself and felt his heart start to flutter. He was *awake,* and he was still hearing both the music and possibly the voice.

Jesus Christ! What in God's name—!

He rose from bed, as if he had received an invitation.

Now the music was in his head like a cancer. He caught parts of it that he had never caught before, as if its source had moved closer. There was a discernible theme, a melody that he could almost repeat. And it seemed so much more prominent. Instead of being at the edge of his consciousness, the music was right *there* in front of him.

Geiger walked to the doorway of his bedroom. The hall beyond was dim. The only illumination was from the nightlight from a hallway bathroom.

"Rabinowitz?" he asked very softly.

No answer. But downstairs the unseen hands continued to play the Steinway.

He stepped into the hallway.

"Rabinowitz?" he asked aloud.

Again, no answer.

Geiger moved to the top of the steps. He placed his hand on the banister and summoned all his courage. He walked slowly downstairs, not knowing what to expect or what he would find.

His eyes, as he looked ahead, reconnoitered his intended path to the closed door of his library. He was shocked and increasingly fearful when he saw light from underneath the doorframe.

Had a friend entered his home to play music? As a prank? At this insane hour? Who?

Still no rational explanation presented itself.

He reached the bottom of the stairs. He went quietly to the door to the den. The playing continued. Softer now. Almost as if it were receding as he approached.

He stood at the door. His heart continued to kick within him. The touch on the keyboard was undeniably, unmistakably, unarguably that of Rabinowitz. That, or the greatest impostor Geiger had ever heard.

Unless, of course, someone had teed up a recording. But who would do that?

He slowly began to turn the doorknob. For a moment, it resisted, almost as if there were a grip on the other side.

Chopin continued.

Then, with a loud click, the latch gave. The door opened to the library.

Instantaneously, the music stopped. As if an invisible conductor had arrested his baton.

Geiger pushed the door and it opened. The room lights, which only a moment ago had appeared to be on, were off. The room was pitch-black.

Rolf reached to the light switch, and before anything could spring forth from the darkness, his hand flicked it on. A line of track lighting across the ceiling brought sudden artificial daylight to the den.

The piano stood mute and alone. Like a big parked car. Geiger stared. The keyboard was closed.

Nothing moved in the room. All the furniture was in place. But he thought he heard a male voice whisper.

"Yes, Rolf. Thank you."

There was no one he could see. Maybe those words had been a thought that formed in his head from somewhere. Not an actual whisper. After all, he kept reminding himself, there was no one there.

He stepped farther into his den.

"Thank you for what?" Geiger asked aloud. "Is something here or not? Where was the music coming from?"

Distant laughter. Like an old man. A rasping, mocking voice. He didn't have to hear any further answer. His gaze examined the piano.

"Was someone here or not?" Geiger asked.

Silence answered. Cold, dead silence.

Then, **"Thank you for coming."** It wasn't a voice this time, it was a thought, a notion, that seemed to take shape inside his head.

"Coming where?" he asked. "Here?"

"Yes."

"Why?"

No answer. Not the slightest. No voice. No Chopin. No thought from outer space slipping into his head.

Nothing.

He waited.

Still nothing.

"To pay respect to your mentor."

The words formed in his head, same as the last ones had. A message from somewhere? Or Geiger's own psyche conducting a dialogue within him. Rolf wasn't certain.

He scanned the room. Something creaked behind him. Something made a noise. Like a foot on a floorboard. But he couldn't see anyone.

Rolf drew a deep breath and steadied himself.

This was his own home, after all, he reminded himself. And though it was late at night, the thoughts he was entertaining were crazy.

Rabinowitz was dead. Rolf had personally helped carry the man's coffin and seen the coffin go into the earth. *Rest in Peace, you old bastard,* he told his mentor. *You can scream all you want, just stay dead.*

Geiger managed a very slight smile. He was starting to recognize the folly of his own thoughts. As he walked to the piano and examined it, he saw no indication that anyone had touched it since he had finished with it a few hours earlier.

"Ghosts do not play pianos," he said aloud.

Then a little surge of fear went through him.

Ghosts?

Why was he even thinking in *that* direction?

Ghosts?

"Yes!"

Rarely before in his life had he even thought much about their existence. Why now?

From somewhere in his subconscious a distant recollection formed and came to him. When studying at Julliard, he had found in the music library early recordings of a nineteenth-century French pianist named Raoul Pugno.

Pugno, too, had been a prodigy, making his debut in 1858 at the age of six and winning his first international competitions in Paris at fourteen. Like Geiger, Pugno had had virtually no formal training on his instrument until his teen years. Later, he became a teacher, a composer, and a recitalist of chamber music. He had made many appearances with a Belgian named Eugène Ysaye.

Both Pugno and Ysaye were huge heavy men, exceptional in size and talent. "The two colossi on the stage together almost made it buckle," observed a writer from the *New York Times* in December of 1878.

But the talent of Pugno and his physical size was not what had remained with Geiger. In Paris in 1903, Pugno had been asked to come to the studio of La Grande Compagnie de Gramophone to attempt to make some recordings. Pugno had accepted the invitation, spending the next several weeks in the studio at an unexceptional old upright. He performed a variety of works and ultimately made eighteen highly noteworthy recordings. All were well preserved.

Thirteen years afterward, Pugno died in Moscow. But the recordings remained in Paris. Later, they were transferred to modern tapes and discs with remarkable clarity. In the 1940s, the Julliard School acquired a set.

At age twenty, Rolf Geiger spent all of his free time one week listening over and over to the recordings of the long-dead Raoul Pugno. The latter's touch had been surprisingly light and agile, particularly for a legendarily ursine man. But what was most remarkable to Geiger was that he was listening to Pugno at all.

As Rolf sat in a library lounge chair with headphones across his shaggy blond head, he heard the brilliant finger work and distinctive technique of a man who had died seventy-three years earlier. Even more eerie, Geiger was listening to a man who had been born during the Second Republic in France and the presidency of Millard Fillmore in the United States.

Geiger at the time had entertained an uneasy feeling listening to the recordings, a feeling made even more so since apparently—according to the tapes' history at Julliard—no previous student had listened to them in thirty years.

He was listening to a ghost.

Or at least, that was his feeling.

He had the sense of listening not to just a recording, but *to an actual ghost* play the piano. The feeling within him was that somehow by teeing up these old tapes on a recording system, he had raised a human spirit to make music.

When he closed his eyes one night, bringing his entire being and consciousness into a parochial world beneath those headphones, he held before him a mental image of the long-deceased Pugno playing—a heavy, bearded, bespectacled man in a primitive Paris studio transferring elements of his soul into an old upright.

The image stayed with him with such clarity that Geiger almost had trouble opening his own eyes. There was something gripping, almost supernatural, about old Pugno and his music.

Geiger had managed to open his eyes and return to the present day.

Now, a little less than a decade later, Geiger found himself listening to this strange piano music that either was or wasn't emanating from the Steinway in his own home. And Geiger had the same creepy reaction.

He was again listening to a ghost. But this time, without electronic assistance.

It all seemed very logical. So logical that it was taking a huge effort to pull himself away from it.

Or wasn't it logical at all? Was he actually just being swept away with emotion and musicality?

He wondered. He agonized.

The left half of his brain rose to his rescue and his rational side took over again. He was thinking in that direction—the direction of ghosts and raised spirits—he told himself, because of the trauma of having buried old Rabinowitz, the man who, for better or worse, had been such a focal point of his life. Wasn't it rational for an intelligent man to belabor the ramifications of such a man's passing?

He drew another breath and calmed himself. He was buried in thought and reflection about Pugno and Rabinowitz, life and death.

And spiritual survival. Absently, he thought back to Brother Matthew at St. Agnes' School in West Virginia more than two decades earlier. Matthew had loved to hold long discourses on the fate and existence of the spirit. Like the tapes of Pugno, Geiger wished he could replay some of those discussions now.

Geiger's thoughts drifted back to the present.

He ran his hand over the closed keyboard of the Steinway. He opened the panel that covered the keyboard. He gently traced his fingers across the smooth ivory and ebony surface of the keys. The touch of the keyboard comforted him.

This room was empty, Rolf finally concluded. There had been no music. Rather, all he had heard had been an extension of his bad dream. This walk downstairs had been not much different than the imagined nocturnal stroll he had taken a few nights earlier.

He sat down at the piano bench. He was comfortable there, too.

His gaze settled upon the keys. He had the impulse to play. Maybe just a few warm-up exercises to get the Chopin out of his head.

He tried to decide. What would he play? His concentration deepened and he nearly jumped out of his skin when he felt a hand settle on his shoulder.

"Rolf?"

His heart kicked and his entire body convulsed in fear. Geiger screamed. His head shot to the right and there was a human form there!

It took a second for the full impact to register. A long second.

"Rolf, honey, are you all right?"

He exhaled in relief, looking up at Diana, who had arrived so quietly next to him.

"Sorry," she said. "Did I startle you?"

"Yes. I didn't expect you."

She let her hand drift to his shoulders. "I saw you get up. I was worried. Can't sleep?" She hugged him.

"A little restless," he answered.

"Want to play? It won't bother me. It's like a lullaby. I could fall asleep listening to you."

He smiled.

"You're wonderful," he said.

"You sure nothing's bothering you?"

He smiled again. "Did you hear any music already?" he asked.

"Music?"

"The piano," he said.

"No," she answered, a little mystified. "Were you playing?"

"No."

"Then, Tiger, how could I have—?"

He shook his head.

"I was having a dream," he explained. "A bad one. When I came out of it, I thought I heard piano music coming from somewhere."

"We're alone in this house," she teased.

"I know."

"Luckily for us."

"I know."

"So your imagination is working overtime."

"I know again," he said. He pulled her to the bench with him. "What do you want to hear?"

"Brahms. Lullaby," she said.

He played a minor theme from the lullaby. A mournful one. He played it with sadness and reflection.

"Sometimes," he said to her, "I feel overwhelmed by things. By music. By life. By death. I think you're my lifeboat, my safety valve, my access to sanity."

She smiled and returned his embrace.

"I don't know what I'd do if I ever lost you," he told her.

"You won't," she said, returning his hug.

"If I pray about anything in this world, it's that," he said.

Gently he played more for her. She kissed him and went back upstairs. Two minutes later, he joined her, and slept perfectly through the remainder of the night.

seven

The full name of the most important woman in Rolf Geiger's life was Diana Stephenson.

She had a long graceful body and a bright beautiful face. Brown eyes that were always alive. Though she had yet to see her twenty-sixth birthday, her shoulder-length brown hair was touched with a tiny bit of gray, as if at one point in her young life some extreme shock or trauma had touched her.

She was from northern California, where her father had been a lecturer in music at Stanford and her mother had been in real estate. An only child, she had been gawky and clumsy as an adolescent. She went to schools for academically gifted children, but remembered them more for her lack of popularity than for their challenging curriculum.

She went through life quietly. She read a lot. She listened to a lot of music. She was very plain for the first sixteen years of her life, had no serious boyfriends, no inseparable female pals. Other kids in her classes, when they had nothing else to do, made fun of her.

First for being so plain. Next for being smart.

Then something happened. She blossomed.

The awkwardness of the teen years suddenly gave way to

grace. Features that had been ordinary evolved into beauty. She learned tricks of style and makeup, jettisoned her glasses, and got a better haircut.

Some of the boys who used to tease her now called her and wanted her company. She turned them down. Girls who had once ridiculed her now wanted her help in homework and social advice. She referred them back to their old boyfriends, who were usually the boys who had taunted her for being un-everything including un-cool. Simultaneously, she finished first in her class, and blew out of California to Wellesley.

There she developed a niche. She was a smart, pretty, well-spoken loner. A little quirky. She taught herself the flute well enough to play in a chamber-music quintet. She read pop French novels in her free time, minored in art, and majored in music appreciation. Knowing how to put words together, she had considerable success writing.

Her territory was music criticism. She was first published in a jazz magazine in Boston. Then the *Boston Phoenix* hired her to cover the entire music scene in eastern Massachusetts. The pay was so-so, but the perks were great.

She scribbled with style. Once she was sent to a country-and-western bar that functioned for wayward cowboys in Brookline.

"My dog came home, the bank returned my farm, and my boyfriend gave me my virginity back," she wrote at the top of her review. "I have just listened to a dreadful C and W band in reverse." Diana Stephenson, the world soon learned, had a tongue as sharp as her intellect.

She kicked around Boston for a couple of years after Wellesley, then married an aspiring actor named Gary who said he was twenty-five but who had actually been out of high school for fourteen years.

Gary was short on talent but long on charm. He led her to New York, then to Los Angeles. He had trouble finding work. He encouraged Diana to act or model, but she wasn't interested. She fell out of the orbit of music review. She worked as a waitress in SoHo, then again in Sunset Plaza in Los Angeles. She was very, very pretty by this time, but obviously adrift. Male customers propositioned her every night. And every night she turned them all down.

Gary discovered cocaine and developed a temper. He hauled off and belted Diana one night. An hour later, she moved out of their crappy apartment in Culver City, drove overnight to Palo Alto, and crashed on her parents' doorstep. Literally.

"Oh," her father said when he discovered her the next morning. "You're back."

"I'm back."

"I'm not surprised. What's new?" He hadn't seen her in a year. The early stage of Diana Stephenson's life was over, and so was an unlovely first marriage.

She went back to college and rediscovered music. While living at home she worked evenings in a sports bar, putting her beauty on a paying basis. Halter top and short shorts. Her tips were astronomical and when customers got out of line she flashed a fake wedding ring at them.

She then would wait for the question that all the guys would ask: "Married, huh? Too bad. What's your husband do?"

"He's a boxer," she'd answer. "Light heavyweight. Big and strong and real, real jealous." End of harassment every time.

She barely spent a penny. So she got her master's degree from Berkeley and headed back to New York, looking to write music criticism or reviews for anyone who would hire her.

Any music. Bluegrass. John Cage. Lemonheads. Trisha Yearwood. She knew it all. Along the way, she went to a Rolf Geiger concert. She was bowled over. The looks. The charm. The attitude. The playfully disrespectful way he could pirouette from Brahms to U2 then back again.

She wondered what made him tick, and decided she would find out and get paid for it at the same time. That meant an interview. It took two months, but she finally wrangled one.

The interview happened in New York. She had gone to talk to Geiger after a concert at Carnegie Hall. She had been working on a freelance article about him and was trying hard to peddle it to the *New York Times* Sunday Magazine, a periodical which had not always treated him kindly.

Rolf wasn't giving interviews in those days to regular music writers. He was living alone, recovering from his brief failed marriage, and carrying a full calendar of recitals. He was also trying to escape the long shadow of his mentor, Rabinowitz.

At the time, Rolf's life was one of gift and privilege in public, but not necessarily one of enjoyment in private. He also was weary of being skewered in the press. Yet he liked the way she looked. So he granted an interview to her, partially to see what she would do with it, partially to have someone to speak to after a recital, and partially because he thought she was as sexy as any woman he had ever met.

She was very easy to talk to.

Diana could converse readily on a wide range of subjects, ranging from the New York Yankees to the art of Edward Hopper to the music of Hank Williams Sr. In the interview, she allowed him to explain himself and talk about his music and music in general. Rolf liked her, right from the start. He quickly realized that they were both isolated loners.

She was perfect for Rolf. Diana was one of the first people he had ever met who also knew that ''Don't Worry, Baby'' was actually written for the Ronnettes as a follow-up to ''Be My Baby,'' an obscure bit of sugar-fix cultural trivia that escaped most musicologists.

''Very few people know *that*,'' he commented during their first chat.

''I know a lot about popular culture,'' she said. ''Classics blending with pop. That's why I'm the perfect person to profile you. You're fascinated with both, also.''

''But I know more than you do,'' he said.

She laughed. ''You might think so,'' she said. ''And I might even *let* you think so.''

''Who was the first to sing, 'Are You Lonesome Tonight?' before a live audience?'' he asked.

''Al Jolson,'' she answered correctly. ''In 1928.''

''Very good,'' he allowed. ''Now name the most recent two-sided hit by Elvis Presley and give me the year.''

''' 'Flaming Star' and 'Wooden Heart.' Nineteen sixty-one.''

''Impressive. Are you as good on the classics?'' he asked.

''Try me, baby,'' she teased.

''How did Chopin die?''

''Tuberculosis.''

"What was the relationship between Chopin and the French sculptor Auguste Clésinger?"

"Clésinger was the son-in-law of George Sand, with whom Chopin had an affair. He also molded Chopin's death mask in Paris in 1850."

Rolf blinked.

"What nineteenth-century pianist did George Bernard Shaw meet and pronounce, 'Nobly beautiful and poetic'?" he asked.

"Clara Schumann, wife of the composer Robert Schumann, and herself a better technician at the keyboard."

She smiled. So did he.

"Is there anything you don't know?" he asked.

"Sure," Diana said. "Plenty. And I won't tell you any of it."

"I wouldn't expect you to."

Her mind was of that type: she knew a lot of odd stuff and, as a journalist, knew how to pull it together. He liked that, too. It was the first inkling of falling in love.

So he let her hang around for a few longer interviews, discussing at length some of the dichotomies of his life, how he wished to be taken seriously as a musician, knew he had a great gift, but couldn't resist having fun at the same time. He let her watch him practice. Then, when her article was finished, he asked her to join him for dinner sometime when he was in New York.

She had declined.

He kept calling.

She continued to decline.

He called some more.

She put him off very firmly, and he finally said to hell with her. He reasoned that somewhere a beautiful woman like Diana must already have an appreciative boyfriend.

She sold her article. The *Times* printed it prominently, emblazoning a picture of Geiger on the cover of the Sunday Magazine. The photo was a hot sexy shot from a 1994 recital in Stockholm. In it, Geiger, his flowing dark blond hair illuminated like a halo by friendly backlighting, intently played Liszt at a baby grand while wearing blue jeans, a pink formal jacket, and a black velvet bow tie.

He was as gorgeous as a hot fudge sundae. Within the magazine, under a similar photo, Geiger was quoted as saying, "I have fun dressing goofy and playing loud music." He also named "Little Deuce Coupe" as one of his favorite pieces of music, right up there with *Die Meistersinger*.

The title on the article, which was also on the cover of the magazine, was "The Prodigy Grows Up. Or Tries To, Real Hard. Honest!"

"The title was the editors' title, not mine," Diana explained when Rolf called her to congratulate her on the placement of the work. "I wanted just to call it, 'Fingers.'"

"I couldn't care less about the title," he said. "Plus, it's probably accurate."

She laughed nervously. "You're not calling to scream at me?"

"I would never scream at you. I want to ask you to dinner again."

A slight change of tone, and, "You don't give up, do you? Not *ever?*"

"Not if I want something."

Her best journalistic voice: "What do you want?"

"You."

More silence.

"Tell me your favorite restaurant," he said.

"It's called Le Rossignol," she answered. It was a test.

"The one in Boston or the one in Washington?" he asked. "I don't know one in New York by that name."

"The one in Boston."

"Say yes for Friday night," he said. "I'll do the rest."

"Okay," she said after long thought. "All right. But we're in New York, not Boston, so you can choose any restaurant."

"I already have," he said.

Friday night arrived. Geiger arrived with a car, a driver, and two dozen roses. The car took them to La Guardia. A private plane took them to Boston. Another car took them to Le Rossignol on Newbury Street. The restaurant recognized him and gave them their best table.

"You certainly know," she said, "how to impress a woman on a first date."

"Personally or professionally, anything I do, I want to do better than anyone else."

"Is that a fact?"

"You already know that's a fact. You printed as much in the article," he reminded her.

"I'm just repeating it now for emphasis," she said.

"Repeat it carefully," he said.

The article led to other assignments. The next time they had dinner together, she slept over at his place. Three months later, she had moved in with him. Then came his big tour of 1995. He made a fortune and was reviled by the critics.

Now they shared a gracious two-million-dollar town house in Manhattan and, when they were in California, they had a small pink house in Malibu. Meanwhile he had stopped performing and for many years had no idea in which direction to take his life. He only knew that he had found a special woman and eventually, with her, he would find that direction again at the proper time.

He felt, and she felt, that anything they had could be taken away from them. But as long as they had each other, they could survive or even recover. They fit together perfectly. They were a rare couple: in love without qualification. Perhaps that, too, was an absurdity in modern life, but it was also a realistic absurdity.

At this point in their lives, as Geiger got used to the idea that he would soon return to a tour of the world's most prestigious concert halls, it was difficult for either him or Diana to imagine that there could be any force in nature—known or unknown—that could drive a wedge between them. But then again, the unknown, the forces that lurk just outside day-to-day reality, always constitute a special terror.

eight

Five days later, Brian Greenstone called a press conference at a private room at Le Champlain Restaurant near Lincoln Center. Following a buffet luncheon, with Rolf Geiger present, he made the official announcement of Geiger's World Tour. About two dozen writer-reporters were present from various media that covered classical music. Greenstone's press conferences were rare, but were always luxuriously catered and involved an A-list client who was at the disposal of the assembled writers. Almost all invitees showed. An absence without explanation meant being dropped from the next event.

"The schedule of the tour is evolving very quickly," said Greenstone, heightening his accent to give the proceedings as much class as possible. A smattering of strobes burst like small indoor flares. "Several of the dates remain to be finalized but the basic structure of the tour is set."

Claire handed out the two-page press release. The tour closely resembled Greenstone's original proposal, both in length and ambition.

The inescapable William Baumann of the *New York Times* asked the first question.

"What has suddenly changed?" he asked, crusty as ever.

"For a couple of years, Rolf Geiger barely performed in public. Now Geiger wants a live audience of half the world."

Greenstone and Geiger both hesitated before picking up Baumann's live grenade. In the corner of Geiger's line of view, Diana made an angry expression and turned away from Baumann, whom she found insufferable.

"Well," Greenstone finally said, "fortunately, Rolf is here, so he can answer your question for himself."

That got a few laughs. "Wonderful," said Baumann.

"I'm suddenly in a good mood, thank you," Geiger said, seeking to keep the discussion upbeat. "And I'd like the entire world, not just half of it."

"Any reason, Rolf?" Baumann pressed. "Seriously? Why a tour of this size and why now?"

"Why not?"

"I think it could be said that Mr. Geiger has suddenly felt himself to be in an immeasurably creative and productive frame of mind," Greenstone said. "He wishes to bring his music before the public as soon as possible. Hence, a very grand world tour starting in the early fall."

"Isn't that *rushing* things?" Baumann asked. "Often tours like this take years to arrange. Orchestras need to be contracted, halls booked, conductors signed, current commitments rearranged where possible."

"Bill, generally you're right," Greenstone answered. "But, because of the unique nature of this tour and of Rolf Geiger's abilities, many of the top people and halls wish to make themselves available when they otherwise might not."

Baumann gave it an arch of an eyebrow and turned his attention back to a plate of shrimp Dijonaise.

Greenstone continued, saying that dates in the major cities had already been set. The concert series would begin in New York and then travel to Europe. South America would be next, then Asia. The concluding concert would be in Egypt in March. Billed as a Concert for World Peace, it would be played in the Valley of the Kings with the pyramids as the backdrop.

There would only be admission charged for the immediate three thousand seats near the stage. Beyond that, the stage would be visible for miles. Television rights would underwrite this particular performance, at which Geiger intended to play the *Emperor* Concerto.

"The Egyptian government has been contacted and is very supportive and encouraging," Greenstone said. "We are hoping for the largest live audience ever to witness any music event. Perhaps one million people."

"What else will you play?" a reporter asked Geiger.

"On the tour or in Cairo?"

"Both."

"I'm not sure about the front part of the final date in Egypt," Geiger said. "But I think we're going to have forty-eight dates worldwide. It might end up at fifty. I'll be playing a heavy concentration of Beethoven. But the tour will focus on music suitable to the particular venues. Prokofiev and Tchaikovsky in Russia, for example. Mozart in Vienna. And so on."

"Will you play Chopin?" someone asked.

"Why wouldn't I?"

"Wouldn't that beg a comparison with Isador Rabinowitz?"

"Probably," said Geiger. He felt compelled to add, "If you want to make a comparison, go ahead. Recitalists are compared all the time. It's part of the business."

He exchanged a look with Diana.

"Mr. Geiger, are you certain you won't relent somewhere along the line and sprinkle some pop into the repertoire?" another writer asked. "What if audiences demand it?"

"These will be dignified, ambitious, strictly classical concerts," Geiger answered. "No one should attend expecting otherwise. I want to demonstrate what I can do as a classicist. The repertoire will be limited. But that doesn't mean we can't have fun: Beethoven, for example, used his own compositions merely as starting points for his own recitals, then improvised on his own work. Hopefully, I can also draw large audiences."

Julie Byers of *Downbeat* said, "This concert tour has already had the opportunity to draw some criticism."

Geiger knew what was coming.

"The criticisms are the same ones that you've heard for many years: You've bastardized 'great music' in the past. Now you're turning around and deciding to play in a manner that you've rejected in the past. Some say this whole tour is an exercise in greed. You stand to make about twenty million dollars.''

"Really?'' Geiger said, holding a straight face and pretending to be alarmed. He turned to his agent. "I thought it was *fifty* million, Brian. I've been misled. I want *out!*''

There was some laughter.

"But how can you be taken as a serious musician under those circumstances of formerly playing with such a 'pop showbiz' atmosphere,'' she asked. "And doesn't a tour like this underscore all those criticisms as well as add some credibility to them?''

"Julie,'' Geiger asked with a sigh, "how did I know you'd be the one to ask the first overtly hostile question?''

"Intuition, I guess,'' she answered.

"First of all, I never 'rejected' the more traditional approaches to music. I merely didn't employ them. Maybe I didn't feel I was ready. I can't answer that.''

"How much does the death of Isador Rabinowitz have anything to do with the timing of this,'' Baumann asked.

"It's coincidental,'' Greenstone answered.

"Come on,'' Baumann pressed.

Greenstone sighed. "Serge Prokofiev died the same day in 1953 that Rabinowitz signed his first contract with RCA Victor. Does anyone look for cause and effect with that?''

The laughter around the room defused the point.

"Mr. Geiger enjoys unparalleled popularity worldwide,'' Greenstone said, continuing while he had the momentum. "A tour like this does not come along very often. We're trying to use venues that will allow millions of people to attend.''

Still the piranhas swarmed. "Speaking of millions, Brian,'' asked Maxine Walton of the *New York Observer.* "How much is this tour really worth to your client? Twenty million? Fifty million?''

Greenstone started to deflect the subject again. But Geiger cut him off. "It's okay. I need to address this,'' Rolf said.

Geiger turned the full warmth of his charm upon his questioner.

"First, no one criticizes performers like The Rolling Stones or Springsteen or Hootie & the Blowfish when they do world tours with extravagant grosses. There seems to be something written somewhere that says that classical artists have to play to smaller elite houses and shouldn't seek large audiences. I don't believe that. The three tenors still play to worldwide audiences and no one seems to care. The great tenors Caruso and John McCormack became quite wealthy playing to the largest audiences they could find, as did many modern recital pianists from Liszt and Paderewski in the last century to Horowitz and Rubinstein in this century. So music is music, to my mind. I'm creating a venue that increases interest and awareness in the greatest music of the greatest composers and a lot of other modern artists who play it. No one is forced to buy a ticket or listen to one note that I play.''

The writers scribbled and let their handheld tape recorders roll.

"And at least two of the largest concerts will be largely for charity,'' said Greenstone. "One of the European dates, probably the one at Wembley, we'll do for world famine relief. One of the American dates will also be for U.S. charities that Mr. Geiger favors.''

"Which charities?'' asked Marsha Kessler of *Newsweek*.

Geiger grabbed the question. "Several, including farm aid, breast cancer research, AIDS research, and a few smaller ones that I contribute to privately.''

"It's quite a generous arrangement,'' Greenstone said with a tired sigh to his media contacts. "Sometime corner some of the rock stars you're always writing about so reverently and find out how much they give to charity and how much they blow up their noses. That nasty suggestion of mine was off the record, by the way.''

"What about recordings?'' someone else asked.

Geiger arched his eyebrows. "Well, I would hope there might be some,'' he said innocently. He smiled slyly and looked to Greenstone as a small ripple of laughter went around the room.

"Mr. Geiger's present label, Aurora Records, has indicated that they will issue the entire tour in a boxed set of ten CDs next autumn. We're very close to a formal agreement. Aurora will make the announcement when we have the contract.''

"What will top ticket prices be?" someone from the rear of the room asked.

"Maybe as high as four hundred dollars in London and New York, and five hundred in Tokyo," Greenstone answered.

"Then *what about* the charge that this is an exercise in greed?" asked Baumann again. "If you figure that the tour will net fifty million dollars, you could actually cut ticket prices and viewing and recording costs by fifty percent and come away with a fortune. Charities notwithstanding, you're still freezing out a lot of people."

"Why don't you ask Michael Jordan why *he* charges so much?" someone mumbled in Baumann's direction to a smattering of laughter.

"My primary interest is music, my performance as a musician," Geiger said. "There will be low-cost rows interspersed with the expensive rows in many halls. The five-hundred-dollar seats underwrite the two-dollar seats."

"You're *still* making a fortune," Baumann said.

"It's legal, you know, Bill," Geiger finally said. "Why doesn't your paper cut the costs of a daily edition from a dollar to twenty cents to bring truth and knowledge to a larger audience?"

"Not analogous," Baumann insisted.

"I'd actually prefer just to discuss music," Geiger said. He found Diana's gaze and they exchanged another glance.

"You have to remember," Greenstone chided the room, "what a tremendously demanding project this is from a performing artist's point of view. Mr. Geiger will be traveling for six or seven months, touring the world. He will be under the most intense scrutiny of any classical artist who has ever lived. I would say that this is the most demanding tour, physically, intellectually, and musically that anyone has attempted. Ever."

"Rolf, in the past you've suggested that you'd eventually like to be known as the best pianist who ever lived. Is that part of what this tour is about?"

"Well," Geiger answered sheepishly, "if you'd like to write that about me when the tour is over, and if I deserve it, I won't object."

His remark was greeted with laughter.

"Rolf, do you think you *could* have done a tour like this when Isador Rabinowitz was alive?" someone else asked.

Geiger looked at the man. "What are you asking?"

"Well, Rabinowitz was not only your mentor but your harshest critic. Wouldn't he—?"

"There's really no relation between this tour and the death of Isador Rabinowitz," Geiger explained again. "The two events are coincidental. I'm in my late twenties, and I was weighing the possibility of a tour like this while I was in Italy a few weeks ago. This is the time that I feel I want to do this tour."

"But do you think you'll be more *at ease* on tour now that Rabinowitz is gone?" asked Ken Osterfeld of *New York* magazine. Osterfeld, too, had found the shrimp tray and reloaded a plate.

Geiger felt a certain impatience building within him. He looked to Diana again. She winked at him, and his nerves eased slightly.

"I think I just answered that question as best I could," Geiger said.

"No more questions involving Rabinowitz," Greenstone said.

Geiger glanced around. Mercifully, there were no more hands in the air. The two dozen reporters present were either making their marks in their notebooks, examining the press release, in a holding pattern around the buffet table, or waiting for others to ask questions.

"Is that it?" Greenstone asked hopefully.

Julie Byers raised her hand again.

"Mr. Geiger, is Isador Rabinowitz still a presence for you?" she asked.

Brian Greenstone was angered by the question. Particularly the wording of it. "Julie, didn't I just ask—?"

"It's all right," Geiger said.

He turned back to Julie Byers.

"I'm not sure what you mean by that," he said. "Presence how?"

"I don't mean a physical presence, obviously," she said. "I mean the memory. Again, not to repeat an earlier question, but the level of musicianship that he set was so high, the friction between the two of you was so well known, and the nature of his criticism was so harsh. It would seem that this would be something you still thought about.''

"I think about it, yes. But I have to play my own music and define myself as an artist."

"And you'd even dare to challenge him by playing some Chopin?''

The question disquieted Geiger. He gave it some thought, then a thorough answer.

"Rubinstein played Chopin, too. God knows, in the early part of this century Chopin was seen as a weak and ineffectual romantic, dipping his pen in some maudlin pool of moonlight to compose nocturnes for feather-brained young women—or so it was said. Rubinstein redefined Chopin with a more direct approach and then Rabinowitz reinterpreted him once again. I'll play Chopin my own way, which is probably closer to the way Arthur Rubinstein played him than the way Isador Rabinowitz played him. But it will be my way. No one *owns* Chopin.''

"But you'll play mostly Beethoven?" came a final question. "Why? Anything specific?''

"What can I say," Geiger said with good nature, trying to lighten the moment. "My name is Rolf Geiger. I like the German composers. Ludwig wrote great stuff. I can't explain much more than that.''

He got the laugh.

Geiger surveyed the room. A final question emerged from someone he didn't know. She was a petite, intense, dark-haired woman. She identified herself as Anita Zwerdling from *Rolling Stone.*

"Would it be correct to say that this is the landmark tour for you?" she asked. "The tour that your *critics* have always been asking for?''

He thought about it. "I think you could say that," he said. "But you could also say it's the grand tour that *I've* always wanted to do. All the way around the world. The greatest music of the greatest composers.''

"Played by the finest young pianist of the century," Brian Greenstone added.

"Arguably the 'finest,'" said Geiger quickly. "But I'll try hard to make that case."

"Thank you all for coming," Greenstone said, ending the press conference. "Catch me now or call my office if you have any further questions. My new assistant Claire can help you also."

He indicated the pretty girl standing near the door with extra publicity releases. The press conference was over and, for the first time in his life, Geiger discovered that he was soaked through with sweat from meeting the press. There had been much about the questions—and their implications—that had bothered him.

"Hard to believe, Rolf," Greenstone said in a whispered aside when they had a moment away from all other ears. "All that you've accomplished in music, all the originality and expertise that you've brought to your instrument, and still these people come in here and throw darts at you."

"I'm not serious enough for them," Geiger said. "Well, maybe this tour will change that."

Diana joined Rolf. He put an arm around her.

Then, before he could make his exit, Julie Byers, one of the more hostile reporters, stopped him near the door. She had brought two recent CDs and a felt-tip pen. Geiger patiently autographed both before leaving with Diana.

The next morning, the spin from the press conference was clear. The headline on the first page of the Arts section in the *New York Times* would foreshadow other write-ups to follow in other journals:

**A HIGH OCTAVE SURPRISE! ROLF GEIGER
ANNOUNCES WORLD TOUR IN THE FALL.
HE'LL ASPIRE TO BE 'FINEST PIANIST' EVER.**

Fortunately the general public received the news of the tour with a more favorable impression than the press and musicologists. Switchboards were swamped with early demands for tickets.

In Zurich, where a box office was set up first, all tickets were gone in fifty-two minutes. It was a new record for a classical sellout in that city. Curiously, it was a city where Isador Rabinowitz had lived for five months during World War II. He had always hated the place and had never sold out a recital there in his life. Some of the old man's friends conjectured that up on Morningside Heights in the crowded old cemetery where Rabinowitz had been buried, presumably for keeps, the departed maestro was rolling in his grave.

Others disagreed: they said he was probably kicking at the lid of his coffin, he would have been so angry.

nine

_____

_____

Mezzaforte.

Mezzaluna.

Mezzanotte.

Midnight.

Several midnights later, in fact.

Geiger was home again and trying to sleep. But there had barely been a peaceful night since the funeral.

Odd, weird associations kept flitting through his semiwaking mind, darting around like malevolent fireflies. Geiger rolled in his bed. His arm went out and he sat up in shock when it couldn't find Diana. He opened his eyes in the dark, saw that she was there after all. He pulled her to him for security.

He wanted so badly to sleep and rest, but nasty contrary thoughts kept bedeviling him.

More rambling associations . . .

Mezza soprano.

Mezzatinto.

Mesopotamia.

Mosquito.

Mesquite.

Tex Mex.

Mezzanotte.

Yeah. Mezzanotte. Midnight again.

He closed his eyes and something out of the past forcibly replayed itself.

It was a decade earlier and he was back in Nice, sitting on the terrace of the Hôtel Negresco. It was the moment of his first international piano triumph. The sun provided a beautiful warmth, as did the sound of a soft new female voice.

"Bonjour," she had said. *"Ça va?"*

He had been startled by her presence. He didn't know anyone had moved that close to him so far away had he been in his thoughts.

He turned to see a young woman in her early twenties. He was startled a second time when he had a few moments to appraise her. She was stunningly beautiful, with the smoldering good looks of a Botticelli painting.

"Hello," he said.

She smiled. *"Vous parlez un peu de français, peut-être? Ou Italien?"*

"I'm sorry. No. I don't speak French," he answered, guessing clumsily at what she might have asked.

"You are the American pianist," she said switching easily to English. "Rolf."

"That's me. Yes." Still awkward.

"May I join you?"

He corrected his posture and sat up. No woman loved a slouch. He was worldly enough to know that. "Of course," he said.

She seated herself and lay her purse on the table. The purse: luxurious black alligator with a twenty-four-karat gold buckle that dazzled in the Côte d'Azur sunlight. Hermès. Her purse cost more than Frank Geiger used to make in a month, on those odd occasions when he was employed.

She introduced herself. Everything she did, she did beautifully, including speak English.

Her name was Anila, she said. She was an Italian citizen and a fashion model from Rome. She worked on the most expensive runways in both Rome and Paris. But recently, she said, she had also landed a few movie roles in films by Truffaut and Antonioni. When Geiger confessed that he had never heard of either director, she smiled indulgently.

"Well, you might not know cinema, but you certainly know your music," Anila said. "You played magnificently last night."

"Thank you," he said.

There was a charming colonial lilt to her English. She was actually Indian, she explained, born in Mugraw, and educated at British schools. She had come to Rome when she was fifteen.

It all sounded incredibly exotic. For lack of anything better to say, he admired her purse, though he'd never heard of Hermès back in West Virginia.

"It was a gift," she said. "From a friend."

"Oh."

"But I don't see him anymore." She laughed. "Long gone. Is that the phrase in English? 'Long gone.' " She laughed again. "And good riddance, too."

He nodded and smiled dumbly in return.

"How did you learn to play the piano so well?" she asked, picking up the silence.

"I taught myself."

"You were tremendous," she said.

He had been. And he knew it.

"Thank you," he said again.

Anila looked at him. Rolf looked at her.

Then, his naïveté getting the best of him, he finally confessed what was in his head.

"Look," he stumbled. "You're very pretty and you've been all over the world. I've never even been out of the United States before. I have no idea what to even talk to you about."

Anila smiled again.

"Who needs to talk?" she asked.

"No one, I guess," he answered.

He was more nervous with her, however, than he had been on the stage the previous evening.

That night they became lovers, commencing an intense seven-day fling. The next day, soaring emotionally, Geiger won the piano competition in Nice.

In his town house, his eyes opened again. Anila was gone

and Diana was there. He felt like making love to a woman. The memory of Anila had aroused him. So should he turn on Diana with a lust that had been incited by another woman?

He felt disgusted with himself. Distantly, he could have sworn he sensed the spirit of Rabinowitz reading his thoughts. And laughing.

Oh, yes. He could have sworn he heard the old bastard laughing.

"Fuck them both, Rolf. Pretend you're fucking one while you're fucking the other. Infidelity is that easy!"

Rolf refused even to acknowledge that thought.

Several midnights had arrived and passed after the press conference. Geiger was deeply engaged now in selecting his music. He had organized scores, left them stacked by his Steinway downstairs, studied many of them, eliminated some, and even spent some time hacking around by working the primary theme from "Good Vibrations" by the Beach Boys into Beethoven's Ninth.

Oh, he wouldn't dare! He laughed. Yes, he was going to play the Hollywood Bowl and yes it would be a real howl to do that. A musical upraised center finger to the whole God damned music establishment. All this while he also demonstrated how good he was!

But the classical music mafia would never forgive him for something like that, particularly having promised to stay away from such stunts.

But nonetheless, Geiger fantasized: Ludwig von B? Meet Brian, Dennis, and Carl Wilson, plus Al Jardine and Mike Love here.

Now, listen up, Ludwig. Mike and Al handle the soaring harmonies, while Brian is the eccentric composer, Dennis is the Beach Boy who drowned because he couldn't swim and Carl is just sort of along for the ride. And, boys, pay attention to Ludwig because he composed while deaf and with Paget's disease.

"Good Vibes" with the "Ode to Joy." The Beach goes to Bavaria. Brian Wilson at Das Bauhaus. Well, once again, why the hell not? At least in private.

He also had a little companion piece, fusing Van Halen with

van Beethoven. The two Vans: Together Again for the First Time!

He played it for Diana. Then there was his standing joke in which, while giving a narration of his music he intentionally confused sentences with "Emanuel Ax" and "a man with an ax," during which he played in a hatchet chopping motion and—as would be the result with an ax—hit no note more than once.

They had been beside themselves with amusement. Laughter was wonderful. He loved to sit her at the piano next to him and play for her, a special audience of one. In some ways, *Moonlight* Sonata and the theme from *Swan Lake* were now songs that belonged to *her,* because he either played them special ways for her, or when he was in public they were meant for her whenever he played.

They would goof around at the piano and laugh some more. There was too little laughter these days because the nights were increasingly dark.

Mezzanotte, after all. *Mezzanotte* meant more than the hour of midnight. It meant, the middle of the night. The real dark watches. The hour of the wolf.

"The hour when spirits rise and walk, Rolf. It's when the dead visit the living. We all know that."

He sprang up in bed again. "Who said that?" Geiger demanded, frightened. This time, he could *not* dismiss the thought.

"I did."

The voice was at the edge of his consciousness, a faint but insistent whisper. Almost inaudible.

But there.

"I said, the dead visit the living sometimes, Rolf. Is that so hard to understand?"

Diana rolled over in her sleep. "What?" he demanded again.

Now she found him. Her eyes half opened, joining him in the jagged unsettling darkness.

"Tiger?" Diana said sleepily. "No one said anything. You're talking in your sleep again."

He was as agitated as a dozen scared cats. He blew out a long breath. "Yeah," he said. "Talking in my sleep. Sorry."

He eased down again into the warmth of his bed. He closed his eyes. Or tried to.

The first part of the night had come easily. It had been restful and calm. But as the dark hours of the morning progressed, other forces began to pilfer the peacefulness of Geiger's snoozing hours.

Some force was again taking command of his head. Rolf settled back into bed, but involuntarily he began to dream. The sequences of the reverie made no sense, but the dreams were alive with disturbing images.

He envisioned his mother's grave. It was set in the middle of a highway and a team of construction workers were digging it up. When they opened the coffin, his mother climbed up to the roadway and swore at her son for not burying her in a more restful setting.

Absurdity of life and death, a voice told him.

A second image: Rabinowitz wandered through the cemetery on Morningside Heights. He turned to look into the eyes of Geiger. "Don't think for a moment I'll stay buried here," the maestro said. There were no eyes in his eye sockets.

Just hollows.

" 'Rest in peace'! What a macabre joke that is! Ever done any research on how many subterranean creatures burrow through old cemeteries?''

Hollows where the eyes had been. No more windows to the soul. Just windows to the fleshless skull.

The worms crawl in, the worms crawl out . . .

Everything went black. Geiger twisted again in bed, pursued now by childhood parochial-school doggerel.

They crawl up your nose and out your spout . . .

The unlinked visions continued.

A brightness came upon his subconscious, then a blackness—much like a movie screen going from full light to no light in an instant. When light was present again, something resembling the grave of Isador Rabinowitz was peaceful one minute, then swirling with dirt a moment later, as if blasted up from underneath the ground.

He's coming back again, Geiger thought. *Just like the dream the other night. The old bastard won't stay dead!*

In bed, something tapped Rolf on the shoulder.

"Greetings, Rolf! I'm here! I'm in your home tonight."

Geiger shook in bed. In his dream there was a cold, firm hand on his shoulder.

He shook again. His eyes fluttered open into the darkness.

Jesus! The hand was *still* on his shoulder.

And—*holy Jesus,* he suddenly realized—*it's not Diana's!*

He bolted up from sleep and flailed at the direction of the touch. The feeling suddenly lifted, as if the hand had released Rolf Geiger's shoulder.

Once again, his heart beat like a kettledrum.

He turned the light on and examined the room. He and Diana were alone. Or at least he couldn't see anyone else. He glanced again at her. She was sleeping peacefully, the little piano pendant hanging between her breasts.

He looked back around the room. He felt his heart pump, and he was aware of the wetness on his brow.

Then he settled back to try to sleep. He turned the light off. He held his eyes open in narrow slits in the darkness of his bedroom and waited to see if any images came to him.

None did. Not right away, at least.

His eyes closed, and he drifted again.

More thoughts came to him from a dark ominous somewhere. Now it was as if some other force were guiding his consciousness, throttling his thoughts sharply into reverse, sending the kaleidoscopic patterns of his mind spiraling backward into his own youth.

Technicolor nightmares. The recurrent multihued terrors of his youth. When he had been a boy he had endured many of them. Some recurring. They hadn't recurred for ages.

The first nightmare:

He was a boy again, sleeping in the decrepit small house in West Virginia. He heard a violent dispute. A man shouting, a woman screaming. He emerged from bed and ran to the top of the steps. It was winter. It was cold as death. He looked down the steps and saw the front door open, wind and snow pouring in, his father drunk and his mother on the floor as her husband flailed at her with his fists. Rolf's feet were rooted in

*place. He couldn't help her. In his nightmare, he turned away
and played the piano to cover her screams. . . .*

Then the second vision. Pure terror this time:

*He walked through the same childhood house. At the end of
a long hallway there was his grandmother's piano. He sat
down and started to play. A wonderful feeling enveloped him.
A feeling of escape, beauty and freedom. Then there was a
pounding sound.*

Knocking.

Hammering.

"Hey! What's that noise?"

*He looked up. His father was smashing the piano as Rolf
played. Then his father's face dissolved and it was Isador
Rabinowitz smashing the instrument. "You are not worthy of
such great music," the old man said.*

But which old man?

"Noise."

That's what his father had called it when he had played.

"Noise."

*That's what Rabinowitz had called it when he played. Some-
times. There were moments when life had a terrible symmetry.*

In his bed, Geiger twisted in anguish.

A third dream rose up.

*He was standing in some sort of burial ground and it was
night. Above him, the stars burned like a million tiny torches.
The moon was pasted in the sky like a wafer. The wafer. "Are
you Catholic?" someone asked.*

He cringed.

*"I'm not anything anymore. I lost my religion long ago,"
he answered. "Shed it the way a snake sheds its skin. Just
crawled out of it one day." "Well, look what you've done?"
the someone continued. "You've killed the most precious thing
you ever had."*

"My music?" Rolf asked aloud in his sleep.

"Your woman."

*In the dream, Rolf turned to the coffin. Simple pine. Like a
spinet. The setting was the same as Rabinowitz's funeral. But
it was Diana who was in the coffin.*

"You murdered her!" someone said.

Geiger screamed out in his sleep. "No!"

"Strangled her."

"No!" he yelled out again.

He saw her in the coffin. Her skin was white as marble. A sleeping angel. Something from a churchyard on a winter evening.

Lifeless as ice.

Rolf turned to the speaker. It was Rabinowitz in the garb of a priest. "Monsignor Kelly, where are you? Brother Matthew, I need you. Where is Sister Mary William? Someone help me!"

Rabinowitz smiled.

The music in the background was discordant. There was insane laughter taunting him. A hell of a nightmare from his youth, except—

"This will be real, Rolf."

Geiger's eyes flashed opened. A hell of a nightmare.

He felt himself turn in bed, as if startled.

"Still here, Rolf!"

In the darkness, he tried to sit up, but there was an inexplicable force upon his upper body. It was as if a very strong man had placed two hands on Geiger's shoulders and shaken him.

Geiger felt himself cry out, as in a nightmare. The unseen hands gripped him hard. He felt himself pulled off his bed and onto the floor, where he landed hard. Then the force was gone and he looked up.

"Oh, my God. . . . Oh my God . . . !"

He was certain that he saw a human form before him, hovering in the room.

Something absolutely terrifying and not of this world.

The image came and went. It was gone in an instant.

Rolf Geiger barely had time to recover. He raised his hand and found the light switch by his bedside.

As far as he could see, the room was empty of intruders. It contained only himself, awake, and Diana, sleeping, barely roused by the lights.

He took several seconds to let his heart and nerves settle. His senses were on full alert, waiting for something unexpected.

But the something didn't come. Or at least it didn't come

now. Gradually, Rolf Geiger got to his feet. He walked to the door and looked into the hallway.

He put on the hall lights. Nothing there, either.

He froze again.

The music had begun again downstairs. The same beautiful but terrifying melodies he thought he had heard once before. They rose from his own Steinway.

Chopin. Technically impeccable. A polonaise expressed in a gorgeous tone. With bigness, sanity, directness, and emotional clarity.

"Oh, God above. . . ." Geiger whispered aloud with a trembling voice. He would recognize that technique, that touch, anywhere. A thousand years could pass and it would be equally unmistakable.

"Yes, Rolf. That's true."

"It's Rabinowitz," whispered Geiger. "He's back."

Geiger felt his forehead wet with perspiration. He felt one bead of sweat moving slowly down his left temple. He imagined that it could have been not just sweat, but a drop of blood.

"Come downstairs, Rolf. Come listen to your master up close. This is a special recital. Just for you."

"No. I don't want to," Geiger said.

"Oh, but you must ... Unless you're scared of your superior."

His gaze drifted downstairs again. There was light seeping out from underneath the door to his library again. The same as the other night when he had also thought that he had heard a *mezzanotte* nocturne.

Rolf Geiger spoke bravely to whatever presence was there.

"Where are you, God damn it!" Rolf Geiger demanded. "In my library? At my piano? If you're there, I want to see you."

A beat. Nothing happened. He waited.

"Not bloody likely. Until I'm ready."

A moment of tension and anticipation dissolved into nothing. Aside from the music, the only sounds Rolf Geiger was aware of was the rhythmic thumping of his heart in his chest.

"Hey," called a nearby female voice. "Tiger?"

Diana. From the still-lit bedroom.

He looked back toward her. She was sitting up in bed.

"What's going on in that head of yours tonight?" she asked softly. "This is the second time you've been up."

Downstairs, the music continued. A melody born from departed virtuosity wafting upward from a stolen harp.

"You don't hear anything?" Geiger asked.

"What?"

He walked back and sat down on the bed. She placed a hand on his shoulder. Her brown eyes searched his.

"You don't hear music?" he asked.

She listened. "Outside?" she asked. "From the street?"

"No. From downstairs in my library."

She shook her head. "Did you leave something on?" she asked. "Radio? CD player?"

"Someone's playing my piano," he said.

She listened again.

"Now?" she asked, mystified.

"Now."

"You hear it *now?*"

He nodded. He heard it.

"Rolf," she said, "I don't hear anything."

"You have to."

The music was resonating in his ears, the volume pumping up as if to irritate him. Geiger held a mental image of the old man aggressively pounding the keys.

"But I don't," she pleaded. "There's nothing there."

"It stopped," Geiger said.

Diana's expression showed concern.

"Tiger, why don't you climb into my side of the bed," she said. "Come in and hold me, okay?"

Geiger withdrew slightly. He looked disappointed. "You didn't hear *anything?*" he asked.

"No."

He sighed. He felt a tumbling sensation within him.

"Let me at least go down and turn the light off," he said. "Then I'll climb in with you."

"It's a deal," she said. "Hurry back."

Geiger left his bedroom and went again to the top of the stairs. No music played down below. But as he looked down he could have sworn he saw the door to the library just closing, as if someone had been in there, come out to the front hall to eavesdrop, then had returned.

The light still showed under the door.

He felt himself age ten years on the spot.

Something's there, he told himself. *Something's there.* Bravely, he started down the steps.

His own footfall was silent in the darkness. His hand glided on the waxed banister as he descended.

Halfway down.

Then two steps from the bottom of the stairs.

Then he was in the middle of the downstairs entrance hall and only a few feet from the closed door to his library.

The music commenced again. An étude.

It sent a shiver through Geiger. He recognized the piece. ''Aeolian Harp.'' This étude had been one of Rabinowitz's favorite pieces. The old master had played it at their first meeting. Now Rolf was hearing it again.

The artistry staggered Geiger anew. He followed the wondrous melody, in the middle of which a tenor voice broke clearly from the chords and joined the principal theme. It was rather like an undulation of the A flat major chord, brought out more resonantly here and there with Rabinowitz's foot on the pedal.

Rabinowitz's foot? What was he telling himself?

The thought distracted Geiger from the music and back to the reality in front of him. He wasn't listening to his onetime teacher; he was listening to a ghost at his piano.

Yes, a ghost. That's what was confronting him now. Geiger accepted it. That was the new reality of what was opposing him.

The ghost of Isador Rabinowitz was in his home.

The worst part about it was that now it all seemed so normal. Within the context of everything else that had transpired, it was so logical. The only explanation for what he was seeing, feeling, and hearing was a supernatural one.

Geiger, still standing in the half darkness, wondered how soon he would look directly at the specter.

Soon.

Would it be there when he pushed open the door to his library, busy at the keyboard?

Maybe.

Would it be ghastly white? Translucent? Indistinguishable from a living creature?

All three.

A moment passed. Perspiration burst again from the Geiger's forehead, this time as if someone had opened a thousand tiny faucets.

Rolf Geiger wasn't able to speak. There remained a dreamlike surreal quality to all of this. It reminded him of a bad dream in which one is riveted in place with a great evil approaching, but one is unable to move or scream. Rolf Geiger also felt as if something—some force—had wrapped its tentacles around him, much in the way a piece of music can capture a performance hall.

Yet, Rolf Geiger knew *this was real!*

The music resounded in his ears. Beauty and horror at the same time. It was as if his head were in a bell and a gigantic new clapper had gone berserk.

"Hell's bells, Rolf. Just for you!"

Geiger could wait no longer. Whatever was waiting for him, whatever form Rabinowitz was in, Geiger was prepared for the confrontation.

He threw open the door to his library. Instantly the music stopped.

The lights went out. Quickly, Geiger reached for the light switch.

The lights along the ceiling fired bright beams in each direction.

He waited. His heart was racing again. He stared at his room and searched for movement.

There was none. Everything looked to be exactly as he had left it late the previous evening.

For almost a full minute, Geiger stood in place. He felt himself a stranger in his own home. He waited anew for a movement or a sign that would not satisfy him in coming.

Then slowly, cautiously, Geiger crossed the room.

To his suspicious eyes, his Steinway seemed to have a strange aura around it, almost an extra glow. He drew back for a second and took a deep breath. Then he spent several seconds trying to convince himself that he had been imagining all of this.

He went to the keys of the piano. Somehow, music was still ringing in his ears. He put his hand on the piano, trying to sense any sort of vibration from having just been played.

My god! He thought he detected something. Someone *had* been playing here. Someone had just stopped.

He reached into the well and placed his hands on the strings. Sure as hell. He thought he detected a vibration, be it ever so slight.

Then Rolf noticed something else.

When he looked at the scores on the table beside his Steinway, he grimaced. Who the hell had been messing with his music?

Diana? Edythe Jamison? Had they dislodged things earlier in the day and he hadn't noticed? Or had the music been rearranged after he had left the room at eleven that evening?

If so, by whom?

He had no objection to either Diana or Mrs. Jamison going through any part of his home. But he wished that if either touched any scores, the music should be returned to *exactly* the same spot.

He had left things as he had for a reason. There was order within his disorder. It vexed him that the music had been disturbed. It was the type of thing that Rabinowitz used to do to rivals—rearrange their music—just to distract them. Just so there would possibly be that little extra hitch in their performance.

He sighed.

Whoever had rearranged things had also placed a piece by Mussorgsky in the bow. He glanced at it.

Pictures at an Exhibition.

Geiger shuddered anew. Coincidence or cruel joke. This was one of Rabinowitz's several signature pieces. In giving an informal performance, he would throw this one off with the "Aeolian Harp" Etude and a polonaise.

Geiger stared at the music for several seconds. He felt an enormous shudder of fear surge within him.

What was *that* doing out? Yes, he had looked at it earlier this evening, but he thought he had put it away. He thought he had buried it deeply, in fact.

And now that he thought of it, this was exactly the Chopin that he thought he had heard playing.

"How in hell did that get there?" he mumbled aloud.

"What?" an invisible voice asked.

"I said, 'How in hell—?' "

"That's what I thought you said."

A heavy momentary silence came across the room and enveloped Geiger. A complete stillness, almost like a picture freezing on a movie screen.

He shook himself. He still must be half-asleep, he told himself, because he was having this dumb-assed conversation with himself.

Yes, with himself. In the middle of the night his mind was playing tricks. It was not uncommon that he dreamed of music, and obviously, Chopin and the death of Rabinowitz were concurrently on his mind.

Thus the vivid dream involving the music. And just as obviously, he had pulled up this score by mistake and left it there on the piano, and subconsciously he even knew he had done it. That's why he was thinking of this music.

It all seemed logical, he told himself. There was logic to everything.

Geiger reached to the music and folded it carefully away, placing it back in its folder. The funny thing was, he actually thought he remembered doing this already. But he must have folded something else away and left this out. Neither Diana nor Edythe would *ever* have opened fresh scores.

Oh, well. He knew he had been distracted recently. This only proved it.

He calmed slightly. He looked around the room and tried to attach himself to his old concept of sanity and rationality. Moments earlier he had been thinking in terms of confronting a ghost. Now all he had before him was some disturbed sheets of music and an empty room.

Of course no ghost was in here, he told himself bravely. *There was no way to leave other than the window and the door.*

He glanced to each. *The window remains locked and the door was in front of me. No one passed through it.*

The light, he decided, had been some sort of optical illusion. The music had been an overworked imagination.

He rose from the piano, put everything away, and very deliberately walked across the room to leave.

For a moment, he thought he was aware of something at the edge of his senses. But then he dismissed that, too. He stood in the doorway, fidgeted slightly, waited, and scanned the room.

Nothing.

He turned the light off. He walked through the dark hall. He found the steps that would lead him back upstairs.

Then a horrible feeling was upon him as his foot found the bottom step of the staircase. The mood of the darkness around him had palpably turned against him. No longer was it friendly, cozy, or comforting. It felt malevolent and oppressive. It felt like something unspeakable had turned against him.

He stopped. From deep within him came the overwhelming feeling that he should not climb the stairs. Something horrible would happen if he did. But he took another step upward. Then a second one.

One step at a time. Each step higher than the next.

He was as frightened as he had ever been in his adult life. Subliminally, deep down, he thought he heard something resembling a low snarling sound. Like an animal. A wolf or a dog, warning not to approach.

He broke into another sweat. He felt as if he had a foot in each of two worlds, both of them fraught with terror. One world that he understood, another that he could barely comprehend.

And the two worlds were rushing together right here. On the staircase. With a horrifying, gripping confluence.

Oh, God . . . God protect me . . . he thought.

Empty words. He hadn't prayed for years. Why look for protection or salvation here?

Are you religious?

No. I'm lapsed.

Wouldn't have helped anyway.

He took a third step upward. Then a fourth. Only seven

more, he knew, to the landing of the second floor. Only seven more and he already knew he would never make them.

He knew because there was a force upon him now. Those invisible hands again. Hands. Leaning down in the dark. Pressing hard on his shoulders, forcing him back. And a coldness enveloped him, too. He felt as if a window had just been opened onto one of those icy gray winter mornings in the West Virginia of his childhood.

"No! Leave me alone! No!" he cried out.

"Impudent!" came the response. **"You said you wanted to see me!"**

"No!" Geiger answered aloud. "I've changed my mind. Stay dead!"

"I can't!"

In the darkness, Geiger forged upward. The fifth step. The sixth.

Then—miraculously—he felt himself break free. The force was no longer pushing downward upon him. He had his mobility back.

His feet moved nimbly for the final steps. He reached the landing of the second floor.

He drew a huge sigh. Whatever presence had been there, whatever aspect of his onetime mentor, Geiger had escaped it.

He steadied himself and took one step toward the bedroom.

Then he noticed that there was a figure outlined against a window at the end of the hall. The human figure of an aged man. A man who was dead and whom Geiger had buried.

Geiger felt the disbelief sweep away from him. He saw the figure move toward him in the dark.

"Maestro . . . ?" he said in horror.

The one-word response was spoken very clearly. Rolf wasn't imagining. He heard an actual voice.

"Yes," the visitor said.

The frigid cold returned and the figure came at him in a rush, traveling several feet in less than a second. In the dark, Geiger felt the dead man's body whack up against his own with a tremendous force.

The limbs flailed and the knees moved and the body of

Rabinowitz was as icy as one would have expected from being in the cold ground for weeks.

Geiger screamed like a man being murdered.

His eyes came wide-open and the face took shape right in front of him. Rabinowitz's face. Inches from his own. Back from the dead. Malevolence written all over it and eye sockets as hollow and horrible as they were in nightmare.

The force of the impact registered upon Geiger driving him backward until he tumbled against the wall, screaming.

He screamed so loud that it could have raised any other souls that were walking that night. He hit the wall hard and slumped low and screamed again.

There was no precedent for what he had just seen and experienced.

A collision with a ghost. Icy cold impact. A head-on collision with a dead man's spirit.

Geiger slumped low to the floor and his screams repeated themselves. He looked up again and saw the figure rushing toward him again, and then again the hands landed on his arms. Shaking him. Calling his name. Rolf screamed and he screamed and he screamed until the hands left him and the lights flashed on again and then the hands found him a second time.

"Rolf! Rolf! Rolf . . . !"

The voice called his name. It was the harsh voice of Rabinowitz until magically it changed into a female voice, raised in concern and anxiety, not in an attempt to harm him.

He managed to open his eyes again. He was still slumped against the wall of the second-floor hallway. But it was Diana who was upon him, holding him and trying to bring him to rationality.

He stopped screaming. His heart was thundering. There was fear all over her face, too.

Rabinowitz was gone.

For several seconds, once he started to calm, she looked at him. His eyes spun like marbles, searching for the danger that had been there seconds earlier. He couldn't find it.

"Rolf . . . ?" she finally said. *"Wake up! Wake up!"*

"I *was* awake."

"You couldn't have been."

"I was awake," he said, sitting up against the wall. "And I saw him. I saw him in the dark."

"Who?"

"And I felt his body next to mine." He looked her directly in the eye. "I saw his face," he said.

"Rolf, *who?*" she asked, her own fear evident.

"Rabinowitz," he said. A long pause as he read the skepticism in her eyes. "He's here," Geiger said. "He's in this house."

"Rolf. This is crazy. And you know it."

He searched for proof. He couldn't find it.

"I know I heard something," Geiger insisted. "I heard Isador Rabinowitz playing Chopin on my piano. And I saw him. He's here. Or his ghost is here. That's why I hear him playing."

"Rolf. Don't be ridiculous. You're scaring me."

"I'm scared, too," he said softly. "What am I going to do now?" he asked. "Rabinowitz is dead. And I'm *still* not rid of him."

"Rolf," she said patiently. "Calm yourself. You and I are the only ones in this house. There is no ghost here, and we are both safe and secure."

His breathing steadied and he listened to her. He wanted desperately to believe. He put a hand on her arm and tried to absorb her calm.

Several moments passed. The terror seemed to lift.

But from downstairs he heard the piano again. It struck up a mazurka. A pair of supernatural hands played Chopin with brilliance and cunning. Amazing harmonies and modulation, a piquancy within the rubato that would have been the envy of Chopin himself.

"See?" Geiger whispered. "*See!* He's doing it again!"

"Doing what?"

"Playing! *Listen!*"

The music thundered. It was as big as the night.

"Rolf," she said, "there's nothing there! There's nothing happening downstairs!"

"There's *music!* Rabinowitz is *playing!*"

"I don't hear anything!" she said. She shook him. "And you don't, either!"

His eyes went wide as saucers. The music down below stopped as abruptly as it had begun. Geiger's eyes wandered over Diana's shoulder, only to find that there, within his home, clearly visible under the electric lights of the hallway, the silent figure of the late Isador Rabinowitz climbed the stairs.

Rabinowitz, or his ghost, was bold and vivid, not translucent at all, substantive and immaculately groomed and dressed, beaming with the same embalmed smile that he had worn for the latter years of his life.

Geiger began to scream again, and he screamed until the specter retreated. It was only a few seconds, but it seemed much longer.

Still no eyes. Just empty sockets.

Like the music that she could not hear, the vision of Rabinowitz was not something that Diana could share. She looked exactly where Rolf was looking and did not see anything.

Which didn't mean it wasn't there. It only meant that she couldn't see it. The contact, it seemed, remained one of mentor and protégé.

Rolf Geiger lifted his voice to the heavens and screamed like he had never before screamed in his life. And he would not stop. As Diana cradled his head and held him tightly, the world's finest living concert pianist howled like a man coming out of a delirium trauma.

Even though he had closed his eyes and refused to look at the specter at the top of his stairs, in his mind Rolf was still seeing the cunning face, the mad-staring wolfish expression and deathly cadaverish features of his onetime mentor.

He screamed and cried until he fainted, and Diana laboriously dragged him back into the bedroom and returned him to bed.

ten

Over the next several days, as late March gave way to early April, Rolf Geiger's nerves were on a sharp edge. Something had changed within him and around him, he knew. Perpetually, he felt as if he had just quaffed six cups of espresso, even when he hadn't touched any coffee. It is always that way when one's sense of reality has been dramatically reordered. It is always that way when one has seen a ghost.

Something within him told him to keep moving. So he went for long walks during the day and early evening and—frighteningly in New York—sometimes even during the night. He started his hikes in his own neighborhood on the east side of Manhattan and sometimes ranged all the way down to SoHo, Tribeca, Greenwich Village, or Chelsea. On these lengthy journeys, he was often lost hopelessly in thought and reflection.

Once, in a maze of wandering that bordered on the dangerous, he strolled all the way up to Columbia University on West 112th Street and Broadway to visit a well-known candy store. He hadn't been there for months, but he had long favored their homemade butter crunch. Suddenly he had an urge for some.

The owner—a man to whom Beethoven was akin to a religion—recognized Geiger the second the recitalist came in the door. He made a huge fuss over him.

Geiger responded courteously. He autographed a candy box and further promised the proprietor a specially signed black-and-white picture—which he did later send, one of about a hundred that he mailed out each year at his own expense.

In the store, once the owner settled down, Rolf bought half a pound of butter crunch. Then, bag of candy in hand, he wandered through the university campus for half an hour before starting back to mid-Manhattan. By the time Geiger arrived home, he had knocked back the entire bag of homemade candy.

He had taken a six-mile walk, just for some candy, instead of sitting down to practice at the piano. Was there not a world tour in the planning stages?

Such actions by the truly famous are only seen as eccentricities.

One enterprising press photographer armed with a telephoto lens had spotted Geiger on his walk and had snapped several shots of him, following him a hundred feet into Central Park while Geiger did his best to ignore the man. The photos would appear the next day with the caption referring to Rolf as the "reclusive piano prodigy," which was not so distant from the truth.

To the eyes and mind of Diana Stephenson, Rolf's behavior was strangely reminiscent of an unfavorable episode from her own youth. Her father had sunk into some inexplicable depression and had puttered silently—almost wordlessly—around the house for several weeks.

Like Diana's father some twenty years earlier, Rolf spent enormous amounts of time on small inconsequential things.

Reading fan mail, for example.

Normally Rolf just glanced at the stuff. Now sometimes, as if looking for some submerged truth within each communication, he read the same letters several times before filing them haphazardly in cardboard boxes. The boxes were then stored at the back of the rarely used coat closet in the front hall.

Repairing a faulty electrical switch in his den and library was another small task which newly obsessed him. It took ten hours when it should have taken one.

In contrast, the big things, such as his devotion to music, he seemed to have dropped altogether. The entire day after Rolf had had his 5 A.M. encounter with the malevolent spirit of Isador Rabinowitz, he did not touch the piano or any piece of sheet music. For as long as Diana had known him, about two years, this was the first time this had ever happened.

The same absence from practice occurred again the second day. And the third. He listened to no CDs or radio concerts, either. If there was any music, it was in Rolf's head, and Diana couldn't hear it.

While the long walks through Manhattan were the new order of the day for Rolf, Diana continued meeting her own professional obligations.

She dutifully attended her evening art classes. The lesson that week for Maurice Sahadi's four students was sketching a very handsome male nude, something none of the female students missed. But Diana could not give her full attention to it. She was constantly calling home to see if Rolf were okay.

When he answered the phone, he politely responded that he was fine. When he didn't answer, she worried, and hoped that he was out, not lying on the floor. So far, he hadn't harmed himself, or anyone else.

Almost as bad was the staring, empty look she saw on his face several times when she watched him unaware. Again, this was something new, something that emerged in the hours after "the encounter," as she now thought of it. It was as if he were listening to a distant symphony, did not like the way it was being played, but was helpless to tune it out.

"The encounter."

Or, "the imaginary encounter."

Whichever it had been.

Once, in the evening, before a fire in the living-room hearth, she went to Rolf and snuggled into his lap. Then she leaned forward and whispered into his ear.

"A penny for your thoughts, Tiger."

"I love you very much," he said.

She kissed him.

"Then what else?" she asked. "What else is on your mind? Please tell me."

"I've never before so much thought of the piano as a weapon," he said cryptically. "But it exists also as an instrument of fear and terror. That's how I see it now. Sometimes."

She considered this for more than several seconds. Her deliberation lasted almost a minute, in fact, which, under the circumstances, considering the recent events, and within the heavy silence that now presided in their home, was one hell of a long time.

"Tell me what you mean by that," she finally said.

He shook his head.

"The piano. A weapon," he said. "Fear. It makes perfect sense."

"Not to me."

"Music can raise any emotion. Including fear. Musicians make music, no one else. The piano is the tool."

"Uh-huh," she answered.

He had the faraway look again, the one she didn't like. "So if music can raise an emotion," he proposed, "do you think it could also raise a spirit? Or a soul?"

"An emotion and a soul are not the same thing," she said.

"No?" his eyes wandered the living room of their town house and settled upon a set of photographs in silver frames upon a shelf.

Graduation day from St. Agnes' School in West Virginia. Seventeen-year-old-Rolf flanked by his mother on one side and Brother Matthew on the other. In another frame there was a picture of Geiger in Nice those many years ago, on the moment of his first major international triumph. "Sometimes I wonder," he said after too long a pause.

Diana nodded.

She didn't like the direction of the thought. It was too sinister for her. There was a persistently macabre undertone to all of Rolf's thoughts now.

She let it go. It was a scary time in the young life of Diana Stephenson. Funny ideas were creeping into her head, too, from somewhere. For example, this was the first time in her life that she had ever considered the possibility of coming home to find someone she loved dead. It scared her that such a thought could enter her head. Perhaps she was picking up odd vibrations from

112 East Seventy-third Street, too, just as Rolf asserted he was. It was as if a little unseen voice were maliciously whispering bad things to her.

Might she be better off, she wondered, with a different man? Rolf had an artist's temperament, including the occasional arrogance and volatility that went with the territory.

Did she need this?

Diana was a beautiful young woman. Intelligent and strong. Since her late teens she had never had any shortage of suitors. If she moved out and was available again, there were probably *hundreds* of wealthy attractive men who—

She stopped herself in mid-thought.

All of this was nonsense. She was here with Rolf because she loved him and wanted to be here. He was exciting and good to her. He loved her and told her so frequently. He was unselfish and contained none of the brutality that characterized so many men. He would buy her gifts and flowers for no reason. If he were having emotional problems dealing with the passing of Isador Rabinowitz, it was her mission to be there for him.

To help.

To lend strength and support.

End of case.

Even to *think* of leaving was nonsense. Yet, Rolf continued with his own brand of nonsense—insisting adamantly that he had seen the ghost of Isador Rabinowitz in their home.

Complete nonsense. Where in hell were such notions coming from?

The subject of the ghost came up several times over the course of the ensuing days. Rolf fervently maintained that he knew what he had seen and that "it," meaning Isador Rabinowitz, was frequently there.

Not in the flesh, maybe, but surely in spirit. And not in the warm and cuddly "Casper" way or the "Someone-To-Watch-Over-Me" way. Rabinowitz's presence, Rolf explained to the woman he loved, was a persistent antagonistic malevolent presence, as welcome as a demon at a fundamentalist church social.

Rabinowitz was much the way he had been in his lifetime. Rolf still insisted that he occasionally heard the piano come to life, with no one in his den and no one at the keyboard.

No one who was visible, anyway.

"Sometimes I'm sitting right there in the library and it starts to play," Geiger said out of the blue one evening. "It *just starts to play*. La da da. La da da dee da. Can you imagine that?"

"No. But I think *you* imagined something, Tiger," she answered.

In continuing the discussion, hoping to purge it with daylight, she in turn had said all the right things.

Diana had been in the house for all those times and had seen and heard nothing, she reminded him.

No ghost. No music.

She even insisted that it had been she who had switched around the sheet music on his piano, though she didn't quite remember having the *Pictures at an Exhibition* out and atop the piano.

"Of course, you can't remember that," Rolf had insisted. "Rabinowitz made that switch. You didn't."

"A dead man made that switch? That's what you're telling me?"

"Yes."

"That's not possible, Tiger," she repeated. "Don't you see how crazy that sounds?"

"I know what I saw," he said.

The logic and the conversation went in circles.

So did a few other things.

Rolf's language, perhaps from frustration, became sprinkled with the odd obscenity, something he had rarely done until these recent and troubling times. Diana remembered how he had complained about old Rabinowitz's purple tongue and how he found it embarrassing and distasteful. Now the odd "fuck" and "fucking" flew easily and readily from Geiger's mouth as if thrown by a foreign tongue.

Something else also made little sense to Diana.

As confusion ran rampant in her mind, elements of involuntary suspicion replaced it. Again, it was as if some foreign agent were putting alien thoughts in her ear. She began to consider the nature of Geiger's long, unexplained absences in the afternoon. It occurred to Diana that another woman might be involved.

Occur. That was all.

She didn't really think that was the case, and she was far, far from the point of initiating the subject with Rolf.

Yet he did seem disinterested in sex in the days following "the encounter." The odd unfavorable parallel to her youth kicked in again. When her father had fallen silent for all those weeks two decades earlier, the silence proved to be a harbinger of an even deeper emotional disengagement to follow. After Christmas 1977, when Diana was five years old, her father moved out one night and took up residence with one of the women who worked for his accountant.

"Molly Shanahan, the Town Slut," as Diana's mother once referred to her with a damning sniff. "Wears her skirts up around her waist, the better to show off her personality." For the previous year, it turned out, he and the lady ledger-cruncher had been juggling more than numbers.

And . . .

The absence of sex in her relationship with Rolf smarted all the doubly for Diana right now.

There was that artist's model she and her fellow students were drawing at night at Maurice Sahadi's studio.

The model was highly attractive. He was a dark muscular man from Wyoming, who was proportioned both handsomely and generously. He was just beginning to make a name for himself in New York as a model in print ads. Diana returned home from a few hours of sketching this body on Mondays and Thursdays looking for more than a shower before going to sleep. Some raw physical lust would have fit into her evening just fine.

But Rolf was clearly uninterested. Somehow, viewing a ghost managed to have had a depressive effect on an otherwise-healthy libido.

However, over the course of ten to twelve days, Rolf became alert again and seemed to return to earth. His eyes became clearer and less distant. The shadow of Rabinowitz seemed to withdraw, and Rolf did concede that the old master had not visited again, even though the piano—to his mind, at least—

still played the occasional phantom few bars from time to time. It sounded like someone sitting down to practice, then changing his mind, getting up, and angrily leaving the room.

Rolf's strange walks in the afternoon were not as long as right after "the encounter." Apparently, the fear of a renewed incident seemed less. Better still, Rolf started to tinker—just tinker—with the piano again, sort of as if he had been waiting for a reservoir to fill up again, and now it had.

To signal that the "recovery" was well under way, Rolf reached for Diana's hand one afternoon when Mrs. Jamison was out for an hour. He pulled her to the sofa in the living room.

"I want you," he said. "Right now."

"You finally noticed that there's a woman living with you, huh?" she asked with a wink.

"I'd never forgotten. I just needed to clear my head somewhat," he answered.

"It's clear now?"

"Clear enough."

"You want to go upstairs?" she asked after a few kisses.

"No. Right here is fine."

He made love to her without even completely undressing her.

Uncharacteristically, he said little to her while having sex. His conquest of her was fast and vigorous, which she did not mind. And yet, on the downside, the lovemaking seemed almost forced. Not routine, but not as intimate as usual, either.

If she looked at it the wrong way, it was almost as if it was a physical release for him more than a manifestation of intimacy or an act of affection. Had it been an act of affection, she wondered, or a male act of staking his claim or reestablishing dominance?

And then there were his hands, which, for some reason, he chose to keep firmly on her shoulders and almost upon her neck while he was thrusting inside her. It was a strange bit of positioning and almost scared her. Like his newly found love of profanity, this almost seemed as if it were coming from somewhere else.

But she put aside her thoughts. Despite everything, there on the sofa, he had led her to a series of spectacular orgasms, just minutes before Mrs. Jamison had come back into the town house. So, straightening out her skirt and her hair, still enjoying the rush of excitement that came from the suddenness and spontaneity of their act, still feeling as if she had been joyously ravished by a man she loved, why complain?

It had been damned exciting.

Also exciting was the easing of Rolf's mood.

Diana had been playing with the idea of their getting away for a few days. To anywhere. Just to get out of the city and away from that house where "the encounter" had occurred.

She had thought that he would nix the idea. But when she proposed a short trip, that same evening, he seemed to welcome the notion.

"Where to? And for how long?"

"Ever been to Nantucket Island?" she asked.

A moment's thought. "Yes. But it was a while ago," he said.

"Interested? You and me? For the weekend?"

His smile was the first one in days that looked almost right. His first since the master had purportedly visited.

"Sure. Great idea. Make the arrangements," he said.

"Thanks, Tiger," Diana said. "And welcome back."

"Back where?" Rolf asked, not understanding.

"Home," she said. "From wherever you've been."

"I've been somewhere?" he asked.

He shrugged. He still didn't understand. But some cloud had lifted, or appeared to have lifted, at least temporarily. Diana chose to interpret this as the passing of a tempest, rather than a lull before an even more violent storm. But then she always tried to be positive.

Rolf spent about an hour in the library that evening playing exercises on the piano. His touch on the keyboard was crisp and filled with authority. That was a good sign, too. The house was filled with music again. This time there was no question as to the provenance of the finger work on the keyboard.

Outside, on East Seventy-third Street, in the darkness of the rarely used stone stoop across the street, the watcher had again materialized.

With gloved hands, he still puffed on the carcinogenic Lucky Strikes. He watched the lights go on and off in the windows of 112 East Seventy-third Street and he smiled to Diana or Rolf whenever they looked his way on the street.

Both of them had by now recognized him from the funeral of Isador Rabinowitz, and both had come to the same conclusion about the man. He was classical piano's version of a Deadhead. In conversation with Rolf and Diana, the old man said that he had been present at all of Isador Rabinowitz's concerts for as long as he could remember. But now with Rabinowitz dead, his attention had shifted to Geiger. He was a fan. That was all he was in life now, he said. A diehard fan. Rolf had seen the type many times before.

He was mildly demented, they concluded, perilously fixated, but not dangerous. Occasionally, because he looked so forlorn, they gave him food. What harm could an old man cause, after all, and Geiger had further concluded that the slamming limousine door could not have emanated from such a frail old being.

"So you'll be coming to some of the dates on my world tour?" Geiger asked the watcher one morning.

"The first ones. Definitely the first ones," the man said.

"Not going to travel to Europe and Asia with me?" Geiger asked, making a gentle joke of it.

"Not unless you take me with you," the watcher answered. "I'd go if you took me with you."

Geiger shrugged. "I'll be lucky if I can get myself there," Rolf said in offhanded response.

The man shrugged from his doorstep. "Well then, I can watch your place here while you're gone."

Geiger looked at him carefully. "Yeah. Great idea," he said without meaning it.

There was something in the watcher's remark that Geiger did not like, yet he let it go. In the same way, he let his newly converted "number one fan" remain there on the block, despite the fact that the New York City police one day offered to make the man move.

"Better that I know where he is than where he isn't," Rolf said. And so the watcher was left to his sentry duty. There, as the days passed, he maintained his solitary seemingly meaningless vigil.

Abruptly, Geiger's kindness was rewarded with a slight change of logistics. The watcher moved closer to Rolf's home and took up a position on the sidewalk directly across from Number 112. He settled into his new location. The watcher awaited just the proper moment to change the course of Rolf Geiger's career and life.

eleven

Thirteen mornings after the appearance of Rabinowitz's ghost, midway through an April that was proving to be gloriously balmy, Rolf Geiger went to his telephone and dialed Brian Greenstone's office. Claire put him through to his agent.

"Hello, Rolf," Brian said, coming directly onto the line.

"Working hard for me?" Geiger asked.

"Sweat is rolling off my forehead, my fingers are white from gripping the phone on your behalf, and my blood pressure is elevated to three-eighty over two-fifty," Greenstone said cheerfully. "Would that be sufficient?"

"Your fingers are only white?" quipped Rolf, backtracking. "They should be *bleeding,* Brian."

"As they say here in America, Rolf, 'Fuck you.' When I feel like opening a vein, I shall let you and the rest of my client list know. Now. How are things, what's on your mind, and why aren't you hunched over an atonal keyboard somewhere bringing tears to the eyes of the so-called cognoscenti as you bugger some classic composition?"

"Which question should I answer first?"

"Any order would be fine. Or just tell your Uncle Brian about your nonstop love life. Regale me with an anecdote or two about how bloody miserable it is to be twenty-seven, famous, wealthy and live with one of the most beautiful women who has ever drawn a breath, to whom I send my regards, by the way.''

There was a long pause which Greenstone immediately interpreted as trouble. "Frankly, Brian, I have a problem,'' Geiger said.

"Oh, Christ. A big one?''

"No, not a big one. Basically things are all right,'' Geiger said. "But I wonder if we could arrange something impromptu.''

"Oh, Rolf, my boy, name it. Ruin my fucking day.''

"I need an immediate concert date. I know it's short notice. But I want to take a dry run. See where I am right now. Test the audiences before the world tour. Test myself. See what I have. Know what I mean, Brian?''

"What are we talking about? This evening?'' Greenstone asked with obvious irony.

"Something within the next few weeks, if you can arrange it.''

"Hmmm. Spring training? A warm-up?''

"Sort of.''

"You know you do this all the time, don't you? You worry about your skills when you needn't.''

"This is different.''

"I don't mind arranging a concert date. It should be no trouble. But I'm equally confident that your playing has never been better,'' Greenstone said. "This is not something you really *have* to do.''

"I know.''

"Tell me what you need,'' the agent asked. "Large house? Small? You wish to play in front of twelve or twelve hundred? Speak.''

"I want a critical but friendly audience,'' said Geiger. "I need a tune-up. Know what I mean? The house can be big. A concert hall, though, not an arena.''

"Where do you want to play? New York?''

"No, definitely not New York. I want it to be a travel date, yet not too far. Too much pressure and part of the local press will rip me just for sport. Plus anything I do becomes too much of an 'event' in New York. It's on my doorstep.''

"It's an event whenever and wherever you play, my lad," Greenstone reminded him.

"I know. Think it would be hard to set up?"

"No. Of course not. It can be done."

Greenstone knew that all he had to do was find the date and the venue. An "added" concert by Rolf Geiger would sell out within a day in any large city anywhere in the world.

"What would you play?" Greenstone asked. "In case any of the unwashed out-of-town promoters have the temerity to ask."

Geiger thought. "Beethoven. Maybe Opus 109 in E Major. Then the Tchaikovsky piano concerto. If it's a nice early summer night and we need to tart things up to sell tickets I could play some Chopin or do the *Moonlight* Sonata. Or maybe use it as an encore."

"Keep talking," the agent said. "It sounds lovely."

"The repertoire would depend on the quality of the orchestra available, the conductor, and how much rehearsal time we would have. The pieces should be well-known so that the orchestra would be ready to play."

"Of course, of course," Greenstone said thoughtfully. "Let me see what I can do."

"Do you foresee any problem?" Geiger asked.

"Only one," Greenstone answered.

"What's that?"

"I have to be quite the diplomat as to where this concert is initially offered. This is the first time in two years you'll have played to an audience larger than two or three hundred. So it's a *very* significant event, is it not? A lot of people are going to have their knickers in a twist if I don't ask them first."

"I understand," Geiger said.

"But that's my problem," Greenstone added quickly. "Let me see what I can do. Give me a day." He paused. "Now I need something from you."

"What's that?"

"Your handwriting. There's some contractual material here from Aurora Records for you to sign, hopefully after you go through the pretense of reading it. Should I send it over or would you care to make another memorable in-person appearance in my office?''

''I was in your office as recently as two and a half weeks ago.''

''And the girls in the whole damned building are still buzzing like queen bees. Does that mean, 'Send it over'?''

''No,'' Geiger said. ''I'll come by. I've been getting out doing a lot of walking recently.''

''Don't I know it, don't I know it,'' Greenstone muttered. ''You were most recently seen in the deplorably vile and disreputable pages of the *New York Post,* wandering aimlessly through public places like Central Park and carrying a bag of candy like a would-be child molester.''

''You saw that?''

''The whole *fucking* city saw it, Rolf. Come by this afternoon and please duck the damned photographers if you are able.''

Geiger went out to walk in the middle of the afternoon. The April day had turned intermittently drizzly. Rolf carried a red-and-blue golf umbrella that he would only unwrap and launch under torrential conditions. So far that day, torrential conditions had not arrived.

He stopped by his agent's office toward four. He sat in the big red leather chair in Greenstone's inner office for several minutes, signing papers sent over by Aurora Records and efficiently presented by Claire. For some reason, Rolf's eye followed her in and out of the room every time she moved. He noted everything about her, her earrings, her skirt, her blouse, her jewelry, and her shoes. The curve of her calves, the way her skirt showed off her figure.

In return, she gave him a friendly hello and a cordial smile. Something about her almost made him feel old.

''We have some money for you, too,'' said Greenstone at length. ''Filthy lucre, of which I have siphoned off the filthiest ten percent.''

The income was royalty money from recording contracts in France and Germany. It had come in at lunchtime, Greenstone said merrily. Twenty-eight thousand dollars and change. Green-stone's office would deposit it for Rolf, saving him the tacky troubling effort of walking a check to a busy New York bank.

"Given the concert date any more thought?" Rolf asked.

"I've given it thought and I've made preliminary calls," Greenstone answered. "And I'm not telling you a damned thing for another few days. Do me a favor? Shut up and be patient. Trust me. I want things to settle. All right?"

"All right."

"What else?" Greenstone asked.

Brian was, when all was said and done, a remarkably percep-tive man, both in business and in personal relationships.

Rolf hunched his shoulders. "Nothing else," he said.

"It breaks my heart when you lie to me."

"I'm not lying to you."

"You're bothered by *something*," Greenstone continued. "I see it in your eyes and your expression. It's upon you, like a watermark. It's not concentration, for that's a different look, Rolf. What might this be? Is it just this concert business? This tour? Your music? I have a hunch there's something else. I have at least ten seconds to listen if you care to tell me."

Geiger was momentarily taken aback. He didn't know how to answer.

"You don't wander around the damned city for no reason, my boy," Greenstone said soothingly. "Now talk. Confess. But only if you care to."

The sentences started to form in Rolf's mind.

Well, yes, Brian. You see, my mentor Isador? Your former client? The fellow I laid in a grave a few weeks back? The man you used to call "the most unbearable pianist of the twentieth century"? Well, he's not completely dead, it seems. Rabinowitz comes over and haunts my home, terrifies me with deathly images, bangs on my piano, frightens my lover, and swears that I will never pull off this tour properly. That's all that's troubling me, old chap. Doesn't sound like much when I explain it, does it?

"Rolf?" Greenstone pressed, lowering his head and waving a hand slightly as if to catch Geiger's lost attention. "What planet are we on today? I asked you a question."

"Oh," Geiger said, shaking himself back to the present. "Right? Sorry. I was distracted for a moment."

"I was asking you what's wrong," Greenstone said. "And you were about to tell me."

"Nothing's wrong," Geiger said sullenly, getting to his feet. "I just want to perform again. Soon. So I'm anxious for you to set things up."

"When you're ready to play, we'll have a venue," Greenstone said. "Count on it."

"I will."

The two men embraced, then Rolf left the office.

Several minutes later, Geiger was out on Fifty-seventh Street again. The skies had opened finally and rain was falling steadily. He pulled his tan Burberry raincoat tightly to him against the rain, but still resisted the use of the umbrella. He had moved about a hundred feet down the sidewalk away from Greenstone's office building when he heard a woman calling his name.

Which was in no way unusual.

"Mr. Geiger? Mr. Geiger?"

He almost didn't turn and look. His friends knew to call him by his first name, and he could do without any strangers today. But there was something familiar about the voice, and the tone of it suggested urgency of some sort.

So he glanced over his shoulder and stopped short.

He turned as Claire trotted quickly toward him from Greenstone's office. Her arms were folded against the wet blustery day. Her navy blue skirt only made it halfway to her knees. As she moved, she was a flurry of beautiful young limbs darting amidst the wind and the raindrops.

"Claire?" he asked, surprised.

She came toward him and arrived breathlessly.

"I'm terribly sorry," she said. "I completely forgot . . ."

She panted for breath.

"Must be important," he said with irony.

Several passersby were watching him, having recognized him in the rain. The west side of Manhattan was murder for being recognized, with one of the highest concentrations of classical music fans in the nation.

"That writer. The one I mentioned," Claire said, still panting. She was not only out of breath, but she was also getting soaked.

"Sorry?" Rolf asked.

"Remember? Phillip Langlois? That was his name. The man who wanted to write a biography of Isador Rabinowitz?"

"Oh. Yes. Him. I remember."

"He phoned again," Claire said. "He says he's going to be in New York."

Geiger sighed in disappointment. "I'm really not in the mood for him or anyone else," he said.

"He says it's quite important," she said. "Apparently, he's racing two other biographies to press. He wants to interview you as soon as possible."

Geiger rolled his eyes. Then he looked back at her. He could see a certain disappointment in her expression. She had, she realized, come out here for nothing. It was written all over her face.

"You're getting very wet," he said. Raindrops made round gray marks on her blouse. They splashed on her face, arms, and bare legs.

"It's all right," she said.

"No, it's not," he answered. He pulled up the umbrella and pressed a button to open it. It whooshed into the air and covered them. He held it forward, but she stepped closer to him to be under it.

"Thanks," she giggled.

"Do you have his phone number?" Geiger asked.

The number was on a piece of paper in her hand. It was already wet. Rain swept across her face as he looked at her. She smiled back as he took the number. Never, when he was growing up in West Virginia, did he ever imagine how many beautiful women there were in the world and how many of them would at one time or another stand before him.

"Thanks," she said. "He sounded nice on the phone. He really did."

"They all do when they want something."

"I told him I'd try to explain the urgency to you."

"You succeeded, Claire."

She looked at him with apprehension for a moment. "I'm sorry. Did I do the wrong thing?"

He smiled. "You're fine," he said.

She was getting even wetter. But she wouldn't turn and go back to the office. Instead, she and Rolf spent a moment looking each other over. Her eyes were wide and merry, which set off her short dark hair to great effect. The beads of rain that ran against her skin made her flesh look satiny and perfect.

"Tell me something," Geiger said. "Did mean old Brian send you out in the rain just to hand me a piece of paper?" Geiger asked.

"Not exactly," she answered.

"Well, you're not on your way home at four-thirty in the afternoon."

"Mr. Greenstone actually said I could phone you," Claire said. "But I told him, since you had just left—"

Rolf was catching on. "You said you'd trot after me?" he guessed.

She nodded enthusiastically, trying not to laugh.

"And trot you did," he said. "Right?"

She waited for a second. "Right," she said.

He let a few more seconds pass. He was aware of more people watching him with Claire as they passed, then talking among themselves. He lived his life, it sometimes seemed, against a background curtain of people watching.

"So tell me something else," Rolf said to her. "Something I don't know."

She sighed and seemed ready to bare her soul for him, or anything else he wanted.

"I have all of your recordings," she said, almost as a confession. "Sometimes I put on your CDs for hours, and I just listen and listen and listen, and I imagine that I'm in the front row of one of your concerts." She paused. "Your music, the way you play, really moves me."

"Thank you. You're very kind."

"I'm a huge fan, Mr. Geiger. I couldn't believe it when I came to work for Mr. Greenstone and discovered you were his top client." She paused and added as a coda, "You take my breath away."

"You're also getting soaked, Claire. You're going to be wet *and* breathless."

"Yeah. Yes. I know." She hunched her shoulders. "Well," she said, "it was worth it. I wanted to tell you. Thanks."

She started to turn.

He spoke impetuously. "The least I can do is buy you coffee," he said.

She was momentarily flustered. "Well, oh, sure. Whenever you have the time and—"

Then she realized that he meant now.

He took her arm. "Come on. Brian won't mind. You're helping a client."

"Helping a client do what?" she asked.

"Keep dry. Stay in a good productive mood. Remain sane. Come along."

He did not let her protest further.

Instead, he steered her not to the coffee shop that was right nearby, but to the bistro that was a door farther away. It was an expensive snooty white-tablecloth two-star joint which actually Geiger didn't much care for due to its pretensions. He had been taken there a few times and stuffed with an overpriced lunch by recording executives. The maître d' recognized Geiger immediately and snapped to attention even though he was eating his own late lunch.

He greeted Rolf like a long-lost brother.

"A table up front or something in the rear, sir?" the maître d' asked. On display, or something discreet, he meant, depending whether Rolf wanted to show off a beautiful young woman or hide in a corner with a mistress.

"Up front is fine," Geiger said.

The staff was starting to set up for the cocktail and dinner hours, but a table was quickly arranged. It was a small cozy one with warmth. Fresh flowers landed in the center almost immediately.

The staff also provided Claire with a fresh dry shawl. The gesture surprised her. She didn't know whether or not to accept and so she looked to him for help.

Rolf nodded very slightly and thanked the waiter.

Claire put the shawl around her. Geiger deduced that she

had not been in New York too long and was not yet accustomed to being taken to the better places by her dates. He pictured her in a sweatshirt and jeans with a guy her own age wearing a reversed baseball cap. He managed not to smile.

Then he pictured her in a T-shirt and cutoff jeans and had to catch himself and issue a course correction. She was a bright young girl. Quality all the way. It was only a matter of time, he mused further, before males of her own caliber spotted her.

As they spoke, she reminded him of Diana four years younger. Geiger watched as she quickly latched on to the service and attention the waiting staff provided. He ordered coffee. She ordered tea. The restaurant provided a plate of small freshly baked cookies with the coffee and tea. Two diners, a man and a woman, leaving their off-hour lunch, glanced at the celebrity pianist seated in the front of the restaurant as they exited.

Their eyes landed hard upon him, made recognition, and stayed. They glanced at Claire, then returned to him. Geiger could read their bourgeois thoughts. The woman thought the girl was lucky. The man thought Rolf was lucky, having such a beautiful mistress. Again, Geiger felt himself on display.

Claire spoke of college and moving from graduate school into the world of entertainment. Her full name was Claire Graham and she was from San Francisco. This was her first job in New York. Geiger had guessed right. She was still thrilled with everything in the city and in awe of it at the same time. The onset of jadedness wouldn't set in for another few months or until she'd had one or two painful affairs, he reasoned. But he didn't tell her that.

"So am I the first famous person you've met?" he asked.

"Almost," she said. "My girlfriend and I went to this bar over on First Avenue the other night and two of the New York Rangers tried to hit on us. But you're the first famous guy to buy me tea."

He shrugged and kept a straight face. "Who said I was famous, and who said I was paying?" he asked.

She looked stricken, then realized he was kidding. He kept up the conversation. He listened to what she had to say.

As she chatted, the front of Geiger's mind was processing music, the art of the piano, how much he enjoyed playing, and—

in response to her various inquiries—how much he needed to practice. Meanwhile, the back of his mind played with the notion of how easy it would be to get Claire into bed. He didn't often have such impulses with women he had just met. He was involved with someone he cared about and he encountered great-looking women all the time. So why was this different?

Temporarily though, he resisted. He wouldn't even admit to himself that having sex with Claire was something that interested him.

After twenty minutes, which was about as long as he figured he could hold one of Brian's employees prisoner, he set her free.

The rain had subsided when they stepped out of the restaurant. But as a special gift, he pulled her into a small store and bought her an umbrella. It was an exceptionally nice fold-up one with a good wooden handle and a plush leather case, clearly extravagant, imported from Spain.

Then, unable to keep her awe in check, she asked him to follow her into the newsstand of her office building. She bought a copy of a classical music magazine which had his picture in it and insisted that he autograph it for her.

He did.

"I can't wait to tell my parents about this, Mr. Geiger," she said, which almost twice ruined the moment.

All of this happened to the amusement of the Bengali news dealer, who barged into the conversation, and then asked him to autograph a copy of *People* magazine. The latest edition had contained the picture of him wandering through Central Park with the bag of butter crunch.

"Do me a favor and stop calling me, 'Mr. Geiger,'" he finally requested of Claire. "Okay?"

"Okay," she said. But she was as yet unable to call him by his first name.

Claire went back to work. He watched her go into the elevator. When she turned and the elevator door was closing, she looked his way. Rolf was still watching her. He was equally surprised that she had caught him. Something made it difficult for him to pull his eyes away.

She gave him a wave and a motion with the umbrella. It was

sort of like a friendly salute. He raised his hand slightly and waved back.

Then he turned and walked home. The rain stopped and the sun broke through.

He felt excited about something and couldn't even tell what. Thoughts of Claire ran through his mind. If nothing else, she had diverted him from the memory of "the encounter," something that usually was never far from his thoughts.

But the nature of his thoughts about Claire truly shamed him. He caught himself again, corrected them again, and silently scolded himself. He would damned well keep his interest in Claire in check, he vowed. He reminded himself that she was a fan and an employee of his agent and, as far as he was concerned, that was a perfect role for her.

She probably had a boyfriend. Or several. He shouldn't confuse her interest in his music with an interest in everything else. She had been fun to have a cup of coffee with, just as it was always fun to make a new friend.

That was all. He kept telling himself all of this. He needed to convince himself.

But it did occur to him that if this was how casual adultery happened, and if this was how relationships tumbled apart when a man fell for another woman outside of his current sleeping arrangement, well, this was the first time he understood how it could happen.

And it certainly was easy.

twelve

Three days later, on a Friday morning late in April, Rolf and Diana flew to Nantucket Island for the weekend. The trip involved two flights, first New York to Boston, then a connection to the island. It was the first time Geiger had been on an airplane since his return to New York from Paris a few weeks earlier.

At one point, shortly after takeoff from New York, Rolf looked out the starboard side of the aircraft and squinted at the sun above the wing of the plane. For some reason he thought of the classic Greek myth of Icarus, who flew toward the sun but perished when the wax by which his wings were attached melted. Then, following a more worldly association, he thought back to his last flight and the lightning that had flashed through the plane.

He shuddered as he thought of it. This flight to Boston was short and smooth, however, as was the subsequent hop to Nantucket. No balls of fire, no thunderstorms. Not even a jolt of bad turbulence.

They arrived in the early afternoon, rented a jeep at the airport and registered at the Gray Lady Inn on Federal Street in the main town. The inn's owner and manager, a trim young man named David Corwin, personally registered the guests. Diana had made the reservations several days earlier.

Both Rolf and Diana were looking for relaxation and escape. Blessed with longer daylight at this time in the spring, they took the jeep out to a secluded beach on the south shore and shared a long walk.

Much of the time, Rolf was silent, though he held Diana's hand as they strolled. The ocean crashed within twenty feet of them and Geiger constantly thought he heard music and a rhythm to the surf.

"Penny for your thoughts," she finally asked.

"The tour," he said. "I'm thinking about the tour. Think I've gotten myself into more than I can handle?"

She shook her head. "No," she said. "There's nothing with a piano you can't handle."

"Thanks," he said. "I like to think that, too."

His response struck her as odd. Somewhat qualified. Normally, he would have not needed to even solicit the supportive opinion.

"The best in the world," she said, leaning tightly to him. "At the piano, as well as many other things."

His hand left hers and wrapped around her shoulder. He held her very firmly, arm around her, for several hundred yards. The beach was nearly deserted. At one point a black Labrador ran to them, barked playfully, then ran at full speed down the beach to join its owner, a tiny figure far down the beach. Even from a distance, the figure seemed bent and slow, an old man exercising his dog.

The day was blustery and the sun darted in and out. But being away from New York, and being able to force the visions of Rabinowitz to a distance, were important.

When they stopped walking, they found a long log, the wreckage of an unearthed tree that had fallen into the ocean during a storm. It had drifted and dried.

They sat down on it. Diana found a small flat piece of driftwood that was a few feet away. She picked it up and looked at her lover.

"Hold still," she said.

He did.

She sat a few feet from him and pulled out the small set of colored pencils that she always kept with her. With a few lines and strokes, she drew a profile and caricature of Rolf, sitting on the beach, the ocean in the background in blue.

She labeled it, "Nantucket, April, 1998," and handed it to him.

"I love it," he said. "And I love you, too."

"Mmm," she answered. "Let's not get back to the room too late tonight, okay?"

"Okay."

Lately every time a moment of affection and intimacy arose, an image of Rabinowitz had flashed into his mind, unsettling him. Now, today, while he was telling Diana how much he loved her, an image of Claire Graham flashed before him, too. He wondered who was controlling his mind.

But the long walks did help.

They were back to the inn by six. On a previous trip to Nantucket, Geiger had dined at the restaurant at 21 Federal Street. The restaurant's address was also its name: Twenty-one Federal. The restaurant had been excellent three years earlier and was equally excellent on this evening. The management had Geiger autograph a menu. There was a piano in the bar from which Geiger, though tempted, managed to stay away.

They took a short walk through the main center of town. At this time of the year most of the stores were closed in the evening, but Nantucket Bookworks had its doors wide-open, inviting them in. They spent a half hour browsing. At one point, Rolf looked up and his heart gave a start. There was a back room in the bookstore, filled with toys and books for children. A young woman with short dark hair, moving just at the edge of Geiger's vision, had just walked into the room.

Geiger blinked. He had gotten a good look at her. He was sure it was Claire.

At first he didn't know what to do, so he did nothing. He wondered if Claire had seen him, seen Diana, and had ducked into the back room to avoid him.

He glanced at Diana, who was at a section of art books near the front door. Then he glanced to the rear chamber again, moving slightly closer. The woman's back was to him now, but from the three-quarters profile he had glimpsed, she had looked just like Claire. Or at least he thought she had. Rolf went to Diana's side.

"I want to leave," he whispered.

She looked up in surprise. "We just got here," she said.

"I want to leave anyway."

She moved her lips close to his ear and flicked her tongue in it. "If you're that horny," she said, "I'm going to make you wait even a little longer."

"It's not that. I just saw someone I want to avoid."

"Who?"

"A girl named Claire." He nodded in the direction of the back room.

"A former sex partner, I assume, Tiger."

"She's nothing of the sort," he answered. "She's just out of graduate school and works for Brian."

"Is she a bitch or something?"

"No. Quite the opposite. She seems very young and very nice."

"Then go say hello. I don't mind. If you don't come back," she kidded cheerfully, "I'll know she was a very special woman."

"I don't want to say hello. I want to leave."

"Oh, don't be antisocial. Go say hi, while I spend some money. She'll be thrilled."

He sighed.

"She'll probably call her parents to tell them. Go give the girl her cheap thrill, then come back here and I'll slip you some sex."

He sighed doubly. Diana could be one of the best teases he had ever met.

"Now, go," she said.

Rolf walked slowly to the rear of the store. He turned a corner and found himself in the small section of the store where children's books were kept.

No Claire. But there was an adjoining area where there was a quixotic and distinctive collection of greeting cards. Geiger saw the woman's shadow through the doorway. He could tell by the silhouette that it was the woman he had taken to be Claire.

He drew a breath. What was going on? Why was this making him apprehensive? It was just a simple hello to a girl who worked for Brian. That's all.

He turned the corner and saw the short dark hair, green parka, and jeans. He took two steps forward, reached and tapped the woman on the shoulder.

"Hi," he said.

The woman turned. Geiger felt a wave of shock go through him. He didn't understand. How could he have been so wrong?

The woman who faced him in response to his tap was not Claire. Nor did she look like her. She had a very pale, pretty face. She was maybe in her late twenties, and her eyes were friendly. She looked familiar, but Rolf couldn't place her—as if he had seen her in a dream, or a famous painting. She was equally surprised to be looking at him.

"Yes?" she asked.

He began to answer, but before his eyes, the features of the woman's face rearranged themselves for a moment and he saw his own mother as an old woman, had she lived. He flinched in deep shock as he stared into her sorrowful hurt eyes, exactly the way she used to look after his father had administered one of his frequent poundings.

"Yes?" the woman asked again. *"Yes?"*

"What?" Rolf asked, shaking himself. The woman's face flew apart again and reassembled to something less familiar and with less emotional baggage.

Now she was amused. *"You* tapped *me* on the shoulder," she said. "Remember?"

"I, uh, I'm sorry," he fumbled, still astonished. "I thought I recognized you. But I'm mistaken."

Her lips parted in a smile. "Quite all right," she said politely. "No harm."

He could tell: she even recognized him. Her eyes hooked him. She was very familiar but the identity eluded him.

"I love your music," she said. "Beach Boys with Beethoven. What a hoot."

He managed a smile. "Thank you," he muttered. "You're very kind."

"I hope you start performing again," she said.

"Yes. Yes," he struggled. "Well, thank you. I might."

"I was *certain* I knew you," he said again.

"I'm afraid not," she said. "But I'm flattered anyway."

"Sorry," he said.

"I enjoyed meeting you," she answered.

She gave him a smile that suggested that she wished he could stay longer.

He walked back through the store, confused and looking everywhere to see whether there was another combination of short dark hair, green parka, and blue jeans.

There wasn't. He arrived by Diana's side.

"Did you find your sex-starved college student?" she asked.

"Very funny. I was wrong. Different lady." He didn't offer any details because he didn't understand the details.

"Oh," she said softly. "Too bad." After another moment, she changed the subject. "Look at this," she said. "Isn't this fantastic?"

It was a thick, fifty-dollar book of Nantucket photographs, taken and compiled by an outstanding local photographer.

He gave it a look.

"I like it," he said, visions of Claire still in one part of his mind, the identity of the mystery woman in another part.

"It's gorgeous," she said. "It has pictures of everything we've seen today."

"Don't let me stand in your way," he answered. "There's empty space in the bookcase back in New York."

"You're a doll," she said.

But his focus was still far away. He was craning his head looking toward the back rooms again, trying to get a look at the woman whom he had tapped. How could he have ever been so mistaken? His eyes and subconscious must have conspired to play a trick on him, he concluded. Thinking subconsciously of Claire, he had seen her where she wasn't.

Or was he just plain losing his mind?

They stayed at Bookworks another few minutes. Rolf bought

two hardcover novels and Diana bought the book of photographs of Nantucket. They returned to the inn by ten.

When the door to their room closed, the bag of books slipped from his hand and dropped to the floor with a heavy thud. Rolf took Diana in his arms. He drew her very tightly to him.

"Still horny?" she asked.

"What do you think?"

"Good," she said.

Held tightly, she knew the answer. He began to kiss her.

Her response to him was as passionate as his advance. They tumbled enthusiastically into bed and made love. Toward midnight, they both fell asleep, Diana tucked closely under his arm.

The next day was not as wonderful.

In the morning, on Saturday, they rose after sleeping late and had brunch in town. In the afternoon, they explored various other parts of the island—'Sconset, Madaket, and Smith's Point. The island remained quiet and sleepy from the winter. The wind off the ocean, while they were on the beaches, still had a sharp edge to it.

Late in the afternoon, when they were concluding a walk along the oceanfront in Madaket, another black dog appeared.

Like the previous day, it was a Labrador. It ran to them and barked, though not as playfully this time.

Geiger shooed the dog away. The animal recoiled and barked adamantly. It almost looked as if it were positioning itself to attack them. It started to lunge toward Diana.

Geiger quickly stepped between her and the animal and blocked the dog with a hard knee to its shoulder. The animal turned on Rolf and snapped, barely missing his left hand—the hand he needed to play the bass clef sections on a world tour.

"Hey! Get away!" Geiger shouted at the dog. He hit the animal with a knee again, much harder this time, sending it sprawling. A second snap by the beast nearly nailed his right wrist.

"Jesus!" Geiger fumed. "If people own an animal like this, can't they keep it on a leash?"

One good chomp on the hands of Rolf Geiger and some insurance company would be in bankruptcy trying to pay the cost of the world tour. He noticed that the dog had no license and no collar.

The animal turned in a looping pattern and came back a third time. Diana ducked behind Rolf. Before the animal could jump, however, Geiger formed an open palm and whacked the dog as hard as he could on the side of its head. Not to injure it but to teach it some manners.

The Lab yelped, snarled, and spun backwards, landing hard in the sand. The animal barked at Geiger again, then, as if in response to a command that only it could hear, it turned and ran away from them, sprinting down the beach as far as it could go.

"That was incredible!" Diana said breathlessly. "Why would anyone own an animal like that?"

"Let's hope the dog's not going for reinforcements," Geiger said, watching the dog escape. He stared at the fleeing animal. For a moment, it looked like a wolf racing over a field.

Then Geiger's eyes widened anew.

"My God," he said. "Look at that!"

Now they both stared down the beach, seeing the same figure in the distance as on the previous day. The same old man.

"Was that the same dog as yesterday?" Diana asked incredulously.

"It sure looks like it," Geiger answered. "Didn't *act* like it, though."

She shook her head. Geiger's hands found hers. In the distance they saw the old man put his dog on a leash. The distant figure, with its dog, stood and watched them.

Rolf felt a surge of recognition, then fear.

"Wait here," he said to her.

He walked slowly down the beach toward them. He drew within a hundred yards, feeling his heartbeat accelerate as he drew closer. There was little doubt in his mind. This was the same man he saw on East Seventy-third Street in New York, the same old man who was at the funeral of Rabinowitz.

Geiger drew close enough to almost make the identification for certain. This old man wasn't just watching him, he was stalking him! Geiger moved within twenty-five yards.

Yes! Positively! It was the same old man.

In indignation, in fear, Geiger shouted at him. "Hey!"

Rolf quickened his pace.

The old man turned abruptly. He walked briskly toward the inland side of the beach and slipped behind a high dune. Geiger accelerated and followed. He caught a glimpse of the man on a path that led farther away from the shore, before he turned a corner by an old beach shack. When Rolf reached that point several seconds later, the man and his animal were nowhere to be seen.

Geiger stood for almost a full minute, looking in every direction. But the old man and his animal had vanished. Completely.

He settled himself. He tried to tell himself that he had imagined the identity, just as he had apparently *thought* he had seen Claire in Nantucket Bookworks the night before, only to be proved wrong.

He walked back to Diana and took her hand.

"They're gone," he said.

"Good riddance."

"If we're lucky," Rolf commented, "they both got torn apart by a pack of rabid seagulls."

The remark struck Diana as particularly funny and removed much of the tension from the incident. As they walked back to their jeep, they were already laughing about the distant old geezer and his ill-mannered mutt. They conjectured that the old guy worked for some local nut group that had set out to undo everything that the local chamber of commerce sought to accomplish.

They returned to their guesthouse and changed for dinner. They ate at Twenty-one Federal again and, once again that evening after dinner, Geiger's eyes and subconscious seemed to be perpetrating devilish tricks on him.

On Main Street on Saturday night, they encountered a series of street performers. From a block away and across the street, Geiger thought he recognized something.

"Incredible," he muttered. "I don't believe this!"

What he thought he had seen was the same clown-violinist he had seen several weeks earlier on East Seventy-third Street, the performer with the ghostly white visage and the vanilla violin to match. To Rolf, the musician in Nantucket even appeared to be wearing the same clown suit with the large white polka dots.

Without explanation, Geiger took Diana by the hand and pulled her through some parked cars.

"What's going on, Rolf?" she asked. "What is it now?"

"I have to see this! And so do you!"

He pulled her along with great urgency, walking down the block to take a closer look at the player. When they arrived, however, the musician looked quite different than Geiger had expected.

There was no white on his face and the violin was actually an electric fiddle. His shirt bore polka dots, but they were smaller than those of the clown on East Seventy-third Street, and this violinist wore jeans and a fedora.

He turned to Geiger when Geiger arrived and winked at him, as if he knew him. He didn't. When he spoke he had a Southern accent.

"I love a good mystery, Rolf," Diana said. "But would you mind telling me what you dragged me down here for?"

Geiger looked at the fiddler as he started to play. Then he told a lie. "Thought I knew the fellow from Julliard," he said.

"Like you thought you knew the girl last night?" she asked.

"Very similar," he conceded.

"You can't be trusted out alone by yourself anymore," she teased.

"You may be right," he answered.

The inexplicable events had not yet stopped happening. When they returned to the Gray Lady Inn, they were surprised to see a police car sitting outside. Then they were even more surprised after they walked in.

It was past 10 P.M. but the lobby was loud with animated voices. Controlled chaos, about two dozen people there, half of them in shock, the others morbidly amused. Everyone seemed to know everyone else, even the other guests.

There was a uniformed policeman named DaSilva and a good-looking sandy-haired detective named Timothy Brooks, who seemed to be in charge.

"What happened?" Geiger asked.

Brooks raised his eyebrows.

"Have a look for yourself, if you'd like a sight you'll never forget," he answered. He motioned into the sitting room where Rolf and Diana had been a few hours earlier.

Diana and Rolf glanced at each other, then walked through the crowded lobby to the doorway that led to the sitting room.

"Just go to the door. No farther," Brooks called after them. "There's a veterinarian at work in there. With a patient."

"A *vet?*" Geiger asked.

Rolf and Diana moved to the doorway. Other people gave way so that he could see. The big plate-glass window that overlooked the meadow had been shattered. On the floor was the perpetrator.

A deer.

A mature buck lay on the carpet, with dark red blood running from cuts to its head, neck, and shoulders. The animal was on its left side, obviously sedated, but breathing hard. Several piles of shattered plate glass—big, dangerous, jagged shards of it— lay around the room.

Brooks appeared behind Geiger. "That animal must weigh seven hundred pounds," the detective said.

"What happened?" Diana asked.

There had been a handful of witnesses. The best among them were a honeymooning couple named Basilio from Weymouth. They had been sitting in the solarium when the incident occurred.

The buck, they said, had come charging out of the nature preserve on the west edge of the meadow behind the inn. The animal had raced across the meadow as if pursued by something that had frightened it terribly. It ran in a circular pattern for several seconds, moving in giant, frantic leaps. Several witnesses thought it might have been injured, but, as it turned out, it hadn't been.

But no one could see anything pursuing it and no one could imagine what might have so scared it. Deer hunting was forbidden on the island, no one had heard any shots, and there were no large dogs or other predators.

The animal had seemed crazed. It ran around in a final circle, then turned abruptly—again, almost in response to some unseen foe—and charged directly at the inn.

"I mean, *directly*," Louanne Basilio said. "That deer never swerved once it turned toward the inn. Just came right straight at the plate-glass window."

"Right at it," added Detective Brooks routinely, "and then through it." He paused. "I've seen a lot of strange things on this island, but this is a new one on me."

"Wonder what it saw," Mr. Basilio said.

Brooks shook his head. Everyone apparently had had an excellent view because the inn had had the rear light on, illuminating the meadow. One theory was that the deer had been attracted to the light, then blinded by it.

A gardener who had been working outside the Gray Lady confirmed the account. The animal had seemed to charge the inn. There had been a tremendous crash when the deer hit the plate glass. The collision with the window had stunned the buck, at the very least, and it had collapsed panting and bleeding onto the carpet, where it still lay.

"How long ago did this happen?" Geiger asked.

"About twenty minutes," Brooks answered.

By chance, the vet lived a few doors away and, summoned by Mrs. Irwin, had rushed over right away. Dr. Lee Goran had already tranquilized the animal and was examining its wounds. A woman from the Nantucket ASPCA stood by also, looking over the vet's shoulder. A decision was being made as to whether the animal would have to be euthanized or released. Meanwhile, an accumulation of curious onlookers stood by in the next room, standing vigil.

Geiger looked to Diana. "Incredible," he said.

"Poor thing," she said, shaking her head.

They were both thinking the same. The second lunatic animal incident in a matter of hours.

Coincidence?

Something in the island water?

Rolf put his hand on hers. Neither he nor Diana could hear the conversation around the deer, but from the way the vet was working on the animal's cuts, things seemed to be going in the buck's direction. The vet wouldn't have been stitching cuts if the animal was going to be put down.

David Corwin, the proprietor, reappeared and walked to

Brooks. "How's it going?" he asked softly. "Is Bambi Senior going to live or can Twenty-one Federal put venison on the restaurant menu?"

Brooks grinned and hunched his shoulders. Two women in the room shot Corwin a withering look and walked away. When they were out of earshot, he spoke again.

"I wonder if the animal huggers will pay for my window and my carpet," he said.

"Probably not," Brooks said. "But you might do okay under your insurance policy."

"I can't wait to be informed that a deer through a downstairs window is an 'act of God,' " he said evenly.

Geiger and Diana stayed and watched. A few minutes later, the deer wobbled to its feet. Miraculously, Dr. Goran led the animal back out through the hole created by the shattered glass. The animal wobbled to its feet outdoors and then sat down again.

"The tranquilizer wears off in fifteen minutes. The deer will wander off again. As long as it stays away from cars, which it should be smart enough to do, it will steady itself and survive."

Rolf and Diana went back up to their room for a few minutes, then decided that they didn't want to be back inside yet. They walked back into town, to stroll on the pier. A handful of people recognized Geiger and gave him a double take. No one asked for autographs. All the time, Geiger kept a lookout for the violinist. They even walked by the street musicians again. But if they had seen him once, he decided, it had been an hallucination.

They were back to the inn by ten o'clock.

Geiger went into the bathroom and showered. He was soaping himself, with eyes closed, when he felt something touch him.

Nerves tingling, he jumped. Then he smiled.

"Room enough for two?" she asked.

"Always," he said. "If it's you."

It was Diana, completely undressed, stepping in to join him. He liked to shower with her. He massaged her back and pulled her into a tight embrace as the water splashed them.

He pulled her wet body as tightly to him as he could. For the first time in several days, he thought of nothing other than her and the female physical presence in front of him.

He reached for the water and turned it off.

"Should I carry you to bed or throw you in bed from here," he asked.

"You may carry me, then put me down gently. Then you can be as forceful as you want."

She kissed him.

"But dry me off first, okay?"

"Of course."

They shared a towel, then tumbled into bed. He again pulled her as tightly to him as he could before making love to her as passionately as if this were their first time together.

Later, toward 2 A.M. he came awake in the soft blue light of the room. For several minutes, he lay very quietly thinking.

He was half-awake, dozing more than sleeping, in a comfortable inn on a quiet island. Around him in the room were objects and furniture which, if not familiar, were conducive to rest.

His hands were behind his head, folded on the pillow as he stared above him and let his gaze drift around the room.

He was struggling again, trying to put events in order.

Diana was lying very close to him. Her bare arm was facing him. He looked at her for a moment and tried to decide if he wanted to make love to her again. With her naked body so close, he started to feel the arousal. She liked it very much when he awakened her in the middle of the night with a sexual urgency that said, *Now, I want to have you right now.*

Yes, he was tempted. But a series of events were coming together in his head, trying to explain themselves.

He wondered.

What had driven the deer to charge into the windowpane downstairs? By anyone's account, this was no ordinary event. Was it unrelated to what was going on in Geiger's life? Or had he drawn something to this inn, something that had made a wild animal go into a frenzy of fear?

What had been lurking in those woods beyond the meadow? Something half-dead? Something half-human? Something with a foot in two different worlds?

Like the ghost of Isador Rabinowitz?

A powerful shudder went through him.

Why had he *thought* he had seen Claire in Nantucket Bookworks? He reviewed what was in his memory and, by God, he was sure it had been her. Few twenty-two-year-olds are quite *that* alluring. He was even starting to sense something strongly sexual and ethereal about Claire. Something that he was having a tough time suppressing even while he loved another woman.

He began to entertain a funny hunch that his strange feelings toward her were somehow associated with everything else that was going on—everything else meaning his haunting by Rabinowitz.

Yes, he was sure it had been her.

He recognized the shape of her backside, the legs that she walked upon so saucily in her short skirts. The curve of her neck and cheek. How could it have been her one minute and another woman the next? Why had he imagined the other woman's face as his mother's?

He *had* imagined that, hadn't he? The dead didn't inhabit living forms to revisit the world, did they?

Did they?

His thoughts drifted.

Then there had been the violinist. The street musician. Once again, Rolf had been sure of what he had seen. That incident had been even stranger. He had rushed across the street and the musician he had seen wasn't even there!

How was he to interpret that?

What was the spin?

Had he seen something from another world? Another reality? Or had it just been some weird coincidence. A street performer whom he had once seen from his window on East Seventy-third Street in Manhattan turns up in Nantucket, then slips away before Geiger can rush up and speak.

Well, come to think of it, those events weren't so far-fetched. The explanation was not that irrational.

But the combination of all three?

He shuddered again. This one was a deep shiver. It roused Diana, who opened her eyes.

"Tiger?" she asked.

"Yes, honey?"

"Why are you awake?"

"Thinking," he said.

"Don't think too much," she said sweetly. "Unless it's about me."

"I'll make it about you," he said softly. "Now go back to sleep."

She closed her eyes and snuggled close to him. A moment later, she opened her eyes and looked at him. She propped her head up on her hand.

"No," she said. "I won't go to sleep. I want to know something."

"What's that?"

"What kind of man was he? What kind of life did he have? Before you knew him, I mean?"

"Who?" he asked.

"The man whom you're always thinking about, whether you admit it or not: Rabinowitz."

He felt a sinking sensation. "Why are you asking me that?"

"Because sometimes I feel that he's here with us."

"*What?*"

"What I mean is, Tiger, that he's gotten into your psyche so deeply," Diana said. "I live with you. I sleep with you. I'm intimate with you. I want to know what kind of man got so far into your mind."

Several seconds passed before Geiger could answer.

"Sometimes I think I never knew him at all," Geiger said to the dark room. "I knew the sour old musician, the great recitalist who wanted me to fail. I don't know what was further inside that. He didn't *permit* people to see inside him."

"Do you think he was dangerous? Devious? Mean?" she asked.

Geiger deflected the question. In the corner of the room something shifted. A crack on an old floorboard. All four of their eyes settled upon the spot for a beat. Nothing was visible.

"A lot of people thought so," Rolf answered.

"But what do you think?" she asked.

"I think all those adjectives applied in one way or another."

"But where did all that malice come from?" she asked.

"I don't know." It was a philosophical point for all midnights. "Where does evil come from, where does genius come from?" he asked.

Another second passed. "So he was like those Russian dolls. The matruskas," she said with sympathy. "One inside another inside another, till you get to the last one."

"Sort of," he said. "What I never understood about the dolls was which was the real one. The outermost or the innermost?"

"Or was one a reflection of the other?"

"And one never can see into the final one, either. That one doesn't open," she said.

He sighed. "You think too much, Beautiful," he said to her. He pulled her close and kissed her.

"I do, do I?" she asked. "Then why is it you who's lying awake with his thoughts?"

"Point," he said.

"Point," she agreed.

He savored the touch of her head against his shoulder.

"Know what I'm going to do?" she said sleepily. "I'm going to go over to Lincoln Center next week when we get back to New York. I'm going to find out everything there is to know about Isador Rabinowitz."

"Why?"

"I want to know why he's gotten so deeply into your head," she said. "I want to know so that I can help you chase him out."

She closed her eyes and settled back to sleep. He tried to do the same, but he was still bothered. Increasingly, it seemed to him that he was on the edge of some new experience, and the first viewing of Isador Rabinowitz was only a harbinger. It had not been an isolated incident and certainly not the end of anything.

Shortly thereafter, he had his confirmation.

With Diana breathing evenly as she slept next to him, Geiger's eyes again came open.

Somewhere, when his eyes were closed, he was hearing piano music. It sounded like Rachmaninoff, played by a master.

For several seconds he lay very still and listened. It was at the edge of his consciousness, he decided, but it was there. It was right *there*.

He half expected something to happen within the room. For

a moment, the sound of the music grew louder and the room, it seemed to him, grew very cold.

It was as if someone had opened a door to the winter. He thought he sensed a presence in the room. When Geiger had been a teenager, Rabinowitz had always wondered about Rolf's sex life. He had frequently asked to hear about it.

Standard questions sprinkled through a recital, attempting to test his concentration: "Do you now fuck her? Is she good?"

Was the spirit of the old master now here to watch him make love to Diana?

Of course he was, Rolf decided. In context, it made perfect sense! Geiger whispered aloud.

"You've followed me!"

A voice in the darkness. **"Yes."**

Geiger's nerves surged.

Yes, Rolf was sure he had heard an answer! The old man was present somewhere nearby. The music continued. A Chopin étude, this one played with a sad and sinister touch.

"What do you want?" Rolf asked.

"She makes love to another man these days, you know," the voice told him.

"What?" Geiger asked.

"The woman lying next to you. Another man mounts her and fucks her."

"Go away, damn it!" Rolf whispered to the darkness.

"No woman is true to a single man. You're sharing her."

"Lies!"

Geiger shifted in his bed, trying to exorcise the most unbanishable of thoughts.

"Think about it. Think *where* this would be taking place."

"I refuse," Geiger said.

Rabinowitz must have leaned harder on the keys, because the volume stepped up.

"Then I will *show* you."

An unwanted image accosted Rolf's sleepy brain. He envisioned Maurice Sahadi's art studio, crowded with young male artists. But tonight it was Diana who was the model. She was completely undressed before a dozen strong men, none of them painting, each of them madly desiring her . . .

"Exactly!"

. . . and Geiger was completely shaken by the idea.

"Sharing her. That's right, Rolf. You are sharing her."

Geiger shuddered violently, one of those weird nighttime shakes that brings a man out of sleep.

"The only solution will be for you to murder her!"

Rolf bolted upright. His eyes were wide-open. The image, the thought, of Diana in death was too much for him to bear.

And he could still hear the music. Distantly.

"I'm imagining you," Geiger said to Rabinowitz.

"No. I'm very real."

"Prove it!" Geiger demanded. "Prove that I'm not imagining you!"

He heard the old man laugh.

Incredibly, Geiger thought he sensed movement in the dark room. Low movement that he couldn't see. Like the movement of an animal. It was coming near him.

Very near. Then it was there.

Something tugged at his scalp. An invisible cold hand seemed to close around his heart. He felt an icy fear sweep along the back of his neck and he flinched. For half a second the foul odor of the dog on the beach assaulted him. Then it was gone. The sensation threw him into shock.

"Proof enough?"

Speechless, his heart kicking, Geiger threw his left hand to the lamp at his bedside. He jarred it, then fumbled with it, trying to turn it on.

"Till next time. *Auf Wiedersehen!*"

Very distantly the cackling voice faded, like the sound of an aircraft disappearing into the distance.

Geiger found the light switch. He clicked it and a yellow light bathed the room. Simultaneously, the room temperature rose again. The light swept away the image of Diana with all those men. Geiger no longer sensed the presence of the ghost, even though he knew it might not be far away.

Rolf listened to the thundering of his heart. He let things settle. The light did not wake Diana.

He waited, expecting something unspeakable. Nothing happened. Then, cautiously, he turned the light off and lay back.

He closed his eyes again, letting the piano concerto, borne on distant wings of questionable intent, bear him off to sleep.

The next morning he awoke shortly after nine.

Diana had dressed nicely. Tan shorts and a pale blue long-sleeved sweater. He loved the way she looked. They packed and prepared for their flight back to New York.

Checking out, Geiger asked if there were any pianos anywhere in the area. In any room or at some inn nearby that might have been playing music late.

David Corwin, at the front desk, pursed his lips and shook his head.

"Nothing that I know of, Mr. Geiger," he said. "I hope you weren't disturbed."

"No. Not at all."

"Rolf is so close to music," Diana chimed in, "that sometimes he hears it clearly in his head. Even when there's none playing."

Geiger didn't entirely appreciate the observation. Diana regretted it as soon as it was out of her mouth.

"Yeah. I'm a regular nutcase," Geiger said dryly. "But my fans don't worry about that. Only the people around me."

Both Diana and David Corwin laughed awkwardly.

Outside a few minutes later, Diana asked, "Should I apologize or are you just your usual testy world-class-musician self today?"

He grimaced. "I'm testy," he said. "I thought I heard something last night. Sorry."

"It's forgotten," she said.

They went to the airport, caught the connection to Logan and were on the one o'clock plane back to La Guardia. On the flight, Geiger heard the music again. He recognized the touch of Rabinowitz and the harp of his own Steinway.

The master was playing on the instrument in Geiger's home, Geiger theorized. He was doing it right now while they were in the air 250 miles away.

But Geiger could hear anyway.

That was how Rolf Geiger "knew." If the piano playing in

his home was continuing while he was away, the haunting would continue also.

And gradually, he knew, it would intensify to the next level.

Shortly before they landed in New York, Diana turned to him. Her hand settled on his.

"Feeling better, Tiger?" she asked.

"He's still pursuing me," Geiger answered softly. "Rabinowitz follows me everywhere I go."

For a moment she had a hopeless look in her eye. Then she turned and stared out the window.

"I know," she said when she looked back. "He's in your head."

"I want him out of my head and out of my life," Geiger pleaded.

"I know," she said softly. The horrible unspoken image returned to him of mortal harm coming to Diana. He shuddered again.

When she spoke again, she had changed the subject to her art class with Maurice Sahadi.

Neither of them mentioned the name of Isador Rabinowitz for the rest of the day. The evening back at their town house proved uneventful. It wasn't until the next morning that they noticed that the watcher across the street had vanished.

He had left a small pile of cigarette butts behind him, but he did seem to be gone. *Hopefully,* Diana thought to herself, *for good.* The more she thought about the gnarled little man, the more he scared her. Just like Rolf's increasingly irrational behavior.

thirteen

On Monday morning, shortly after Mrs. Jamison arrived, Brian Greenstone phoned.

Rolf took the call in his upstairs office. Greenstone had spoken to a half dozen out-of-town promoters about doing a mostly Beethoven concert within the next six weeks. All were keen to book a date. Four had emerged as strong possibilities.

"I've narrowed it down to Miami, Boston, Washington, and Philadelphia, Rolf," Greenstone summed up. "Any of those cities are possible. I'd have to get back to them right away. The dates would be in either late May or early June."

"Sounds good. Keep talking," Geiger said.

The date in Washington was a Monday at the Kennedy Center. Monday was generally not a good evening for a recital, though Rolf Geiger with a Beethoven program would have easily sold out the Center any night of the week. After listening to the particulars, Geiger vetoed Washington for other reasons.

The notion of playing in the capital, Geiger felt, would put too much pressure on the date. It would seem "too official" and would give the appearance of an early starting point for the big tour, even though it wasn't. Washington critics could be surly, also.

"Have to agree with you, lad," said Greenstone. "If Washington were the only opportunity, we might do it. But your reasoning is fine."

Geiger and Greenstone eliminated Miami, too. While Geiger liked the city, Beethoven in Miami in June wasn't the right equation.

"I prefer Miami in the winter, when it isn't as sultry," said Geiger, "and when the rest of the country is wrestling with snowblowers."

"Have to agree with you again," snorted Greenstone. "I don't care much for Miami at all, though I do admit it has its advantages when one has ice up one's nostrils here in the north."

"So where does that leave us?" Geiger asked.

"It leaves you in the caldrons of your colonial insurrection, if I dare say. Boston or Philadelphia," Greenstone said. "These are the better bets, anyway. Got a calendar in front of you?"

Geiger did.

The date in Boston was the last Wednesday in May before Memorial Day. A good date, though on the downside, much of Boston would be occupied with graduations at that time of year. The location was Lowell Hall at Harvard. One thousand seats. Not too big, not too small. Definitely possible. But not perfect.

Boston critics were not terribly friendly, either, treating some visiting musicians the way the local sportswriters treated the Red Sox. Geiger had heard all the stories he needed about Boston music critics from Diana, who still knew many of them. In the back of his mind, it still rankled that a *Boston Herald* reviewer had once pronounced Geiger "psychotic" for a rendition of "Bolero" interspersed with themes from the Grateful Dead.

"The Academy of Music in Philadelphia has a potential cancellation for Thursday, June 11," Greenstone continued.

"I like Philadelphia," Geiger said absently.

"Of course you do. It's East Coast, early in the month, and best of all, the Academy is the most prestigious building in the city. Nothing major competing, plus the art museum has a big show in the summer. So there will be plenty of tourists, and many of the tourists will be young and female. That works nicely for you. Makes you a perfect audience, in point of fact. The Philadelphia critics are very fair and, as you just reminded me, you like the city.''

''Seems like an ideal date,'' Geiger answered. ''Why is there a potential cancellation?''

''The soloist who was going to perform wants to go on a trip to Greece with his boyfriend who's a college student. Ticket sales were slow and the Academy wants out, also, par-*tic*-u-lar-ly if they can book a potential sellout. That means you. You'd be doing everyone a favor to grab the date, including possibly yourself.''

''Does that mean the orchestra's available, too?''

''Indeed, it does, since the orchestra was booked for the lascivious violinist.''

''Sounds good,'' said Geiger.

''I wouldn't be recommending it if it weren't.''

''Can we set it up?''

''I'll make the calls this afternoon,'' Greenstone said. ''Or maybe tomorrow morning. The Academy is *very* anxious, so I don't want them to think *we* are too anxious. I think they will deal with us most generously. I happen to know, in fact, that they got off the phone with me under the illusion that Boston and Washington had the inside track.''

Geiger smiled. ''Shame on you, Brian.''

''I don't know how they came to that misimpression.''

''Shame on you, Brian,'' he repeated.

''I didn't *tell* them that, lad, I just let them come to that conclusion. Now, put down the bloody phone and pretend we didn't have this conversation.''

''Perfect,'' Rolf said. ''Perfect.''

''Oh, and there's something else, too,'' Greenstone added quickly. ''I want you to think about this.''

''Go ahead.''

It flew through Geiger's mind that it was something involving Claire again, but it wasn't.

''Despite what we discussed previously, I'm looking at the possibility of *starting* your world tour in London.''

Geiger was surprised. ''Rather than in New York?''

"Precisely."

"Any reasons?"

"Several."

"Name two."

"I can get Wembley Stadium for September first. This is huge. They'll be having football matches at about the same time, but the stadium can be made ready."

"I don't want to run second to British football," Geiger said.

"You won't. There will be a lot of excitement, including the football, but you'll fit in nicely and we'll get spillover publicity in the rest of Europe."

Greenstone paused.

"But the larger reason is that I definitely want to start you off with very strong press notices for playing unadulterated great classical music in a mega-arena. If you've been watching, the British press hasn't hit you as hard as your own American one has."

"I *hadn't* noticed," he confessed. "I stopped reading all of them."

"My brethren still find you charming, even when you're playing," Greenstone purred. "Why, I can't imagine."

"How nice."

"So, go there, play magnificently with traditional works, conquer London, and it gives the English press the chance to say, 'See! See there! This Rolf fellow *is* wonderful and we here in the U.K. knew it all along!' New York will be grudging with its praise unless you've already been pronounced sensational around the world. If we come off good press in London, we're halfway home in New York, also."

"So what do we do with New York? End here?"

"Maybe. Or maybe we end in Cairo. The *Emperor* at the Valley of the Kings, as you suggested. Or Tokyo. I love Tokyo. I could retire on what we might make in Japan alone."

Greenstone laughed.

"Anyway," the agent continued, "this is all 'TBA.' To Be Arranged. So we need to talk more about the back end of the trip, Rolf. The main thing is, the Brits will treat you fairly, which is all we are seeking. And the country will feel honored to have you commence your tour there. Pigs-in-clover, that's what it will be. Oh, and I can probably pull a taut string or two and have Charles and his current concubine attend. Would you like to meet them?''

"Don't know. Maybe. Should I?''

"I already *know* they wish to meet you. I wouldn't leave anything like that to chance.''

The assertion left Geiger momentarily speechless. His last contact with royalty had been in Scandinavia on the 1995 tour when a local princess wrote down her phone number and let it be known she would be home alone after a concert. Geiger had wisely misplaced the number.

Meanwhile, as Rolf turned over the memory of this, Greenstone forged ahead.

"So, look, see my game plan?'' the agent asked. "The favorable European notices will be spinning back to the U.S. Do well in Europe and you'll be pronounced culturally kosher for the slavering American audiences. Thus it will be all the harder for the vampires in the American musical establishment to be out of sync. Harder for them to write bad reviews. Not that you deserve them, Rolf. I'm just advising you as a client. End of fiery sermon.''

Greenstone paused finally.

"Of course,'' he said by way of conclusion and benediction, "you'd be a total ass to ignore such profound thought and luminescent advice from your uncle Brian.''

"I wouldn't dare.''

"Good.''

"London was Rabinowitz's adopted city,'' Geiger mused.

"Was it? Well, the old bastard is dead, so who gives a shit? He's easier to represent as an estate than as an individual.''

"During the war. Before coming to the U.S.''

"During the war, *what?*''

"Rabinowitz lived in London during the war.''

"Well, too bad the Huns missed him. And, hello, London is also *my native* city,'' Greenstone said. "And that's where you should debut the tour. You've got glamour, money and you'll draw a humongous crowd. It's the way to go, lad.''

"Okay," Geiger said. "You sold me. London. I'll do London first."

"You're cooking, Rolf," Greenstone told him. "You're cooking."

In his home, Geiger set down the phone. His agent could have been considered a world-class windbag were it not for the fact that he knew what he was talking about. If Brian Greenstone claimed a tour was going to be a success, he was invariably right.

Geiger sighed for a moment. He went downstairs and looked for Diana, then remembered that she always went to the health club on Monday mornings. Rolf discovered that he was apparently alone in the house Mrs. Jamison had gone back out again. She put in forty hours a week, but sometimes—like now—Rolf couldn't figure her schedule.

But he knew he would survive the day even if she didn't come back. He and Diana were to attend a preview that evening of the Renoir exhibit at the Metropolitan Museum of Art. He had obtained an invitation to the preview. The actual opening wasn't till later in the week.

He moved from his office down to his library. There was a stack of fan mail that he had left near the piano. He reread some of it. Then, beginning to feel ambitious—and untroubled by Rabinowitz so far today—he moved to his bookcase.

He started to select some scores. From his shelves, he pulled Beethoven's Sonata in A Major #2. The work might be part of the program for Philadelphia if the Quaker City date worked out.

Well, he reasoned, why not? He might as well start looking at some music.

fourteen

Diana Stephenson returned to their town house from the gym shortly before noon. She showered, changed, grabbed a piece of fruit and some yogurt, then left again early that afternoon.

She walked through Central Park to Lincoln Center. There she continued on to the Theater and Performing Arts annex of the New York Public Library. She went to the third-floor research gallery and tried to remember the specifics of what she was seeking.

There would be a wealth of material on Isador Rabinowitz, and she would not be the only person researching him now, so soon after his death.

Hadn't she learned as much as she needed to know about the departed maestro? Couldn't she ask Rolf *anything* about the old man? The high points of the man's life were well-known. As a music scholar, she had her own working familiarity with the man. So why was this even necessary?

Then she recalled.

She was looking for insights more than anything. She wanted to know what it was that had stayed within Rolf's psyche. What invisible piece of the man had remained after his death?

If she could find it, perhaps she could sit down with Rolf

and lead him past it. The challenge of surpassing the maestro was enough to grip Geiger's personality. But was there more?

On the third floor of the library annex at Lincoln Center, Diana signed in with the librarian on duty. He was a short, wiry man with closely cut gray hair. He assigned her a work space at a long flat table. She set down a notebook and a pair of new pens at her assigned place.

Then she went to the massive card catalogue for the theater and performing-arts collection and found several listings for material on Isador Rabinowitz. Among them were several files of old clippings.

She designed a strategy for her research. She knew the bold strokes of the man's life, his childhood in Europe, his flight from the Nazis, his residence in London during the war and in Vienna afterward. Why not see if she could pick off the stray detail that could lead to an enlightenment?

Yes, she decided. That's what she should do. She would read through five of the old folders on Rabinowitz. She knew his recent history. Now she would peer into the past.

She was aware of other movement in the room. Other researchers were constantly coming and going. She paid little attention to the movement until she had written down the call letters of the files she wanted. Done, she turned and her gaze traveled the room to find a man of about thirty-five sitting three long tables away from her.

He was good-looking, with dark hair and a square jaw. He wore a blue pin-striped shirt and a tie. He was watching her intently. When she caught him, he lowered his eyes to the file he was reading.

"Oh, really?" she mused.

Diana smiled to herself. She was both flattered and annoyed. She had another male fan, which was not unusual. She frequently caught men watching her. A couple of times a week, men tried to pick her up. In stores. In museums. Sometimes it was okay. Sometimes it was irritating. Never was she interested and never did she encourage it. This man at the library table had apparently been watching her from behind. Who knew for how long? Who knew for what purpose?

Well, she told herself before getting on with her work, *at least he's nice-looking.* This was better than drawing a creep.

She filed her call slips with the librarian, who sent them to a library clerk who would retrieve them from the stacks. She went back to her desk table and waited.

A minute passed. Then another. She was facing the man at the table who had been watching her. Twice he looked up to see her looking at him. The second time, he smiled. That caused her to turn away completely.

Several minutes later, the librarian reappeared. He now had a name tag which identified him as Harold Milsap, Assistant Reference Librarian.

Milsap cradled an assortment of folders in his thin arms. "Here we are," he said as he arrived.

The files she requested were contained in large envelopes, nine by twelve inches, each containing a collection of newspaper and magazine clippings. She knew from previous research projects, particularly in the arts, that these old-clipping collections were sometimes priceless. Sifting through a bunch of them sometimes put into focus aspects of a subject's life that had been missed by others.

Milsap set four files upon the table in front of Diana. All of the files showed age. None had labels, other than Rabinowitz's name, a reference code for storage, and a notation of how many clippings were in each file. One folder was very thin and contained only a few clippings. Many of the clippings were from the 1960s or before.

Harold Milsap arranged the files in front of Diana so that she could see the titles on their spines.

"File request number 156. Am I correct?" Milsap asked.

"You are," Diana answered.

"These are your research requests," he continued, looking them over. "Or at least this is what's available. Isador Rabinowitz seems more popular today than before he died."

"That happens," she said.

The librarian spoke in an intense hushed voice. "You asked for five files. Subject matter, Rabinowitz, Isador. One file is still in use elsewhere here today."

"Someone else is researching him?" she asked.

Mr. Milsap gave a nod to a research table toward the other end of the room. As luck would have it, the dark-haired man in the blue pin-striped shirt, Diana's newest fan, had the other file.

She glanced at him, but apparently he had given up on her. He was sitting quietly now, intently leaning forward, his gaze studiously on the material in front of him. If he was truly reading a clipping file on Rabinowitz, he was totally absorbed by it.

"The gentleman right there," Milsap said. "He's doing some sort of research, also."

"Will he want these files eventually?"

"I couldn't say. I know he saw them yesterday. He might be finished with them."

"He's been here before?"

"Four days in a row," the librarian said. "He's reading everything we have on Isador Rabinowitz."

"Is that a fact?" she mused.

"That is a fact," Harold Milsap pronounced.

"Thank you," she said.

She turned slightly and took another look at the man. He was *very* good-looking. He still didn't look up.

Milsap went back to his desk.

Diana opened her first file. Carefully counting out the fifteen clippings that the file contained, she arranged them in order in front of her. She was always meticulous about such research. She picked up one of the pens and prepared to take notes.

The top file was the thinnest. It contained clippings from recitals by Rabinowitz in the 1950s. They were reviews and personality profiles. Mostly puff pieces, journalistic wet kisses.

Diana read through all of them. In keeping with the homogenized image that America wanted for itself in the fifties, each article had a similar spin: Rabinowitz, the genius, had suffered greatly in Europe before and during the war. Now he had brought his genius to the shores of North America and the nation was all the better for it.

"Oh, brother," Diana whispered to herself, thinking back on the stories that Rolf had told her. Three wives, countless mistresses, three legitimate children and two others that weren't, all of whom would end up hating him. Lucifer of the Larghetto, Satan of the Scherzo.

She reassembled the fifteen clippings and tucked them neatly back into the folder. She set the file aside with no more insight than when she had begun.

She picked up the second file and waded through thirty-two more clippings. More of the same.

She found a headline from a news story,

MAESTRO RABINOWITZ
BECOMES U.S. CITIZEN

with a few paragraphs of text attached.

The item was from *Time* magazine in 1953. The article, which pictured Rabinowitz with a bevy of beautiful, amply cleavaged women at the Stork Club in New York, brought the public up to speed on the great man's arrival and career in America. Despite the fact that *Time* pointedly reminded its readers that Rabinowitz was a Russian-Viennese Jew, he was now as American as a hot dog. "Or at least as American as the brilliant physicist, Albert Einstein, to whom he is frequently compared."

Rabinowitz? Einstein?

Diana almost gagged on that one.

Next came some more of the credit-to-his-race bullshit. Diana noticed that the picture at the Stork Club, the one with all the babes, also featured J. Edgar Hoover, who apparently had helped accelerate Rabinowitz's citizenship application. Hoover wore his usual sinister closet-creep grin.

Presumably, thought Diana, *the women are with Rabinowitz.*

She checked with some notes on Rabinowitz's life that she had made before the library visit. The pianist had been married to his second wife at the time. He hadn't divorced her till 1957. The women in the photo were all leaning toward Rabinowitz, who was quite handsome as a man in his late thirties. None of the women seemed inclined toward J. Edgar at all or in any way. They probably had found him creepy, too. Plus a little scary.

Diana reassembled the thirty-two clippings and closed file

number two. She had already spent an hour on this. She was getting nowhere. She yawned for a moment and glanced around the research room. The good-looking man at the distant table was still there. He didn't look up.

"Well," she joked to herself, "there went my opportunity to have a quick affair with a stranger this afternoon. Love at the library, sex in the stacks, banged among the books, and I missed my mark."

Concentrate, a voice told her.

The subconscious command came into her mind so clearly that it jounced her out of her fluffy unrealistic fantasy. These thoughts at the edge of her consciousness were irritating. They didn't even feel like her own.

She leaned back into her files.

"A quick affair with a handsome anonymous stranger," she mused further. "Never had one and probably never will."

No?

Despite her evident beauty and the many opportunities she had had, or perhaps *because* of these factors, Diana had never just hopped into the sack quickly with a would-be lover. All of the relationships in her life—and there had not been that many compared with some women she knew—had been lengthy, involving a period of getting to know the man, developing a bond, then making the decision to sleep with him. Quick impersonal sex was not her style. Not her way of doing things.

But soon it will be, my fair Diana, the subconscious voice told her now.

"What?" She answered. She looked up. She was now in an inane dialogue with herself.

Soon it will be.

"Soon it will be *what?*"

No reply.

She shook her head. One side of her subconscious was now in open revolt against the other. Good girl, bad girl? She wondered what had put this line of thought in her mind, then realized it had probably come from the man sitting at the other table and the publicity shots of Rabinowitz with a gaggle of high-maintenance chorus girls. She yawned again. If she needed something good and stiff in the middle of this afternoon, it was a good stiff cup of coffee. A nice caffeine fix. That would have been a good deal more useful than an affair in the afternoon. But there was no caffeine possibility in sight.

She glanced at the man two tables away. She had lost his attention completely, it now appeared. She almost felt disappointed, in spite of her better sense. She went onward to the third file.

No big surprises here, either.

Looking at another batch of kissy-facey positive write-ups, Diana developed a deep respect for the publicity people and handlers who had relentlessly sanitized Rabinowitz's public image during that era. She had heard all about the private Rabinowitz from Rolf—the tyrannical nature, the physical abuse of his family and women, the vile language, the insistent, persistent bullying of students, peers, agents, employees.

Everyone.

The way he used to place his hands menacingly on the backs of the necks of students or musicians, suggesting that choking them to death would be the appropriate response if their musicianship didn't measure up.

What a monster. What glowing personal write-ups. If half this stuff could be believed, canonization should not be long in the offing.

She found something else, in reference to the old bastard.

> . . . a personality and warmth as charming and incandescent as a waltz by Strauss . . .

wrote *Look* magazine in 1965.

"Oh, yeah. Right," she said.

The "Dark Angel" stuff about the man didn't surface until he was well into his seventies. By then he was so celebrated that everyone—well, *almost* everyone—made excuses and explanations for him. Post-Watergate journalism: it was finally permissible to print the truth. No more equivocation by the knights and princes of the keyboards. By the late seventies it was considered fair game to print dirt on almost anyone.

And yet, going by the files in front of her, Rabinowitz still eluded journalistic justice. *Esquire* had done an edgy piece on him in 1984. But even that one tended to explain him away in light of his artistic brilliance.

Diana closed the third file and opened the fourth. This held nineteen clippings. She counted them out, arranged them neatly, and then stood up. She was getting tired of this. She left the clippings on the table and walked away to find a water fountain. Then she went downstairs and outside for a moment for a breath of air.

Renoir tonight at the Metropolitan Museum, she thought. How she looked forward to it. Renoir had established himself as a genius without being a monster. So why had Rabinowitz needed to become one? Perhaps there was no good answer to that.

She went back upstairs to the third floor and her work space. She sat down again and sifted through the final assortment of clippings.

A little bit of interest here: She found references to Rabinowitz's "legal difficulties" in the late 1940s and early 1950s. She assumed the reference had to do with his wives or perhaps his entry into the United States. Heaven knew that Rabinowitz was not the type of man to bother with the letter of the law when he set out to do something.

She had even found a quote in the *Esquire* article which even summarized his attitude.

> "Laws, morals, accepted ways of doing things; these are contemptible and thoroughly irrelevant 'petit bourgeois' concepts which should not be allowed to inhibit those possessed by genius. I don't put my fingers on the keys to a piano in the same way as mortal men. I don't put my feet on the earth in a same way, either . . ."

"Oh, *really!*" she muttered. "Please tell us how *truly wonderful* you are."

The word *egomaniacal* came to mind, but she chased that away, too. The term was too mild for Herr Rabinowitz. For the first time, she started to comprehend the "Dark Angel" term that had been used for years within the classical music industry and behind Rabinowitz's back. Writers had probably shied away from using the term in print out of fear of Rabinowitz and fear of his influence through his recording label. Or, as a music professor at Berkeley had once said of him, "If he hadn't been a Jew, he would have been an excellent Nazi."

And, what about this "possessed by genius," the words he had used in reference to himself?

She took a moment and wondered about the wording. Why hadn't he said "he, who is a genius"? Was there a subtle clue to something there? Or had it just been Rabinowitz's quirkiness of speech, his devious way of sending around in circles those who tried to figure him out?

"My lasting beauty will be judged from my poetry at the keyboard, and . . .

—Rabinowitz had been quoted in another interview, this one upon the occasion of his seventy-fifth birthday in 1989—

. . . not from any aspect of my personal behavior or demeanor."

" 'Screw all of mankind while I'm alive, in other words,' " Diana mumbled. " 'Then remember that I was a great artist.' What bullshit!"

After another quarter hour, Diana started to gather the nineteen clippings from the final file. She was almost finished. She also was filled with a growing revulsion for the subject of her inquiry, but she did feel that some sort of clearer picture had emerged, though not the one she had come seeking.

It was apparent that any personal experience with Isador Rabinowitz was an event of enormous intensity, especially when the glowing public image crashed into the vile meanness of the private man. She wondered how Rolf had managed to tolerate being his student and chosen protégé for the seven torturous years he had been under Rabinowitz's influence.

Somehow, all of this refreshed her view of Rolf. It made her feel closer to him. And, looking at all this from one perspective, she was surprised the old man had left as few emotional scars as he had. Viewing it from another angle, she had a much better understanding of the man she lived with and loved.

No wonder he liked to weave themes from Chuck Berry—particularly "Roll Over, Beethoven" and "Brown Eyed Handsome Man"—into passages of Ludwig van B's *Ninth Symphony*. It was Rolf's way—obviously one that he had developed under Rabinowitz's tutelage—of retaining his own sanity. Plus, as she thought it through further, it was a nifty way of simultaneously saying, *Fuck You,* to the old man and the music mafia that protected his villainy for half a century. There were many ways to save one's soul.

Diana was finished. She assembled the final clippings, counted them carefully and—

—and—?

"What?" she asked herself. Something was wrong.

Earlier she had counted out nineteen.

Now there were twenty.

She looked around. No one had set down any file on her table. No one was anywhere close to her. In fact, there was virtually no change in the room between the time she had gone downstairs and the five minutes later that she had returned.

She counted the clippings again. There were twenty. Either she had miscounted the first two times—unlikely—or one had been added.

She glanced through them again.

She had read them all, it seemed. What hadn't she noticed? What was—?

Her hand froze as it settled on something that never touched upon Rabinowitz by name. She read the headline.

SURVIVAL OF DEATH

Unlike every other clipping in the folder, this one had no marking to indicate its origin. It was just *there*. She had carefully kept track of everything she had read, and she was certain that it hadn't been there when she had gone downstairs.

She started to read.

OSLO, NORWAY. (AP) *May 17.*

Seven dozen European scientists and philosophers, meeting today in an extraordinary session at the Torkelsjohen Castle in Oslo, joined together to express a strong commitment to a modern spiritualistic reinterpretation of Christianity and Judaism. Central to the theme of the communiqué is the tenet that the soul, rather than passing on to the next world, remains at least for a short time within the physical confines of this world. Several case histories and experiments were cited which signaled significant evidence of contact with individuals who had been physically dead less than a year.

Writer-philosopher and Nobel Laureate Fridtjof Nansen, who chaired the proceedings, stated that the soul—

Diana stopped reading as she felt a funny twinge.

Where *had* this come from? And why was it nestled in with the other material on Rabinowitz? She turned it over as she examined it. There were absolutely no markings as to where it had been published. It didn't even seem as old as the other clippings, and, infuriatingly, there was no year marked upon it.

It was as if it had just been placed there. Just for her.

She tried to ignore its implications.

THE DEAD WALK AMONG US, DIANA. Untalented Rolf is not so crazy after all, ACCORDING TO SEVEN DOZEN SCIENTISTS AND PHILOSOPHERS.

She stared at the clipping for another moment. Then another strange feeling assailed her, one of being on view.

She raised her eyes and her heart jumped.

As she stared at the waiting area around the elevators, where three people were standing, one of them—an older man—turned quickly away from her.

He turned, it seemed, to prevent himself from being recognized.

But across the work desks, books, and card files, and through a plate-glass wall, she recognized the tattered soiled coat and the rumpled trousers. She knew her East Seventy-third Street watcher when she saw him.

Suddenly the extra clipping made sense.

He had placed it there! *Why!*

She bolted to her feet and moved rapidly around a corner toward the bank of elevators. She left the research room at a dead run.

One set of elevator doors opened and the three people waiting entered to descend.

"Wait! Hold it!" Diana yelled.

The doors started to close as she rushed toward them from the side, unable to gain a clear look at the passengers. The metal doors slammed completely shut as she reached them. She punched the doors with her fist, then madly pressed the door "Up" and "Down" buttons. But the elevator had gone.

Several seconds later, another set of doors opened for a different elevator car.

Diana rushed in and pressed the button for the first floor. The car made one infuriating stop during which a fat woman ambled on. Then it continued. Diana ran out of the elevator, through a ground-floor reading room and around the corner toward the exit from the library.

Far up ahead of her, going through the revolving door, she thought she saw the escaping watcher.

She ran through the entrance area, through the security checkpoint, and out the revolving door in pursuit. She was just seconds behind the man. But outside, she stopped.

She couldn't find him. He was gone.

Vanished.

She looked in each direction. There were not that many people around. But somehow he had slipped away. She heaved a deep, angry sigh. How could he have disappeared so quickly?

Something passed between her and the sun. The spring day suddenly felt cold. Diana turned and went back into the library, then took the elevator back upstairs. She took the same elevator car into which she had seen the old man disappear. She thought it still carried his stench.

When Diana returned to the research room on the third floor, she was both confused and angry. Her material was undisturbed.

She quickly assembled all the clippings and picked them up with their folders. She walked back to Harold Milsap, the librarian.

He sat at his desk and looked up expectantly from a magazine.

"Finished?" he asked.

"Yes."

He reached for the files. "Thank you," he said.

She hesitated.

"May I ask you something?" she inquired.

"Of course."

"Did you notice if anyone walked past the area where I was working? I was away for about five minutes."

"You were away twice. Once you walked. The second time, you ran."

"The first time," she said.

"I didn't see anyone. But I wasn't watching." He tapped a finger very slightly on his desk. "Something missing?" he asked.

"No. The opposite."

"The opposite of what?"

Diana handed him the clipping. "This *appeared* where I was working. I'm *certain* it wasn't there when I left."

He frowned. She handed him the clipping.

SURVIVAL OF DEATH

Milsap read the headline and the first paragraph, an ironic smile breaking out as he read.

"Mmm? Well," Milsap said. "This *is* uplifting." Then he shrugged. "But I don't suppose it should be in an Isador Rabinowitz file," he agreed.

"It wasn't there when I went downstairs," she repeated.

"Well, I have no idea where it came from," he said. "Magic, maybe?"

"I'm not amused."

"You're upset, aren't you?"

"Quite a bit," she retorted, growing angry. "You didn't see anyone come in and put it down?" she asked.

"No."

"I had the sense that an old man might have dropped it off."

"I'm an old man," he said playfully. "It wasn't me." He smiled.

"Older than you. Bent over."

"But you didn't get a good look?"

"No," she said. "I was reading. I *thought* I recognized an old man who was up here. He may be stalking me. That's why I'm asking you to treat this seriously!"

"Look," Harold Milsap said, relenting. "If this is troubling you, I'm sorry. Please be calm. There's really nothing uncommon about this."

"No?" she asked angrily.

"No. People lose clippings out of one file, then they stick them in another. Or the clipping fell to the floor from one file and someone picked it up and placed it among yours. It's not a problem. We'll keep it here at the desk till we decide where it belongs."

Diana felt a presence appear quietly beside her.

"All right," she said, calming and easing slightly. "It just seemed very strange."

There was a man standing next to her. She glanced at him and flinched slightly. It was the handsome man in the shirt and tie. He had been watching everything.

She quickly gathered her composure.

"Problem?" the man asked.

"You were in this room when I went out," she said. "You didn't see anyone place anything on my table, did you?"

"No," he answered amiably.

"And you didn't put anything there, yourself?"

"Why would I?" he asked.

"I don't know," she said.

A long pin-striped arm reached past her. The man moved with grace and strength, she noticed. He picked up the clipping and read part of it.

"Not from my files, either," he said to Diana. "Although I noticed that you're on the same topic as I."

"Yes. I noticed, too," she said.

"I'm finished with my file if you need it." He offered it to her.

"No. Thank you. I've seen enough."

He laughed slightly. "I wish I could say that," he said. His English was polished with a British accent, which surprised her.

"What are you writing?"

"A biography."

"On Isador Rabinowitz?"

"The one and only," he sighed.

She took a long chance. "Your name isn't Phillip Langlois, is it?"

"Yes, it is. And I assume you read it off the librarian's register," he said, not surprised at all.

"No," she said. "You've been trying to contact a friend of mine. Rolf Geiger."

"You know Rolf?"

"I live with him."

"Ah, I see," he said thoughtfully. Enlightenment swept Phillip Langlois's face. He produced a small leather case and withdrew a business card. On it, he wrote his hotel phone number in New York.

"Well, unhappily I might have guessed that such a lovely woman would not be unattached in this city," he said. "But I'm pleased to meet you."

"Same," she said aloud. *What a flirt. But smooth,* she thought. She glanced at his card. She couldn't completely decide whether he was full of charm or full of himself. She concluded it was a harmless mixture of both. So she let him get away with his flirtations.

"Look, call me," he said. "Anything you want to know about Isador Rabinowitz, I'll be glad to let you know. If I can help you, then maybe you could help me ask for an interview with Mr. Geiger. Does that sound fair?"

Milsap looked back and forth between the two of them, feeling like a referee at a tennis match.

"It's a deal," she said, accepting Langlois's card. "Definitely a deal."

He offered her hand, and she accepted it.

On leaving the library, Diana noticed that her pendant had broken and was gone from the chain. She had worn the silver piano pendant almost every day since Rolf had brought it back for her.

She was heartbroken. She was also certain it had been there when she had arrived at the library. She remembered fingering it while she was waiting for the files.

Distraught, she retraced her steps in the library and on the street several times. She couldn't find the pendant. Over and over, she searched the areas where she had run after the man in the tattered coat. No luck. She filed a report with the lost and found at the library, but she surmised that someone must have picked it up, and kept it.

Finders, keepers.

Later at the bus stop on West Sixty-fourth Street, she waited for the crosstown bus that would take her home. She thought about the silver pendant and knew that she would not immediately have the heart to admit the loss to Rolf. That evening, she decided, she would stash the chain in her jewelry box. Maybe miraculously, she told herself, the silver pendant would reappear.

The bus arrived and soon her mind went in a different direction.

As the crosstown bus entered Central Park to traverse the city to Manhattan's East Side, Diana saw a familiar figure sitting on one of the stone walls that bordered the park.

It was the old man. The watcher. Just sitting there.

His eyes were focused on the bus and seemed to lock with Diana's eyes as the bus passed.

How he knew she was there, and how he knew where to look for her, was something that she could not comprehend. And like so much else that was happening, it chilled her flesh and her soul.

fifteen

Diana arrived home in the late afternoon. She found Rolf in his library, still looking through a batch of fan mail that had been sitting out for a week.

"How did your day go?" he asked her.

"In terms of what I found on Isador Rabinowitz, nothing new. Unless the fact that he once had his picture taken with J. Edgar Hoover comes as a surprise to you."

"Nothing comes as a surprise to me," Rolf said.

"I also met one of the writers working on a Rabinowitz biography."

"Which one?"

"Phillip Langlois."

"Isn't he the one who's been trying to interview me?"

"Yes. He told me that." She paused. "I have his phone number," she said. "He's staying at a hotel in New York right now."

"What did he seem like?" Rolf folded away the letter and placed it in a box. It needed to be filed away in the downstairs coat closet with the rest of the fan mail. For the time, however, he set it aside.

"He seemed okay. Are you going to give him the interview?"

Geiger shrugged. "Probably. Maybe that will give me one friendly writer."

"Or maybe your own biographer someday."

He grinned as she walked past him and kissed him. Then she settled on the piano bench next to him.

"I thought maybe I'd meet him again," she said. "See about this book he's doing. Then I can give you a better idea about whether you really want to be interviewed by him."

"Makes sense, I suppose," he said.

"I can see what else I can learn about Rabinowitz, also."

"Don't we know enough already?"

"Maybe. Maybe not. Want to have dinner before the museum or after?" she asked.

"You choose."

"After," she said. "I also had another 'incident' at the library."

"Like what?" he asked.

"The old man who has been watching this building. I think he followed me."

Geiger stiffened. *"What?"* he asked.

"I thought I saw him on the research floor of the performing annex. Then a clipping turned up in my research material, one which hadn't been there earlier. Something creepy about survival of death. Then he was sitting on the stone wall of the park, watching my bus when it came back to the east side."

Geiger took this all in for a moment. A little surge of fear went through him, and he imagined that he felt pair of icy hands brush the nape of his neck. A little wave of goose bumps followed. What Diana was telling him seemed unreal. He tried to find some plausibility somewhere but couldn't.

"And you're . . . uh . . . ?"

"Sure that it was the same man?" she asked, finishing his question.

"Yes."

She looked away for a moment, then her gaze returned. "I'd swear it in court," she said. "But of course I can't prove it."

He thought about it again for a moment, then gave her hand a squeeze.

"What is he, Rolf?" she asked. "Some demented old fan?"

"Yes. Probably," he said, hoping that was all. "Every performer attracts a few screwballs. This one's mine."

"He scares me, Tiger," she said.

"Was he out there when you came home?" Geiger asked. He motioned with his head toward the front of their town house.

"No. He's not magical, I don't think. I left him on the West Side."

Geiger nodded, bothered by her phraseology. "Magical"? What did *that* suggest? Why had her perceptions inclined even-so-slightly in that direction?

"We'll have to deal with him," Geiger said, thinking aloud. "We can't let him bother us. Maybe I'll talk to the police. Maybe I'll pay him to stay away. I don't know, but I promise you we'll get rid of him. Okay?"

He put an arm around her shoulders and hugged her.

"Okay," she said.

A few minutes later, Diana went upstairs to dress for the evening at the museum. Rolf stayed at his Steinway. He began to gather his concentration again and settle into a score for Beethoven's Piano Sonata in A. The work was a favorite. He was already thinking ahead and would play the piece at the Academy of Music in Philadelphia if the date could be arranged. He felt his concentration on music sharpen for the first time in several days. He stayed at the Steinway till after six.

When Diana was ready to leave, she came downstairs. She was beautiful in a dark green dress. Rolf told her so. His preparation took less time. He threw on a sports jacket and they were gone. They both scanned their block for the watcher when they left, but—to their relief—he was nowhere to be seen.

Rolf and Diana walked along Seventy-third Street to Fifth Avenue, then up Fifth to the museum.

The evening was pleasant and the walk took twenty minutes, which they both enjoyed. There were photographers outside the main entrance to the Met. They spotted Rolf immediately as he started up the long stone steps. He managed a smile as he entered with Diana. The showing this evening was a private one for invited guests, two of whom—both young women—asked Geiger to autograph their programs. He obliged. The curator of the Renoir exhibit also came over to introduce himself. He mentioned other shows he was planning and said he would be happy to place Rolf's name on a standing list of celebrity invitees.

"That would be wonderful," Geiger answered. "I'd appreciate that."

"Consider it done, sir," the curator said. He gave Geiger a cordial nod. He had elevated obsequiousness to an art form.

This was a Monday night and Broadway was dark. Two well-known actors were there. One was knocking the city dead in a somber drama about a murder trial; the other—a high-testosterone matinee idol—was starring in a musical that had just opened and was doing a million dollars a week in business. Geiger appreciated their presence because they drew attention away from him and allowed him to walk through the gallery with Diana with a minimum of fuss. New Yorkers could stare and gawk just like people in any other city, Rolf knew. He appreciated anything that lessened the experience.

Diana ran into one person she knew, a female magazine editor with whom she had had her difficulties. The editor gave her an icy hello until she realized whom Diana was with. At that point her attitude warmed remarkably.

"Do let me know what you're working on," the editor said, her eyes sliding ceaselessly back and forth from Diana to Rolf and back.

"I'll give you a call next week," Diana said politely, ending the conversation.

"Do," said the editor. "So nice to see you."

Rolf suppressed a smile and gave Diana's hand a squeeze.

"No intention of calling her, right?"

"How did you guess?"

"I know you," he said.

There were fifty-eight canvases, drawn from collections all over the world. Geiger and Diana took their time looking at the entire show, though Diana's insights into the works were far more astute than Rolf's.

Diana was partial to many of Renoir's earlier works, the portraits of men and women from the 1870s. Those who had been immortalized in oil had wonderful Gallic names which resounded over the century:

The graying, bearded Victor Chocquet. A hauntingly pretty Jeanne Samary. A fresh-complexioned young man named Georges Rivière. A sultry but innocent young woman named Thérèse Bérard. And the nameless, but equally beautiful, lady with a veil, turned three-quarters away from the artist and the world.

Geiger shared Diana's fascination. But what arrested his attention was a canvas titled *Les Filles de Catulle Mendès*.

He stood for many minutes before it.

The work was a warm, elegant 1888 composition of three young girls gathered around a *belle époque* piano. Two of the girls were small. The third, whose left hand was on the keyboard had beautiful long golden hair. The middle child carried a violin. It occurred to Geiger that the music of these three girls had long ceased to be heard. They had lived their lives and gone to their graves. And yet two of the girls were staring into his eyes over the course of more than a century.

It wasn't creepy. It was rather beautiful, the way the artist had captured some part of their souls, something that now could never be taken away. But Geiger also wondered where their lives had gone, or to where their spirits had flown. He wondered if anyone anywhere still heard their music. He was reminded of the tapes of Raoul Pugno that he had listened to at Julliard.

Diana joined him. "Penny for your thoughts, Tiger," she said.

He hunched his shoulders.

"I like the pictures of seminaked women bathing, if that's what you're wondering," he said.

She elbowed him. "You would," she said.

But his actual thoughts—on three little girls and their music from 110 years ago—were too complicated even to start to unravel. As Diana and Rolf exited a few minutes later, Diana steered him to a quote in French from Renoir on a plaque near the entrance. In it, the artist referred to "the instincts of my fingertips."

It was an interesting point. Like great music, the creation of fine art demanded not only spiritual instincts and grand creativity, but also physical and tactile ones.

They left the museum at half past eight and headed home. When they were within a few blocks of 112 East Seventy-third Street, they stopped at a favorite small restaurant on Madison Avenue.

They had a light but satisfying dinner, then returned to the home they shared. Again, no watcher. Geiger carefully activated his alarm system and locked the front door behind him.

Rolf listened to his phone messages. There were six, eight if one included no-message hang-ups. "Phantoms," he used to call these empty messages, though he no longer cared for this terminology. The six messages contained nothing that couldn't wait until the next day. One was from Mrs. Jamison, who said she had a dentist's appointment in the morning and might not be in until ten.

Rolf went into the library and sat down at his Steinway. Diana joined him, snuggling onto the big comfy sofa with a book. She loved to read and have Rolf practice in the not-so-quiet background. She didn't find it distracting to have the music played so close by, and he rather liked having her near. The pursuit of his art was elusive and solitary enough. It pleased him to have a beautiful woman present.

This beautiful woman in particular.

"My muse," he liked to call her.

He settled in at the keyboard and again sought to unravel the mysteries of Beethoven's Sonata in A.

He unfolded the score and leaned forward from his bench. As he concluded some warm-up exercises and began to play, Diana rose to pick up the collection of fan letters that he had left on a nearby table. She would put them in the back of the coat closet on the main floor, where he preferred to store them.

Moments later, just as his fingers were readying themselves, Geiger became aware that Diana was now in the front alcove.

He heard her opening the door to the coat closet. Then the click of the light going on. He sensed a second's pause as she reached to the rear shelf in the closet to put away the fan mail, before hearing her close the closet door.

The tranquillity of the evening was shattered by Diana's

scream. It was a bloodcurdling yelp of terror that threatened to rattle, then shatter the glass throughout the house.

Diana's scream shot through Rolf. It propelled him from his bench at the Steinway, kicked his heart into his throat, and sent him running.

All he could think about was that Diana must have seen *him*.

Rabinowitz! The dead man was walking, finally visible, manifesting himself to someone other than Geiger!

Geiger *knew* Rabinowitz was there.

Somewhere.

"Diana! Diana!" Rolf yelled.

He burst from the library and saw her. She was recoiling against the closed closet door, her face white and her hands raised to her eyes in anguish.

"No, no! Get out!" she screamed. Then her terror was so complete that she couldn't speak. She could only gesture madly.

She pointed across the large entrance foyer to where a human figure stood just inside the front door.

The bent old figure came into focus. Geiger's angry eyes settled on the man standing in their home, the cause of Diana's screams.

When he recognized the man, his own stomach surged and leaped.

"What the—?"

Rabinowitz?

No?

It was the watcher. Somehow—*somehow*—he had gotten into their home.

Geiger's fear turned mercurially to anger. "What the hell are you doing here?"

Diana was so shaken that she was trembling. Rolf could see it. The intruder was only ten feet away from her.

"I don't mean you any harm," the old man said, backing slightly.

"Get out of here!" Geiger demanded. "How the hell did you get in?"

"The door was open."

"Like hell it was!" Geiger answered furiously. "I locked it."

"I came right through it!" the man insisted.

Geiger took up a position between him and Diana.

"It was *locked*," Geiger insisted.

The man smelled horrible. Geiger recoiled slightly.

"Rolf, be careful!" Diana said. She opened the closet hurriedly and pulled out a baseball bat.

"Out!" Geiger insisted to the man.

"I'm returning something," he said.

"Outside!" Geiger said. "Anything you have to say, you say outside."

The man protested. Geiger pushed him. There was something foul and awful to touching him. And something was wrong with his eyes.

At first Geiger couldn't move him. Then the man retreated a step. For someone who looked aging and frail he was surprisingly difficult to budge. Something strong and powerful locked in an old body. Then the watcher gave way.

"All right. I'll go," he finally said.

Geiger held on to the man's fetid old coat and pulled him to the front door. Geiger had the idea that he wouldn't have been able to move him had the old man not cooperated. There was something unspeakably strong beneath the surface.

Geiger opened the door. Voluntarily, the old watcher stepped through. He lurched one step down the front steps of the town house, then turned.

He looked up with imploring but now-gleaming eyes, eyes that seemed to change as Rolf watched.

"I found this," the watcher said. "I wanted to return it."

He reached out with a closed fist, then opened his hand. Geiger looked downward. In the watcher's palm was the small silver piano pendant that Rolf had purchased in San Remo.

"Your lady lost it," the watcher said.

Geiger was startled. Then he reached forward and carefully—with two fingers—took the pendant. The old hand withdrew.

"How did you know it was hers?" Geiger asked.

"You brought it back from Europe."

Geiger bristled again and felt an even deeper fear.

"How did you know that?"

"I read it in one of the newspapers."

"Which one? Which newspaper. No one printed *that!*"

The old man shrugged cryptically. "Somehow I knew," he said.

Geiger glared at him. "Don't ever come into this house again."

"Unless invited?"

"That won't happen."

"Unless invited?" the old man pressed.

"Yeah!" Geiger snapped, just to get rid of him. "Unless invited!"

The old eyes glazed. He gave Geiger an indignant look and turned away. He walked down the steps, turned, and made his way down the block.

Geiger, calming now, blew out a long breath. He stood on his front step as he watched the man go a few paces from the steps of 112 East Seventy-third Street. The old watcher stopped and turned. There was a new expression in his eyes when he looked up at Geiger. Something new that Geiger hadn't seen before.

"I'll go," the intruder said. "And you won't see me again. Not in this form, at least."

"What the hell does that mean?" Geiger asked.

The watcher laughed quietly. A car passed.

"I have more than one piece of jewelry," the watcher said. "More than one thing that glows or sparkles."

Geiger was trying to decipher the intruder's meaning when the old watcher held up his right hand. Geiger felt a bolt of shock streak through him. There was—for the briefest of moments—a dazzling sparkle from a finger on the man's hand. Like the glimmer of an emerald. Then the man lowered his hand and the reflection from the stone—if it really had been one—was gone.

It left Geiger speechless. The watcher turned and walked to the end of the block, toward Park Avenue. There Geiger lost him in the shadows and headlights.

Geiger stepped back into his home and closed the door.

"Jesus!" he muttered to himself.

Diana, still shaken, came to him. He held her.

"The door was locked," she said. "You locked it, Rolf."

"I know."

"I don't know how he got in."

"I don't either," he said, staring fearfully into the middle distance. "It's all right. He's out of here now."

But it wasn't all right, and Rolf knew it. Nor did he have any answer for her next question.

"How could I have not seen him?" she asked. "How could I have not seen him standing there the moment I left the library?"

"I don't know," he answered with a shudder.

"Where *was* he?" she demanded.

"I don't know," Geiger repeated.

Diana pulled away from Rolf for a moment and looked him in the eye.

"I want him removed from this block," she said. "I don't feel safe while he's around. I don't want to see him in here again or anywhere else." She paused. "Will you call the police or should I?" she asked.

"I'll call," he said. "I'm not convinced it will do any good. But I'll call."

sixteen

Detective Janet Solderstrom pulled her unmarked car to the curb before 112 East Seventy-third Street. She stepped out of her vehicle and drew a breath. She was a large woman, broad-shouldered and sturdy, standing almost six feet. She had frequently been mistaken for a man back when she walked a beat and wore a uniform. She had learned to curse like one, too.

She knew the block, having worked in Manhattan since the early 1990s. This neighborhood was peaceful and professional, the type of place where she was rarely summoned for anything violent. Yet housebreakings weren't uncommon.

She knew what types of people lived around here. They were attorneys, bankers, diplomats, and other professionals, with a few celebrities tossed in. These were people with money and power. They considered themselves to be the social superiors of ordinary police officers, she knew, even though many of them were only one generation away from the working class. Worse, they frequently didn't take female detectives seriously. Sometimes Solderstrom didn't hold their prejudices against them. Other times she did.

She walked to the front door of the town house and rang. She waited.

Solderstrom looked at the neighbors' houses and scanned across the street. She felt a low rumbling of displeasure within her. The money these people spent! They threw around millions of dollars to live on a block like this. In some cases they hadn't even made their own fortunes. They'd inherited. Or, she felt, ripped it off in some sleazy real estate or stock transaction. Every once in a while one of them would go out of control some night on booze or cocaine and kill someone, then hire one of their high-priced "mouthpiece" neighbors to try to beat the law.

Where was justice? Janet Solderstrom ached for the opportunity to bring down one of these hot shots.

She knocked louder the second time. Several seconds after her follow-up knock, the door opened.

A young man in his late twenties with a handsome but haggard, tired face loomed into view and answered.

Solderstrom pulled her gold shield from the breast pocket of her worn jacket. "Police Department," she said. "I'm Detective Janet Solderstrom."

She was such a large woman that she filled the doorway. Dressed in a plain brown suit which could have been a man's, she had pulled-back hair and a hard, pinkish face. She gave Geiger a tight smile.

"Of course, of course," Geiger said. "Come in."

"Thank you," the detective replied.

Geiger led Solderstrom into his home. She was ready to dislike him immediately, living in a place like this. But as she followed him, she felt her own attitude ease slightly. No, she didn't like wealthy people *per se,* but this young man didn't seem as condescending as so many of the rest. Maybe he'd be okay.

What she couldn't figure out was why he looked familiar. There was something about him. When he led her to his library and she saw the piano, and all the awards and accolades that were scattered around, she put two and two together to get four.

Geiger was capable of being impeccably polite. After a few seconds, he turned and offered a hand.

"I'm Rolf Geiger," he said. "Sorry if I seem upset. But I *am* upset. That's why we called the police."

Diana came into view and introduced herself. "I have no idea how many police would be involved," Geiger said. "Are there more coming?"

"Only if I call for them," Solderstrom answered. Her hands went on automatic pilot, pulling a ballpoint pen and a small notebook out of a jacket pocket.

"So you had an intruder? A burglar? What's the story?" Solderstrom asked. "Is this a good place to talk?"

"Right here is fine," Rolf Geiger said.

He motioned toward a new sofa. They sat, and he went through the events of the day. He briefly recounted his visit to his agent's office, Diana's trip to the library and so on. They had come home from a museum exhibition and been home for a while when their house had been intruded upon by a quirky older man.

A watcher. A stalker. An aging fan who looked harmless but who was growing increasingly aggressive.

Diana told about his appearance at the library, and how— after the watcher had taken up position down the block a few weeks earlier—he had now moved to a position across the street. All that, until tonight, when they found him within their home.

"He may be harmless, but he's starting to scare us," Geiger said. "And I don't know how he got in here."

"Do you know his name?"

"I only know he follows a lot of classical music," Geiger said.

"If he's located, do you want to issue a trespassing complaint?" Solderstrom asked.

"No," Geiger said. "Look, I was hoping you could just talk to him. Get him to stay off our block."

The detective shrugged. "No official complaint?" she asked.

"It might be easier for everyone," Diana said, "if someone from the police department *talked* to him."

"We want to be left alone," Rolf said. "That's all."

The detective thought about it. "I can talk to him. Where can I find him?"

They led her out of the library and into the front hall. They showed her where the man had been and how he had somehow gotten past the front door. Rolf walked Detective Solderstrom to a window and pointed to the steps across the street, the watcher's usual location.

"He sits *there*. Sometimes for days at a time," Geiger said.

"He shouldn't be hard to find," Diana chipped in. "He's been out there for a couple of weeks."

The detective steadily eyed the empty location. She searched the empty shadowy areas on the sidewalk across Seventy-third Street.

"For a couple of weeks, huh?" the policewoman finally answered. "But he's not there right now."

"I have no doubt that he'll be back," Rolf said. "He's a fixated fan. I think."

"Fixated, huh? I've heard of stuff like that happening," the detective said. "Guess he likes you too much."

"Sometimes people like that become dangerous," Rolf said.

"Did he threaten either of you?" Solderstrom asked.

"No," Geiger said.

"Anything missing?"

"No. In fact, he returned something."

The policewoman turned and peered at him. "Excuse me?"

He repeated the part about the missing pendant.

"Of course, who knows how he got it to start with?" Diana added. They walked away from the window and stood at the precise location in the entrance hall where the watcher had stood when Diana and Rolf had confronted him.

The detective looked back and forth, from one of them to the other. "There's not much I can do unless you file a complaint," she said. She thought about it. "I suppose I can have someone keep an eye on the block," she offered. "If they see anyone camped out across the street, fitting the description you have, we'll have a chat with him. Would that be what you're asking?"

Diana and Rolf looked at each other in relief. "That might help quite a bit," they said. "That might work just fine."

Detective Solderstrom again said she would see what she could do. Moments later, she was gone. Thirty minutes later, Diana and Rolf were upstairs, frightened out of their own home, packing a pair of small suitcases.

That same midnight, they temporarily moved a few blocks away to the Westbury Hotel, registering under the name of Mr. and Mrs. Raoul Pugno. The press did not discover them, and the bell captain and front desk staff were discreet.

"Good morning, Madame Pugno," the staff would address Diana as she went out for a walk in Central Park in the morning.

"A phone message for you, Signor Pugno, sir," they would say to Rolf as he reentered the hotel in the afternoon.

Rolf came and went from his town house during the afternoon. He needed to work at the piano. He did not feel entirely safe in the building. He was certain that the angry ghost of Rabinowitz was lurking there somewhere. But the ghost—if there was one—seemed to control when he made his own appearances. Geiger probably should have been even more scared, considering that a visitation might have occurred at any time. But he wasn't.

Nor did he know what was more frightening: the idea that something supernatural was lurking or the notion that something live and earthly—a seemingly decrepit old man—had broken into their home?

Against the latter possibility, Geiger contacted a security consultant, a short, squat, mean-looking man named Peter Arroyo.

Arroyo, the son of an anti-Castro Cuban exile, was a former U.S. Marine sergeant. He knew a few things about security and agreed to do a complete analysis of Geiger's home and suggest what sort of further security was needed.

Trying to concentrate anew on music, Rolf wondered what was next. He sensed that bad things often came in bunches, and every once in a while, unsolicited, the idea of Diana's death came into his mind. He figured it was much like the free-floating fears that some parents have for the safety of their children. There was no rational reason to think anything would happen to her. But the suggestion of her death had been put into his mind by one of those visions of Rabinowitz. Now he couldn't shake the thought. Every once in a while, he looked at the woman he loved when she was standing next to him, and uttered a silent prayer.

Normally he didn't pray. He had long since given up the faith of the nuns, the priests, and his early influence, Brother Matthew. But he put in a prayer here, anyway, just in case Someone was listening.

Rolf also entertained the idea of some sort of impending doom, an innate sense seemed to tell him that some deadly force was closing in on him. If there were to be a second funeral, he prayed that it would be his own before it would be Diana's. He did not know—at this point in his life—how he could ever survive her death.

To add to his anxiety, the tabloid press, first in New York and then across the nation, was taking the occasional shot at him. Somewhere someone was feeding them tidbits that were just within the bounds of the libel laws:

Geiger was into the occult.

Geiger was on the verge of a nervous breakdown.

Geiger was unable to summon the artistic fervor needed for his next tour, and friends feared for his welfare.

Rolf had been photographed from a distance in New York several times recently, and these pictures appeared with this creative text. It only added to his sense of being stalked, though ironically his "watcher" seemed to have disappeared, at least temporarily. But Geiger was treated in the yellow media much like a wayward rock star, so much so that he was almost convinced himself that this was what he was.

He was, after all, reclusive, and more than a little out of the ordinary. He had been a star in his teens, a sex symbol. He lived with a woman to whom he was not married. He sometimes said strange things.

He was turning, in fact, into a *dandy* target. One more reason, he thought to himself as he practiced at his Steinway one morning, why it was incumbent upon him to get out onto the recital stage again.

Get out there and wow the planet. In some ways, preparation for the world tour was turning into his lifeline for the future.

The next morning, his new security consultant, Mr. Arroyo, stopped by. They walked through the house together.

Arroyo was gravely shaking his head, showing Geiger windows that were secure and doors that had not been touched or jimmied.

"I really don't know. I really no understand," Arroyo said. "We can put new alarm system in. I do everything you want. But you know what, Mr. Krieger?"

Geiger didn't bother to correct the inaccuracy of his name. "What?"

"I do it if you want me to, put some alarm system in. But I think you buying something you no need. I analyze your home and I don't see no way that any bad guys get in. You got good alarm system now on the windows and doors. I dunno. Maybe you should get a dog."

"I'd love a dog. A big mean one with a lot of sharp teeth. But I travel a lot," Geiger said indulgently.

"Yeah. I hear you. I understand. Myself, I don't like dogs, either. Big dogs, they eat a lot. I live in a bad neighborhood. Bronx. I got a gun at home for my wife."

"I'd like some sort of alarm system that's more sophisticated than what we have now," Geiger said.

"I can do it if you want."

"Part of what I'm buying, Mr. Arroyo," Geiger said, "is peace of mind for the woman I live with. Can you understand that?"

"Sure. That's why I bought my wife a gun."

"Yesterday on the telephone you mentioned an alarm system that's vibration-sensitive, and which I could turn on and off from the bedroom."

"Yeah, I can do that one. That's a good one."

"That's the one that shows if there are any movements in the downstairs even while I'm upstairs."

"Is a very excellent system. It don't keep people *out*, you know. Don't keep nobody *out*. You gotta secure your doors and windows for that. But it tells you if anybody's got in. It reads vibration and body heat. That's why it's sensitive to all human or animal movement."

"That's what I want."

"If you want it," Arroyo said, sensing a few thousand dollars' worth of quick work. "I have it and I can put it in for you. Okay?"

"Okay," said Rolf, anxious to get this done. There was nothing quite like a gabby tradesman to waste his time and get the day off to a rotten start.

Arroyo glanced down at his work sheet.

"Oh," he said. "It's *Geiger*. Not *Krieger*." He pronounced them both as if they rhymed. As in, Gee-ger. Kree-ger.

"Geiger," Rolf confirmed. "Two syllables. Guy—ger."

Arroyo apologized profusely, then blew the pronunciation again on his next trip past Geiger's name.

"I had another Mr. Krieger as my customer," Arroyo said. "Man lived down near St. Vincent's Hospital, then bought another apartment in Orange County. I fixed the security on both places."

"Is that right?" Geiger asked, with no interest whatsoever.

"This Krieger was a former army officer. Must've been a general or something. And an excellent tennis player. I opened a closet and must've been two hundred tennis balls roll out. What do you do with two hundred tennis balls. How can you play with two hundred balls at once?"

Geiger said he had no idea.

"I remember, he had a lovely wife. Austrian woman. Or maybe it was Australian. Where do they play tennis?"

"Both. But you're probably thinking of Australia."

"I think that's what it was. Australia. That's probably where he learned to play tennis. Australia. They hit the ball upside down there, you know," he said with a wink. "Hit a shot too high and it falls off the earth."

"Uh-huh. How soon can you get the alarm system in here?" Geiger asked, losing patience.

"Today."

"Let's do it," Geiger said.

Arroyo called in two of his assistants, who brought over an array of electronic boxes, wires, and switches.

By five o'clock they had entirely installed the system. Rolf, thinking the situation through, was increasingly skeptical that this particular system, sensitive to any physical movement or touch, would really solve the problem that confronted him.

seventeen

―――――――――――――――
―――――――――――――――
―――――――――――――――

Rolf Geiger and Diana moved back to Seventy-third Street after five days in the Westbury.

On the first afternoon home, the ringing of the telephone shattered an afternoon practice at the Steinway. Geiger stopped playing and stared at the phone. It wouldn't stop. It rang sixteen times before Rolf finally went to answer it.

"Yes?" Geiger answered.

The benevolent voice of Brian Greenstone came over the line. "Rolf?" he asked.

"What?"

"Sorry. Am I disturbing you? I keep calling this number and no one answers. Do I have a client at this location anymore?"

"Sorry. I've been out a lot," Geiger answered flatly.

"You don't sound so chipper. You all right?"

"I'm all right."

"Don't you understand that I get worried unless you do something to annoy me every day?"

"Okay. I understand," Geiger said. He himself managing a smile. Brian had that effect.

"Well, look, lad," Greenstone said. "I have joyous tidings.

The Academy of Music called back. You're set up for June 11 in Philadelphia, as we discussed.''

The date fell upon nearly deaf ears.

"Does that still sound good for you, Rolf?''

"I think so,'' Geiger answered.

"You 'think'? I could call them on Monday and see how long they can hold the date open if you're unsure.''

Geiger thought about it.

"No. On the contrary. I'm sure,'' he said, warming quickly to the certainty of the time and venue. "Now I need to play all the more.''

"I'll still hold off on the contract for a day or two. Okay?''

"Okay, but not necessary.''

Rolf now had an important professional date toward which he needed to point himself. The problem was, every time he sat down to play in his home, or to plan his program for Philadelphia, he felt as if the old man were somewhere close by, shaking his head in disapproval, listening with the most critical ear in the universe.

It's all shit, Rolf Geiger. Everything you play is shit!

The old man had once concluded a lesson by telling him that. Years later, Rabinowitz had come to a recital and said the same thing aloud from the audience.

Today, and the day before, and probably two days hence, over his shoulder, beneath his consciousness, he would hear that obnoxious *mitteleuropa* voice saying the same thing or working variations upon it.

Today, your playing was not so much shit. It was crap.

"Gee. Thanks,'' Rolf answered.

You are very welcome. Someday you should learn to play music more than noise.

Noise.

"Well, fuck *you*, too, old man!'' Geiger whispered aloud in his library one afternoon, summoning his nerve for a spiritual counterattack. "I'll dance on your grave yet.''

Moments later, as if in response, the A-sharp key above middle C refused to work. *The key wouldn't move!* It was as if something were within the body of the piano, freezing the action.

Rolf got up from the bench, highly agitated, and paced. When he sat down again the key worked. He kept his responses to himself for a time thereafter.

Sometimes, entire days were the colors of the old man's dark spirit. On some days, while dressing on the second floor, Rolf was certain that he heard piano music coming from the library, just loud enough to transcend the extensive soundproofing.

Geiger would run downstairs and look. But the library would always be empty. Or appear empty. He broke into a sweat frequently. He did not sleep well. He kept feeling for the icy touch of a pair of hands on his throat.

Every little creak in a floorboard—day or night—unleashed a little army of terrors. For the first time ever, Rolf found himself turning on the radio or television to spoken words instead of music while home alone. He even found himself leaving extra lights on to ward off the darkness.

One night, while sleeping comfortably, he was jounced by the feeling of motion in his bedroom. His eyes came open like window shades snapping upward. He realized what had roused him. Someone had been moving on his mattress and was now moving in the room.

His heart gave a quiver of fear. His eyes settled upon a filmy figure across the room. He threw out his right arm to find Diana, but simultaneously he realized that it was she whom he was watching.

She was naked and had her back to him. Her skin looked very white in the darkness. Her body was illuminated very slightly by the light from the streetlamps that slipped past the bedroom shades.

Now *she* looked like a ghost, he found himself thinking. He was horrified anew by the thought of her death, because she was as alive as he was. The thought scared him, the ease with which it could hop into his mind.

He watched her. His eyes adjusted to the minimal light. She—and this whole incident—were very much like a dream. Several minutes went by. Diana stayed by the bedroom window looking downward and outside to the street.

She must have sensed his eyes on her body for she looked

his way and smiled slightly. She knew his eyes were open and gazing at her.

"Tiger?" she said.

"What's wrong, honey? Is he out there again? Our 'watcher'?"

"No. He's not there."

He waited to hear what else was bothering her. Specifically, he waited for her to tell him that she had seen a ghost. In the house. Outside the house. But it wasn't quite like that. Not this night.

"I had a very bad dream," she said softly.

"Come over here and tell me about it," he said, sitting up. He moved a hand to the bedside lamp. "Do you want light?" Rolf asked.

"No."

She walked back toward him. He couldn't help but admire the lovely sexuality of her body as she approached him. Naked, she so often reminded him of something from a painting by a French master.

She arrived at the bed and he gently guided her back to him. Her body felt warm and safe beside his.

"So tell me," he said comfortingly. "Tell me about your dream."

"No," she said again.

He embraced her with one arm.

"It must have been *very* bad," he said.

She was so upset she couldn't speak immediately.

Finally. "It was, Tiger," she said, her voice laden with emotion and barely audible. "It was horrible."

"Will you tell me tomorrow?" he asked. "In daylight?"

After a moment's consideration, she answered.

"No. Probably not. I'm hoping it will go away. All right? I don't ever want to tell you about this one."

"It can't be any worse than some of the ones I've had recently."

"I don't know," she breathed.

"Did something bad happen to one of us in the dream?"

He felt her hesitate and then nod. He was afraid to ask who had died. Him or her. He was afraid to put the thought any more concisely in the air.

"Diana, it was only a dream," he reminded her. "We've both been under some awful stress. When you're stressed in your waking hours, you're going to be stressed in your sleeping hours, too. Okay?"

Another long pause and she said, "Okay."

"That's what's going on."

"I don't want to die, Tiger," she whispered. "And I don't want you to die, either. And I've never been so scared of it in my life."

Downstairs, something creaked in the house.

Heat? The furnace wasn't on.

Another intruder?

The *same* intruder?

The ghost again?

Or just one of those old house creaks. Inexplicable, day or night?

He sure as hell hoped so. He broke into a small sweat, anyway, and reminded himself that he had just paid top dollar for a state-of-the-art alarm system.

Whatever was down there, he wondered, could it fly beneath the system's radar?

"Yes, I can."

Rolf held Diana for several minutes, hardly knowing what to say, not wanting to admit that he was every bit as frightened as she, maybe even more.

He tried to hum the *Moonlight* Sonata to her. For a while it worked. It calmed her. So he allowed several more minutes to pass.

"Do you remember that black dog on the beach in Nantucket?" she finally asked.

He was surprised by the question. "Sure. Why?" he asked.

"Did you notice anything strange about it?" she asked.

He considered the question for a moment.

"*Everything* was strange about it," he finally said. "Its behavior. Its god-awful smell. The way it appeared to be so different from one day to the next. Why?"

"It smelled like death," she said. "Didn't it?"

"It smelled like it had been rolling in horse manure," he said reaching to make light of it or everyday rational sense of it in any way possible. "And there are a couple of horse farms right nearby."

"That was the smell of death, Rolf," she said. "I know it was. That was the smell of rotting flesh. That wasn't an ordinary dog."

"Diana . . . The old man who broke in here had a similar stench," he said. "And he wasn't dead."

"No?" she asked. "Maybe he is."

There was something ominous in her voice, hideous in her suggestion. Worst of all, her dark thoughts were dangerously close to his own, underscoring every fear that gripped him.

"You're still in your bad dream," he said. "You're making a lot of nonsense at a scary hour of the night."

"Okay," she whispered. "Then I'll be quiet."

But in truth, neither of them wanted to continue this line of "reasoning" to its next logical plateau.

There was another creak from downstairs. It seemed farther away. Outside on an otherwise-empty Seventy-third Street, a drunk was going by, singing "Good Night, Irene" in a magnificently resonant tenor voice to each passing doorway. As the drunk reached Park Avenue, he began a rendition of "The Mighty Quinn."

"I don't want to die, Tiger," Diana said again. "And I don't want you to, either. Not for a long, long time."

Her words trailed away. The last syllables were very low.

He was about to phrase a reply, but realized that she had slipped back into sleep. The slumber seemed peaceful this time. So he held her protectively while she rested, hoping somehow to shield her from the travail of more nightmares. He ended up remaining awake until the light of dawn was creeping past the window shades.

One more dawn, he thought to himself. And both he and Diana had survived another night.

Later in that same day, still mystified by the events of the early morning, Rolf asked Diana to join him on a short walk. She was more than happy to go with him and get out of the house.

He led her westward across Seventy-third Street to Central Park. When he had guided her to a sufficiently peaceful setting and a matching state of mind, he asked if her mention of the black dog in Nantucket had something to do with her bad dream.

She said it had. They continued to walk.

When he pressed the question and asked how it tied in, when he inquired as to what had happened or what the dream meant, she again refused to answer.

She said something about an image from long ago, a bad dream she had as a little girl, and she said there was something within all of it that she never thought could happen. But which now seemed possible.

He squeezed her hand again.

She sighed.

They walked for a hundred yards in silence. "When will you tell me about your dream?" he asked.

She thought about it. "I dreamed that you decided that I was interfering with your career," she said. "So you murdered me."

He felt as if his ability to speak had been taken away from him. He had never had a sensation like it before.

"And I don't ever wish to discuss it again," she said. "Not one single word."

eighteen

Four nights later, toward midnight, Rolf went to his library and sat down in his reading chair. He spent several minutes sitting perfectly still and thinking. Diana had already gone upstairs to sleep.

Again, he didn't know which was the most terrifying:

The fact that the watcher had entered his home, with no sign of forced entry.

The notion that the ghost of Isador Rabinowitz haunted him.

Or a combination of the two.

How could he ever live here comfortably again?

And what about the dream or vision or intuition Diana had had? She still wouldn't tell him exactly what had gone through her head, as if giving words to it would somehow enhance its chances of occurring.

The truth tormented him and eluded him. Yet, he had to know it eventually.

Had to.

Right now, it was standing in the way of his performing. He had to know what sort of demon or ghost or spirit or fear or quirk in the universe he was confronting.

Somehow, he had to make it come forth so that he could

see it. Force it out of the shadows. Force it out of the gray recesses of his mind. He shuddered again. He thought back to that foul-smelling ill-mannered animal and how it seemed to have snapped at his hands.

"Jesus, life is weird sometimes," he admitted to himself.

More than weird, he realized.

Terrifying. Just when you think you have reality figured out, a window opens to another dimension. And you don't know if you dare to step through. Who the hell knows what you would find on the other side.

The other side. He turned those words over in his head. Life used to be as simple as the infinite variations that an artist could find on a keyboard. Now it was more complex than theologians and philosophers could ever have imagined.

Geiger sighed and rose from his chair.

He wandered to the kitchen and turned on a small color television that sat at the end of one counter. He made a sandwich, then found a bottle of beer in the refrigerator. It was very cold. The way he liked it.

He liked it so much that he had a second one immediately.

He sat down in the kitchen and tried to calm himself.

Deep down, he knew what he was facing. The supernatural explanation was the only one that made any sense.

He picked up the remote control, to channel surf. For one of the first times in his life, he had had enough of music.

Enough about God damned Beethoven. Enough about Chopin and enough about whether or not he would play such and such a concerto in Paris.

Fuck it, he thought. *Fuck all of it. Music, music, music, art, art, art. Who the hell cares?*

What, he wondered, was the value of his craft compared with the value of life? He thought back to a quote he had seen once from an artist who had said that if he had been in a burning museum and could save a Rembrandt or a stray cat, he would choose the stray cat.

Meow. *Aristotle Contemplating the Bust of Homer* is being broiled and baked, but *meow*.

The thought amused him. Of course, he mused further, if

the artist had *owned* the Rembrandt his response might have been different.

Rolf cursed again to himself.

He realized that he had grown much more profane over the last few weeks. He had long considered profanity a highly undignified act. It reminded him of his dirtball relatives in West Virginia and old Rabinowitz, who couldn't articulate *fuck* from *fock*. These days, he seemed to have become profane and didn't much care about it anymore.

Geiger kept flicking the remote control to the television.

Suddenly, bull's eye.

Baseball. The New York Yankees were playing the Philadelphia Phillies in one of these new scheduling arrangements.

Perfect. Interleague play at last.

Geiger was a baseball iconoclast. He liked the Designated Hitter, he liked the new divisions, and he liked interleague play. What he didn't like was pretentious people pontificating about some other era of the game in rusty, sweaty, cigar-stenched old parks.

The Yankees.

Geiger admired the excellence and the tradition with the passion that only adopted New Yorkers can muster. Best yet, on this evening, the Yankees had no special musical significance at all, other than their insistence on playing Sinatra's rendition of "New York, New York" after each game. Geiger even liked that in its nervy in-your-goddamn-face belligerence.

Tonight, as he finished half the sandwich and then grabbed a third beer, he was in the mood for some assertive Sinatra braggadocio.

Make it an Italian special, he contended. From the *genti* who brought him Verdi, Puccini, Rossini, and Vivaldi, now how about some Sinatra brio, with a touch of Rizzuto, a memory of DiMaggio, and a trace of Girardi? All this right now seemed like a damn sight better idea than any rubato, arpeggio, or multo vivace that he could think of.

He tried to do a pan-Italian Yankee lineup. Berra, Pepitone, DiMaggio, Crossetti, Rizzuto. Billy Martin would manage. For reasons of pure mischief, Sal Maglie—who had passed through the Bronx in the latter days of his career—would pitch.

Ah, great, he thought, his attention returning to the present. The Yankees were pounding the Phillies. Who said there was no such thing as quality television?

He smiled for a moment. Then he finished the third beer. He didn't normally quaff suds this way, but Diana was asleep upstairs and he felt he had earned it.

More than that. He felt tonight that he *needed* it. He *needed* to just crash out and get lost for one evening. Then he could put his mind in order in the following days and quickly prepare for the Philadelphia concert.

Philadelphia?

Why, yes. There was even a symmetry emerging here. He was watching Philadelphia play baseball. Would Phucking Philadelphia come to watch him play the piano?

He knew they would. As much of the city as could fit into the creaking but majestic old Academy.

He settled back. Brew helped him think. Sometimes. So he grabbed a fourth.

Seeing the ghost the other day had turned his brain inside out. Yet in some ways, it had been a liberating experience. After all, now that he knew that ghosts existed, and that Rabinowitz was floating around out there somewhere, along maybe with everyone else . . . well, what the hell? Was there any line of thought he couldn't entertain now? If ghosts were possible, hadn't the underpinnings of his religion and his sense of the rational world been completely redefined?

An image of Brother Matthew came before him again, his onetime friend and confidant. He wondered how Matthew would counsel him in this situation.

A mad urge was upon him. Pick up the phone and call the Franciscan brother. He would be easy to find as he was back at St. Agnes' School.

Of course, could a man in Rolf's position just pick up the phone after a dozen years and glide gracefully into a chat about the supernatural?

Then again, why not?

Thoughts seemed to cascade forth from the past. Visions of childhood. Poverty. Abuse. The ability to use his great musical gift to rise above all this.

His reverie lasted for several minutes. At the end of it, he wondered where he was.

He was in New York he reminded himself. He snapped to attention as he sensed the presence of the ghost.

Geiger took a long gulp of his beer. He finished his sandwich. He raised the beer-in-progress to his lips and knocked back half of it with one long swig.

He had a bizarre feeling. He almost felt combative now. Alcohol was a great equalizer.

"Hey, Rabinowitz! Where are you?" he shouted. "Isador! You old bastard! Come on out!"

To any witnesses, he would have looked like a madman. One arm flailed at the air, in case the specter was within reach. Geiger listened to an echo bounce quickly around his home. Then he laughed aloud.

Something made him think of his father. Geiger grinned. Maybe there was a hell for the old man to burn in after all, he reflected. Maybe Frank Geiger and Isador Rabinowitz could line up next to each other at the Great Latrine of Hell and exchange insults as they aimed their streams.

He could count on something anti-Semitic from his father. He was equally confident on something profane from Rabinowitz.

Geiger looked around. Then he rose from the kitchen table and, carrying the bottle of beer with him, walked into his library.

"*Anyone here?*" he called out. "*Anyone* else *here?*" he demanded.

No response again.

"Hey!" he shouted aloud. "*How's life after death so far, Isador?*"

No response. He laughed again.

"You contrary old bastard!" Geiger mocked. "You want to be alive again?" he ranted as the full effects of drunkenness came upon him. "I'll make you wish you weren't!"

Geiger's hands found the keyboard. He zipped off a Chopin Fantasie, playing it the way Geiger wanted to play it. Then he decided to muck it up. He transmogrified it into something ugly, giving it an annoying disco beat.

"Chop, chop, Choppin' at your, door!" Geiger proclaimed

to the tune of "Knock, Knock Knockin' at Heaven's Door."
" 'The Man with the Ax' plays in concert tonight!"

The chords thundered. Geiger assaulted the keys relentlessly.
The whole work was out of whack.

"Can I raise a ghost?" he asked. "Can I offend a sleeping
spirit? Sure! I can always play a little something to raise the
fucking *God damned* dead!"

He played *Pictures at an Exhibition.* One of Rabinowitz's
pets.

"You put the music out for me, Isador. So maybe you'd like
to hear it."

Geiger started playing the main themes, but these pictures
at Rolf's imaginary exhibition were from Mapplethorpe.

That would have the old man sizzling.

Geiger proclaimed it aloud as he hit noisy ugly themes:

Queer couples. Defiled flowers. A crucifix dipped in—
Mapplethorpe, Mezzathorpe.
Heidi high, Heidi ho.
The fucking ghost,
Gotta Go!

"Hey, Isador, you frustrated old goat! How about, Pictures
of an Exhibitionist, instead?"

Into the themes from Chopin, Geiger nestled themes from
Queen. "Radio Ga-Ga" intertwined around an arpeggio. Then
"Bohemian Rhapsody" floating with great finesse through a
Chopin rhapsody.

Mama, mia, Mama mia!

Yeah. The old man could take the late, great Freddie Mercury
and listen to him till he kicked the lid off his coffin.

"Come on, Rabinowitz!" Geiger taunted. "Where are you!
Where the *fuck* are you?" he screamed, cursing with a nastiness
for which he might have once censured the old man.

He crushed the right pedal on the piano. The music filled
the chamber, rattling some figurines on the nearby shelves.
Geiger's hands thundered with a power that might have pulverized the keys and harps of lesser instruments.

Then Geiger burst from the bench screaming, as music
echoed within the heavily soundproofed room.

''Where are you?'' he bellowed again. *''Where, where, where? Come out! I know you're here!''*

Geiger went from closet to closet in the library, throwing the doors open, tearing the contents from within. He crashed around the room, knocking over books and scores, sending a standing lamp tumbling to the carpet. It hit with a crash. Its porcelain bowl shattered.

Geiger stood in the center of the room and got off a long final scream. His heart thundered. The sound of the music he had just made receded like a daydream.

Then he felt a presence. He felt the conduit from one world to the next.

He wandered out to the front foyer of his home. He went to the window and stared out.

The watcher was waiting for him. The old man was standing there, as Geiger knew he would be. Waiting for him. Waiting to be summoned.

''Unless invited.''

Geiger stared downward. By the shadowy illumination of the streetlamps, he could see the features of this unwanted sentry. The watcher's eyes seemed to glow like coals as he glared upward. Geiger's body was bathed in sweat. He could hear the kettledrum of his own heart.

Rolf averted his eyes and shook his head. A conduit from the dead and back to life.

''Invite me in.''

''No.''

''Invite me in!''

''Yes.''

Geiger looked downward through the window to the street. The watcher's face creased with a demonic grin. The figure on the street fixed Geiger with taunting eyes.

''Yes.''

Geiger turned and lurched slightly. He held his hand up and braced himself against a wall. He wove his way back to his library. He went to the center of the room, breathing hard. He was there when his nose picked up again the horrible stench of decaying flesh. The air pressure in the room seemed to change.

Geiger looked up with a start. The watcher was in his home now. He stood in the open doorway of the library. Solid and substantial, as defiant and bold as the clapper on a new bell.

Geiger stared at him. His fear plateaued. What now could happen that hadn't already happened? Geiger watched as the old man's image faded out before Geiger's eyes. The watcher disappeared.

Or actually, he moved. From one location to another. Invisibly through the air. Geiger knew exactly what was to follow.

With his back to the piano, ever so slightly, Rolf heard something.

A tap. A very slight tapping.

It was almost inaudible. An infinitesimally soft touch to a key of the Steinway. An old Rabinowitz mannerism as a prelude to playing.

Removing specks of dust from the keys. Soft as an angel.

What hearing Geiger had!

He had sensed the sound of a man's learned fingers settling upon the keyboard in preparation for playing.

Yes! Rolf knew he had heard it. The sound, barely above a silence, of the flesh—*if that's what it could be called on a ghost's fingers*—settling on the keys.

Rolf spoke aloud to the room.

"You should hold your fingers higher," Geiger taunted. "Your fingering sucks."

Then he cringed. He could see—*he could even hear*—the skin of his visitor's face stretch into a frozen cadaverous smile.

Then Geiger thought he heard a slight laughter.

"Turn around, Rolf."

"Not till I hear you play," Geiger answered.

"Have it your way, you young fraud!"

Geiger knew.

The ghost was now fully present. Same as he had been present all along, same as he had been present on the stairs those several nights ago.

"Present," a very drunken Rolf Geiger now said to himself. "First in my mind, then in my home."

"Next in your fucking soul forever!"

"No," Rolf answered. "Anything but that!"

Then Rolf *did* hear laughter. He heard the fingers come down on the keys. Ever so sweetly, ever so exquisitely, the late Isador Rabinowitz began to play for a small private audience of one.

A brilliant flourish and arpeggio to start. A rubato to bring tears to the angels. A Chopin to make women cry.

"Turn around, Rolf. Observe the excellence of which you will every day never be capable."

Geiger steeled his nerves. He braced himself for what he would see.

"You wished to see me? Well now you will see me."

As he heard the music swell, Geiger turned.

The watcher had been transformed out of his earthly disguise. The true identity was revealed. There at the keyboard was Rabinowitz, solid and substantial, dead for two months, sitting and playing Geiger's Steinway.

Geiger didn't scream. He didn't bolt and didn't faint. For some reason, after all that had happened, it seemed strangely natural. The master was back.

It was the logical conclusion of events. Or if not the conclusion, the next important step. Rabinowitz back from the dead.

To haunt him?

Forever?

"Maybe," said Rabinowitz.

Chopin continued. A ravishingly pretty polonaise. It contrasted magnificently with the terror Rolf felt.

"Next step to whereabouts, young Rolf?" Rabinowitz asked casually from the piano. **"Do you know where you're heading?"**

Rolf broke into a hot sweat. "Why are you here?

"I'm here for you, Rolf," the master said.

"What the fuck does that mean?"

The old man made a tsking motion with his dry dead tongue. His lips moved as he spoke.

"Your language is vile," Rabinowitz said.

"I learned it from *you.*"

The old man shrugged. He threw off a brilliantly piquant rubato.

"You learned *nothing* from me," the ghost insisted. **"And at least, if had you learned *something* from me, I would**

have though preferred it to be musicianship. A seriousness about your art."

The ghost hummed softly, an odd rasping sound, and continued. **"If you have to picked up a habit from me, why couldn't have been it a good one?"** Rabinowitz asked.

"What do you *want* from me?" Geiger demanded.

The old man's eyes, alternatively shimmering and hollow, rested on Geiger. There was a skeletal grin on his lips in response to the question. Then he broke into a joyfully campy rendition of "Heart and Soul."

"That's what I've always wanted," Rabinowitz said. **"Your heart and your soul."**

Geiger cringed again. He began to move slowly in the library. But he had a sense of moving as if in a dream.

He was floating, not touching the ground.

Or am I staggering, he wondered, *drunk out of my mind?*

He seemed to revolve around the piano, even though he was attempting to approach it. Obviously, he concluded quickly, he couldn't control his own movements with the ghost present. As had so often been the case, Rabinowitz was his master.

"Are you sleeping well these days?" Rabinowitz asked.

"Hardly at all."

"That's good," the ghost answered cheerfully. He raised his eyes and seemed to be focused upon his young protégé. **"And I will arrange for you now to sleep even worse."**

"Please don't."

His eyes established contact with Geiger's. Then the eyes were gone for a flash and there was a yellow rotting emptiness in the sockets.

Geiger jerked backwards and felt an equal hollowness in his gut. The sensation was half fear, half revulsion. Geiger stifled a gasp. Rabinowitz's face contorted, the eye sockets filled in, and the gleaming mean eyes were back.

Rabinowitz continued to speak, ignoring Geiger's plea for quiet.

"Imagine that when you die your brain doesn't really die," the ghost continued evenly. **"Oh, to the modern doctors your brain has ceased to have electrical charges. So they think it's dead. But not really. Just your body. So they**

pump you with embalming fluid, put you in a coffin, slam the lid, and let you lie there thinking, unable to move, for eternity.''

''Is that what it's like? Death, I mean?''

Rabinowitz raised a single brow. He played a few bars of a mazurka next. **''You'll find out,''** he answered.

The master kept playing. **''Let's say, I'm familiar with death. Would you like to be familiar with it, too? Sometime soon?''**

''No.''

''Your lady is going to die, you know. And you will kill her.''

''No!''

For an instant, Rabinowitz raised his hands, the hands that used to flirt with Geiger's neck when Geiger was a student. Then the hands descended as quickly as they had come up. Geiger had the impression that somehow Rabinowitz hadn't even missed a beat.

''I'm going to banish you. By thinking about something else,'' Geiger said.

Rabinowitz laughed again, an evil cackle. **''You will only banish me by surpassing me in greatness. And you will never do that.''**

Geiger steamed. At the keyboard, the ghost changed his tempo.

''For example, do you recognize this mazurka?'' Rabinowitz inquired. **''Technically quite challenging. You could never perform it with justice.''**

Geiger turned from the specter and tried to block him out. The intensity of the music heightened.

''Think about this, Rolf,'' Rabinowitz said. **''The guillotine. You are placed in it and your head is chopped off. But the head does not lose consciousness for several seconds. Your final seconds of life are spent contemplating your head's severance from your body.''**

''Go,'' said Geiger. ''Leave.''

Rabinowitz laughed. **''Consider this the way the decapitated man would consider his fate: Some things are constant. I will always be your master. I will always be your better.''**

"You are wrong. You'll be proven wrong."

"Your Diana," Rabinowitz began slowly. **"She copulates joyfully with someone else."**

"That's not true."

"She has sex with the artist, you know. He's an Arab, I believe. Very powerful loins. He's a large man. He pleases her considerably."

Geiger bristled. "That's a lie. All of it."

"I can see the truth. And the future."

"It's a fucking, vicious lie."

"At least he's an artist," Rabinowitz said. **"Not a pretender such as yourself. But a veritable artist."**

Geiger held back for a moment.

"He enjoys her from the back side, you know, as Arabs do. It's a way they claim their women. They're like sheep, the Arabs are, but when they find a nice slutty ewe—"

Geiger whirled and approached the Steinway, his movements a cross between a man in a nightmare and a belligerent drunk.

Rabinowitz laughed gleefully and held his place at the piano bench. His hands never swerved from the keyboard. He glanced up as Geiger approached.

"I'm already dead," he said. His eyes went yellow and hollow again. But he continued to speak. **"There's nothing you can do to me. I don't even feel pain anymore."**

As soon as those thoughts were in Geiger's head, Rolf reached his tormentor. He lunged at him with both hands, as if to throttle him.

But there was nothing there to grasp. Geiger's hands sailed through Rabinowitz, though he looked as solid as any man whom Geiger had ever faced. His hands, as they went into that horrible, inexplicable space that comprised the ghost, felt as though they had been plunged into ice water.

For an instant Geiger remained rigid, staring at his arms which had entered the ghost's plane and come out the back. Another smile curled on the corners of Rabinowitz's mean lips.

Then he was gone and there was nothing in front of Geiger. But he still heard music playing. And he still heard that damnable voice.

"You can't keep me in a grave," Rabinowitz said.

Geiger whirled, white as fresh snow now. The ghost was behind him, formally attired for a concert. He looked just as Geiger had last seen him alive, at the Kennedy Center in 1994.

"I will always be with you," Rabinowitz said. **"You will never escape the grandeur of my shadow!"**

Geiger staggered forward and waved another arm at Rabinowitz. But the specter again remained stationary. And again Geiger's arm swiped through it.

The young pianist lurched sideways and howled, the full terror of this second encounter sinking deeply into him. He screamed again and crashed into the closed door of his den.

He nearly stumbled but steadied himself. There were tears pouring from his eyes now. Tears of terror. He opened the door to escape from the library and tumbled out into the front hall.

A beer bottle crashed at his feet and shattered. He had no idea whether he had left it on the floor and knocked it over, or if Rabinowitz had hurled it at him.

It didn't matter. Rolf staggered to the front door, opened it, and weaved out. Holding the railing on his front steps, he staggered down the front steps. He hit hard against a parked car and came to a painful stop.

At least, he thought, *I'm out of the house.*

Geiger slumped down against the vehicle. He closed his eyes and collapsed into sobs.

He had no idea how long he was there or how many people might have passed. But it did occur to him as he sat there that he was very drunk in addition to being very scared.

He knew, however, that for the rest of his life he would see his arms passing through the body of the dead Rabinowitz. From now on he would always hear those haunting works by Chopin in a different way. And he would always see those hollow yellow eye sockets, coupled with the macabre smile and the distinctive touch at the keyboard.

After a while, he got to his feet. But he was unable to move very far. He resisted the notion of returning to his own home. So he crawled to the town house two doors away. He reclined on his neighbor's front steps and passed out.

Almost.

His eyes flickered a few times between then and dawn. Once

was when a taxi slowed down to a stop, honked, and asked him if he needed a lift home. Geiger's eyes opened just long enough to close again.

The cab drove on.

At another time during the night, he thought he saw his mother standing near him, looking down and sadly shaking her head. At another moment, the violinist in the clown suit appeared. He put a comforting hand on Geiger's forehead and shot off a short scherzo by Paganini.

"Help me," Geiger said to him. Or her.

The clown-musician gave an eerie low bow, filled with feline feminine movements, and vanished into the glare from a street-lamp.

It was, in other words, like almost any other night for a drunk on a stoop in Manhattan. Almost like any other, that is, except for the quality of the ghostly company.

Toward dawn, as he slept, a photographer found him. At about seven o'clock, Diana, half-frantic, half-crazed, emerged from the town house, saw him, and took him back inside.

It wasn't for another hour that he was able to explain the previous evening to her—what he had seen and what he had experienced.

nineteen

Two afternoons later, Rolf was sitting in his library reading a score when Diana appeared. He looked up.

"Detective Solderstrom is here. She says she needs to talk to you," Diana told him.

Geiger sighed. "Oh," he said. "Her. All right."

What terrible timing, he mused. He had just been making progress into his examination of the score when he was interrupted.

"Send her in," he said. Irritated, he folded away the score. He had the now-usual sense of not being alone in the library, the perception that a pair of unseen eyes were upon him, that he was under scrutiny.

Always, he thought. *It's always like this now.*

Rolf had an old Soviet clock on his bookshelf, a little square black relic of Stalinism that he had bought for three U.S. dollars during the Tchaikovsky competition of 1988. He was aware of the clock's peculiar abnormal tick as he waited for the detective. The tick wasn't unusual for a Soviet clock. Diana always described it as the most perfectly useless item she had ever seen. Only twice a day did it give the time and additionally it was ugly.

"Why do you think the Russians let me leave the country with it?" Rolf had always answered.

Outside the town house something passed across the sun. Then the figure of a large woman filled the doorway. Worse, Geiger caught bad vibrations from her right away.

"Mr. Geiger," she said.

Unlike the first time they had met, he now felt a wave of hostility roll toward him.

"I was driving by and I thought I'd stop in," she said. "I was wondering whether you'd seen your intruder again."

Rolf thought for a moment. "Once a few nights ago," he answered.

"Have a problem with him?"

Rolf gave it several seconds of thought. "He was outside. I saw him from my foyer."

"But you didn't speak to him? Or feel yourself threatened?"

Geiger knew the truth—an account of what had apparently happened, culminating in the appearance of Rabinowitz— would be useless. "No, and I haven't seen him again after that," he said.

"Has anyone?" Solderstrom asked.

"Diana hasn't seen him, either, if that's what you're asking."

"I assumed you would have called me if there had been a second incident," she said.

"I would have."

Geiger sensed something uneven about the woman. "What about outside? Around the block?" Solderstrom asked.

Rolf shook his head. So did Diana.

The detective took a moment.

"I'll get right to the point here, Mr. Geiger," she said. "I know there was one person seen sitting out on this block two nights ago and from what my witnesses tell me it wasn't any aging homeless person. By the time a sector car came by, the individual had returned to his home on this block. He was dragged back in by the woman he lives with. Early in the morning. Know what I'm getting at here, Mr. Geiger?"

Geiger knew, and suppressed a little wave of anger.

"I'd had a few beers," he said, "and felt like sitting out. I know that's a little unusual. But it happened."

"You've got a world tour coming, and you're sitting out on the stoops in your neighborhood? I'm having trouble understanding that," she said.

"Please try to."

The detective looked at him very carefully.

"However strange you think that is," Diana offered from the back of the room, "the original intrusion happened. This old man was at a funeral, he followed me to the public library, he had a piece of my jewelry, and he's been watching this house."

"But now he's gone?"

"It seems that way," Geiger said.

Solderstrom's eyes went from Rolf to Diana then back to Rolf. She sighed. "Well, we can't warn him if we can't find him, can we?"

Rolf shrugged. The woman had a point.

"Let me ask you this," Janet Solderstrom said. "I spoke to a couple of the other detectives who used to work Lincoln Center and the theater district. One of the men on Manhattan South knew of an old guy who used to hang around after concerts and shows. Sort of matches the description you gave. You want me to follow up on this, or do we let it slide?"

"I want you to follow up," Diana said before Rolf could answer.

"I do, too," Geiger said.

She looked at both of them and sighed.

"Okay," she said. "If I were you, I'd remain alert. But there's a good chance you scared the living hell out of this individual. He's frightened and won't come anywhere near you again. I don't know. I just thought I'd check with you."

"I appreciate it," Geiger said.

The policewoman excused herself and left another business card. To Rolf and Diana, at the time, it seemed like a nonevent, perhaps even a way of coming to check the inside of the town house again. Detective Solderstrom departed and took her chilly attitude with her.

* * *

The evening arrived.

Rolf and Diana waited for something else unpleasant to happen. But nothing did, and soon, one normal day followed another.

Strangely enough, as Rolf and Diana remained poised for another encounter with the police or another haunting within their home there was no next episode of either kind. Just when they expected the worst, a big empty nothing transpired.

Rolf in particular lived in a constant state of tension, waiting for the moment when something would happen again.

Something terrifying.

After dark, his nightmares were gone, replaced by real fears and real sleeplessness. He felt helpless. He spent much of the time around the house, preoccupied by fear and anxiety, and trying to concentrate on practicing. April gave way to May. Then the date to play in Philadelphia was only two weeks away.

Brian Greenstone reported that tickets had sold briskly in Philadelphia. The recital, as Greenstone had predicted, was a sellout within two days. Requests came in for interviews from the local newspapers—the same newspapers that had pilloried Geiger for his last rock-and-classics appearance at the CoreStates Center. Cautiously, Geiger spoke to some of the interviewers over the telephone, though one of the newspapers sent a woman to New York to interview him in person. Geiger obliged, though he was not helped by the tabloid publication of the picture of him sitting on his neighbor's front steps, apparently drunk.

Diana had her own bout with print journalism, too.

She met Phillip Langlois for lunch. He was gracious and pleasant and told her all the superficial things about Isador Rabinowitz that she already knew. She realized he was picking her brain for information, asking questions slyly, trying to evoke answers that would have involved Rolf. Despite Langlois's charm, she found herself building a wall against him and his questions.

Yet, no matter how sturdy the wall was, it didn't go high enough. She could tell Langlois liked her. He was attracted to her sexually. Under normal circumstances, were she unattached, her response might have been different, but she was living with a man she cared for and respected. Who needed a complication like this?

Langlois confirmed her feelings as they left the restaurant. "Look," he said, "I really appreciate your coming out and spending time." They stopped on the corner and he bought half a dozen long-stemmed red roses from a flower merchant. He handed them to her.

"That's not necessary," she said.

"It's an innocent thank you," Phillip said. "Nothing more."

She wasn't certain how innocent it was. But the flowers *were* pretty. "Thank you," she said.

"If I think of something further about Rabinowitz which might interest you, how can I get in touch?" he asked.

"Through Rolf's agent."

He sighed and smiled.

"Look, I'm not an ax murderer," he said. "If you don't want to give a phone number, I happen to know your address. I know it because the bloody tabloids are always printing pictures of you or Rolf coming out of your building. So would it be all right if I just dropped you a note at 112 East Seventy-third Street?"

"That's all right," she said. "As long as that's the only thing going through your mind."

"What else would be?" he scoffed.

"I have no idea."

He smiled. "Me, neither," he said.

He walked in the other direction. She walked toward Seventy-third Street, carrying the roses. Back in her home half an hour later, she walked in as Rolf was at the piano, working through the middle of the Tchaikovsky piano concerto he was planning for Philadelphia.

The music swelled beautifully and greeted her as she came in the front entrance.

The door to the library was slightly open. She poked her head through. Rolf, as was his custom, did not look up from what he was doing, but acknowledged her with a slight nod. She went to the kitchen, found a vase, and arranged the roses.

She returned to the library, set the flowers on a table near the piano, and took a seat on the bench next to him.

"Hi," he said, still playing.

"These buds for you," she said.

He managed a sly smile and worked the Anheuser-Busch theme into the Tchaikovsky. They laughed at the image of Clydesdales pulling a troika.

"Since when do you buy yourself flowers?" he asked. "I thought I was in charge of that."

She found it easier to lie.

"I bought them for you," she said.

"Cool. Thanks."

He leaned to her and kissed her, flowing seamlessly from the Clydesdales back to Tchaikovsky, never wavering in the tempo or feeling in what he was playing.

"How am I doing?" he asked. "Aside from the tacky beer commercial, am I doing justice to 'Mr. T.'?"

Mr. T.: Rolf's private appellation for Peter Ilyich Tchaikovsky. Wouldn't the music critics love that one? Rolf once called Tchaikovsky 'Mr. T.' in front of Rabinowitz and the old man had gone sky-high ballistic.

"You're treating Tchaikovsky better than his own government did," Diana answered.

"But am I treating 'Mr. T.' better than Van Cliburn?" Rolf asked slowly and with exaggerated concern. "Cliburn used to *own* this piece."

"You're treating Comrade Tchaikovsky *almost as well* as Van Cliburn," she teased. "You've always been my third favorite pianist after Van Cliburn and Jerry Lee Lewis."

She quickly stood, and he playfully slapped her across her backside. His left hand was so fast she could barely perceive the missing notes. She scampered away with a laugh.

She watched his concentration settle back into the music and she left him alone.

And so it went.

She went to her art classes and received two article assignments from New York magazines. She kept busy during the day and allowed Rolf as much time as possible to practice and prepare his program for Philadelphia.

Meanwhile, Brian Greenstone continued to establish dates for the tour that would follow. Thirty dates had been set. Another fifteen to twenty were probable. London would definitely open, New York would come in October, and the tour would end either at the pyramids or in South America. Depending . . .

The music program for the tour evolved, too.

Remaining at issue was the *Emperor* Piano Concerto. It was perhaps Geiger's favorite work of Beethoven, and amply allowed Geiger to measure himself against the greatest who had ever played. It seemed a natural to close the tour in Egypt. But, it also seemed a natural as an opening work at the Royal Albert Hall or Covent Garden in London. Promoters in both places wanted it.

"How about if I play it to open, Brian," Geiger suggested one afternoon over the telephone. "Then I play the recording of the opening performance when I close. That will save me having to even show up for the final booking. Just play the tape."

"Very bloody funny," Greenstone answered.

"Just trying to help."

"Well, don't try to help. Don't think at all, for God's sake, and don't do any heavy lifting with your damned hands. Just practice your infernal instrument. Practice, practice, practice so that you hit all the right notes and don't end up playing in whorehouses."

"Or Las Vegas."

"Same thing."

"Brian, you'd still get your 10 percent. And what's so bad about playing in Vegas. Or in a whorehouse?"

"Which reminds me," Greenstone said before ringing off. "Lovely Claire, your new Number One fan and potential groupie, sends her undying and most impassioned love."

"Don't start trouble, Brian."

"Me? Start trouble?" he sniffed. "Don't be ridiculous."

It was a time when the earlier incidents of haunting first began to recede, and when a sense of rightful place began to reappear in the lives of Rolf and Diana.

Even at home, Diana suddenly had a strong urge to put things in order. She spent a great deal of time on small household tasks like putting shelf paper in a cupboard in the kitchen and pantry. She took the first steps for stripping and refinishing the steps that led to the small attic above their bedroom. She hated to go anywhere near the front-hall coat closet—where the watcher had first appeared within their home—but she did once, just long enough to take all of Rolf's fan letters out and organize them. She put something else back in order, too, taking the small silver piano pendant to a jeweler and having it reattached to its chain.

Since the watcher had held it in his hand, she also had it thoroughly cleaned, both with disinfectant and silver polish. She looped the chain around her neck and went back to wearing it every day.

For both Diana and Rolf, even the terrifying dreams at night seemed to have abated. Overall, the tension within their home began to lessen.

One evening, three days before the date in Philadelphia in early June—after no further *specific* poltergeist incidents in the house—Diana sidled onto the piano bench and sat next to Rolf as he was practicing.

She sat there for several minutes. Listening. Thinking. Working up her nerve.

Geiger was previously notorious for changing his programs at the last moment, playing what he damned well felt like playing because he knew his audience would go along with him.

"That was Rolf Geiger Light," he had explained to her recently, comparing himself once again to beer merchandising. "Now I'm Rolf Geiger Regular and I, like most trained and professional musicians, will adhere to my previously arranged program."

He paused.

"Probably," he concluded.

But actually, he meant it, and the program for Philadelphia was set. He had been down and back to Philadelphia for the last week to rehearse with the orchestra. The program was a little bit of a grab bag, but it was early summer and the audience, he felt, and maybe even the critics, would indulge him that one little quirk.

He would start with a short Beethoven sonata. Then a Chopin polonaise which, in a gesture of goodwill, he would dedicate to his mentor, Rabinowitz, with a few words before playing. The third piece would be a sonata by Beethoven, which would take him to intermission. The second half of the recital would be the Tchaikovsky Piano Concerto No. 1, always a huge favorite in Philadelphia, a fact of which he was well aware. In previous generations, Van Cliburn used to knock the walls off the old Robin Hood Dell with his summer performances of Tchaikovsky.

"So it'll be 'Mr T.' to close the show?" Diana asked, sitting next to him as he brought his hands up from the keys.

"It's 'Mr. T.'," he said. "And I promise not to call him that. Except to you. Jesus, I'm going to behave real good on this trip."

She smiled. She sat close to him, his arm around her while he played.

"Now that the program is planned," he said, "here's something for you. Your own private recital."

He poised his hands over the keyboard, then the hands came down on the keys. Perfect height. Perfect touch. The first few notes were like a legion of fireflies on a summer night.

The *Moonlight* Sonata filled the room, the house, and their spirits.

twenty

The glamorous old Academy of Music in Philadelphia anchors the performing-arts district of the downtown south of City Hall. Modeled after La Scala of Milan, the Academy has presided like a proud dowager on South Broad Street since the 1850s. It is a lavish building that is probably never more beautiful than when it is illuminated by the softness of gaslights on a cold autumn or winter night when the Philadelphia Orchestra, another great orchestra, or a great recitalist is set to go onstage. But it can be beautiful on a summer evening, also.

On the day of his recital, Rolf Geiger arrived in the afternoon by private car from New York. He and Diana had a suite booked at a hotel across Broad Street from the Academy. They spent an hour there while Geiger studied his scores once again.

Not that he didn't know them.

Toward four o'clock, he walked across the street to the Academy and approached the stage door on Locust Street. Several fans were sitting outside.

The stage door is next to the entrance to the cramped amphi-theater section, known locally as ''the nosebleed'' seats. The amphitheater is one of the last great bargains in North American classical music, available for all performances for four dollars per seat on the day of the performance only. It is a favorite of students from nearby Penn, Temple, and the Curtis Institute of Music. The line swarmed with such students.

For a hot ticket—and any sudden concert by Rolf Geiger was a hot ticket—lines start hours before performance time. Such was the case today. Geiger, as was his custom, took time to stop at the line and speak to the people ready to see him play. He spoke to everyone in the line and signed several dozen autographs.

"I hope you all realize there are no fireworks tonight, other than the music itself," he told them.

His fans answered that they understood.

"No more monkeying around. This is a classical repertoire. Beethoven, *Chopin,* and Tchaikovsky."

"What about the encore?" a girl asked. " 'Smashing Pumpkins'?"

"Probably more like 'smashing cellos' instead," Geiger answered. "And anyway, how do I know I'll be asked for an encore?"

Everyone laughed.

"You'll be asked," someone said.

"You're just trying to keep me playing for as long as possible," Geiger bantered back.

"That's right," the same someone answered.

"I won't even be goaded at encore time to slip any pop in the program," he said with a smile. "It's serious stuff from here till the end of the big tour."

"*If* you play an encore, what *might* it be?" asked another young man in line.

"I have *no* idea what I'd play," Geiger said with a wink. "I don't even have an encore ready. Haven't thought beyond the final bars of the Tchaikovsky."

He then lost his straight face and began to smile.

"Of course," he said, "by the time it's ready to close the concert, there will be *moonlight,* so maybe some sort of *sonata* would be nice."

"The entire work?" someone asked.

The crowd laughed.

"How about the first movement? Could I get away with that?" Geiger asked.

"Can we count on the first movement?" a girl asked.

"No," said Geiger. He glanced at a sign that gave the ticket price for amphitheater seats.

"You can't count on anything. And, hey! For four bucks, what do you want, a CD, too?"

"Can we have one?"

In an inspired moment, Geiger found a pair in his jacket pocket and gave them away.

Everyone laughed again. The mood was airy. Geiger loved the excitement and anticipation which preceded a concert. He was further encouraged by the fact that so many people had come out to see him play without the promise of the old gimmicks, pizzazz, and showmanship. Philadelphia had always been a favorite venue: Geiger even had a longtime friend who joyfully taught music at St. Peter's School.

The audience just wanted great music. He was ready to give it to them. It was great to be out here, and he realized how much he had missed the concert scene and the interplay with fans. Philadelphia had long been a great recital town, with fine, knowledgeable audiences. He had been away too long.

By now, three dozen passersby and tourists had stopped to watch, joining the four dozen in line. Rolf had himself a nice crowd already. Traffic began to stop and two mounted policemen came over to have a look. Diana came over and got him.

"I never argue with this lady," Geiger announced. "If she says it's time to go indoors, then it's time to go indoors."

He allowed Diana to pull him away. The crowd applauded him as he departed.

Geiger shook hands with some members of the orchestra, who were already there. The conductor, Robert DaSilva, greeted Geiger with enthusiasm. He was a stocky, affable man with a New York accent. They made final preparations for the evening.

Geiger inspected the stage and carefully examined the Bösendorfer that he would be playing. Normally he might have flown one of his own pianos to this concert. But in negotiations the Academy had promised this fine instrument and they had made good.

A piano tuner stood by. The instrument was in excellent order. With everything set, Rolf then took Diana around the corner to the Sixteenth Street Bar and Grill for a late but light lunch.

At six he returned to the hotel to dress. There are some conductors who would take their limousine across the street. Geiger came out as a beautiful summer evening descended on Philadelphia. Dressed in black tie and tails to play, he took Diana by the hand and crossed Broad Street. They made a beautiful couple.

Traffic stopped and a few horns honked to them. Geiger smiled and waved. He felt once again as if he were on top of the world. Not just the music world, but the entire world. Geiger still had the appeal of a rock star. People stepped out of cars to wave to him.

Before the concert, he sat with the musicians in the lounge below the stage. He watched the clock with a twinge of anxiety. It was seven o'clock, then seven-twenty.

He found himself a Diet Coke, sipped most of it and lost interest. At seven-thirty the Academy's doors opened.

He waited patiently, making small talk with anyone who approached him.

At a quarter hour before he would play his first work, Rolf went to the curtain at stage left and peered out into the house. Six tiers of seats, stretching toward the mural of the sky on the ceiling of the grand old building. To look at the Academy from the stage, he recalled, was an awesome experience. The building was ornate, huge, inspiring, and intimate at the same time. The seats were a deep red, matching the carpeting, and the wood-work a warm dark oak. So what that the ancient paint on the ceiling was peeling a little? Geiger peeked out a second time and saw that the building was full, and crackling with excitement.

"Counting the house?" Maestro DaSilva asked as he walked by. DaSilva loved to banter back and forth with Geiger.

"Just seeing if I know anyone," Geiger replied in jest.

"No," DaSilva countered, "and none of them know you, either. They just came to see me conduct."

"Why should they watch you, Maestro? The *orchestra* doesn't even watch you."

"You got a point there," he said, and disappeared to flirt with a pretty red-haired woman who was the second violinist.

"Tiger, you *almost* look nervous."

He turned and saw the most beautiful face in the world.

"Hey," he said.

He put his arms around Diana and gave her a squeeze. "Want to sit on the bench with me while I play?" he asked. "I'd like that better than going out there alone."

"I don't think that would be considered serious musicianship," she reminded him. "Bringing your squeeze on stage?"

"Screw serious musicianship," he said in a low voice.

She laughed.

"One minute, Mr. Geiger," the stage manager, Bernard Vickers, announced in passing. Vickers was a very tall, very thin man, upon whom clothes hung very loosely. Rabinowitz had once described him as "a grapevine with a suit on it."

Geiger gave Vickers a nod. Unfortunately, Geiger thought of Rabinowitz's nasty grapevine remark whenever he saw Vickers.

"I want a kiss before I go out there," Geiger said.

"Yeah? From whom?"

"Only one," he said to Diana.

She gave him one. Then a second. Abruptly, she realized, "You *are* a little jittery, aren't you?"

He shrugged. "A little." Then he added, "Hell, this is something new. Know what I mean? In the past I always felt I could improvise, take the tone of the house, feel the pulse of the audience, and take it in any direction."

"You still can."

"No," he said. "I used to be able to take it in *my* direction. Tonight I have to take it in the *right* direction."

The houselights went down.

"See you later," he said. She had a seat in a private box with one of the directors of the Academy.

Rolf drew a deep breath.

Yes, he had hacked around in San Remo before an audience of two hundred giddy European admirers. Tonight, however, this was *music—serious Goddamn music!*—before critics and a large sophisticated audience in a major eastern city.

Then, his time had arrived. Rolf took two strides forward

,and felt the thrill of live concerts return in a surge. He stepped into a spotlight that brought him onto the stage.

The applause was huge.

It came at him in a swell, much like a wave, and for a moment something caught in his throat. But he went to the Bösendorfer, placed a hand on it and gave the audience a smile and a slight bow. It had been a long time since he had stood this way before a comparable American audience. And he felt all the better for it.

He sat and readied his hands. They were a trifle more moist than usual.

Then he began to play. Geiger came in with a perfect touch, hitting the opening allegro with vigor and spirit. He was off to a fine start.

As he played, he was pleased. The music was flowing brilliantly. He hardly knew which pleased him more—the flow and continuity of the thoughts or the brilliant counterpoint that seemed to flow effortlessly from his fingers.

There was also the passion. The execution. The extraordinary expression.

The opening work passed brilliantly and the audience erupted with fabulous applause when Rolf finished.

He left the stage amid accolades. When he returned, he hushed the audience and dedicated the second work.

"As you know, this is my first public performance in the U.S. in three years," he proclaimed boldly. "It is also my first appearance since the passing of one of history's great pianists. Isador Rabinowitz."

There was some applause, interrupting Geiger.

"I would like to dedicate this next work in particular and this evening in general to the late Maestro Rabinowitz."

There was applause again, though in this same building Rabinowitz had once thrown a Stradivarius—followed by a torrent of obscenities, and then by a cellist—down the steps into the dressing room when the violin's owner had displeased him.

The Chopin polonaise went seamlessly. The audience responded and the evening was in fine form.

A Beethoven piano sonata was third on the program. Here,

too, Geiger triumphed. When he stood at the sonata's conclusion, bowed and walked off stage, the entire audience was on its feet.

Geiger was smashing and the offstage activity at the intermission reflected that, also. Diana grabbed Rolf and embraced him. The orchestra congratulated him and DaSilva—sipping a suspiciously large gin and tonic—gave him a sharp thumbs-up.

Everything was cooking. The mood at the intermission was triumphant. The break passed quickly.

Then, twenty-five minutes later, the orchestra began to file onto the stage. The first violinist and concert master, the last orchestra member to appear, was met by a warm ovation. Conductor DaSilva, a local favorite, despite his New York birth, followed to considerable applause, taking the position on the podium so many times previously occupied by Stokowski, Ormandy, and Muti.

Then Rolf Geiger returned to play Tchaikovsky. He drew a standing ovation when he walked back onstage.

He sat down to play. This was, without question, one of his great nights of musical victory. Perhaps this was a turning point in his career, he told himself, the moment when he could put his improvisations and variations behind him and play the piano better than any man or woman had ever played.

If so, this was exactly what he wanted.

He felt every bit of the excitement. This significant triumph in Philadelphia would be a prelude to fifty others around the globe, he now sensed. He *knew* he was better than any other man alive. Within another eight months, everyone in the world would know it, too.

He took his place at the keyboard of the gorgeous Bösendorfer. Then something strange happened. The mood onstage seemed to shift for an instant.

The atmosphere darkened as if something were passing through.

Like a cloud. An indoor cloud.

Rolf could have sworn he felt something icy—like hands or strong fingers—flirting along the line of his shoulders.

Toward his neck.

He cringed and shivered. It was powerful this touch! Immensely big and powerful! He looked to DaSilva, who looked back at him and waited.

Geiger gave the conductor a nervous nod. He shook himself and attempted to drive away that eerie touch that came from behind him.

"Go away," he muttered quietly.

DaSilva looked back, having heard the whisper. The conductor frowned slightly, not understanding. Geiger shook him off and indicated that he should begin.

The conductor authoritatively raised his baton, held it for a beat, and brought it sharply downward. Geiger's fingers found the keys and instantly brought the Academy back to the Russia of 1875, when this piano concerto was composed.

Geiger had a sense of hyperrealism as he was playing.

His fingers knew where to go without him directing them. His touch was free, spirited, amazingly pure and accurate. His fingers seemed to sing as they rippled passionately over the keyboard.

Geiger swelled with pride and enthusiasm. It was brilliant. His performance could not possibly have been going better. And this brilliance would only serve as a fantastic springboard to—

To what—?

The feeling that was within him was now something more than excitement. He listened again to the music, the music that his hands were creating. He felt the rhythm in his hands and measured the flow of his fingers.

And he realized . . . . .

. . . .*the music was not his.*

The interpretation was not his.

No, no, no, he told himself. *This cannot be! A dead man cannot be in my body. Rabinowitz cannot be playing. I am Rolf Geiger and I am alive and Isador Rabinowitz is dead and this cannot be happening!*

But it was!

He heard the unmistakable touch of Rabinowitz upon the keys. In every note, in every bar and syllable. Even the touch of Geiger's foot on the pedal reflected the execution and the interpretation of the dead man.

. . . the legato, the cantabile . . .

It wasn't Geiger's. It was Rabinowitz's.

Who in God's name was playing?

How in the Devil's name could this be?

What the *Living Hell* was going on?

Geiger tried to compensate with his fingering and he discovered he could not. His own touch at the keyboard, the brilliant touch that had been with him all his life—the one that had swept him from a frozen small stinking town in West Virginia to New York, Paris, and Vienna—had deserted him.

The old man's vicious spirit was moving his hands.

Rolf's hands barely felt like his own. It was as if something else were moving them. His gaze rose frantically from his work to find Diana in the audience. The fear all over his face told her that something terrible was happening.

But she didn't know. Not right away. She could feel that it was there, but she couldn't recognize it. Not like he could. But then, he was the only one who *really* knew who was playing.

Rolf's eyes returned to the stage. He glanced to DaSilva. The conductor knew something was wrong, but couldn't tell what. He gave him a slight shake of the head.

And yet, and yet . . .

Rolf Geiger felt the audience hanging upon his performance. He knew to them it was going extraordinarily well. Brilliance poured from his fingers, but not *his* brilliance.

He proceeded, barely missing a breath. Yet now, instead of pleasure and excitement welling within him, it was fear.

Where was his own execution?

Where was his own standard of playing?

Where was his own spirit?

Where were his own hands?

First Rabinowitz had gotten into his head. Now his body. *Next the soul?*

The sheer horror of the thought made him glance down. His mind was stricken. The hands playing before him, the hands attached to his arms, were not his own young powerful vibrant hands.

Geiger nearly screamed! The hands before him were the hands of a very old man!

A dead man.

Or more accurately, a man so excruciatingly bitter that he refused to remain dead.

They were Rabinowitz's hands playing this Tchaikovsky. Lined, wrinkled, gnarled—

and!

—even bearing the famous green emerald ring!

Rabinowitz was playing. He had taken over the concert!

Geiger felt frozen. Only he could see this! He tried to pull his hands away, but the hands continued to play.

Tchaikovsky soared.

It soared the way Rabinowitz had always wanted it to soar. Geiger could hear the brilliance, but also recognized the lack of spontaneity and the constraint.

Rabinowitz's dark trademarks. The old bastard's fingerprints. His death grip on music.

Geiger looked down again. The aging hands played, for the aged misanthropic spirit. The emerald in the ring sparkled in the lights and winked like the eye of a demon. Geiger's hands and body responded to a command that was not his, a possession that belonged to Rabinowitz.

Geiger grimaced.

He fought with the impulse to stand and run from the piano. Then, when he gave in to that impulse and wanted to flee, his body would not obey.

The possession was complete. In utter terror, Geiger watched for the final few seconds as the hands at the keyboard, bedecked with the emerald ring, continued to play.

Grandly! Magnificently! And now in the inspired style of the *young* Rabinowitz.

In all the delicate nuances of the work, the fingers at the keyboard seemed like feathers. Yet in the passages that required more strength and character, there was a forcible grasp and a tenacious élan that actually evoked gasps from the audience. Not a single note was slurred. Each note stood out like a cut, multifaceted diamond. The entire concerto swept and sparkled like a freshly fallen Moscow snow.

The music boomed

Tchaikovsky, Tchaikovsky, Tchaikovsky!

One of the many composers that Rabinowitz had "owned."

Geiger approached the final measures. There was a final cascade of octaves and chords. The hands played across the keyboard. Geiger was making no effort to play. He watched in terror as his hands moved without his control. The hands pulverized the final notes and swept upward in triumph.

The emerald ring vanished as did the lines on the flesh of Geiger's hands. He felt something unspeakable leave him. He was finished.

More than finished.

For a moment, there was a beat of silence in the Academy. Then the old house erupted. Like a wave receding backward, spectators in the rear of the orchestra came springing to their feet. The applause was instant and thunderous. It rose from the downstairs and swelled upward into the cavernous old ring of amphitheater seats halfway to heaven.

"Four dollars a seat, Rolf. Your white-trash old man could have bought two on the day he died!"

Geiger's lips moved, trembling first, then giving rise to a curse.

"Fuck it," he whispered.

"Shot in the neck, wasn't he? Maybe you should try the same."

"I said, 'Fuck it,' " Geiger mouthed again.

DaSilva saw it, and, not understanding, thought it was an oath of exhilaration. Patrons in the front rows were either amused or shocked. Some, both.

Geiger pulled back his hands. He felt a tug on them, as if they were being held by something unseen. He yanked them down. The spirit of Rabinowitz seemed to release them. Geiger had control of them again.

He stood.

He staggered. He looked blankly at the audience and the avalanche of flowers hurled toward him. An armada of beautiful young women rushed the stage and were held back by security people.

Rolf nodded. He was bathed in sweat and emotion. He couldn't find a smile.

The onetime prodigy stepped tentatively away from the bench upon which he had played. He gave a nod to DaSilva. He reached out, his hands trembling, to both the conductor and the first violinist. He held the violinist's hand for a moment and thanked her.

Then Rolf turned back toward the audience.

Everywhere before him there were eighteen hundred spectators standing in approval, hands upraised in tumultuous applause. The echo of "Bravo, bravo," carried downward from the amphitheater and family circle. It rebounded across the parterre audience and embraced him. The applause was wildly enthusiastic and relentless.

No one made a move to the exit.

Geiger stood in the midst of all this, a disbelieving figure who suddenly felt very small. The orchestra saluted him and withdrew. But he motioned to the orchestra with a sweeping gesture and demanded that they come back onstage to share the moment with him.

With trembling hands, he again thanked conductor DaSilva. DaSilva again saw something strange in the young pianist's eyes but did not understand it.

Then Geiger fled.

He exited the stage and proceeded quickly downstairs to the dressing room, catching no one's eye as he ran.

He went into the dressing room and closed the door behind him. Above him, the applause thundered longer and steadier. He could hear the shouts for an encore and he trembled at the thought of those hands

—Rabinowitz's hands—

returning.

He couldn't play an encore. He couldn't. Not tonight.

For that matter, he wondered breathlessly, how could he ever play again? Was he so possessed by the spirit, even the body, of Rabinowitz, that any note that he could ever plunk out at the piano would only be another man's music?

Suicide was suddenly a very comforting thought. At least it

would put him on an even plane with Rabinowitz—angry and dead.

Geiger collapsed into a heavy club chair. He felt his heart race. He felt the sweat all through his shirt and formal attire.

Slowly, riddled with fear, he held up his hands before his eyes. The hands that contained his genius. He gazed at them. They were his own again. They were back. For the moment, at least.

The roar continued above him. The audience was stomping its feet for more. If the tumult was changing at all, it was only getting louder.

Bad form, he thought to himself. *Very bad.* The audience was demanding his return for an encore and he was nowhere to be seen.

Oh, but what could he play?

How could he play anything?

Moonlight Sonata? "Für Elise?"

Would one of those get him off the hook?

And whose hands, whose spirit, would play?

Deep within him, there was a fear unlike any that he had ever known before. Then he felt something sweep past him, much like a draft from a door that had sudden opened.

Oh, God. The spirit! It was back!

It was almost as if there was something cold playing at the nape of his neck. Something icy. Like fingers that had been dipped in snow.

He knew whose.

He drew a long breath. It was the moment of a great triumph, yet he knew that he hadn't even played that evening. Rabinowitz had played and Geiger had been robbed of his triumph.

How, he didn't understand.

Why, he didn't understand.

What the future held, he could only conjecture.

And still the audience above him roared.

He thought of a target pistol that he kept in New York. It crossed his mind, for the first time in his life, to use it on himself.

"Why don't you?" asked a voice. **"In the neck, if you please, like your racist Jew-baiting old man!"**

"Shoot myself?"

"Why don't you? You'll never be as great as I. I would never permit it."

"Where in hell are you?" Geiger asked the empty room.

Upstairs the audience was still stomping. Pounding. Insistent. They didn't just *want* him back. They *demanded him back.*

Or, more accurately, they wanted back whoever had mesmerized them with Tchaikovsky.

It was painfully clear to him now. Any greatness he attained would only be the legacy of Rabinowitz. He could never play again on his own. The world tour would be an exercise in humiliation, nothing more.

The gun back in New York. The pistol. One good bullet through the brain . . .

At least no one would ever know why. . . .

The knock on the door to his dressing room startled him.

Geiger recognized the touch: Diana.

"Rolf?" He heard her voice. Then a third rapping, insistent as the applause.

He sprang to his feet and went to the door. He unlocked it and threw it open. She stood before him, with Bernard Vickers, the Academy stage manager, several feet behind her.

"What's going on? Are you okay?"

"I'm okay."

"Something's wrong," she said. "Tell me."

"I'm all right," he insisted.

"You're not all right. I love you, and I can tell. What happened out there?"

He shook his head.

"Did you *see* something?" she demanded with conspiratorial urgency. "Was something *there?*"

He knew exactly what she meant. He wouldn't answer. "What about you?" Rolf asked. "Did *you* see something?"

She shook her head.

Her hand found his. "Your audience is begging," she said. "The orchestra is waiting."

"As is Maestro DaSilva," said Vickers.

"Of course," said Geiger, still badly shaken. "Yes, yes. Of course." He struggled for his composure.

Diana leaned to him. "Something *is* wrong," she said, "and I want you to tell me. Later."

"Maybe," he said.

"Promise me," she said.

"Maybe," he answered.

She sighed.

"Mr. Geiger ... ?" Vickers said again. He indicated the pathway that led back up to the stage.

"Of course," Geiger said, again trying to recover. "Yes, yes. Of course."

A million thoughts were upon him. None of them good. "Please," he said to Diana. "Lead me."

She did, taking his hand and guiding him back. The orchestra was again offstage. They gave way when they saw him and formed a path. He walked through them. They applauded also.

Snippets of conversation from his peers:

Absolutely fantastic!

As good as anyone now ...

Didn't think "the brat" could be that good ...

The applause from the eighteen hundred, which had continued now for ten minutes, was subsiding only slightly. It exploded again when Rolf Geiger walked back onto the stage.

He appeared stunned to those who knew him. Even some customers in the parterre boxes noticed. He walked to the piano. His mood had changed.

"What the hell am I doing?" he asked aloud.

Offstage, DaSilva was surprised. A slight murmur rippled through the audience.

"*Moonlight?*" the conductor called softly. That was what the plan had been. Enough people heard the word to garner a smattering of applause.

"*Moonlight,* huh?" Geiger asked.

But again, he felt the icy hands of his master upon his shoulders.

The touch was cold and firm as usual. The presence was overwhelming.

Geiger glanced down and saw that his hands were his own—this time. But the hands remained on his neck and behind him.

"I think not," he said. "*Moonlight* Sonata's such a clichéd piece by now. Sort of for slutty teenage girls to sniff at."

Geiger looked offstage at the orchestra. Some of the musicians were conferring. Geiger spoke in a low hiss.

"Just everyone shut the hell up," he snapped. "I know what I'm about. If you guys had the guts to be soloists, you'd be out here!"

Shocked, the musicians fell silent. The first few rows of spectators reacted similarly.

Then Geiger turned to the audience. " 'The Dying Poet,' " he said.

He looked back to his keyboard and began to play.

His Chopin unfolded gravely, with poetry and aristocracy— a small jewel of a performance. Worthy of a Rubinstein, a Horowitz, a Liszt, or a Rabinowitz.

And all the time, he played with Rabinowitz's hands on his shoulders, close to his neck. He could feel the eyes of the ghost peering over his shoulder.

As Geiger came to the obbligato, his music filled the grand old music hall. Though Diana, watching from the wings, saw his lips move, no one heard the words he spoke.

"I'm ready to see you again, Rabinowitz," Rolf Geiger said to his departed mentor. "I'm ready to see you and talk to you."

No one other than Geiger heard the response.

"Soon. When I'm ready," Rabinowitz answered.

Geiger completed the encore with a flourish.

Then he stood, thanked his audience, and was gone again. He went to the dressing room with Diana and they quickly gathered his things.

He was out the door fifteen minutes later, hurriedly scribbling sloppy autographs as he brusquely pushed his way to his limousine.

"Out to dinner, sir?" the driver asked.

"No. Back to New York."

"Rolf?" Diana demanded.

"Just shut up," he said to her. She was stunned. And hurt. When she tried to get close to him, he wouldn't touch her.

They stayed in Philadelphia just long enough for her to go up to the hotel suite and remove their clothing. Then his driver took them back to New York. All along the way, on this the night of a tremendous artistic triumph, he was sullen and angry, as if a personality other than his own had taken complete control.

Halfway back to Manhattan, Diana began to press the issue, but he wasn't ready to talk about it.

"Who the hell do you think you are?" she finally snapped at him in response. He looked at her quizzically, but when he tried to respond, she was now in turn angry.

"Forget it," she snapped. "I don't want to hear it."

"Fine with me," he snorted.

That night, Rolf Geiger had no further comment or explanation about what had happened on the stage of the Academy of Music. Nor was he happy, the next day, when Brian Greenstone called him and started fishing around a bit.

"I heard it was sensational, old boy," Greenstone thundered, "but some of my intimates tell me it was a little confusing at the end. Told me you seemed to have a bit of a bee in your lovely bonnet. Care to regale me with an explanation?"

"No, I don't," Geiger said. And he hung up the phone on his old friend.

Inadvertently, the music critics came very close to an explanation. Both the *New York Times* and the *Philadelphia Inquirer,* in the next morning's editions, made the same observations.

The performance had been mature and brilliant, they agreed. The technique sounded so much like Isador Rabinowitz that a listener could close his eyes and picture the deceased master at the keyboard.

"Rabinowitz was Geiger's great, if unloved, teacher," William Baumann concluded in the *Times.* "If young Geiger has decided to get serious about his art as he now indicates that he wishes to, it perhaps says something about the young man's intelligence that he should adopt and master his mentor's great and distinctive technique."

"Fuck you, Baumann," was all Geiger could say over breakfast the next morning when he came across that comment. "I'll play it the way I fucking feel like playing it!"

Geiger spoke with a bitterness never before seen by anyone, least of all Diana, who was a witness to this. "Someone ought to set fire to your house and murder your children,'' he added calmly, addressing an imaginary Baumann in their home.

Then Geiger picked up the telephone, called Baumann's voice mail at the newspaper, and left the same message in person.

Diana rose from the breakfast table when she heard his words and went back upstairs. She locked herself in her own bathroom and cried for two hours. For all this time, Rolf stayed downstairs in the library, poring over Chopin at the piano, alternately cursing, reading the score, and playing.

Never once did he think to go upstairs to see if she were all right. And never once did she dare go down.

''Greatness,'' grumbled Geiger to himself as he made beautiful music at his Steinway, ''has its price. And I'm now willing to pay it.''

twenty-one

A week after the perceived triumph in Philadelphia, Rolf sat in his library on a bright summer morning. It was past ten. Diana had gone to her health club. Aside from the music, which flowed generously from Geiger's Steinway, and the occasional utterance from the pianist, the town house was silent. Even the city beyond East Seventy-third was calm.

Anyone viewing the handsome young virtuoso at the piano would have guessed that he was alone. Rolf, however, knew otherwise.

There was no score in the music rack of the piano. Geiger was busying himself with warm-ups—physical and intellectual calisthenics. Trill exercises, simple and chromatic scales, and exercises for the throwing of the hands, for which he used a two-part fugue of Johann Sebastian Bach.

Geiger watched his powerful young hands run up and down the keyboard. He listened with an intensely critical and demanding ear as the right notes came together in the proper context and music flowed from the Steinway. This went on with marked concentration for twenty to thirty minutes. From there he moved to the piano passages of the *Choral Fantasy* by Beethoven, a probable part of his London program.

He played it passionately and impeccably. When he was finished, he raised his eyes from the keyboard.

Rabinowitz was standing there in the suit in which he had been buried.

"Well?" Geiger asked.

"Well what?"

"Well, what did you think?"

"Competent," said the ghost of the maestro.

Geiger eyed him now without fear. It seemed very normal that he should be there. "It was better than 'competent,' " Geiger said.

"You struck every note with a rigid exactness," Rabinowitz said. At this interval, the ghost drifted around the room. **"Perfection makes you sometimes a little cold,"** Rabinowitz continued. **"Or at least, it makes your interpretation cold. Play this again. Try to not care how many notes you miss. Bring out your conception of the work. Make it vivid. Happen it. Again."**

Rolf's hands returned to the keyboard. He reattacked the piece with more swagger and increased elegance and imagination, but less precision.

"Good, good," he heard the ghost say. The old man's voice was all around him. He at one point felt his mentor's hands settle on his shoulder, just by his neck.

"Play the prestissimo at the end in broken octaves," the ghost instructed.

"What?"

"Fuck! Do it, damn it!" Rabinowitz ordered.

Geiger reached and followed instructions. His own hands were a flurry before him. The sound that swelled from his Steinway amazed even him. It gave him goose bumps.

He glanced up. Rabinowitz was gone. His eyes went back to the keyboard, he went back in the score and played through the same passage again in broken octaves. He was amazed.

When his eyes rose again, Rabinowitz was a handsome young man, much the way he had looked when he had fled Austria in the thirties. He was sitting on the piano.

Weightlessly.

"**Don't look so much at me, explore your music! Explore your music!**" the ghost snapped.

Geiger's eyes returned to the score. He went back to the beginning of the piano sections of the *Choral Fantasy* and played the work straight through.

Then, at the end, he looked up.

The ghost stood there, its arms folded.

"**Good,**" Rabinowitz finally said. "**That was good.**"

"What about the broken octaves?"

"**Don't use them there.**"

"Why not?"

"**They don't belong there. It's show-offing. It will only impress American audiences who know nothing.**"

"If I don't use them there in the *Choral Fantasy,* where do I use them?"

"**In the *Totentanz,***" Rabinowitz said. "**Lizst's *Dance of Death.***"

Geiger cringed slightly and shifted restlessly on his bench. "What are you talking about?"

"**Your London program.**"

"Who's playing it? You or me?" Geiger asked.

The ghost was suddenly gone from the piano. Geiger glanced around the library and found him in the chair across the room, looking middle-aged, the way he had looked as a famous performer in the 1950s when he had frequently been Jack Paar's guest on the *Tonight Show.*

"**Unfortunately, you,**" the ghost said. "**It would be better if I played, but—**"

"You're dead. You're not here."

"**And it is you who are keeping me alive,**" Rabinowitz answered. "**But then, why are you talking to me, Rolf, if I'm dead and not here?**"

The ghost's tone was mean and taunting. Then Rabinowitz disappeared so abruptly that Geiger felt a change in the pressure of the room. He looked around the library, all directions, and couldn't find the ghost.

"All right," Geiger finally said. "Come back. Show yourself."

The face materialized inches in front of Geiger's.

It was so intense and disagreeable an image that Geiger recoiled in horror.

"**You're playing London under my tutelage,**" said Rabinowitz. "**You will achieve greatness under my instruction. That is the *only* way. You deviate, and I will take over the keyboard again, the way I did in Philadelphia.**"

"Whose success was that?" Geiger asked. "Philadelphia? Mine or yours?"

"**The newspapers credit us both,**" Rabinowitz said. "**Of course, *I* was playing.**"

"No. *I* was playing in your style."

"**Same thing.**"

"Not true. I can achieve greatness on my own," Geiger said softly. "I can and I shall."

"**If you're so sure, then why don't you?**"

Geiger had no response.

"**And why haven't you?**" Rabinowitz taunted further. "**You left my instruction eight years ago. Why no greatness on your own? Tell me, young man, why?**"

Again Geiger didn't answer. Possibly he didn't answer because he knew.

He hadn't dared. He hadn't aspired. Rolf had wanted to conquer the pianistic world but hadn't dared take the first serious step until the old man was dead. And now ironically he, Rolf, was keeping the old man alive.

"**Well then, there!**" the ghost insisted. "**There we have the truth between us, yes?**" He made a clucking sound like a chicken to rub it further in.

Suddenly Rabinowitz was an old man again. He was sitting on the piano bench next to Geiger.

"**As the piano is your instrument,**" he told Geiger, "**you are *my* instrument. That much is very bright.**"

With disdain, Geiger turned away from the ghost. When he raised his eyes again, Rabinowitz was in full view, right in front of him.

"**Now, what about the London program?**" Rabinowitz asked. "**The *Choral Fantasy* is acceptable. What else?**"

"It's an all-Beethoven program."

"**Mistake. You need to show range in London. English**

audiences will include a few people who have some sophisti-cation."

"The second piece is Concerto No. 4 in G."

"Expendable."

"It's a beautiful piece."

"Maybe. Don't play it."

"The *Emperor* is the main work."

"I don't like it."

"It's what I want to play."

"The *Emperor* is bombastic, pretentious, and pedes-trian." He paused. **"Plus, it's cheap. Cheap, cheap. It challenges no audience and thus no recitalist. You cannot play it."**

"You used to play it."

"When I desired to. Everyone knew I was great, so I could play it and get away with it."

"So that's when I'll play it, too. When I desire to. And I desire to in London on September first."

"You will only get yourself in trouble at times when you think. You must obey me and obey the music."

Geiger simmered.

"You *cannot* do this tour without me, do you understand, Rolf?"

Geiger's left hand went to the keyboard. He played a strain of the *Emperor*. Then his right hand found the keyboard and he embroidered the melody of "Don't Be Cruel" and "Suspicious Minds."

"What is this noise?" Rabinowitz asks.

"The *Emperor* meets the King," said Geiger, knowing it would annoy him.

"Which King? Martin Luther?"

"Presley."

The specter was vehemently angry, which pleased Geiger.

"You are jerking off!" Rabinowitz thundered furiously. **"Intellectual masturbation. Same as you've always done! Whore! Slut!"**

Geiger added a leitmotif from "Blue Hawaii."

"You dick around. You have the intellect of a honky-tonk player!" Rabinowitz insisted.

Geiger persisted.

"'Me and you and 'Blue Hawaii,' Maestro," said Geiger. He sang along in the fashion of Elvis. "'Come with me, while the moon is on the sea . . . '"

Rabinowitz roared.

Furious, he knocked a pile of scores from where they stood on a nearby table. Nothing offended the old man quite like catchy successful American pop music, which he considered a cultural abomination.

". . . 'The night is young,'" Geiger crooned. "'And so are we . . .'"

The scenario was nothing new. It was the same as many of their "lessons" and "learning sessions" from fifteen years earlier.

"You will eternally play garbage, left to your own devices," the old man ranted. He seemed to be in three places at once, three different incarnations, three different stages of his own lifetime. **"Only if *I* play will you rise above it."**

"That's a bloody lie," Geiger snapped. "You never *let* me play. Always orders. Always instructions."

"You never have the *balls* to play as good as you would! No soul! No heart, either!"

"Then fuck you once again," Geiger said. "Turn me loose."

Curiously, the ghost retreated when Geiger insisted upon the *Emperor* portion of his London program.

"What else will you play?" Rabinowitz wanted to know.

Geiger was thoughtful. "Maybe I *won't* play the Concerto No. 4," he mused. "That leaves an opening. So I would still be looking for the third piece."

"I told you, imbecile. Liszt's *Dance of Death.*"

"Why the *Totentanz?*" Geiger asked again.

"To further embarrass yourself, it is obvious," he snarled. **"Technically demanding. Very showy. I played it most masterfully. Think you could rise to it?"**

Geiger thought about it.

As a teenager, he had seen André Watts play the *Totentanz* at Philharmonic Hall at Lincoln Center in New York. It had been electrifying. The music had been riveting and Watts had always been a great showman. As was frequently the case, Rabinowitz had a point.

Geiger looked at the ghost. "Do *you* think I could?" he asked.

Rabinowitz laughed.

Outside the library, in the vestibule of the town house, there was the sound of a door closing. Diana returning home. Rolf recognized her footsteps.

"Totentanz," he said aloud. "The *Dance of Death.* London 1998. Rolf Geiger's World Tour."

He thought about it for a moment. His fingers came down on the keyboard and he played a few of the bars he could remember.

Dance of Death and Diana appeared at the doorway. He glanced up.

A confluence of ideas: Diana's *Dance of Death?* he mused. He liked the alliteration, though the thought made him cringe.

"How's it going?" she asked softly.

He grunted.

She gazed into the library and saw no one other than Rolf. The muscles of his face and neck were tense with concentration. She had a packet of morning mail in her hands.

She asked again. "How is it—?"

Rolf slammed his hands down onto the keys in mid-phrase. The Steinway thundered with his rage and anger.

"Don't interrupt me, all right?" he snapped. "Can't you see things are different? What the hell am I doing in here, dicking around with Carole King crap?"

She stood frozen at the library door. Tirades such as this one, little explosions of temper, had become common in the week since Philadelphia, but they never ceased to leave her speechless. Once they had never happened. Now they happened several times a day. Unhappily, Diana was feeling increasingly as if she should just stay away from him.

But her own anger rose in her defense.

"I'm *sorry!*" she said. "But I thought I heard you talking."

He looked around the library as if she were crazy. Even Rabinowitz had turned invisible to Rolf.

"To myself, if anyone," he said. He paused. "How was your workout?"

"What does it matter?"

"You've already distracted me. Tell me about bouncing around with all those other firm butts and abs."

"Some other time," she said. "Here. Your mail. From your adoring, unquestioning fans, no doubt." She bundled it and tossed it into the room, like a woman feeding a caged beast in the zoo. The mail landed with a thump, then several pieces flew in various directions.

Rolf watched dispassionately and made no move to pick anything up. Diana left the doorway. Geiger heard her go upstairs, a slight stomp to her feet.

He calmed. He set his attention back to the music. He looked down.

Where was he, he wondered.

"Dance of Death," came a nearby voice.

"Yes, of course," Rolf said aloud.

He tried to pick it up again. He struggled. He had studied the piece years ago but couldn't remember it well. He struggled. His hands faltered.

"Need help?" Rabinowitz asked.

"Maybe."

Then, before his eyes, his hands aged again, the emerald ring appeared. His body sagged slightly but he felt a surge of brilliance course through his hands.

The hands played.

The old hands took over again. Technically inspired. Glowing with virtuosity, making Geiger recall the piece. He played by himself. The old hands disappeared and Geiger's took their rightful place.

He ended at a mid-interval near the end of a bar. Rabinowitz was correct. The Liszt piece would be the perfect third for London.

He looked up. The ghost was before him again.

"You're right," Geiger said. "Good choice."

"So your program is now established for London?"

"Yes, it is."

"Good. Good," Rabinowitz muttered.

His eyes drifted in the direction in which Diana had vanished. **"Do you love that woman?"** he asked.

"Yes, I do."

"You mustn't."

Geiger's eyes burned at the ghost. They burned so censoriously that the ghost faded. Then the specter rematerialized on the other side of the library, speaking again as a handsome young man.

"Personal attractions are not good," he said. **"Personal relationships are poison when genius is to be realized. I many times have told you that.** *Many* **times. It is significant more now than—"**

"Spare me," Geiger said.

"You don't wish to heed my warning?"

"No."

"She is unfaithful to you," Rabinowitz attempted.

"Talk to me only of music," Geiger said. "Talk to me only of the piano. Of personal relationships, you never knew anything."

"*Women cheat!* **This one in particular."**

"You lie."

"I will prove it," Rabinowitz said. **"I will show you. I will—"**

The voice of the ghost cut off as Geiger went abruptly to his feet. He crossed the library and approached the window.

"Rolf . . . ?"

The ghost drifted in front of him. Geiger evaded him and stepped to the window. Rolf reached to the shade on one of the high windows, grabbed its cord, and jerked it. The shade shot skyward.

"She is a slut, Rolf. She is in bed with many men aside from you!"

Geiger whirled.

"Speak to me only of music," he insisted again.

"In time I will *show* **you about such a woman!"**

Geiger arranged for a generous river of cleansing sunlight to flow upon the ghost.

A moment passed.

The substantial image of Rabinowitz stayed in place for

several seconds. A look of extreme anger and ferocity washed across the spirit's face.

"Now vanish," Geiger said. "You are no longer wanted."

Then—before Geiger's astonished eyes—the young Rabinowitz aged to his middle years, then to his sixties, then to his later years. Then to the day he died.

"**She cheats on you,**" Rabinowitz tried again. Then he disappeared, though the thought and the words continued to ring in Geiger's ears.

Upstairs in the bedroom that she shared with Rolf, Diana flopped down on her side of the bed. She arranged her mail and sifted through it. Among the day's arrivals, she found an envelope bearing the return name and address of Phillip Langlois. She set it aside unopened until she had read a letter from her father and another from a sister. She looked at a catalogue from one of the New York museums before going back to Phillip's correspondence.

She opened it.

Dear Diana,

Mr. Rolf Geiger has never returned my repeated requests to his agent's office for interview time. This is his privilege, and I do understand that he must be terribly busy right now with preparations for his upcoming tour. But I do hope he might reconsider. If you have the opportunity to mention favorably that you and I met at the New York Public Library and that I'm not a monster of the tabloids, I would be most highly appreciative. I do very much covet the interview opportunity in light of the book material on Isador Rabinowitz which I am developing. In the meantime, I wonder if you might have lunch, coffee, or tea with me sometime soon at your convenience. This might sound slightly mad to you, but I have a theory reflecting upon the life of Isador Rabinowitz which would suggest that you, Diana, may be in personal danger. I don't mention this to alarm you,

*and forgive me if I DO alarm you. But danger is danger
and I would be negligent if I did not pass along to you
what I know.*

Respectfully yours,

Phillip Langlois

She read the letter twice, not knowing exactly what her
reaction should be. His penmanship was clear, concise, and
bold. Enclosed with the note was another business card, marked
with his hotel phone number.

Her first reaction to the communication was that she was a
little dazed, particularly coming off Rolf's minitantrum of a
few minutes previously. Then she was irritated. She had a
feeling that Phillip was a man who was long on charm and
short on substance. This theory was quickly replaced by one
that reminded her that he was a reporter for the *Telegraph* in
London, and he would certainly know the way to snare a woman
into a story. Both of these theories gave way to the sense that
he was also a man on the make, one who was interested in her
sexually.

From somewhere came the image of her in bed with Phillip
Langlois. She wondered what it would be like. Where had such
a nutty image come from? Had Phillip sent it along telepathi-
cally? Or had it risen from her subconscious?

She read the note a third time, hoping it might yield an
extra insight with increased familiarity. It didn't. It didn't yield
anything the third time except the invitation for lunch, coffee,
or tea that had presented itself the first time. She read for
motivation and couldn't clearly find one other than the one he
had given. That is, he held the theory that she was in some
sort of danger and he felt obliged to warn her.

An exercise in altruism, that's what the letter was, a pro-
Phillip voice within her proclaimed. And Phillip, her Galahad,
her Lancelot, was doing nothing more than riding to her defense.

Yeah, sure, whispered another voice within her, this one
highly skeptical. She was twenty-six and divorced, not twenty-
one and unwary of men of the world. She had seen enough of

primal male motivation in her time to recognize a touch of it here.

She thought about him a little more as she lay on her bed and fingered the handwritten note. Might as well face it, she concluded, Phillip oozed sexuality in a hunky-guy beneath the shirt-and-tie sort of way.

She played around with her thoughts some more. She wondered about Rolf and his recent tirades. Was this, she wondered, just a glimpse of what might follow with Rolf? Gary, her first husband, and only husband so far, had been too given to his career—or lack of one—to pay her the respect and attention she needed. Now was Rolf set to push her into the background in a similar manner? Would he always be *too busy* to treat her in the wonderful way he had treated her in the past?

She wondered.

As she lay on the bed reading, her fingers left the letter and found the small silver piano that lived between her breasts. She twisted it thoughtfully. All of which made her ask herself, as she had asked herself more than a few times recently, what she wanted from Rolf.

How long could the relationship sustain itself?

What was she going to do, tag along as his girlfriend for a few years until she hit her mid-thirties and he replaced her with a younger version of herself?

It was a nasty reverie, all brought on by Phillip's letter. She wondered where such thoughts were coming from recently. Was there now something within the atmosphere in the town house?

She cringed again, recalling Detective Janet Solderstrom, who continued to phone and drop by every few days, and didn't seem to care much for Rolf.

A line of inane verse barged into her head from parts unknown:

> Janet, Janet.
> From another Planet!
> Light a fire of suspicion
> Then stay and fan it.

Well, that particular detective *did* seem to be from another world sometimes. But might she have been onto something?

Might she? Maybe?

But what?

Diana tuned away from her thoughts for a moment and in to the music from downstairs.

Rolf at the keyboard.

God! What bizarre piece was he now playing? This was nothing she had ever heard before. Where was *this* coming from? There were more strange and scary things going on, it seemed, than just her bizarre recurrent nightmare with its lupine predator that wanted either to rape her or devour her.

As she turned over her thoughts and fears, the piano piece downstairs—it sounded like Franz Liszt jacked up on amphetamines—continued for several minutes in all its fire and fury. Then it stopped.

Silence from down below.

She heard Rolf on the steps coming upstairs. She tucked the letter from Phillip Langlois back into its envelope and nestled the envelope back among her mail. It took a place between the correspondences from her sister and father.

Rolf entered the room, gave her a glance, and said nothing. He went to his dresser to retrieve something, but she couldn't see what.

She sat up on the bed and watched her lover, eyes on him intently. When he turned around, his eyes locked on hers.

"What?" he asked uncomfortably.

She shrugged. "Just wondering if you were going to say anything," she said.

His gaze remained firm and unyielding for a moment. Then something gave way within him. His expression changed, so did his mood, and so did his demeanor.

He walked over and sat down on the edge of the bed.

"Yeah," he said. "Guess I *should* say something. Sorry I barked at you down there."

He gave her a hug.

She responded. "I'm sorry I interrupted you," she said.

He shrugged. "I have a lot on my mind. London can't be a disaster. It's going to be a long concert. Three major works.

Some of the stuffy old farts in the music establishment will tell me I can't do all three, or shouldn't do all three, all in one night.''

"So why do all three?"

"I want to show that I can," he said.

She nodded.

"And I want to get all the works I want to play in this one tour. So that means practically doubling up on dates in some places. Like London, to start.''

"Rolf, are you sure you should do it that way?"

"I'm sure."

"I don't want this to kill you, you know," she said.

"Why do you say *that?*" he asked.

"Well, because I *don't,* Tiger."

He flinched slightly.

"The piece you heard me playing is the *Totentanz.* Franz Liszt. The *Dance of Death.*"

He felt her shudder. "What put that in your mind?" she asked. "I've never heard you play that. Why play it in London. And why a piece with such a macabre title?"

He drew a breath and stood. "Something I thought of," he said tersely. "An instinct I have. The right piece of music at the appropriate time." He seemed to think about it for another moment. "What can I say? It's an instinct. I live my professional life by instinct. So why go against it now?"

"I can't argue with you," she said, "if you think it's right."

A thoughtful look crossed his face and he said nothing else, leaving Diana alone again in the room. She glanced in the direction he had gone, then looked back to her mail. She listened to Rolf walk back downstairs to the library.

For the next several hours, music flowed from the Steinway. Some passages repeated themselves, some bars, and the occasional grand piece of music—specifically the *Choral Fantasy*—uninterrupted and beautiful. It almost seemed a crime that such magnificent playing fell upon so few human ears.

In the evening, Rolf made dinner for himself. Diana went to her art class with Maurice Sahadi. She returned home around ten and Rolf was still playing. She readied for bed by herself and climbed in at eleven-thirty.

Before turning the light out, she reread the day's mail. She still didn't know what to do about Phillip Langlois.

Rolf came upstairs about midnight. She was almost asleep. He sat down on the edge of her side of the bed and placed a hand on her shoulder. She had a funny sensation. It didn't feel like his hand, even though it was.

It felt somehow different, though that was a silly thought. She rolled over and could see him in the dim light.

"Tiger?" she asked, not knowing what was going on.

He smiled.

"I want you," he said.

"You want me or you want sex?" she asked.

He smiled strangely, which added to her confusion over the moment. It was as if he had developed a new smile, one she didn't like.

"How about both at once?" he asked.

Normally she didn't have to think about it. Tonight, she did. But, "Okay," she said. "Climb in here."

He did.

But the sex was perfunctory. He said little during it and acted like a man going through the motions. It occurred to her in the middle that he could have been with any woman and it wouldn't have made any difference to him. It was hugely dissatisfying. When it was over, he went right to sleep, saying little else. She lay there for thirty minutes wondering what was wrong until sleep claimed her, too.

The next two days, he spent earnestly at the piano, saying very little, hardly acknowledging that Diana even lived there with him.

She was willing to grant him his space and not say anything. She went to another gym class, another art class and to two movies with friends.

On the third day, she telephoned a very surprised Phillip Langlois and told him that she had some time. She would be happy to meet with him, even though Rolf's schedule was still enormously cluttered.

Langlois seemed pleased. Very pleased. They set a date five days away.

"I'm looking forward to it," she said.

"Same," he answered.

When she set the phone down, she wondered what she had done. "Most affairs start over lunch," her mother had once told her. Nothing she had seen in New York over the last few years particularly disproved Mom's Axiom of Sexual Dalliance.

During the phone conversation Phillip had given her a wide choice: breakfast, lunch, coffee, drinks, dinner. She had made her own decision.

She also wondered where the emotional intimacy she had shared with Rolf had gone and when, if ever, it would return. It was a question she would have to answer for herself. She was certain that Phillip Langlois would pose plenty of other questions in the interim.

Meanwhile, the date was set and she found herself looking forward to it. For lunch.

twenty-two

"Have you ever heard the name Laura Aufieri?" Phillip Langlois asked.

The British author sat with Diana Stephenson in one of the modest places on Third Avenue just north of Bloomingdale's. It was a hamburger joint with red-and-white-checked tablecloths, but with enough salads on the menu to draw a female clientele.

Diana thought for a moment, then said she hadn't.

"I suspected you hadn't," he said. "Not very many people have. Laura Aufieri nearly cost Isador Rabinowitz his career. Although," he continued, "Laura lost more than Rabinowitz did."

"I'm not following," Diana answered said. "And this must be fairly old news."

The waiter arrived with food. A meat pie for him. A pasta salad with shrimp for her.

"Well, it's an old story," Langlois began. "But I'm not sure how old it is as 'news.' But let me backtrack a minute. I have this theory that Rabinowitz and Rolf Geiger are basically very similar in psychological makeup."

She started to scoff, but he insisted that he be allowed to continue.

"You see," Langlois said in his best analytical voice, "they were both prodigies, but came to their gifts very late. Not like most prodigies who perform on the piano when they're four or five. Then, as young adults, they were romantics and iconoclasts at the same time. Fooled around with their gifts, fooled around with ladies, had an unsuccessful early marriage here and there, then went for greatness."

He paused. He had a draft Bass ale in progress and his hand kept finding it.

"This is what fascinates me," he said. "When Rabinowitz made his move to become a world-class recitalist in the 1940s, *that's* when his personality very quickly changed. For the negative. I've been watching the things in the newspaper recently, and everything has a very eerie ring. It's like watching Rabinowitz all over again. The intensity. The lack of humor. The change of personality."

He paused. More ale. Between swigs his tone alternated between dead calm and breathless.

"Well, come on, Diana, you *live with* Rolf Geiger," he said eventually. "Am I not correct that Rolf has changed recently?"

She tried to dismiss what he was saying. But she was having trouble doing so.

"He has a world tour coming up. It's not unusual for an artist to be preoccupied or even moody. Much of that is concentration. If you think about it, it's to be expected."

"Right," he said, not believing it.

"Perhaps I know better than you," she said.

"Maybe," he allowed. "And maybe not. Look, this is not some unfounded ramblings that I'm giving you today. I've done extensive study. Rabinowitz was a student of Rachmaninoff. You can see it in their techniques: beautifully organized performances, impeccably delivered, rarely capricious, uniform from one season to the next and guided by a sense of sonority and a strong left hand. But when Rachmaninoff died in 1943, that's when Rabinowitz started both his quest for greatness and his descent into a perpetual meanness. It was as if when the mentor died, the student was unable to accept the death or step up and try to surpass the mentor professionally."

Another gulp of Bass as Diana started to pick at her salad.

"I'm not a psychologist," he said. "I'm a journalist. And I know when I see two individuals on parallel roads."

She thought about what he had said for several seconds while Philip started to eat.

"Suppose I'm listening to you," she said. "What direction are you going with this?"

He proceeded very carefully.

"If you'll forgive my bringing this up, I'm waiting for someone to get killed."

She bristled. "What?" she snapped.

He repeated. She felt anger first, then a wave of fear.

"I have a feeling you're going for a very cheap analogy," she said.

"Oh?" he asked. "You know, I've been an investigative reporter for many years. I notice things. And I notice that you look like a very frightened woman these days."

Again, she protested.

He waited. "Hear me out, please? Without interrupting."

She crossed her arms and waited.

"In 1944 in London," Langlois said, "the handsome young Rabinowitz was approximately thirty years old and just making a name for himself. He was involved with a young woman named Laura Aufieri. Her body was found in the home in Mayfair that Rabinowitz kept at the time. She had been strangled to death."

She felt something sickening crawling around her stomach. "So?"

"She was a woman with whom Rabinowitz was having an affair at the time. A long-term affair." He held the sentence a beat. "But once he was out of that romantic relationship, through her death, he went on to bigger things in terms of his career."

"Why wasn't Rabinowitz arrested for the murder?"

"He was."

"*What?*"

"That's part of where this whole 'Dark Angel' terminology came from. Tragedy. Violence. Strange goings-on always followed the man." He thought for a moment. "There was another woman who died suspiciously in Rabinowitz's past, too, way back in Russia. But all records disappeared during the Stalin era. So who's to know what happened?''

"All of this is supposition," Diana insisted.

"Sure. But even this 'Dark Angel' nickname is a little spooky. Rachmaninoff in his lifetime was known as 'the *arch*-angel.' ''

"So did Rabinowitz go to jail?" Diana asked.

"No. No charges were filed. Lack of evidence. And naturally, because of who he was, a budding young virtuoso on the piano, the police cut him a wide degree of slack. But he was questioned nonstop for two days.''

"You're implying that Rabinowitz did it, right? And that Rolf will do the same thing? Is that what you're saying?''

"As a reporter, I'm just noting the eerie confluence of facts. In fact, I didn't say anything. You just came to the same conclusion as I did.''

She ran a hand to her face, not caring for the direction of this story.

"If this was such a big deal," she asked next, "why wasn't it in the newspapers and why isn't the story widely known here?''

"Libel laws in England," he said. "The stories of the death of Laura Aufieri were in the newspapers, and the address in Mayfair of Rabinowitz's home was printed." Langlois unwrapped a folder and started pulling clippings out of it. He pushed two before Diana. Across half a century, the face of a murdered woman looked out at Diana.

She cringed again. Laura Aufieri was approximately Diana's age. The slain mistress also bore a resemblance. And she, too, Diana noted, had been in the arts as a musical actress.

She looked at the material for several seconds, then raised her eyes. Her salad was losing her interest.

"Why would Rabinowitz have killed her?" she asked softly.

"The theory was, that he felt she was standing in the way of his career. The personal relationship was costing him passion from his musicianship. He had no love or any emotion to give to anything except the piano. Laura may have protested the end of their relationship or Rabinowitz may have lost his temper. Who knows? Maybe she was pregnant. Maybe she was involved with another man. That rumor surfaced, too, stating that Rabinowitz murdered her in jealousy—though God knows he found it increasingly difficult to leave young women alone, himself.'' He paused. ''Look. What's indisputable is that Laura Aufieri was murdered.''

Diana blew out a breath, overwhelmed and still highly skeptical. ''I still don't know what to say. Or how to react.''

''That's what I thought you would say.''

''What else *can* I say?''

''A year ago I sued the Metropolitan London Police Department to have documents declassified,'' Langlois continued. ''Rabinowitz was the chief suspect and subject to arrest. He then moved to the United States and stayed here until the London magistrates let the case grow cold. There may have even been bribes involved. Oh, and, in *this* country,'' Langlois added, ''Rabinowitz struck up a friendship with the head of the Federal Bureau of Investigation, J. Edgar Hoover. Apparently, Mr. Hoover made sure that there would be no cooperation forthcoming from American police agencies in the case.''

''Fascinating,'' she said, enduring a disquieting sensation as she remembered that picture of Rabinowitz with Hoover that she had seen in the library. ''But this is still a story from more than fifty years ago.''

He pursed his lips thoughtfully. He looked back down at the pictures of the dead woman.

''Is it a case from fifty years ago?'' he mused. ''Or is it a case from this coming autumn? You're a beautiful woman, Diana, and whether you know it or not, Rolf may feel you're in his way. I'm worried about you.''

Claire's eyes rose as the handsome but weary young man came through the door to Brian Greenstone's agency. Then her face lit with a smile.

''Hi,'' she said.

''Hello,'' Rolf Geiger said in return.

A moment passed as they assessed each other. ''Is Brian in?'' he asked.

"He's in," she said, a slight tone of question attached to her sentence. "Is he expecting you?"

"No. Not specifically. I said I'd come by sometime today," Geiger said brusquely. "See if he can see me now."

"I'll let him know," she said.

Rather than pick up the phone, she stood, turned and walked to Brian's door. She wore a dark blue sleeveless short summer dress. Geiger gave it an eleven out of ten.

A moment later she reemerged. Rolf was still standing by her desk. She gave him a nod and a smile. Geiger was free to go on back to Brian's office.

"Ah, the gods stroll insouciantly among the mortals again today," Greenstone said by way of greeting. "Probably looking to wreak havoc upon the earthly sphere."

He indicated a chair where Geiger was to sit.

"Knock it off, Brian," Geiger said.

"Oh. Cranky again, huh?" said Greenstone. Geiger sat down. "Well, it beats me. Young, handsome, about to become obscenely wealthy, ten million women under the age of thirty get wet for you merely on sight, and you choose to be cranky. All, right. Be that way. See if I care."

Geiger settled into the chair.

"You wanted to confirm the musical program in London. I have the program if you'd like to relate it to the promoters."

"That's wonderful. Share it with me first then I'll share it with them."

"Beethoven's *Choral Fantasy* to open the program. Then Liszt's *Totentanz*. The *Emperor* is the main piece I want to play, so I'll probably play it third, after the intermission. Or maybe I'll take two intermissions. I don't know right now."

"Intermissions could be arranged later," Greenstone allowed.

"I might even change the order of the program on the night of the performance. Depending on how I feel. Think they'd have a problem with that?"

"Well, you might want to let the musicians of the London Philharmonic know so that they have the music in the right order. I don't think you want to play the piano solos from

Totentanz in the middle of the *Emperor*. Seems to me that's what you're trying to get away from doing.''

"It was a serious question, Brian.''

"I doubt very much that they would have a problem. If you change the order of the works on the night of the performance it might be seen as quirky. But the program, in its size and range, is already quirky. So I doubt if anyone is going to run up onstage and stop you.''

"That's fine,'' said Geiger nodding.

"You think you might want to do this *Totentanz* thing— which is the *Dance of Death,* I believe—last?''

"Maybe.''

Greenstone shrugged. "You'd have to consult with the conductor, obviously. But I'm sure you'd be on the same page.''

"Ah. That's another thing. Tell me again who's conducting,'' Rolf said.

Greenstone blinked. "Rolf, do you have early Alzheimer's or something? I'm finding your behavior mildly erratic, and if you wish to consider that a bit of classic English understatement, feel free.''

"What are you talking about?''

"The conductor was one of the first things we arranged.''

"So who is it again?''

"Heinrich von Sauer, grandson of the great pianist Emil von Sauer, as you will recall. He will be flying into London from Munich just for this program. Heinrich will be, I mean. Not Emil, who is long buried.''

"Von Sauer, huh?''

"One of the finest in the world.''

"Who approved him?''

"You did.''

"Is he already signed?''

"Yes! Of course, he is!''

"So we're stuck with him?''

"Rolf! Wake up, man! This was set a month ago, and even if it hadn't been, you should jump at this. Von Sauer is excellent. Works with a piano virtuoso—that would be *you,* I believe; *you* are the piano virtuoso in this sentence—as well as anyone in the world. We are indeed fortunate to have him.''

"All right, all right. What venue are we playing."

"Covent Garden, as you again well know."

"Explain again why."

"Because it's *there,* damn it."

"I want a real explanation. Why not play, you know, that other one? The big one over near the British Museum?"

"Is this a crude reference to the Royal Albert Hall, which is not near the British Museum at all, but rather is in South Kensington?"

"Yes. I guess so."

"Covent Garden has more cachet, and by osmosis, so might you, if you can behave your suddenly very dark destructive influences and do a sensational performance there."

Geiger considered it.

"The Beatles played the Royal Albert," said Greenstone, expanding. "McCartney before he was respectable. So did The Who, so did Rubinstein, so did Horowitz, Cliburn, and so on. That's rather the point. I, or I should say *we,* since you and I decided this, *we* did not want any confusion over whether this was a pop or classical performance."

"Uh-huh."

Greenstone paused.

"Now that I think of it, you've played the Royal Albert, too," he added. "At Easter of 1991 in dark blue sequinned jeans and a strawberry pink formal jacket. I recall that your *shtick* that evening was to weave seventeen separate leitmotifs from Jagger-Richard into a piano transcription based on the main themes from *Parsifal.*"

"I remember. I liked that stage. You know, I always also liked that line about how many holes it takes to fill the Albert Hall."

"Bully. Fine. Come here quoting Paul McCartney any time it flips your switch, Rolf, but Covent Garden is set this time around. It's rented and it's fucking 'SRO,' which in your case means, 'Sold Right Out.' So this, like Heinrich von Sauer, is an indelible part of your future."

Geiger looked away into the far distance, then his attention returned.

"It's tough for me to tell you this, Brian, because we've

been friends for so long. But I don't like the way some of this has been set up.''

"What the hell are we talking about?"

"I've been paying attention to the musical program. I've left the business arrangements to you. And I'm not happy with some of your choices.''

"Is this about *money*, Rolf?"

"Partially.''

"Jesus, Joseph, and Mary!" the agent snapped, his voice rising in anger, then quickly coming under control again.

Greenstone leaned back at his desk and drew a deep breath to calm himself. His ample midsection rumbled slightly. His vast wall of patience was starting to crumble.

"Well, aren't *we* the greedy little prick today?" Greenstone chided, losing it again for a moment. Then he chose a rational conciliatory approach. He had never had such a problem with Rolf Geiger before. Not one.

"Look," he finally said, "mind telling me what's gotten into you?"

"Maybe some common sense," Geiger said. "I'm going to be playing three concerto-type works in one program. Shouldn't I be compensated for it?"

"My boy. Let Uncle Brian put a few fiduciary things in perspective. You will be making a guarantee of twenty-five thousand pounds sterling, or, in terms that may sound more tactile to you, a minimum of thirty-eight thousand dollars. I hasten to add—I am veritably *falling out of my fucking chair to add*—that this is the highest guarantee ever paid to a solo performer in the United Kingdom for anything aside from the major outdoor arenas. Do I make myself clear?''

Geiger tapped on the arm of his chair.

"Clear, sure. But what about those outdoor arenas? Tell me again why we're not playing Wembley or some big football stadium.''

Greenstone stared at him uncomfortably. "Have you suffered a blow to the head recently, Rolf? You are not yourself.''

"Don't be a smart-ass, Brian. You see the issue here! Why am I not booked into a larger hall? The three Goddamn tenors were pulling down a million dollars each at Giants Stadium in 1996.''

Greenstone was inordinately angry. But he spoke slowly, choosing his words very carefully.

"First off, lad. You are not a tenor. Or if you are, it doesn't matter because no one wants to hear you sing Gershwin or Puccini or Manilow or any frigging thing else. But they do wish to hear you play Beethoven. All that's fine. But you and I decided early on that this tour was to be a class act. No stadiums, which are basically highly conducive to making money and negatively conducive to fine music. This was to be the Greatest Pianist playing the greatest music, under circumstances under which the audience could *hear* the music and, if we are very lucky, may even be in a position to *appreciate* it. Recall?''

"Sort of.''

Greenstone gave him a sigh and a hopeless look. There was irritation, but also concern.

"You've forgotten. You've legitimately forgotten? My God, Rolf! What's going on with you? It was one thing to be wandering around the city with a bag of candy, presumably looking for preschool girls, quite another to be missing-in-action on your professional commitments!''

Greenstone sighed. "Talk to me, damn it,'' he said. "Tell me what's wrong.''

Geiger slouched slightly in his chair. He ran his hand across his face and then his hair. Greenstone studied his client and knew that something was badly amiss.

"My God, man. If you don't mind my saying so, you also *look* awful. You appear like you need rabies shot, that's how you look.''

"Lay *off* me, Brian.''

"I'm not trying to lay *on* you, Rolf. I'm seeing a lot of tension. I'm seeing a lot of things I don't like, to tell you the truth. I'm seeing Rabinowitzisms, which were unseemly enough with the original cast.''

Geiger glowered at his friend and agent.

"My man, I know you have probably been practicing and rehearsing intensively until the notes are running out of your ears,'' Greenstone continued. ''But you have to come up for air a bit. You will not be able to start this tour and succeed upon it if you are dead on your feet before it begins.''

Geiger looked up. ''Dead, huh? On my feet? What are you talking about?''

''A figure of speech. A metaphor, I submit.''

''I didn't care for it.''

Greenstone—psychological warning lights flashing all over the place now—eased considerably. ''Then I withdraw it, Rolf. With my apology.''

Geiger tensed again, then eased back.

''How's Diana?'' Greenstone asked.

''Why do you want to know that?''

''I want to be reassured that your private life is tranquil. Is it?''

''It hits a few bumps here and then,'' Geiger allowed.

''And Diana?''

''She's okay.''

''Just okay?''

''Yes. Okay. Or well. Or fine. Or lousy. Or whatever you want me to say.''

''Ah, so. I see.'' A long pause. The agent's eyes narrowed. ''But Diana's in New York? She's over there on Seventy-third Street keeping house with you?''

''Yes.''

''Rolf, are there any personal problems I might help you with?''

''Personal problems?''

Geiger seemed on the point of saying something else.

But then something both curious and shocking happened right before Brian Greenstone's astonished eyes. The light from the window that faced Seventh Avenue must have hit his client from a funny angle, because Geiger suddenly looked absurdly old. It was as if the pianist had aged half a century or more in a few seconds, his face morphed into a tangled twisted road map of lines and wrinkles. Greenstone flinched in shock at what he thought he saw.

Then Geiger moved and the disturbing, confusing vision was gone, replaced by the haggard face of the younger man, riddled with concern and preoccupation. The face that Geiger had worn when he entered. Simultaneously, Geiger's attention to this meeting was at an end. And so was the meeting.

Geiger rose without warning.

"I guess that's everything," he muttered. "I have to go practice. Keep me informed."

"I will, Rolf." Greenstone was dazed. He had found the entire impromptu conference hugely disconcerting. The sudden conclusion of it made it only more so.

"What did I come here for this morning?" Geiger asked absently.

"To discuss your music program. London. Opening night of the world tour. September one."

"Ah. Yes. Did we discuss that?"

"At length," Greenstone said, his eyes locked on his client. "*Choral Fantasy, Totentanz,* and the *Emperor,* as the spirit moves you."

"Yes," Geiger nodded. "Yes, that's right." He smiled broadly for the first time throughout the visit. " 'As the spirit moves me.' That's a good one, Brian. I like that."

Then he turned and departed, leaving Greenstone in a state of worry and abject bewilderment.

"Hi," Claire said as Geiger emerged from Greenstone's office.

"Hello," Rolf answered. "Hello and good-bye."

She smiled brightly. "I'm going to lunch," she said. "Will you go down in the elevator with me?"

He stopped and looked at her again. She was leaning over her desk, straightening some phone messages. He reconsidered his previous scoring. In that dress she scored maybe a fifteen out of ten. And best of all, no bra. Her eyes rose and met his, catching him assessing her.

He tried to pretend she hadn't caught him and wasn't able to read his mind. Fifteen *in* the dress. And *out* of it?

She smiled. "I, like, don't really care if you look at me," she said softly. "I like it. I'm flattered."

"You're hard to miss, Claire," he said. "Yes, I will wait."

"Thank you."

She took Brian's messages in to him. Then she came out,

grabbed her shoulder bag, and left the office with Rolf. They went to the elevator and waited in silence for a moment.

Each time his eyes settled on her, she smiled.

"Claire?" he finally asked. "What are you looking for from me?"

She shrugged impishly. "Anything you want to give me," she answered.

"What's that mean?"

"You mean, what would I *really* like?" she asked. "In my wildest dreams?"

"Yes."

"If I tell, you'll be embarrassed," she said. *"I'm already* embarrassed."

"Then let's both be embarrassed," he suggested.

She laughed.

"I'd like it if you came over to where I live sometime soon," she said. She added, "I'd make you feel right at home. I'd do whatever you asked me to do."

The elevator arrived as if on cue. It was empty.

A sixteen-flight descent in an aluminum room without windows. Claire chatted the whole way down. There were no stops, no other passengers.

Claire had a place down in the Village, she said, her first pad since leaving academia. It was on West Tenth Street not far from where it intersected with West Fourth Street. The place was on the ground floor, two tiny bedrooms, a bath, one small living room and a cramped kitchen with no food in it.

Claire shared her digs with another girl named Carla, a high-school friend from West Hartford, she said. Carla had just graduated from the University of Connecticut and worked as a waitress in one of the seedy restaurants around the corner on Bleecker.

They hit the lobby. Claire remained at Rolf's side. And at his ear.

The living situation was very much of a twentysomething arrangement. A couple of young girls with their first place and all the bawdy on-the-pill merriment that such a situation can evoke. As Rolf listened, the setup sounded a little young and footloose even for him. But kind of exciting, also.

"We have a real good relationship," she said. "Carla and me. Carla's there most of the day. She keeps house better than I do. Then she goes out to go to work about five. I come home about seven. So we entertain guys at different times."

"Uh-huh."

They were outside on the sidewalk.

"Which way are you going?" Rolf asked.

"Whichever way you are," she answered shamelessly. Her smile was now as pretty as it was mischievous. She was about five-four and her hair was honey brown with a nice glow in the summer sunlight, even on busy West Fifty-seventh.

They turned east and began to walk.

"I'm going to show you something that's special," Claire said. "I've never shown this to another guy. Look at this."

They stopped.

Claire dipped into her purse and came out with a billfold. She opened it and found a picture of herself and her roommate. She pulled it out from its compartment.

"Here's the two of us," she said. "Me and Carla. In Nassau last March."

As informal girlfriend-with-girlfriend shots went, this one was a zinger. Claire and Carla were sitting together arm in arm on a flaming red beach blanket. The sand was bright around them and so was the blue sky above and behind them.

They were wearing oversize sunglasses, big floppy straw hats, wide smiles, and bikini bottoms. Claire appeared to be the one in pink. Carla was in turquoise. Neither were in very much of either color, and they laughed at something that must have been terribly funny at the time to the two girls who had doffed the tops of their swimsuits for the photographer.

Carla was as pretty as Claire. Both girls had beautiful skin and no tan lines.

She let him have a good look, then tucked the picture back into her wallet.

"If you want to see more, you have to come by in person," she teased. "I mean, you were, like, fucking me with your eyes upstairs there, weren't you?"

He was too surprised to answer.

Claire surged forward.

"If you'd like to have Carla and me at the same time," she offered politely, "that's okay with me, we don't mind. Just let me know ahead and she'll switch shifts at work. I'll fuck you by myself or we'll both fuck you. Whatever you like. I just want you to come over."

She leaned forward and kissed him, pressing her breasts against him as she leaned. At the same time, as gently as she could, her left hand brushed across his crotch. It had the intended effect.

"Between the two of us," Claire promised, "we could make you come five times in a night," she said. "Unless I get greedy and want to do that all by myself. So call me, okay? I want you to come visit."

"Claire, are you aware that I have a girlfriend?" he asked.

"Uh-huh," she answered. "And I don't give a shit. If she's dumb enough to let you walk around the city by yourself, I don't feel sorry for her."

Then she tucked a piece of folded note paper in his shirt pocket.

"Bye, handsome," she said.

He watched her walk away. The next thing he knew, he was unfolding the paper from his pocket and reading it. Her address and phone number.

He watched her disappear into the midday crowds on the street and watched the men whom she passed. She was an eyeful. Several of the men turned their heads to gather a second look at her.

He tucked the address back into his pocket, turned, and walked in the direction of East Seventy-third Street, still trying to put the events of the morning in order.

twenty-three

_____

_____

_____

Rolf sat at the piano in his town house and played the *Dance of Death*. Summer had progressed and London was only a month away. Each date of the tour was set now, from the September first opening in London to the final in March. Tokyo would be the last date on the tour and there Geiger would conclude with Rachmaninoff's Third Piano Concerto, one of the most difficult and demanding pieces ever written. It was of this he thought as he practiced the *Totentanz.*

The thoughts made the ghost of Rabinowitz materialize again.

"Not a good idea," the ghost said as he stood over Rolf. **"Rachmaninoff Three. You are not up for it."**

"I am," Geiger said. He played Liszt as he argued Rachmaninoff. "Or at least, I will be."

The ghost gave a dreadful little snort. One of anger and contempt.

"Watch your fingering! Watch! Hands. *Hands lower!*"

Rabinowitz growled like a disgruntled wolf. **"You are striking single notes with a force that makes the instrument moan,"** Rabinowitz said. **"Look! There! You are jabbing at the keys!"**

Geiger drew a breath and corrected himself. Sometimes he could envision Rabinowitz. Other times he could only hear him. Sometimes the ghost appeared as a young man, one whom Geiger could recognize only from the old photographs. Other times he would appear very old.

Very old and highly cantankerous. And always contentious. But unable to be pleased at any age.

Meanwhile, Rolf Geiger's fingers danced along the keys. They danced as if they had never been set so free before. The *Totentanz* was as demanding a piece as Liszt could have imagined. Geiger knew that he was playing it with fire and passion. And he believed he had the interpretation. His ears felt hyperalert. The piece was turning into a magnificent effort.

The ghost stood by. His hands touched upon Rolf's neck.

"Go away," Rolf said softly during a hushed adagio passage.

"Make me."

"I will."

"You cannot. You need me."

Geiger could not see behind him and did not care to look. But he sensed that a smirk rode upon the dry, dead lips of Isador Rabinowitz.

"Not forever," said Geiger.

The fingers tightened on Geiger's shoulders. They were designed to scare. To intimate. The fingers that had made pianos sing like angels across the world were fingers that also suggested homicide.

"Forever," asserted Rabinowitz.

Many minutes went by. Geiger thought he heard something. But Diana had gone to the gym. Or somewhere. She was spending increasing numbers of hours away from their home. They seemed to get along better that way.

"Do you want me to leave completely," she had asked him over the Fourth of July weekend.

"Leave? Move out?" he had asked.

"Yes," she had said.

"Why would you do that?"

"You don't seem to need me," she had said. "You don't seem happy with me."

"I sometimes don't know what I want," Rolf had answered after much thought.

"Me neither," she answered.

For a period of two weeks, while they lived together they barely spoke. For sleeping, she moved into the guest room. It just sort of happened one day, this miniestrangement. Yet it was clear that it had been happening slowly all along. Incrementally day by day since the tour had been scheduled.

Since Rabinowitz had returned.

Greatness at the keyboard, Geiger had reasoned in summation, was attainable only on old Isador's terms. Was this why he had administered his own life the way he had, from one abusive failing personal relationship to another? Lowered into the ground at the end by a core of onlookers many of whom had hated him?

But meanwhile, his piano had lifted its voice in ecstasy for six decades.

Geiger massacred a G chord. He winced.

"You're thinking about *her* again," Rabinowitz said. **"You're thinking about a woman. That is why you blasphemed your music."**

"I'm thinking about my life," said Geiger, correcting the chord, retreating several bars and starting over.

"Your life is the keyboard. Same as mine was."

More minutes went by. Geiger concentrated deeply. The piano was at the forefront of his mind, a multitude of thoughts and relationships at the fringes of his consciousness.

"I want the answer to some questions," Geiger asked his mentor.

"And what would those be?"

"I want to know about being dead," Geiger said. A long hesitant pause, and then, "Is there peace? Is there joy? Is there a consciousness or a loneliness?"

His questions fit the passages he played. A weary soulfulness came forth in his voice and in the piano's harp.

"You'll know soon enough," Rabinowitz said.

"That answer is unsatisfactory. You've always asked me questions and posed challenges. But you don't give me answers or solutions."

"I do. But you are foolish and don't assimilate."

Geiger raised his eyes and flirted with throwing some Jim Morrison into Franz Liszt. Rolf could use the piano as a weapon, too, he now knew. But he refrained.

As if to provoke, as if to suggest a perverse reversal of the natural order of time, Rabinowitz showed himself as a small boy. Three years old. Nineteen-eighteen. The year of the Bolsheviks, the year of the Armistice in Europe.

"I'm still waiting for an answer," Geiger said.

"I am listening to your music. Your technique. It is almost good today."

"It is better than that. Give me an answer or I will banish you."

"And how would you do that? Banish me?"

"By removing you from my thoughts."

"You will only remove me from your thoughts by surpassing me as an artist," Rabinowitz countered. **"And that you will never be capable of—"**

"An answer about death, or I will abandon the piano and go watch baseball. Then you will be far from my mind."

There was a blast of an unpleasant odor in the room. Something like the fetid flesh of a dead animal. Then there was an intense cold. Rolf steadfastly played through it.

At one point, Rabinowitz's hand, the right hand, the one with the emerald ring, appeared at the piano and tried to grasp Geiger's. But Geiger played right through it, taking its power away, never focusing his gaze upon it.

Then, on the other side of the room, two books flew from a table, landing on the floor with a loud thud. Still, Geiger played.

"Death," said Rabinowitz. **"That is what you wish me to speak of?"**

"Is it lonely?" Geiger asked.

"Such questions from so young a man."

"Is it lonely?" he repeated.

"If your life was lonely, then your death is, too. You will dig your own grave and die as you lived."

"Appropriate," said Geiger.

"The funny thing is, you no longer feel pain. Emotions,

yes. But no pain. And no fear. What is there to fear after you die?"

Geiger turned it over in his head. "You might fear an eternity of . . . of . . . of what?" he finally asked.

"Invalid question," answered the ghost. **"There is no eternity because there is no time. If you died in 1938 or 1998 it makes no difference. You have no sense of how long you've been on this side."**

Geiger thought of what the ghost had said. He reached the end of the third movement of the *Totentanz.*

He paused, then set his fingers to play the fourth and final part. His musicianship flowed.

"Now tell me what you want," said Geiger, still busy at the keyboard. He mastered a prestissimo section.

"What I want?"

"Why are you here?" Geiger asked.

"You summoned me."

"I did *not.*"

"You think you didn't. But you did. The dead belong to those who keep them alive. So for that much, I am grateful."

Geiger considered the thought.

"You stand here and you seem to help me technically," Geiger said. "But I think you are actually here for a different reason. To stop me from surpassing you."

"I don't need to be here for that."

"Yes, you do."

Again the hand swiped at the keyboard. Geiger kept playing.

"My surpassing you did not happen in your lifetime," Geiger said. "You helped see that it didn't. Now? Now unless I empower you to stop me, no one will stop me. Do you follow my logic?"

"Your logic is twisted. You do not have my talent."

Geiger smiled. "My logic is coming into the light. And London will prove what I can do."

Rabinowitz vanished for several minutes, as if in anger. Then he was back.

"Where do you suppose your woman is?" Rabinowitz finally asked.

"Don't start that again," Geiger said.

"Nothing to start, Rolf," the ghost insisted. "But it's for you to stop."

"There's nothing going on. There's nothing to stop."

"You let another man make love to your woman. That doesn't bother you?"

"She is not . . ."

"It's a disgrace," the ghost said. "That's what it is. You may be left with only one resort to save your honor."

"What's that?" Geiger asked.

"You will have to kill her," he said. "The proper moment is near, and that is what I would suggest. There are ways of doing it that you won't get caught. You will live well without her."

The ghost nodded.

"Yes, yes, yes. I do believe that is the only solution," urged the ghost.

Geiger listened to this through a veil of exhaustion. No matter how many times he turned it over in his mind, no matter how many facets of it he counted, it all came back to the same thing.

The thought horrified him.

"Do you believe I'm capable of murder?" he once asked the ghost.

The ghost roared with laughter.

"We are *all* capable of it under the right exigencies," Rabinowitz answered. "You . . . me . . . Could you kill in self-defense?"

"Probably."

"Then why not in defense of your life's genius?"

Geiger was not convinced. Nor did he wish to be.

Meanwhile, his mind was starting to push in dark new uncharted directions, provoked incessantly by Rabinowitz's accusations. The fantasy recurred to him of Diana being the figure model at the art gallery. He tried to picture her in the course of adultery with another man. He pictured her easing out of her clothes and standing before an unknown bed as another man, fully clothed, took her in his arms, pulled her into bed, began to kiss her and make love to her.

He recoiled from the thought.

Diana in bed with another man.

The ghost gleefully intruded.

Pure Rabinowitz: **"The horns of the cuckold rise so beautifully from your head, Rolf. He has his pleasures exactly right where you have yours."**

Geiger pulled his hands from the keyboard.

He rose abruptly and hurled a bookend at the specter. The bookend passed hard through the ghost and hit a wall. There it broke and shattered an antique vase.

The ghost was gone and there were shards of plaster and crystal all over the floor.

Moments later, Geiger was surprised when Diana opened the door.

"Rolf?"

"What?" he snapped.

She looked around the room. Geiger stood at his piano, the broken crystal on the floor several feet away. There was a huge dent on the wall and a cracked marble bookend lay on the floor.

As they both stood there staring, the unchecked books took off on a merry slide sideways. Several tumbled off the shelf.

Rabinowitz's invisible hand? What had given the books the push? Geiger could hear Rabinowitz chortling.

"What happened?" Diana asked.

"Some things got broken."

"Want me to get a broom?"

Geiger glanced at the wreckage. He saw Rabinowitz standing near it, looking down, admiring the mess he had caused.

"Tell her that if she fucks another man you will kill her," he said.

"No," Geiger said, answering both of them as one.

"She is already fucking one of them. Maybe two," Rabinowitz said. **"Accuse her now! See how she reacts!"**

"No!" he snapped again.

"I heard you the first time," Diana said.

Rolf sighed. He felt a tension mounting with both Rabinowitz and Diana present at once. He thought of how to explain the mess on the floor.

There were two ways. The lie and the truth. The first option seemed easiest.

"Goddamn score. Doesn't make much sense. I lost my temper."

"Try to keep calm, Tiger."

"I am calm."

"Doesn't look that way."

She entered the room and moved toward him. "May I come in?"

"If you want."

"Whore!" said Rabinowitz.

"Do you hear anything?" Geiger asked.

"What do you mean?"

"A voice," Geiger asked.

She cocked her pretty head.

"Something out on the street maybe?" she said. But she found nothing else audible.

Rabinowitz appeared right behind her. **"Claire is much more succulent,"** Rabinowitz said. **"You should stop delaying. Go down to the girls in Greenwich Village. Their hot lithe bodies are bronzed from the summer sun now. They still await you."**

"When did you come in, anyway?" Rolf asked her.

"About a half hour ago."

"Why didn't you let me know you were back?"

"You don't like to be bothered when you're at the piano."

"Well, I like to know who's in the house."

"Next time, I'll ... I'll ... Oh, screw it, Rolf! You're increasingly impossible! I don't know what to do!"

She stunned him. She turned and marched away. She slammed the door. Moments later, he felt the vibrations of the front door slamming shut. She had left again.

"Very good," said Rabinowitz.

"Fuck you," Geiger said aloud, to either, neither, or both.

He began to wonder. Why *was* Diana so irritable?

What *was* going on?

Why *didn't* he go see Claire at her place?

Why *wasn't* Diana there when he needed her?

Who, he wondered, had come into her life?

Whom was she seeing?

It was the only thing about which the ghost seemed to have a point. Several days in August followed the same pattern.

Rolf would practice and the ghost would visit. They would talk. As Geiger's precision at the keyboard increased, the venom of the ghost's tirades against Diana would intensify proportionately. He would sometimes elevate Rolf to a mean, homicidal frenzy.

When Diana was out, which was now almost always, Rolf would pour his rage into his music. When she came home, he would smolder, barely speaking to her.

"I think," she said again one day. "I should move out."

"No," he said. "I want you here."

"Will you treat me better?" she asked.

"I want you here," Geiger said. "You know how you will be treated."

"Oh, the abject disgrace of having your woman move directly from your bed to the bed of another man," mused the ghost one day. **"Such humiliation. Better she die somewhere than disgrace you in public like that."**

Sometimes, Geiger no longer felt the sense of horror over Diana's death. Only a sense of sadness and permanence.

"And inevitability," said Rabinowitz boldly. **"As inevitable as Covent Garden."**

Which brought up another point. For the first concert of his tour, should she come with him? Should she stay behind in New York. Several times the subject came up, alternating with whether or not she should move out.

On some days, she was going. On other days she was staying. Rolf overheard her discussing his behavior on the telephone with her family, who, she later revealed, cautioned her that all great artists could be difficult: thus she should try to settle him. But the situation between them had all the earmarks of a relationship that had once been vibrant but which was now coming apart at the seams.

"What do *you* want to do?" Rolf would ask her.

"I want you to have a tremendous appearance at Covent Garden," she said.

"Does that mean you stay or come with me?"

"Whatever helps you more," Diana answered.

"If she stays behind, she can spend the nights with her lovers," Rabinowitz suggested.

Geiger was now hooked thoroughly into an existence defined by his piano on one side and a jealous rage on the other. Chords of anxiety constantly sounded through him, giving rise to anger and distrust. His mood each time he looked at her had the wailing tone of an unchecked car alarm on a cold city night.

One day when Diana was out, Rolf prowled through the guest room. He sifted through correspondence and found several from Phillip Langlois. He had no right to read any of them. He read them all. They were letters of increasing emotional intimacy and of a growing friendship. They indicated no sexual liaison, however.

Not yet.

He thought about the situation. Now he *knew* the identity of at least one of the men she was seeing. And knowing brought home the reality of it.

Rabinowitz stood over his shoulder as Rolf read every word of every letter. Geiger had never met with Phillip Langlois. He knew nothing about the man. Rolf wondered what he looked like.

"Go find out," Rabinowitz said. "Go watch her with him."

Two days later, when she left to have lunch with "a girlfriend" Geiger followed. He saw her enter a small restaurant on the east side. He took up a position in a coffee bar across the street and waited till she emerged.

Two hours later she emerged with a handsome man a few inches taller than she. He held Diana's hand. He gave her a kiss and a long hug when they parted. Geiger reacted with anger and sadness. If she weren't sleeping with this man, soon she would be.

Rolf went home and arrived an hour before she did. He never admitted that he had even been out. All afternoon, all evening, he poured his attentions and his anger into his music.

"I tell you, she is sleeping with *more than one,*" the ghost taunted. "How long before this appears in the newspapers? There is no disgrace like being doubly cuckolded in public."

"Vanish!" Geiger screamed.

Rabinowitz laughed. The ghost was thoroughly in his head by now, at last in full possession of his soul, his personality, his mind.

"You may play Beethoven until Heaven applauds," Rabinowitz said, **"but your woman will drag you low into the mud."**

That evening was a fertile one for suspicion, also.

Diana's art lesson had ended at nine, and yet she had not come through the door by ten-thirty. Rolf had waited in the library, hunched at the piano, but was now unable even to practice properly until he had heard her come in. It was now a rainy summer evening and well after eleven-thirty.

A few minutes before midnight, she stood at the door to the library, her tall frame wrapped neatly in a trench coat, her dark hair at shoulder length, watching him, giving him a smile and waiting for a welcome in return.

"Hi, Tiger. How's things?" she asked.

"Fine," he said flatly. "How did it go with you?"

"It went well."

"Stop somewhere on your way home?" he asked.

No immediate answer. "Maurice fed me," she said.

"Fed you what?" he asked, looking up.

Instinctively, she didn't like the tone of the question.

"Dinner," she said. "Or a late supper. Whatever you'd call it. There's a little place on Spring Street around the corner."

"What did you have?"

"A bowl of soup and a glass of red wine," she said.

His questions now took such an accusatorial edge that she sickened of them very quickly.

She paused. "If you don't believe me, the name of the place is Mistinguet's and I've been there before and the waiter's name is Joel. If you call and ask if he's seen me, he'll remember."

"I'm not interrogating you," Rolf said, easing slightly.

"You could have fooled me," she retorted.

Then she eased off, and answered in a gentler voice. "Maurice has three students. He took us all out," she said.

"Three women?"

"As it happens now, yes."

"Did he sell some canvases?" Rolf asked, unmoved.

"Why?"

"He's strangely solvent for an art teacher. Last time I saw him he was angling to find other new students. He looked rather threadbare."

"I wouldn't know about his finances," she said with a hopeless sigh. "He treats us well. He's a good teacher."

"Do you like him?" he asked.

"Rolf," she scolded gently. "Don't be a pain. It's not like that."

"How is it, then?"

"He's my art teacher. That's *all.*"

She left the room. He looked at her leave and imagined how he would have felt if she were leaving him for good.

It's not like that. The statement ricocheted around in his mind and found infinite ways to reverberate.

It's not like that.

No? Lately, he didn't know how it was.

Or how it wasn't.

He felt like he needed her more, but he equally had the impression that she was intentionally spending more and more time away from him. Art. Magazine articles. Lunches. She even mentioned a book she wanted to write. God knows what ideas Maurice This or Phillip That were putting in her head. And now she seemed always to be tardy coming home from an evening meeting.

"Just long enough to jump in and out of a hot bed," Rabinowitz chided him.

He reminded himself that there needn't have been anything to it. But her recent behavior, her strange hours of absence, were at variance with what had once been the norm. And that was what he noticed.

Midnight arrived and passed.

Rolf looked at the keyboard before him and somehow felt bored with it. Disappointed by its potential this evening. He sighed and felt extreme unease with the conversation that he had just had with her. But he didn't know what to do about it. His thoughts stampeded. Then they spiraled.

Sometimes entire vistas of deceit formed in front of him, kaleidoscopic images that gained coherent shape, blew apart, and subsequently reassembled: Maurice was Diana's not-so-secret lover. Or maybe Phillip Langlois was. Or maybe they both were or maybe it was just one or the other and he would never know which. Maybe she left Maurice Sahadi's studio and ran around the corner to tryst with Phillip. Maybe she liked to go to bed with both of them at once, just for the intensity of the experience. He thought of her naked in the arms of either of the other men and felt a rage building within him.

He had no way of knowing all the places where Diana went or what she was doing. It occurred to him that he could have her followed, or follow her himself each time. But he further reasoned that there was no one he could trust to follow her and there was no way he could do it himself. Not without losing all his practice time.

Plus, if she ever found out, she might leave him on the spot, which was what he feared in the first place.

"**You will have to kill her,**" Rabinowitz reminded him. "**It is really the only logical solution.**"

"It would ruin my life," Geiger answered.

"**If you do it properly, it will be a small blip in your existence. You will then be free to continue playing.**"

"But am I a potential murderer?" Geiger asked.

The ghost laughed. "**Of course you are! That is your fate!**"

Geiger stared across the library and willed the ghost to appear before him. When it did, it was fully substantial. The elderly Rabinowitz.

"You created such beautiful music in your lifetime," Geiger said. "But you have no humanity at all."

"**Sometimes one has only a single choice, Rolf Geiger. One or the other: Artistic genius. Humanity.**"

"I don't believe you," Geiger said.

"**Name a man with both,**" the ghost challenged.

"Bernstein. Rubinstein. Renoir," Rolf answered.

"**Picasso. Wagner,**" Rabinowitz countered.

"Go now," Geiger said softly.

The ghost protested, but went.

In his library, Geiger steadied himself for several minutes. A plan was falling into place now, one which would define his future.

He found the score for the *Emperor* and placed it in the music rack. He attacked the piano passages and commenced the opening allegro with spirit and passion. He played the first part of the concerto, and as he worked at the piano a thought formed somewhere within. He was reminded that he had never felt this sort of jealousy before, not until his conversations with Rabinowitz had put the notion in his mind.

He heard water running upstairs. Diana was showering.

"Why?" he wondered. "To wash the cologne of another man from her body?"

Then he reminded himself that she *always* showered at this time in the evening.

Two hours later, he tired of his music.

His hands lifted from the keys. He closed the piano and went upstairs. He found Diana in the upstairs guest room. The light was off, and she appeared to be asleep. Time was when she never went to bed without him, then more recently there was a time when she at least came down to say good night.

Now she just quietly retired, as if he weren't there. He stood at the doorway looking into the room. Then went to her and sat down on the edge of the bed beside her.

He looked down.

The old voice came as if on cue. **"Strangle her now."**

He admired her lovely brown hair as it was spread over the pillow. He thought back to the days before he had visualized the ghost of Isador Rabinowitz. He recalled the time when nights brought to him love and warmth and sanctity and quiet.

Back before all these demons seemed to have come forth into his world.

"Now! Do it now! Kill her!"

He placed his hands on her shoulders, looking downward at her lovely face.

Rabinowitz's commands came like wails from a banshee. *"Before she wakes!"*

He was not surprised when her eyelids fluttered and she came awake. "Rolf?" she asked, surprised. She was a little frightened. He could see it.

His hands were on her. Touching her hair. The soft delicious warmth of her neck and shoulders flowed into his palms.

"NOW!"

"You're very pretty, Diana," he said.

She sighed sleepily. "Thank you. That's sweet. You woke me to tell me that?"

"Any man would find you very beautiful. So few would be lucky enough to have you."

She wasn't certain what he meant by that.

She moved one of her hands to his and gripped it.

"I want you to go to London with me," he said. "I think that would be best. For both of us."

She smiled.

"All right?" he asked.

"All right," she said.

He leaned down and kissed her on the forehead.

Then he rose and left the room.

He walked back downstairs. He went back into the library. When he sat down and closed the door, Rabinowitz was present as soon as he lifted his eyes.

"When will you obey?" the specter asked. **"When will you commit the murder? When will we have an end to this?"**

"London," Geiger said. "We'll have an end to all of this in London."

The ghost seemed alternately pleased and disappointed. Geiger began to play again. He played through the night, over and over, until passages that had already been nearly perfect shone like jewels every time light fell upon them.

He was practicing now like a madman. When Diana found him slumped asleep at the keyboard the next morning, that was also how he looked.

twenty-four

_____

_____

_____

"**S**he's back," Diana said.

Rolf looked up from the keys to the Steinway. "Who's back?" he asked.

Diana hunched her shoulders and made a clumsy hulking motion as she walked.

"Oh," Geiger said. "The detective."

Not just any detective, but Detective Janet Solderstrom.

The large blond woman stood in her usual brown suit in the entrance foyer of the town house. Her back was to Rolf as he came out of the library to meet—if not greet—her. Diana remained in the background.

Solderstrom was standing before a handsome Cape Cod seascape by John Hutchinson, the Massachusetts artist. The detective's plump fingers were either on the frame or on the canvas. Geiger couldn't tell and she moved her hand quickly when she heard Geiger approach.

She turned to face him.

"Hello, Detective," he said without warmth.

"So?" she said. "Playing the piano, huh?" She phrased it as if it were some sort of surprise. "Wish you'd play something I know. But we probably don't listen to the same type of music."

She gave him an icy smile. Something about her made Geiger bristle. Almost instantly. Just the sight of her. When Geiger thought further about it, he realized *everything* about her made him bristle.

"As you may know, I have a concert in London on September 1," Geiger said.

"Yeah. Yeah. Right. That's part of what I'm here to discuss. I'd like to get this case closed before you take off."

She looked over his shoulder at Diana. Her pupils were little beads of animosity. Then her eyes slid forward again and stopped on Geiger.

"This trip of yours," she said. "I've been reading the newspapers. You're going to be gone for six months."

"No," Geiger corrected. "The tour is seven months. New York remains my home. I go to other cities. I perform. I return. I leave again. The schedule extends for seven months, but my absence does not."

"Oh. So you leave, you come back, you leave again?"

"Yes."

"Must be very tiring."

"It can be."

"Do you enjoy it?"

"Enjoy what? Travel?"

"Playing piano. Music. Do people notice if you hit a wrong note? I would think it would be a lot of work, trying to get all the notes right every time."

The irritation level was rising. Quickly. "It's what I *do,*" he said. "I'm a pianist."

"Like, you give concerts, right? That's what that means. I mean, I've seen you in *People* magazine and I saw you on the television one time when you were walking through Central Park with some candy. What show was that on?" she asked.

Geiger refused to answer.

"*Entertainment Tonight,*" Diana said from where she stood by the library door.

"That's the one," Solderstrom said. "That's where I saw you. Did you know they were taping you?"

Geiger realized a sinking sensation in the pit of his stomach.

"Detective, are you here to talk about the break-in here or about my career?"

"Well, one has a bearing on the other," she said.

"Why is that?"

Her answer, after a moment, was filled with challenge. "I wanted to make sure you were only going to England on this trip."

"What difference does it make?"

"We wouldn't want you to be out of touch. In case we needed to ask you a few more questions."

"I'll be available," Geiger said.

Geiger noticed that Solderstrom had a little tic to the pinkish flesh beside her left eye. It betrayed her anger when she started to get steamed.

"It bothers me," Solderstrom continued. "You file a police report, and now you're going to travel the world. You people with money do stuff like that. Then if I put in weeks of work, you're around the globe, don't come back, and our case goes down the sewer. Can't blame me for getting pissed."

Diana was becoming as angry as Rolf. She walked to his side, and the detective found herself looking at two pairs of enraged eyes instead of one.

"Sorry you feel that way," Geiger said.

"If it were up to me, I'd have your passport lifted. I don't like your attitude, Mr. Geiger."

"Well, that's great. I don't like yours."

Janet Solderstrom eyed him harshly. "Anyways," she said, "I got something to show you."

She reached into her pocket and sifted through some photographs. She assembled a group of five.

"This is sort of a lineup," she said. "Except it's pictures. It's not in person. I'm going to show you some pictures, and you tell me if any of these people are your trespasser."

"All right," Geiger said.

The detective handed them five photographs of what appeared to be older men. They all looked homeless, or at least severely down on their luck.

Both Diana and Rolf froze when they arrived at the fourth photo. There was their watcher.

Unmistakably.

"Him," Diana said, holding up the picture.

Detective Solderstrom looked to Geiger.

"I agree. That's him."

The police woman took the photograph back. "Thought it might be," she sniffed. "Okay," she said. "I hear you."

"So now what?" Diana asked.

"Now I disappear again and you wait. I might have some news for you real soon. That's if you're in the country and not too busy."

"We'll be here," Rolf said.

"Both of you?"

He felt an ominous suggestion in her tone.

"Both of us," he said.

"Well, that's good. Some relationships aren't so permanent anymore. I'm glad yours is."

She turned and moved back to the door. Mrs. Jamison appeared from the dining area and went to open the door for the detective. But Solderstrom opened the door herself and was through it without offering them the courtesy of a good-bye.

Twelve hours later, Diana rolled over in her bed. She tossed. She was still in the guest room, the bedroom next to Rolf's. The night outside was quiet. The last thing she had seen when she had looked out the window was an array of stars, plus a yellow moon.

So why couldn't she have peace? Why was something coming for her again from another stratum of reality? What was approaching her could travel through walls, doors or even flesh.

It was a thought. A notion. A feeling.

A vision. Plus something grotesque from childhood.

Another horrible image was coming together again in her subconscious mind, and she didn't like it. She knew it was going to be frightening. She knew it before the image took over her.

She rolled again in bed.

She could almost hear herself thinking.

Oh, Rolf . . . Oh, Rolf, lover! Please help me, Tiger . . .

"Diana?"

"What?"

"Would you like to die tonight? Or would you like to live in fear?"

"Neither."

" 'Neither' is not an option."

Come close to me and I'll kill you, Diana thought.

She heard manic laughter in response.

"*Kill* me? Impossible. Why, I'm already dead."

"No please!"

She experienced the sensation of tumbling and she knew she was drifting off into the darker regions of sleep. Then she was lying somewhere. She was all dressed up and motionless on white-satin sheets.

Her eyes were closed. In her dream, many people came into view around her and she suddenly realized that the people around her were crying.

Her parents. Rolf. Her sister.

Her friends.

And, to make it complete, Rabinowitz.

"He killed me and he killed you," the old maestro said.

"*Who* did?"

"Rolf. Crazy fucking deceptive bastard!" said the old master. "He gets away with *everything* because of who he is."

"What are you saying?"

"I'm saying that the same Rolf Geiger who makes love to you will also kill you."

"No. Not true," Diana protested again.

In her dream, Rabinowitz laughed and tried another tack. "All right. Want to know how you will be killed?"

"No!"

"Good! I'll tell you!"

She turned over rapidly in her sleep and dismissed him momentarily.

Weird associations ran through her head. "I used to have a husband. His name was Gary, and God knows where he is now!"

She saw herself lying perfectly still and lifeless in a coffin, hands folded across her chest. Rolf stood by dry-eyed, stood looking as if he were pleased.

She tried to cry out. She wanted to escape.

But the dream—*A nightmare, Diana, or is it the future?* someone asked—gripped her fiercely. She realized that she was at her own funeral.

Diana turned sharply in her bed again, arms flailing, crying out in her sleep.

Don't leave now, Diana. This is the future.

Diana felt a scream in her throat, ready to break loose.

She felt herself sinking again, sinking in the manner that Isador Rabinowitz's coffin had gone into the earth. Four cozy dirt walls forever. She gazed upward and Rolf was shoveling dirt down on her dead body.

She bolted upright in the bedroom. The room was dark. Very little light from outside.

Her eyelids flickered open.

"Diana?"

In the dim light she recognized Rolf.

"Jesus, honey . . ." he said. "You were gasping and screaming and rolling all over the place. What the hell are you dreaming about?"

It took a moment for her to realize.

She had passed through a thick layer of dreams. Now she was back to a dark summer night. She leaned forward into the arms that waited for her.

She sobbed. Rolf embraced her. After several seconds she tried to relate the vision that had again pursued her, how horrible it had been, and how it had seemed that death had been so inevitable.

"It's okay," he said. "Nothing's going to happen. I promise. *Nothing.*"

"Tiger, what's going on in this house?" she asked breathlessly. "Where are these thoughts coming from?"

He turned on a light. A friendly yellow glow embraced the room.

"I wonder," he said philosophically. "Is something supernatural really here? If we have a ghost, it's angry and trauma-

tized. It wants us to be the same way. So it has different ways
of terrifying each of us.''

She leaned back against the wall and gathered herself. Then
she embraced him again.

''You're very convincing,'' she said.

''Thanks.''

She sighed. ''I'd be sunk without you, Tiger,'' she said.

He smiled to further comfort her, but his own smile was
short-lived.

His gaze traveled the floor and found a pair of feet. Not feral
feet, but the feet of Rabinowitz. The old man's ghost was
visible to him, the glow still incandescent in Rolf's own eye.

He motioned to Diana.

''See anything right there?'' he asked. He indicated the spot
where Rabinowitz stood.

She looked straight at the spot.

''No,'' she said.

''See?'' Rolf said. ''Of course you don't. We're alone.''

''Liar,'' the ghost said.

She looked away.

''When will we have some peace?'' she asked Rolf.

**''Peace? When will you execute this bothersome
woman?''** the ghost demanded.

''London,'' Geiger said. ''This will all get resolved in
London.''

Once again, he was answering both of them simultaneously,
and himself in the bargain. And he knew he was telling the
truth.

The schedule for the tour was set by August 20. Fifty dates
across the world, September through March.

The dates had been arranged so that Geiger would not have
to be on the road the entire time. He would do cities in clusters,
then return to New York, then do another group of cities one
to two weeks later. The schedule took into account breaks for
Thanksgiving, Christmas, and New Year's Day of 1999. He
would arrive in London three days before his concert at Covent
Garden, for example, stay for an extra day, return to New York,

then return to Europe ten days later. The schedule also allowed him time to make final preparations on scores.

There were a few final details to conclude before leaving for London. Rolf went by Brian Greenstone's office again two days before departure to pick up the airline tickets that would take him and Diana to London. He would also sign several contracts while at his agent's office.

Claire, as usual, was all smiles and attention for him. Brian provided her with the paperwork for him to sign and stood dutifully by as he read and signed. Today, she was ready to give a sprained neck to any man who passed her. She wore a pair of blue jeans that were so snug that they appeared to have been spray painted on. Up top, she wore a filmy yellow blouse. Nothing else, it was apparent.

"All set," Rolf said when he signed the final document. He stood to leave. She was between him and the door.

"I'm a little disappointed," she said.

"About what?"

"You know. I *invited* you. You never came over."

"You're right. I didn't."

"The invitation still stands," she said.

"Claire," he said, "you're not a woman of great subtlety, are you?"

She shook her head. "Nope. I say what I think, and I tell you what I want."

"Then would it make sense to you," he asked, "if I told you this: I'm on my way to London in two days. And the only thing I'm going to be banging on for the next week or so is the piano?"

She pursed her lips, smiled a little, and nodded sweetly.

"Yeah. I hear you. I'd understand that," she said. She thought it over. "Maybe when you get back you'll feel different," she suggested. "Maybe you'll be, like, real tired and all and want to come over and settle in and let me make you feel real happy."

"Maybe," he said.

He might have added that he doubted it. But somehow it was too much trouble.

twenty-five

Rolf and Diana flew first-class to London from New York. They took the 10:00 A.M. flight which brought them into Heathrow at nine-thirty in the evening, GMT. A car and driver arranged by the concert promoters in London picked up Rolf and Diana at the airport and drove them to Claridge's, where they would stay.

The concert was in three days.

The next morning they awoke comfortably. They were registered in a roomy, solid suite on the third floor overlooking Brook Street, directly above the entrance to Claridge's ballroom. Two huge bay windows and a narrow balcony and porch allowed them to step outside from their suite—just slightly—and look down at the other arrivals at the hotel. Even though this was the end of August, the hotel was packed with the wealthy and influential from various nations: Saudi oil barons, multinational bankers, Swiss who-knew-what, beautiful women of indeterminate nationality who seemed to wait under the canopy at the main entrance and to speak to no one, and the occasional American film director or actor. Rolf had stayed here twice before when playing London and was as comfortable as any man could be at $1500 per day.

Well, it was the promoter's money, after all, he reasoned, so why not enjoy it? Television rights to the Covent Garden concert had been sold to the public broadcasting system in the United States and various live- and cable-television outlets in Europe. With the package so big, only the most jaundiced-eyed and anal of accountants could have nudged an eyebrow at the extortionate hotel expense.

On his first day in London, Geiger went to Covent Garden to meet his conductor, Heinrich von Sauer and members of the orchestra.

Von Sauer was a sturdy jowly man of about sixty. He had a tangle of white hair framing his sprawling face and a big low belly. He spoke many languages, but none perfectly. His German had a Swiss-Austrian lilt to it. His English had a Slavic accent, but he had learned French in Germany and conveyed strange echoes of the Third Reich when he spoke of Debussy. His Italian was a disaster as he'd learned it in Belgium from a Flemish mistress, or so he liked to explain. And on it went. Nonetheless, he was comprehensible and intelligent in all the near-tongues he spoke. Geiger had liked him on the previous occasions they had worked together. They also agreed upon their approach to all three pieces of music.

"There is just one thing that remains," von Sauer said. "Order."

"What sort of order?"

"Which comes second, which comes third? *Totentanz* or the *Emperor?* There seems some confusion remains from New York."

"Right now, I'm thinking *Totentanz* third, following a second intermission."

More brilliantly ruptured English: "I'd like to tell the orchestra at certain."

"Tell them. We close with *Dance of Death.*"

"Appropriate. And you will probably be asked for an encore. Unusual as that is, that is often your predilection, as well as that of your public. Not that it involves the orchestra, but have you an idea? I am so wondering."

"I was thinking of the *final* movement of the *Moonlight* Sonata," Geiger explained.

Von Sauer nodded inscrutably, intrigued and impressed.

The first movement of the *Moonlight* Sonata, with its calm settling passages, was more a signature piece than appropriate encore material, even though Geiger had broken accepted custom in the past by playing it. The final movement of the *Moonlight* Sonata, a stormy whirlwind that forced the fingers of the pianist to fly across the keyboard like a crazed bat, was an arresting choice.

"Inspired," von Sauer said. "We are alike thinking on this."

"Hope so," said Geiger.

A rehearsal took place that afternoon and another was scheduled for the next morning. There would be a final one on the morning of the concert.

Diana always found things to do by herself in London. She disappeared to museums and art galleries, then went by Covent Garden to meet Rolf for dinner on their first evening after arrival. Seeing some theater on the first night might have been nice, but was not possible in light of jet lag and the demanding nature of Rolf's schedule.

Late on the second afternoon in London, Rolf managed to slip away to do some shopping.

He purchased only one item for Diana. It was a silk scarf at Liberty's, red and blue with a montage of musical patterns upon it, not the least of which was a grand piano. The scarf was a beautiful sturdy piece of fabric—both delicate and strong.

He examined it carefully in the store, even doubling it up several times and examining how well it would work if it were made into a rope or garrote. A pair of strong male hands using this could strangle a woman perfectly, he mused. Wouldn't Rabinowitz be pleased?

Geiger paid for the scarf and, after leaving the store, threw away the packaging. He would present the scarf to her himself at just the right moment. That moment, as he now saw it, would be between the second and third works of his London performance.

He walked back to Claridge's from Liberty's with his inevitable plan for Diana's immediate future running through his mind. He crossed Regent Street carefully. The London buses, cruising close to the curb from the "wrong" direction, made ghosts out of more than a few inattentive foreign visitors each year.

He arrived back at Claridge's at six. He and Diana went to a comedy in the West End that evening, then paid homage to Oscar Wilde's ghost at the Café Royale for a late supper.

They returned to the hotel around midnight. They settled onto the big sofa in their living room. They opened a split of champagne that had been sent from the manager and placed on ice.

"Want to see what *I* bought today?" she asked.

"Sure."

She hopped up from the sofa, then reappeared a few moments later in a bright red teddy.

"Like it?" she asked.

"Come back over here and you'll find out," he said.

She came back over and he took her in his arms.

"I bought you a little something, too," he said. "But I'll give it to you during the concert tomorrow."

"During?"

"It will be more memorable that way."

"You're sure?"

"I'm busy now, anyway. It's time to take things off, not put them on."

She laughed. "Your hands are so talented and valuable," she said. "I guess I shouldn't push them away."

"I guess not," he said.

For both them, it was a perfect ending to a memorable evening. They took the champagne with them to the bedroom, and made love for the first time in two weeks.

Diana took it as evidence that the dark mood that Rolf had fallen into had finally lifted. Rolf saw the act as a renewal of their relationship, a reminder of how much he loved her both spiritually and physically.

Given all of that, on the eve of the concert at Covent Garden, the scarf and his plans for the second intermission the next day, fit perfectly into place.

*   *   *

It was not unusual for Rolf to be restless the night before a major concert. Geiger awakened at that dangerous hour of the early morning. Past 3 A.M., not yet four. It was an hour when sometime truths emerged from sleep, and, in his recent experience the hour when ghostly spirits occasionally emerged from worlds unknown.

Diana slept peacefully under his arm. But from where he lay in bed, he could see that there was a strange light in the next room. And he distantly—almost subliminally—heard music.

A magically euphoric violin.

He lifted his arm and rose from the bed, leaving her warmth behind.

He took a moment for his eyes to adjust to the dimness in his bedroom. Then he walked to the living room. The light was a strange bluish yellow and it came from the London night outside the hotel.

For another moment, he waited, half-expecting Rabinowitz to emerge from the night. And for half an instant, Rolf thought he felt Rabinowitz's hand on his wrist in the darkness. But when he moved his wrist, there was no obstruction. And there was no trace of Rabinowitz anywhere else.

Geiger was alone. Or assumed he was.

Something compelled him to the bay windows and doors that overlooked Brook Street. He walked to the glass doors and looked out. All he could see were the brick upper stories of the buildings across the street, plus their black rooftops.

He reached to the lock on the portals and opened them, stepping out on the small balcony. He thought of Claire and for some reason he also thought of Anila, the young Italian girl who had been his first lover at the Negresco in Nice many years earlier.

He thought of his first wife, sexy Barbara, with whom he had not communicated for years. He had heard she had married and lived in Westchester County with a husband and son. He thought about the fragility of all human relationships.

Then he felt a shiver. He stepped forward and looked downward. He felt another deeper shiver because there in old Mayfair something all too familiar was taking place down below him.

His eyes started to track a figure across Brook Street even before the full impact of it registered upon his mind.

The human form he was watching was completely inappropriate. A refugee from a Fellini movie.

Geiger was incredulous. It was the clown again. The polka-dotted clown. Looking up at him, violin in hand, playing a tune of enticement that presumably only Geiger could hear.

Ghosts, Geiger thought to himself. *Let one ghost into my head and I let a legion of them into my head.* There was no doubt in his mind that this was what he was watching: another ghost.

It was definitely the clown he had seen twice before. First, on a bright three-quarter-moon night on Seventy-third Street, just before the haunting with Rabinowitz had begun. Then Rolf believed he had caught a glimpse of it again in Nantucket.

The clown wore the same getup as both previous times. A baggy jump suit, black with big white polka dots on it. White face. The violin. Oversize shoes and a wide flat hat.

Here was a complete reenactment of what Geiger had seen in New York, and he searched his soul as to why this would happen. And he looked at it in terror this time because he knew this performance *was* for him.

He remembered the name of the clown: *Umberto.* A good strong Italian name that had come straight out of nowhere.

The clown looked up at him. Then the ghostly musician cradled the violin in his left arm. He held the bow aloft and put bow to strings and began to play.

For several minutes, Geiger watched, transfixed; if in fact this had any possible measurement in time. The tune the violinist played was deeply romantic and passionate. It strangely fit all of the emotions he had felt for Diana while he had made love with her, while he had held her incredible body in his arms.

Geiger broke into a violent sweat.

He wondered if the clown were mocking him or trying to arouse further romantic passions in him. He felt a trembling within his own body. He turned quickly away, unable to look any longer. He rushed back into the hotel and closed the win-dowed doors.

But then came the violin music again, carried on the wind, and through the closed window. The instrument was in the hands of a master, and so were Geiger's emotions.

He turned again, reopened the doors to the balcony, and looked back down and saw that no one other than the violinist was on the street.

No one—not one other person—was present to give any notice to the clown playing such beautiful music.

It was as if this performance were just for him.

Just for Rolf Geiger.

Deep down, he knew it was. The clown kept playing.

Geiger took this in for another few seconds, then turned. He left his hotel room. He didn't wait for an elevator. Rather, he ran down the massive staircase at the core of the hotel and made a damned fool out of himself as he raced out through the deserted lobby onto Brook Street.

He stood for a moment.

From the opposite side of the street, the clown-violinist stared at him, waiting for him. There was again no doubt in Rolf's mind that he was looking at a ghost. The ghost stared directly back at him and waited.

The music had stopped. A lone passerby watched him.

The night porter from Claridge's appeared beside Rolf. "Is there anything we can help you with, sir?" the porter asked.

"No. No," said Geiger gently. Then he asked, "Do you see anyone across the street? Or hear any violin music?"

The porter looked across the street but didn't appear to see anything.

"Sir?" the night man asked again.

"It's all right," Geiger said.

He stepped from the sidewalk. A large taxi turned the dark corner quickly and cruised right in front of him, practically crushing his toes. Late revelers returning to the hotel, Geiger assumed. Geiger glanced into the cab and saw his suspicions more than confirmed. There was a thirtysomething English rock star with three ravishing girls, all about nineteen, and none of them his most recent wife.

Rolf didn't wait for the hack to discharge its passengers. He moved around them and crossed the street. He was anxious to confront the clown.

"Who the hell are you?" he would demand.

"Why are you here?

"What do you want?

"Why are you stalking me?"

But when Geiger arrived on the opposite side of the street, the music was no longer audible. The violin was gone, and so was the clown.

Geiger felt befuddled.

He searched in each direction. Then he saw the hunched lonely figure of the clown walking away from him toward nearby Hanover Square. Geiger took off in brisk pursuit.

Once, the figure stopped and looked back at him to make sure he was following. Geiger accelerated his pace. The clown was a hundred feet away from him. Then eighty. Then fifty.

Geiger further closed the gap. He trotted after the phantom, a preposterous figure in polka dots, as it ambled through the thick London night. Before reaching the square, the clown turned on South Molton Street, a small smart arcadelike side street with fine shops, a block from the hotel.

Geiger continued to follow. He was reminded of the mythical supernatural beast which would take the form of a vulnerable animal to lure would-be predators to a lonely high ground. Then it would assume its real form. The hunted would turn upon, and destroy, the hunter.

Was this some sort of ghostly trick? An emissary of Isador Rabinowitz? Geiger could not stay away.

The onetime prodigy was now on South Molton Street. He closed to within twenty feet of the violinist. The violinist stopped halfway down the block.

Then the player turned.

Cautiously, Geiger walked to the clown. The white face looked toward Geiger. It was not a face that he recognized. The ghost's lips were thin, pink, and very lifeless. A meager smile emerged from them. Geiger stood only a few feet away.

Somehow Geiger did not feel the urge to speak. He sensed no malice from this vision and he felt that whatever this spirit was seeking to relate, a message would manifest itself.

He was correct.

He stared at the vision and a bizarre feeling overtook him. He realized for the first time that underneath the makeup, underneath the polka-dotted suit, the clown was a woman.

A very pretty woman.

"Who are you?" he asked.

"Laura Aufieri," she said.

"Who?"

She smiled. "We have someone in common," she said. Then the clown turned again. Geiger knew that he was to follow.

With a start—he realized where he had seen her before. In Nantucket. In the bookstore. She was the woman he had mistaken for Claire and approached. Even back then, the ghost of Laura Aufieri had been stalking him.

She led him farther down South Molton and into an even heavier mist. She cut through an alley and Geiger continued to shadow her. For a moment there was a light rain, which disoriented him. She trotted slowly. He kept pace. He made one turn, then another, and they came out on a block that was filled with an eerie light. Geiger noted where he was, on Whitlowe Street where it intersected with Folger Place.

The woman in front of him was walking slowly now. She went into a doorway that was lit differently than all others on the block. It was four doors from the corner.

Geiger followed.

He stepped into a building that had apparently not changed since World War II. It smelled of mustiness and the furnishings in its entry areas were aged. There was thick carpeting on the steps and blackout curtains on the front windows.

He followed Laura up one flight to a landing. Now there was a spring in her step because she was a much younger woman in her twenties. She even slightly reminded Rolf of Diana.

She stopped at a door on the first floor. It was unlocked. She entered and looked to see if Rolf was still with her. He was. He was aware of her eyes now, in particular. They were very pretty, as was she.

He walked through the door. He had a sense of being in her home, or a flat she kept. She was transformed and dressed differently now, wearing a skirt and blouse that would have been fashionable during World War II. As Rolf looked further, he realized that this whole room was like that. He had stepped into an evening from fifty-some years ago.

In the front hall, something took his breath away. It was a theatrical poster from October 1942. The Duke of York Theatre in the West End. Laura's name was headlined in a musical review. Her picture on the poster showed her in the clown outfit, obviously her most famous role.

Then Geiger stepped into a living room, which was warm from the glow in a small fireplace. Laura smiled to him, but Geiger's heart gave a start because there was movement in a nearby chair.

A man in the chair, previously perfectly still and unnoticed, set down the *Times* of London and glared at Rolf.

Isador Rabinowitz. Geiger was shocked, for this was a Rabinowitz that he had seen in old photographs. It was a Rabinowitz of about thirty, the nasty malicious womanizing brilliant artist who had fled to England from the Continent to escape the Nazis.

"Why are you *here?*" Rabinowitz demanded of Geiger. "You have no goddamned right to be *here!*"

Geiger heard himself speak. "But I *am* here. Laura asked me to follow," he said.

"She did *what?*" Rabinowitz roared. "Laura! *Laura!*" Rabinowitz rose in a fury.

"Protect me!" Laura said to Geiger.

Rolf was confused. "Protect you how?"

She shook her head and began to cry. "Oh, you can't, you can't," she said. "I'm already dead. But *I* can protect *you.*"

The logic escaped Geiger.

Rabinowitz grabbed the woman and she screamed. Geiger's feet felt frozen in place. Rabinowitz filled the air with profanity and vilifications. He slapped Laura hard across her face. She staggered. Geiger made a move to help her, but the deadly tableau began to play out before his eyes.

Rabinowitz dragged her into the next room and Geiger heard her continuing screams. The light in the next room took on a pinkish macabre glow. Rabinowitz's shouts triumphed above Laura's.

There was no way for Rolf to measure what followed in real time. But he next found himself at the door to the bedroom, looking in. A vile vicious Rabinowitz clutched the unfortunate woman around the neck. He was shaking her and shaking her, and when Geiger made another move to interfere, he realized again that he couldn't. He was watching an event from half a century ago. No more could he have interfered than he could have stepped into the canvas of a painter.

Sadly, he bore witness to the murder.

Laura was lifeless. Her head was turned and inclined to her shoulder at an impossible angle, like a frail bird whose neck had been wrung. Rabinowitz's powerful brilliant hands slowly released her and her body slumped to the floor.

"There," Rabinowitz said softly and with great satisfaction. "There. Let that be a lesson for women who interfere with a man's art."

His expression was grave, but confident. He turned toward Geiger. The woman on the floor looked like a slain angel. Rolf could no longer bear to observe. He turned away.

He heard Rabinowitz calling after him, but he did not stop. He departed the flat and walked down the front steps. When he left the building, he was confused as to which direction he had come. Everything seemed different, and he realized that this was because he had now passed back to the current day.

So he aimlessly wandered around the small back streets of Mayfair for many minutes. When he found Oxford Street, he regained his bearings. He found South Molton from Oxford.

He looked at his watch. It was 5:00 A.M. and a dark blue was in the sky. He walked slowly on South Molton, his head down, his gaze lowered, the monstrosity of all he had seen replaying in his mind.

Halfway down the block, minutes from his hotel, he found himself in front of the window of a shop that sold antique jewelry.

Geiger looked at the display. Then, gradually, he realized that he was not alone. His eyes focused slowly on the window and he saw the reflection of Laura again. She was back in her clown role and carried her violin. He wondered if she was now blessed to wander for eternity in the life form that had made her happiest.

She smiled to him.

"I'm so sorry," Rolf said. "I understand what happened. I know he was a murderer."

She didn't say yes or no. Instead, the ghost looked toward the shop window, seeming to indicate something. There was metal security lattice across the plate glass to avoid a smash-in. But a great deal of small jewelry was visible beyond the glass.

"What? What is it?" Geiger asked.

The ghost's eyes were kindly and peaceful now, and a very deep blue. They were intensely romantic eyes, though with something very vulnerable in them. Geiger held the notion that the ghost's expression now fit the poignant violin serenade that she had played earlier.

The ghost carried her violin under her left arm. She reached out with her right. She extended an arm through the metal and through the window.

Her index finger came to a gold ring. It was a woman's diamond ring, the main stone in a classic Tiffany setting with red rubies surrounding it.

Geiger's eyes set upon it. He looked hard at the ring.

"What?" he asked again. "What about it?"

The ghost smiled more widely. Rolf glanced back to the shop window. Laura withdrew her hand.

Geiger blinked.

The ghost did not exactly speak. But she conveyed a thought.

"Do you believe in guardian angels?" she asked.

Almost involuntarily, Geiger answered. "If I believe in ghosts, I should believe in all spirits. Including angels. Shouldn't I?"

The thin lips smiled.

"Yes. You should," she told him. "Sometimes great evil can be undone before it happens."

The clown raised a finger to her mouth to indicate Geiger should hush. The blue eyes glanced toward the ring again.

Geiger's gaze followed the lead of his companion. He looked at the ring for several seconds.

"You love someone, don't you?" he heard Laura.

Another thought was upon Geiger. He raised his eyes and could no longer find her reflection in the shop window. So he turned back to the specter and started to speak.

"Look," he asked, "what are you trying to tell—?"

He stopped in mid-sentence, stunned.

Rolf was alone on a quiet shopping street at the advent of a London dawn. Not another soul anywhere near.

Back in New York on the same day, Detective Solderstrom had what she wanted. Death certificates here, death certificates there. She had prowled through the great labyrinth of Manhattan records on Grand Street until she had exactly the death certificate she wanted.

When she had it, she drove back uptown to her precinct and showed it to her sergeant.

"These fucking rich people on the east side," she said to her commander. "I can't believe the crap they put us through just for a little publicity."

The sergeant was familiar with the case of the break-in at the home of Rolf Geiger, the onetime prodigy and now quirky superstar rock and classical recitalist. When the sergeant saw what Janet had found, he cursed right along with her.

Their "watcher," the man whom Geiger had insisted he had been seeing all summer, the one who had even walked into the town house, was identified as an old man named Liebling who had followed the classical music scene in New York for six decades. The problem with Geiger's story, the problem with his identification of the photograph that Solderstrom had shown, was that old Mr. Liebling had passed away quietly in his sleep back in February.

"Tell me," the sergeant said. "Do you think old Liebling's ghost is walking around? Or, wait a minute. Maybe it's just old Leibling's corpse that's been walking around, and some other evil sprit has been inhabiting it."

"Very funny," said Janet Solderstrom without the slightest

trace of a smile. "Very funny," she growled a second time. "But I don't discount anything in this city and with these fuckhead music people."

"Or maybe your rock pianist just doesn't know how to make a positive ID," the sergeant said.

The sergeant had a good laugh, which she did *not* appreciate.

"Know what I'm going to do?" Janet Solderstrom concluded. "I'm going to be waiting at the goddamn airport when that Geiger comes back. And I'm going to give that smart-assed blond kid an earful. If he ever comes back."

"Sure, Janet. Do what you want," the sergeant grumbled. "Tell him he's been getting stalked by a ghost. See if he believes that. Or, what the hell? If you want to drop it completely, who's gonna complain?"

twenty-six

When Rolf Geiger walked onstage to play at Covent Garden, the audience greeted him warmly. The handsome old theater, with its plush red interior and dark wooden railings and facades, was alive with excitement. When Heinrich von Sauer raised his baton that evening at Covent Garden, Rolf was ready.

Geiger played the *Choral Fantasy* with depth and emotion. He could hear the ripples of appreciation flow through the audience. He felt good playing that night, and was convinced that his own feelings were reflected in the music. The orchestra and chorus were excellent, too.

At one point in the second movement, Geiger raised his eyes and saw Rabinowitz, ever the stern master and instructor, standing not far from the conductor. Geiger lowered his eyes again and tried to remain focused on what he was playing. From the ghost of Beethoven himself, nearly two hundred years earlier, Geiger adopted the manner of holding down particular notes and combining these with a soft gliding touch that imparted a vivid tender feeling to the fantasy.

"It's good. It's good," Rabinowitz spoke toward the end. It was better than good.

The audience roared its enthusiasm when Geiger brought the

piece to a close. When he stood, he was witness to more applause than he had heard for the last two years. He glanced to the critics in the stalls, however, and noted that all of them were still writing. *Ready to rip me to shreds the next day?* he wondered. He would find out when it was too late. And for that matter, what the hell? Tonight he would play to please himself, and let the world follow if it wished.

Diana was sitting in a private box this evening, guest of some air-headed duke who was an involuntary patron of Covent Garden. Geiger didn't mind. She was off to the right of the hall, and his eyes could settle upon her whenever he pleased. If he felt he was playing for her, he could put more passion in the music.

Geiger went downstairs to his dressing room at the first intermission. Diana came down, too, and a few of the members of the orchestra were invited in, also. They stood around for several minutes, sipping soft drinks and munching pretzels, two of the perks of live performance.

The stage manager came by and gave the five-minute warning. Members of the orchestra evacuated the dressing room first. Diana was left alone with Rolf for a minute.

"Come back down at the next intermission," he said to her. "I have something for you."

"What are you talking about?" she asked.

The scarf was in his pocket, unwrapped and ready to be slipped firmly around her neck.

"What a surprise it will be, this necktie party!" Rabinowitz gleamed from across the dressing room.

"Just be here," Rolf teased. "Just you and me. That's how I want it."

She gave him a kiss and said that sounded great.

Bombastic and fulsome as the *Emperor* might sometimes be, Geiger brilliantly played the second Beethoven offering. He accentuated the romantic elements, and created an *Emperor* in a beautifully expressive style. He colored the work exquisitely and resisted the temptation—which Beethoven himself often could not resist—to tinker with the changing tempo.

Rabinowitz stood by silently, appearing here onstage, then

there, constantly moving around the orchestra. Apparently, only Rolf could see him. Only Geiger knew he was there.

But with the concerto, Geiger succeeded again. The audience was on its feet after the second work of the evening and sent the young virtuoso offstage feeling as if he were two-thirds of the way to conquering the world. Or at least the part of the world that was London.

At the second intermission, Rolf again walked down the steps toward the dressing room, intent on what he was about to do. Several stagehands watched him as he passed. Some said words of congratulations to the handsome young pianist. A few applauded. All of them bore witness to the fact that when he entered his dressing room, the chamber was empty.

He went in and closed the door.

"**Now?**" asked a voice.

Geiger's eyes rose. Rabinowitz was present. The spirit was by the near wall, clad in white tie and tails.

"Yes," said Geiger now.

"**Oh, lovely,**" said the ghost. "**Murder as a prelude for the *Dance of Death*. Tell me, what will you do for an encore? Theme from *Die Götterdämmerung*, I would hope.**"

"You'll know soon," Geiger answered.

He sat for a moment at his dressing table. He would have liked to pour himself a brandy, but he never permitted himself a drop of alcohol before playing. And he wouldn't tonight. So far, it was a triumph. He had played magnificently. The third and most demanding piece was last. All he had to do was—

There was a knock on the door. He recognized the hand.

"Come on in," he said aloud.

Diana opened the door and peered in. "Tiger?" she asked.

"Enter," he said. "And lock the door."

His hand dipped into his pocket for the scarf.

She closed the door behind her and locked it. She looked particularly beautiful. And her neck was bare.

"What's going on?" she smiled.

"**Death is what's going on,**" said Rabinowitz. "**Yours, you compromising whore.**"

Rolf grinned strangely. "Memorable night, isn't it?"

"Yes." She paused. "Are you all right? You're acting weird."

"Well, I'm fine," he said. The ghost hovered nearby. "See, the thing is, this is a big night. A triumph, I hope. I want to make it memorable for you, too.'

"It already is, Tiger," she said.

"Even more." He stood. "Come kiss me," he said.

"Perfect," said the ghost.

She came over to him as he stood. Diana closed her eyes.

"Eyes closed till I tell you to open," he said.

"If you say so, Tiger," she said.

He kissed her. Then he kissed her a second time. He reached behind her with the scarf in one hand. His other hand joined the first. He raised the scarf up around her shoulders.

"Tiger . . . ?" Her eyes flickered.

"Keep them closed," he said. "This is a surprise."

"You have talent as a murderer," Rabinowitz said. **"My hat is off to you. Now . . . "**

He pulled the scarf up around her bare neck.

" . . . pull it tight and strangle her!"

"You're very beautiful," Geiger whispered. He moved the scarf in place around her throat.

He began to tighten it.

"Rolf?" she asked with a lilt in her voice. "What are you doing?"

"NOW!" thundered the ghost.

"It's a present," he said. "I bought it at Liberty's. Look. Piano prints."

He gently tightened it until it lay the way he wanted it, safely and delicately around her neck.

He stepped away from her. She looked in his mirror and admired the silk garment he had so tenderly placed upon her bare neck and shoulders. He held her protectively from behind and kissed her on the back of the neck.

"It's beautiful," she said.

"So are you. Don't ever forget that."

Rabinowitz raged. Geiger ignored him.

There was a rap on the door from the stage manager. Five minutes till the next drop of the baton.

He turned her and faced her. "I wanted you to know," he said, "over the last couple of months I was picturing you with other men. With Maurice. With Phillip. I was incredibly jealous. It made me realize how much I loved you and wanted you with me."

"Rolf, honey . . . ?"

"So I wanted to tell you that here. Tonight. When it's important. At a time that you'll always remember."

"You can tell me that anytime you want," she said. "And you have to know that there is no other man in my life. It's just you."

"Of course I know. That's the way I want it."

There was a crash behind them as a lamp slid from an end table.

It caused Diana to jump. Geiger looked back and saw the glowering visage of Rabinowitz.

"What was that?" she asked.

"See anything?"

"No."

"Rabinowitz spinning in his grave," he said. "Can't stand a bit of tenderness. Come on. Let's go upstairs. Time to play some tunes."

He took her hand and led her to the door. At first the knob wouldn't give. The door opened and the fearsome shimmering form of Rabinowitz stood in Rolf's way.

Diana walked through the form first. Then Geiger passed through it, not hesitating a step. Distantly, he heard a tremendous wail of pity and terror as he proceeded. But Rolf was more anxious to get to the piano than ever before in his life.

He jogged up the steps to the stage, carrying himself like an athlete who couldn't wait to start a great game. He walked out onto it almost before the lights were able to follow him.

The audience rose as Diana worked her own way back to her private box. London gave Rolf Geiger a standing ovation as he came onto the stage and stood near his piano. He raised his hands in appreciation and savored the applause for several seconds. When he turned to the piano, Rabinowitz was on the bench.

Geiger sat down anyway. Rabinowitz remained on the edge

of the bench, or at least Geiger still saw him there. A snarling unhappy presence.

"You'll fail with this," Rabinowitz told him. **"Just like you'll fail with every other major work. You're an amateur, Rolf."**

Geiger looked at von Sauer, who was regarding him quizzically and sensed—not for the first time—something odd.

"You all right?" the conductor asked.

"Hey! I'm pumped up, man," Geiger said to his conductor. "Let's go."

"Fool!" exclaimed Rabinowitz.

Without warning, Geiger turned to the audience and held up a hand. He indicated that he wanted complete quiet.

"We all have some ghosts to exorcise," he said. "And ghosts can take some strange forms. I'm going to exorcise one of mine tonight. Maybe I'll chase some others for you, also."

There was some chuckling, but Geiger's expression showed he was serious. Then, as the baton of Heinrich von Sauer came down, a solemn hush took over Covent Garden. The audience knew that a torch had been passed to a new generation of recitalists.

"Bloody fucking lunatics!" Rabinowitz roared in Geiger's ear. But the younger man could hear only his own playing. That, and the vision of Franz Liszt, who had written *Totentanz* more than a hundred years earlier.

Geiger played it the way *he* wished to interpret it.

He sat at the piano as a young master, dazzlingly handsome once again, his dark blond hair just appropriately askew, his fingers dancing along the keys like little euphoric angels. And all the time, Rabinowitz, coming from somewhere, ranted and howled at him in fury.

Geiger was prim one moment, and boiling with sensuality the next. His fingering demonstrated a degree of velocity rarely seen before, and he played the fiery andante and presto sections with a power and mastery that sent waves of electricity through the old hall.

At one time—though only Rolf could see it—as he came to the most demanding sections of the *Totentanz,* the ghost tried to take charge. As Rolf looked at the hands before him on the keyboard, the skin on the backs of his hands started to wither.

Age spots appeared.

The emerald ring manifested itself and, for a few measures, the old man was back.

He had won. Rabinowitz had wrested control.

Geiger's eyes rose to his right. They drifted to the box where Diana sat. A slight smile crept across his lips. He drew a breath as he played and with more power, with more muscle, with intense precision and emotion.

He tore into the final passages of the *Dance of Death*.

Words formed on his lips. They were not audible beyond the stage, for the orchestral accompaniment buried them.

"Go," he said to Rabinowitz. "Go now back to your grave. And stay there."

"No," the ghost answered. **"I will never go. I will haunt you forever."**

"You will be in my thoughts and my musicianship," Geiger said. "But you will never again haunt me."

"I will!"

"You are dead. I am alive!"

"No!"

Geiger's eyes found two cellists, a man and a woman, who were watching him curiously. They knew he was in a dialogue with . . . with . . . *something*. He winked at the cellists, astonishing them. Their eyes shot back to their music.

He moved toward completion.

The ghost was silent now.

Rabinowitz stood by the piano, holding on every note, listening to Geiger's hands bring forth the intense morbid rhapsody within the piece. But the ghost knew he had lost. Geiger had brought himself to the *Dance of Death*. Not Rabinowitz. And he had brought the entire audience within Covent Garden with him.

"Are you Catholic, my boy?" insinuated the old man. **"I hate Catholic boys."**

"Screw you," Geiger whispered, wondering if any front row audience members could read lips.

"You will fail here, and you will fail at life," the old man said: a final desperate effort to sabotage the performance.

"No, no, no," Geiger whispered back. "I will conquer both. Unlike you, I will conquer life, love, *and* music!'

"Bastard!" the ghost roared.

But all his screams, threats, and shouts were ineffectual now. Geiger had passed him by.

"You are no longer," Geiger whispered, "in my mind. Thus you are no longer."

The old man howled profanely. But he was badly wounded in spirit, and his image began to recede before Geiger's eyes. At first Rabinowitz had been substantial and imposing. But as Geiger kicked into the final bars, and as waves of excitement pulsated through the theater, Rabinowitz—in all his grandeur, with all his accomplishment—was suddenly reduced to something small and mean.

Rabinowitz raised his eyes to Geiger and kept them yellow and hollow upon the young man. But this, as an intended distraction, also failed.

Geiger concluded the piece masterfully, bringing to it a flourish worthy of a bullfighter with flying cape and plunging sword.

He hit the final phrases and sent a knockout blow toward the audience.

The ghost was gone. Words came to Geiger that would ring forever.

Rabinowitz's fading, faltering voice: **"You couldn't have done it without me,"** opined the old man.

"At first, no. Now, yes."

Geiger's hands thundered down upon the final chords. He brought the *Dance of Death* to its frenzied conclusion.

Then, like a magician, he pulled his hands from the keys to show that he was mortal, there were no tricks, and that this inspired pianism had been the work of one young man who had worked so hard to refine and define his skills.

His hands and *his* soul. No one else's.

Then Geiger was on his feet. And so was the entire audience within Covent Garden. The old place exploded, and even the smattering of lords and knights in the stalls rose to acclaim the young American virtuoso.

Geiger stood onstage as flowers were hurled. A phalanx of female spectators surged toward the stage but could not get past the security people who formed a short human cordon at the ring of the stage. Vast bouquets of flowers cascaded downward from high up in the grand circle, and individual roses and lilies fluttered downward. Two dozen bouquets from the stalls landed near Geiger's feet.

The applause was so overwhelming, that Rolf almost tried to hide, turning and applauding himself for the orchestra, for Heinrich von Sauer and for the various sections of the orchestra.

Twice Geiger tried to leave and twice the audience brought him back. He eventually settled in for a short encore and did the final movement of the *Moonlight* Sonata, as planned.

Another sixteen minutes of applause followed.

He returned to the stage once with von Sauer and then a final time, dragging with him an involuntary female partner in a scarf and black gown. The audience roared its final approval for the night, then reluctantly took the hint.

Rolf was with company and wanted to go. The audience finally let him. As he left the theater, he looked everywhere for Isador Rabinowitz. But he saw no sign of the old man. Nor did he expect ever to see him again.

twenty-seven

Half an hour after takeoff from Heathrow, Rolf Geiger peered out the side window in the first-class compartment of his New York–bound British Airways jet. The aircraft passed over the west country of England and found its proper highway in the sky, the flight pattern that would take Rolf back to New York for ten days.

After Labor Day, he and Diana would return to Europe. Dates in Paris, Rome, Munich, Bremen, Copenhagen, and Stockholm would follow within the next three weeks. The audiences would be knowledgeable and demanding. Geiger looked forward to the new challenges.

The sky was blue and bright outside the jet. The seat next to him was empty. Diana had gone upstairs to the lounge. Geiger was alone with a multitude of thoughts.

Geiger had a remarkable sense of fulfillment, even though only one concert date had been completed and forty-nine remained. The previous morning's press in London had been unanimous and euphoric. Geiger had triumphed at Covent Garden.

Welcome to the new master!

—the *Daily Telegraph*

Three great pieces, one unparalleled performer.

—the *Guardian*

Rolf Geiger has mastered Beethoven, Liszt, London, himself, and the world of classical music all on one dazzling evening at Covent Garden.

—the *Times of London*

Bravo, Mr Geiger and welcome back! You, sir, may be the finest who ever sat down to play!

—*BBC-2*

It was heady and impressive stuff. Big wet kisses in the daily British press. Even the critics who had been so quick to trash him two years earlier now proclaimed him as the world's greatest living pianist. And the irony was, to Rolf, it no longer mattered. Brian Greenstone had faxed him a number of reviews that had appeared around the world following the London concert. Rolf, while not ungrateful, had almost been dismissive of them

Greatness was too vague a term, Rolf had decided. And maybe too heavy a burden for any one man. Similarly, it was fleeting as a breeze. He had seen many athletes, many performers, playing long after their prime. Geiger would do his tour, do it with the highest standards of precision of which he was capable and then go on. Laurels would wither, he knew. Other things were more lasting and important.

But, moreover, he enjoyed the sense of finally having seen his mentor Rabinowitz in his entirety. Equally, Geiger had the sense of having broken free of him and his oppressive spirit.

Geiger gazed continually out the window. The airplane climbed into the sky. There was something about air travel that always put him in a deeply reflective mood.

Now, today, Geiger wondered about many things, just as he would always wonder about the worlds around him.

Had Rabinowitz's ghost *really* been there? Or had the vision been in Geiger's head?

Had Rabinowitz really pushed Geiger to a higher more spectacular realm of musicianship? Or had this just been Geiger's psyche playing with itself, rationalizing and agonizing, dealing with the parallel memories of a loveless father and a loveless mentor?

Had there really been a ghost there to move Geiger's thoughts and his musicianship along? Or had Rolf found love, peace, his future, and the salvation of his soul through the scores of long-dead composers?

After all, no one else had seen Rabinowitz since the day the old maestro died. Not even Diana, though she felt that she, too, had sensed *something* and had suffered her own share of bedeviling dreams.

But for that matter, didn't a pianist raise a spirit every time he newly interpreted a score? Geiger thought back to the recordings of Raoul Pugno, those creaking tapes from ninety years ago, and thought he knew the answer.

But what of Rabinowitz personally? And what of his music, the beautiful playing, the forceful melodies, the exalted rhythms which had propelled him to the position of the greatest pianist of his age, until the younger pretender had lifted the mantle from his shoulder?

What was all that? What had been his genius? Had it been a gift? A talent? A curse? Or—taking the matter further—had it all been a pernicious mask, something to cover a malevolent spirit that had never surfaced?

Geiger had the impression of having seen Rabinowitz in his lifetime the way some men see a piece of great music. Some look at the larger movements of the score, but fail to note the underlying themes, the leitmotifs upon which the melody was based and pegged. They play the music. They touch all the correct notes. But they don't understand the emotion of the symphony.

The airplane climbed.

A thousand questions besieged him. A dozen answers suggested themselves to each, and each answer in turn suggested a dozen new questions. Sometimes, when thinking about Rabinowitz, Geiger felt as if he were locked in a wilderness of mirrors, with each mirror held up to the next, curving, bending and reflecting onward to infinity.

Then, as the airliner leveled off eight miles in the sky, he had a quixotic notion of finally liking Isador Rabinowitz and respecting him.

Rabinowitz, his personal evil aside, had been a man after all. He had had something to say, had had his place in the world, and had made his statement and his mark. Undoubtedly, Rabinowitz had purchased his genius and his greatness with his humanity. But he would be remembered as one of the finest musicians ever.

Who was Geiger, who had lived little more than a third of Rabinowitz's years, to reject the way Rabinowitz had led his life? When Rabinowitz had been Geiger's current age, he had been a young man of twenty-nine in England. The defining moments of his life had yet to occur.

But the more Rolf Geiger examined the contradictions of his mentor's life, the more he puzzled over it. At first he tried to make his interpretation in romantic sympathetic terms, seeing the artist who had fled the gas chambers and horrors of central Europe. Music had offered Rabinowitz's life a symmetry, he told himself, an opportunity to put events in order. Those parameters had allowed Rabinowitz's genius to emerge.

Then Geiger rejected this. He saw that definition as too sparse and not taking enough into account, particularly the malice and viciousness with which the homicidal artist had conducted his private life. So in the end, Rolf was left with a complex score with many elements, some aggressively attacking the others, which would emerge differently with every interpretation. He could see Rabinowitz's spirit as something very small and mean: a man who could not stand the thought that someone younger could be better. So he set out to stop the younger man, even from the grave. Then again, what was the ghost doing other than defending the man's life's work?

Finally, Geiger thought back to the incident on Whitlowe Street, when he, Rolf, had wandered the London night on the lonely restless eve of his greatest performance. Subsequently, he had used a map to find that location again before leaving London. He had gone there on foot and alone and, to no surprise, found the house he had "visited" a few nights earlier.

The building no longer looked as it had when Rolf had visited. It had been modernized and refurbished several times over the last few decades. A young German couple now lived on the second floor. The only thing that gave Rolf a further start was the round blue sign on the front of the building, noting that the great artist Isador Rabinowitz had lived at this location from 1940 until 1945.

In the aircraft, Geiger shook his head. Like Beethoven, Rabinowitz would never be played the same way twice.

Geiger's attention turned to the present. He had his own life to live, his own ears to fill. This was his future. His mentor was finally buried.

Rolf settled for an image of Rabinowitz receding in his mind, until the image became something very small and very large at the same time. In the image, the great man himself was seated at an upright, again much like Pugno alone in a studio years ago.

The man. The person. His music.

He would recede more as the years went by—much like the image of an angry possessed man going through the door, slamming it, and leaving for a final time.

Geiger turned his attention back within the airplane and examined a final question.

What was the burden of excellence? Of genius? Of being the best in the world at anything for a lifetime?

Was it too much for any one man to bear? Is that what Geiger had tried to throw off, the soul-clutching aspects of that burden? Was that what he had evaded for all those years when he filtered Billy Joel into Stravinsky? And, if Rabinowitz's ghost had driven him to escape that, could the old master have been seen as malevolent after all?

You couldn't have done it without me?

Those words would replay forever in Rolf Geiger's heart. Once again, there were wide-open areas for differing interpretations.

A woman appeared beside Geiger and slid into the seat next to him. He turned to speak, expecting Diana. He was surprised when it wasn't she.

"Hello," said the woman. Geiger had seen the face before.

"Hi," he said. He wasn't sure who this was.

"I know there was a lovely lady sitting next to you," the

visitor said. "Your fiancée, I'm sure. Well, I'm sitting two rows behind you on the left. I just came over to say hello. It seems this is the only place we ever meet."

She was in her fifties, dark hair and American. Nicely dressed. A Donna Karan suit.

"Do you remember me?" she asked.

For a moment, he didn't. Then he had it.

"Oh, right," he said. "Yes, of course. Air France. Paris to New York. Last March."

"That's correct. With all the fans you meet, what a *fabulous* memory!"

"We had a fireball rolling down the aisle," he recalled. "Not that we needed one."

She nodded and smiled. "I guess I'm your Fireball Lady," she said cheerfully.

"What can I do for you?" he asked.

His eyes wandered past her for half a moment, searching for Diana. For all he knew, every man in the upstairs lounge was trying to pick her up. Let a woman like Diana out of one's sight and naturally other men would notice. But he was secure enough to know that now it didn't matter. No one else was going to get anywhere with her.

"Do for me?" the Fireball Lady asked. "Nothing. I just . . . Oh, I went to your concert the other evening. Covent Garden. Sat right in the stalls. You were just . . . just. . . ."

She shook her head, searching for the right accolade. "Just tremendous!" she finally said. "That Liszt! That Beethoven! You knocked me out!"

"Thank you."

"And that part about ghosts that you mentioned in regard to the Liszt music?" she said. "*Dance of Death?* Was that it?"

"That was it."

"Was that something spontaneous that you said? Or was that planned?"

"A little of both."

"Do you actually *believe* in ghosts?" she asked. "You know, whether they really exist or not?"

He sighed, smiled and shook his head.

"I've had some experiences," he said. "Too complicated to mention. So maybe, yes. Maybe I do. And yet I don't know how to fully answer that question."

He looked past her and still didn't see Diana.

She nodded. "Well, look," she said. "I don't want to intrude. But there's just one thing . . ."

Once again, he knew exactly what was coming.

"I have a little niece named Barbi Ann," his fan said. "She lives up in Scarsdale, New York, and *loves* that piano sketch and autograph you did for me last March. Remember it? I promised her that if I ever ran into you again—*and I really didn't think I would!*—that I'd see if maybe—"

"I don't mind at all," he said gently. "I'd be honored. Do you have a pen?"

"Oh, wonderful."

She found another thick note card and her Mont Blanc pen. He signed,

To Barbi Ann,

Much Love,

and drew another piano. Life did have a funny way of repeating itself.

He looked at his signature. It hadn't changed much since March, and yet he felt so different.

Rolf Geiger

He handed the card back to his occasional air companion in the skies above Europe.

"Thanks so much," she said, savoring the fresh souvenir. Then in her usual conspiratorial whisper, "Clear skies today. No lightning. No shitty turbulence, let's hope."

"Let's hope," he agreed.

She excused herself and went back to the row two behind

him. The seat next to him was vacant again. What *was* Diana doing up in the lounge?

He reached to his luggage and found a small box from the jeweler on South Molton Street, the one that the ghost of Laura Aufieri seemed to have led him to. He placed the box on his lap under a newspaper. He looked around.

Still no Diana.

He remembered the fireball that had ripped down the aisle of his Air France jet six months earlier. A man now given to new insights and superstitions about the world around him, he wondered about the provenance of the lightning.

Like a talent, like a skill, like a sense of genius, could any man fully understand where such a fireball had come from?

There were the rational scientific explanations, and they would satisfy most people. Electricity in the atmosphere. Moisture in the clouds. Thunder. Lightning. Manifestations of a physical rational world.

Sure.

But Geiger wondered if the rational reasoning were really the proper explanation. Was there actually something else? If a ghost could take various quasi-human forms—its own form at different ages, a nightmare man-wolf figure, a watcher— could it also have taken the form of a fireball? Or might some unsatisfied human spirit have dispatched the fireball?

As warning perhaps?

As a bit of ghostly pyrotechnics?

It had scared the hell out of Geiger the first time it had happened. Yet he had also taken with him the lesson that he could survive it a second time.

There was a movement near him. He looked up. Sunshine in a different form: Diana was back.

"Hey," she said, sliding back into her seat.

"Hi," he said.

He gave her hand a squeeze. "What's going on up there?"

"An Israeli film director tried to pick me up. Then a French guy who claims he's a Rothschild. Next time I go up with you."

"It's a deal," he said. He thought for a moment. "How'd you get rid of them?" he asked.

A sly smile crossed her face. "I told them I was engaged."

He laughed. "What made you tell them that?"

"It sounded good," she said. "And I figured it would work."

"Hell of a coincidence," he said.

He pulled the box out from under the newspaper. "I was going to have trouble getting this through customs, anyway. So I needed to give it to you now."

Astonished, hesitating slightly, she stared at the box.

"See, the thing is," he said thoughtfully, "I wouldn't have gotten through the past few months without you. I wouldn't have buried the ghost of Rabinowitz, I wouldn't have played as well in London, and I wouldn't have learned how to love again." He paused. "Sometimes life is very simple."

She took the box in her hand.

"So open it," he said.

Her eyes found his.

"I had a rotten first marriage," Rolf said. "So did you. I'm ready to try again with the right person. I'm hoping you are, too."

"I'm ready," she said. From the swiftness of her response, he knew she had already thought about it.

"Then *open* the damned box."

She pulled away the blue ribbon and lifted the lid. There was a small jewelry case within. It was brilliant red velvet. She opened it and they both looked at the ring. A beautiful diamond was surrounded by small rubies in antique gold filigree.

She looked at it for several seconds, a sea of thoughts and emotions overcoming her.

"I found it in a jewelry store in London," he said. "There's at least one story that goes with it. Franz Liszt once owned it and gave it to a woman he loved."

"Wow," she said. "That's priceless."

"So are you," he said.

She looked at him and nearly melted.

"I want you with me all the time on this tour," he said.

She blinked. "All forty-nine more dates?" She laughed.

"It's a much longer tour than that," he said. "Time was when I thought I'd retire once I did this tour. Well, I don't know if I'm going to conquer the world in fifty shots. And if

I do or if I don't, it doesn't matter, because I'm not going to retire. I want to share music with you and I want to share a life with you. So it's a long tour, Diana. It's more than seven months.''

She was not able to speak. She gave his hand a squeeze. Intimacy eight miles aloft, 880 feet per second now over Scotland, pondering a rapidly accelerating future.

''If you accept, try it on.''

She did. She held out her hand to see how it looked. It looked better than any other ring possibly could have. She leaned to him and kissed him.

''I love it,'' she said. After several moments she noticed there was no marking on the box.

''Where did you find it?'' she asked.

''In a jewelry store on South Molton Street.''

''It's a beautiful ring,'' she said.

Diana looked upon it with fascination. He looked at the thrill and glow in her eyes.

''I hardly know what to say,'' she said.

Then she thought further about it. ''What made you go there?'' she asked. ''How'd you find that particular store?''

He smiled. He told her a short ghost story, one involving a white-faced clown with a violin and a funny polka-dotted outfit. And damned if she didn't recognize the name of Laura Aufieri.

It was a story that she listened to with rapture and which he would retell to her again over the course of many years. But it was their story, a private one, and a footnote of a larger episode of restless sprits, a grander tale which was not as pleasant as the shorter one that it contained.

It was a story that only they could share or completely understand.

Their section of the aircraft became bright with the sun. The engines eased to a quieter hum as the aircraft settled into its cruising speed. The sky around them was a limitless blue and, like the sky, the tour before them stretched without limit.